A Memory of Blood and Magic

K.N. Brindle

andalso
press

A MEMORY OF BLOOD AND MAGIC

For more information contact info@andalsopress.com

Library of Congress Control Number: 2024914993

ISBN: 978-1-965275-01-6

For Molly, who makes everything possible.

And for Sarah, who was the first to believe in Arin.

Author's Note

This is a work of fantasy fiction. As a citizen of that genre, it bears certain traits which should be expected by readers. There is emotional and physical conflict and violence. There are battles. There are deaths of loved-ones.

Having said that, this isn't a story about fateful quests or chosen ones or dark lords. It is a story about people.

This is also a story which looks head-on at the challenges faced by many in our very real world who are struggling to find their identities and their place in it. Depression, suicidal ideation, and self-harm are real factors in characters' lives. There are depictions of sexual assault and trafficking. There is discrimination, abuse, and use of in-world epithets. As the author, I strove to ensure that these depictions are meaningful and necessary to the story and that none of the terrible things that happen in this work are gratuitous.

Most importantly, this is a story about trauma. About both the pain and the healing that can arise from learning to accept the reality of the traumas that have shaped our lives. And it is about finding within ourselves the strength and self-kindness that we need to reach that acceptance.

*"Out of suffering have emerged the strongest souls;
the most massive characters are seared with scars."*

—Kahlil Gibran

Part One

THE FIRST THING you need to know about me is that I killed my family.

My parents should have known—I was two weeks late and turned sideways. The midwife told them my mother and I would both die, and if there was to be any hope, they would need to call for the hedge-witch from down past Meers. This was a dire decision to make, and fraught—no one would dare go begging of a witch except at utmost need. But after hours of listening to my mother's agonized labor, Father set out for Old Marga's.

You may wonder how I know this, as I had not been born yet. I had some in bits and crumbs from Mother and Father. Some from my older brother, Ranji, who was five—just old enough to hear the talk if not to fully understand. And some I had from my somatic memory many years later, after I began studying.

Even having recommended it, the midwife excused herself

before Father made it back several hours later with Old Marga. Calling on a witch is always distasteful, even if sometimes necessary. I know now that birth magic is some of the easiest to enact. It took little effort for Old Marga to bring me forth using Mother's agony as the source, channeling her labor pains to align my body within Mother's and draw me out.

I'm certain my parents assumed they would hold their new daughter, pay the witch, and have all the peace they could muster with a squalling newborn in the tiny house. But Old Marga drew a wizened finger through the gore and birthing blood from my crown to my groin and sucked it in their crooked mouth for a moment as if savoring well-aged wine, and then spoke my doom to my parents.

"This one'll be a witch when they's grown."

At first, my parents did not understand Old Marga's proclamation. When they did, they recoiled in horror, protesting.

"But, she's a girl. That's clear!" my father said.

The witch only grinned the wider. "Oh no, they's a mixie... no doubt, no doubt. You'll see. The blood don't lie." And with that, Old Marga took the small bag of coins and walked out.

One

They named me Arin and raised me as a girl, and for the first few years I knew no differently. How could I? *Girl* and *boy* seemed only arbitrary distinctions to a child only learning to walk and talk. And no one would ever speak of having called on a witch to aid a human birth—it would be a mark of utter shame. Most would rather lose babe and mother both.

My childhood was mostly unremarkable. I had the same olive tint to my skin as my family and most others in the area, though mine, like Father's, was lighter and more muted than some. Freckles and sunburn came more easily than tans for both of us. Sure, my hair was a little darker than Mother's and curlier than Father's, but I was by no means an unusual child to look at, though I remember many comments growing up about my long eyelashes and gray eyes.

My parents were smallholders on the Freelands. The village nearest our farm was Meers and we went to market in Maplewood. As smallholdings go, I remember it being comfortable and homey. We lived in a small house Father built, with one tidy room with Mother and Father's bed, a great hearth and chimney of river stone, and a fine table that my father made himself. My brother and I slept on cots in a small garret tucked in the rafters under the thatch that we reached by climbing a series of pegs driven into the mortar between the stones of the chimney.

Most days were as alike as any day on any farm. Eggs to be collected, goats milked, animals fed and tended. Milly, our cart mule, shared the fenced yard with the goats and chickens.

Endless work always waited for us in the barley and vegetable fields. As I grew, I took on a share of those chores I could manage. At first it was the egging, then the foraging as Mother taught me the rules for safe berries and mushrooms. Come harvest, it took all of us to gather and set by what we needed in food, seed, and trade goods.

The first time I heard the word "mixie" was when I was six. Ranji was teaching me to tend the goats and it was time for milking. We had spent the morning corralling and sorting the does, with Ranji pointing out which were making milk and which hadn't yet been bred, and idly imparting wisdom gained in his eleven years.

"You gotta always keep the buck away from the does, 'cept when they's making kids, or the milk tastes bad." And, "If you let the kids suck too much, the nanny goes dry, so we milk 'em first, then let 'em suck."

I watched as he expertly separated a nanny from the flock, guiding her with his knees to the corner of the yard near the fence, where the milking stand was waiting. Prompting the nanny up on the stand with an end of carrot, he trapped her head in the yoke and brought down the milking bucket from a hook. All the while, he kept up a running narration for my benefit:

"They don't mind it, they's always happy to get a treat."

He grabbed two teats with his finger and thumb, showing me the grip, and pulled two squirts of milk off to the side before starting the rhythmic pulls to fill the bucket.

"A steady count is the thing, kinda like a heartbeat. Not so diff'rent from people. You was born and all you could do was squall and suck, squall and suck. Sometimes I'd wonder if you'd ever let go of mommy's tit. But nannies don't lullaby their kids—unless... I wonder if a nanny bleating is a lullaby? I guess this'll be you someday when you get babies of your own. Though, maybe not, you bein' a mixie."

I was so puzzled by this last word that I didn't notice at first that Ranji had stopped his rhythmic milking and his endless narration. I had no notion what he meant by it, but his face showed me that he had said something wrong. There was a miasma of doubt, discomfort, and fear surrounding us.

I knew from Ranji's own reaction that I couldn't ask him or Mother and Father about it, and indeed we never talked about it until years later. It took me a long time before I felt sure enough in myself to speak about it.

It was time to harvest some of our crops, and Father had finally decided at seven years old, I was old enough to give real help in the fields. I was in the peppers, tiny knife in hand and stooped to reach the low-hanging ones. It was an awkward process even for me who didn't need to bend far: Grasp one of the bright red fruit with the left hand, press the knife-edge to the stem with the right, squeeze the stem between knife and thumb to cut it, and drop the pepper into the canvas bag hung over my shoulder. And repeat. And repeat and repeat and repeat. Farming is a life of so much repetition it's a wonder that old farmers ever pass on—seems that they'd just stay alive forever out of habit.

Red peppers. Mother taught me to only pick the ripe ones. I was so focused on finding the red peppers, so immersed in my task and lost in the numbing repeat of grasp, press, cut, drop, that I can't say how it happened. But one casual repeat, and I was staring at my left hand where a stripe of bright red blood was welling up even before the pain started. I had never seen so much of my own blood before. It was just the same color as the peppers. The shock of that held my tongue for long enough that when I finally cried out as the pain caught up to me, Mother looked up and screamed to see me.

I couldn't at first tell why her face held such horror. It was a deep cut, and hurt, but I had seen my father take worse. Then I noticed. Blood-red. Pepper-red. Not just the blood on my hand. My hand itself. Both hands and arms. My sleeve and homespun shirt, and trousers, and leather shoes. All bright, uniform red. No color of dye was ever that rich and bright, even if we could possibly afford it, which we certainly could not. My clothes had been un-dyed wool, more dirt-colored than anything else only moments before. Wonderingly, I reached up and pulled down a pinch of curls so I could see by tilting my head with eyes sideways: even my hair was bright pepper-red.

Mother reached me then, grabbing my shoulders and shaking me. "Stop that, Arin!" she cried, her voice holding worry and desperation and fear.

Only then did it occur to me to wonder how I had become all over red, and at once everything returned to normal. I was myself again, my hair was its usual shade, my clothes were their usual dusty gray, and my hand still hurt. Now, so did my neck from her shaking, and my arms where her fingers still gripped like a vice.

Her grip eased with her face, and she moved to take the knife I still held in my right hand. She poured water over my cut from her water bag and pressed a kerchief to the wound, binding it tight. All the while she muttered, "It's okay my dear. All is well. Not to worry."

But even as I settled from the shock of it all, I could hear it in her voice: the same fear from before, papered over now with love and tenderness, but there all the same.

When I reached my ninth year, my family each surprised me with a gift. It was not a common practice in our family that I recall. But that winter, whether by some conspiracy or by chance Ranji, Father, and Mother gave me something special they thought I would cherish.

Ranji and I were working together to turn the soil in the barley field. Ranji moved first down each row, driving a long pole fitted with a wedge into the dirt. With each thrust, he would lever the pole forward or to the side, pull the wedge out, take a step and repeat the process.

I followed behind him, using the hoe to break up the clumps and even out the row. I had a bag hanging from my shoulder, and any weeds that had found their way into the field since harvest, I pulled by the roots and stuffed into the bag to add to the straw for chicken bedding.

The field ahead of us looked dry and packed down. Behind, it was dark and rich and soft. Father had explained to me that when the freeze came—any day now—the cold would kill off any grubs that had been growing in the ground, waiting for a chance at the roots of our crops. Working in this way, we made steady progress down one row and up the next.

I was lost in the rhythm of the work, so I didn't notice that Ranji had paused until I caught up to him. He was kneeling in the dirt, one hand grasping the pole and the other sifting through the loosened earth at his feet. I moved to peek over his shoulder just as he stood.

He turned to me and leaned the pole against his shoulder and poured a splash of water from his leather flask into the palm of his hand, working something there. After he had let the water drain away between his fingers, he showed me what he held.

It was a small stone—about the size of his thumbnail—and smooth. The winter sun caught its wet surface and it gleamed purple and gold. It was beautiful.

"This is for you," he said, grinning. "My present for your ninth name-day."

"Thank you!" I took the small stone, rubbing its smooth surface between my fingers. It was the most beautiful thing I had held. I took a moment just to look into its iridescent shimmer in the light, before throwing my arms around my brother. "Thank you!"

When we had finished turning the field, we both returned to the house together to wash up. Though we used pole and hoe, and the air had the crisp chill of coming winter, the work had left us sweaty and all over dirt. Mother always insisted that we start each chore with clean hands and clean face.

When we had each dipped out cold water from the rain barrel into the wash bucket and scrubbed ourselves blue in it, we made our way to the yard. Ranji would check the thatch on the goats' lean-to shelter while I saw to the chickens.

Their small coop was sound enough, but we were at the point of the year where each night was colder than the last, and instead of cleaning out their nestings, Mother had taught me to pile fresh straw over the soiled. Through the deep cold of the coming months, the soiled straw would begin to compost, adding some heat to the coop.

The hens clucked their offense at me as I disrupted their domain. I checked for eggs as I worked and emptied my bag of weeds, mixing it into the straw set aside for nesting and packing it in an even layer. When I was finished with the bedding, I swept out the small run inside the coop and scattered a handful of feed and grit.

Father caught me on my way back to the water barrel to wash off again.

"Pips!" he called. It was his nickname for me. Mother always seemed to scowl when she heard him say it. "So, you're nine today!"

I finished washing up and smiled at him. Father was always happy, always smiling, and his deep voice filled me with comfort. "I am."

"Well I never. Seems yesterday you were just a little nips hanging on your mother. Now you're practically grown!"

He leaned in conspiratorially. "Now, your mother's hard at work on something for you I hear, and I won't spoil the surprise, but I have a little something for you too. A nine-year-old who works so hard on this farm needs a good knife."

My eyes widened and I looked down into his hand to see a small pocketknife, the little blade cleverly set in a whittled wooden handle with a pin to fold on and a small split ring to lock it open and closed. I took the offered knife and ran my fingers over the handle, feeling the smooth flats and edges of the wood, imagining Father working the shape down with his own knife.

I opened and closed the blade, letting my hands become familiar with the action. With it open, I tested its edge on my thumbnail as Father had taught me, just touching the blade to the nail, and applying a little sideways pressure: if the blade dragged across the nail, it needed sharpening. But this one was sharp and finely honed and didn't move at all.

I closed the blade and threw myself at Father, wrapping my arms around him in a hug. "Thank you thank you thank you!" I squealed.

I felt his comforting hands on my back and he said quietly, "Always, Pips. Happy name-day."

I could hear the smile in his voice.

Dinner that night was a favorite winter meal of salted goat, stewed all day in a rich sauce of goat milk, mushrooms, and herbs until it was tender and the aroma filled the house to bursting. Mother had baked bread, setting a flat stone in the fireplace beside the stew pot and throwing on it small rounds of dough she flattened by hand. We ate in comfortable silence, dipping the hot flatbreads into our bowls to sop up all of the hearty stew.

Father kept the fire crackling and the window open, and we sat together at the table feeling the glowing warmth fill the house and the deep chill of winter settle into the hills around us. Our home felt like a bastion of love and comfort against the darkness that crept over the farm.

When the meal was done and Mother, Ranji, and I had washed up the bowls, she sat me down and moved to the chest that she and Father kept their clothes in at the foot of their bed.

"Arin, you are nine now," she said with a smile. "In three weeks, we celebrate Winterfeast, and your ninth Winterfeast is a special celebration." She drew from the chest a small bundle wrapped in her summer shawl. Mother pulled a chair around so that she could sit before me and placed the bundle on her lap.

She reached up to stroke my wild mane of curly hair. I liked that it tended to grow *out* more than *down*. The curls wove and interlocked themselves so that my hair, though longer, looked much like my brother's.

"Your hair has always been so wild," she said. Though she echoed my thoughts, she did it with a grimace. She combed my hair with her fingers, separating the curls and untangling it. "You'll have to start brushing it, if we're going to give you a proper braid."

I felt my face warm and an odd feeling creep into my stomach.

"Here," she said. "This is for your ninth Winterfeast." She unfolded the shawl and shook out the folded cloth within. It was a feastday dress, fine cream-colored wool with lavender ribbons trimming the neck and sleeves. The bodice was embroidered with blue marigolds, likely by her hand. "Don't you love it?"

I felt like I had swallowed a stone and it sat in my stomach as a cold, dead weight. My shoulders were so tight they ached. I looked down at my shirt and trousers, the same rough and practical clothes that Ranji wore, and closed my eyes.

I hated it.

"It's beautiful," I said. It was, I did not lie. But I did not want to wear it, Winterfeast or ever. I didn't understand why, or where this sudden aversion came from.

I forced a smile to my lips and took the dress from her, folding it delicately and wrapping it back up in the shawl before placing it on her lap once more. "Please, keep it in the chest for now, I don't want it to get dirty."

Mother smiled and rose to put it away.

I put my hands to my head and vigorously scrunched my hair back into its wild nest, trying unsuccessfully to undo what she had done to it.

The following weeks gradually became a bitter war between us. Each morning, she made me brush out my hair before I started my chores, counting the strokes until she was satisfied.

When brushed, my hair went from a wild but light tangle to a thick, heavy cap that hung partway to my shoulders. I felt it on the back of my neck when I turned my head and felt it when I lifted my hand to wipe sweat from my brow.

At first, each morning after I set out on my chores, I would deliberately muss it back into comfortable disarray. When I was working outside, I had the ready excuse that this was simply the natural result of doing my difficult, sweaty farm tasks.

But there were days when, beyond fetching water for cooking or washing, my chores kept me indoors and side-by-side with Mother. On those days I suffered her attentions as stoically as I could. It was difficult.

Every chance she could, she found some excuse to stroke my hair and comment on how pretty it was, and how exciting it was that I would soon wear the traditional braid: "Your hair is so lovely Arin. I can't wait to see you in your first braid." Or: "We'll tame those curls soon enough. How beautiful you'll look with it braided!" And: "I've set aside ribbons in blue and yellow to weave in like my mother did mine."

Her doting grated on me. I couldn't say why at the time, only that her vision of who and what I was felt wrong in a way that left me deeply confused.

The morning of Winterfeast, Ranji woke me with an elbow to the ribs and crawled over me in my cot to climb down out of our garret. I groaned with sleep and the chill that had seeped into the rafters.

I changed my sleeping gown for my shirt and trousers, checking the pocket for my folding knife. Father had helped me twine straw into a thin yarn and wrap it tightly around the purple stone to fashion it into a necklace. I took this down from its peg and slipped it over my head.

When I climbed down the pegs, Mother was already at work stoking the fire for breakfast. I ducked out to the privy and returned to the wash barrel. Winter had finally arrived in truth, just in time for Winterfeast. I was the last up and out, so I had no need to break the ice that formed over the barrel, but the water was still cold enough to make me gasp.

We settled around the table for breakfast mash and tea, and Father talked us through the chores we each had for the day. It was a shortened list this day, with a whole afternoon and evening of feasting and celebration on the longest night. We would stay up late to welcome the dawn, a tradition in anticipation of a fertile new year.

Mother twisted her mouth but didn't say anything at my wild hair. I skipped my daily brushing, with the excuse that it would only be mussed again by my morning chores, and she would brush it out tonight for braiding.

After breakfast, we all set out to finish our tasks. Mother sent me foraging. I wandered the woods with my foraging bag and I'm sure my eyes missed much of what I was sent for. It wasn't the cold, gloomy morning light that filtered through the trees. There was light enough to see, but my mind was not on the plants and fruit of the forest.

I was thinking about the dress and my hair. Now that the day was upon me, I dreaded what Mother had planned for me. I didn't understand why I had to be cooed over and fancied.

What was *nine*? I didn't feel any different from last winter. Why should I suddenly wear braids and ribbons and dresses?

My stomach clenched at the thought of the beribboned dress with its bodice and frilled shoulders. It was pretty enough. I thought Mother's similar dress lovely when she wore it on feast and market days. But imagining it on *my* body, imagining *my* hair done in tight plaits, made me feel...

I could not name what it made me feel, but it was something *wrong*.

I continued wandering, but my stomach and my shoulders were becoming more and more tense. I felt my breathing coming in shorter gasps and I could not keep my mind from that sense of wrongness.

Finally, I sat down on the cold, hard ground with my back against a tree and tried to catch my breath. I felt my eyes growing hot, and when I put my hands to my face found tears there.

How long I sat with my face in my hands, I don't know. It was long enough for me to begin to feel a small seed of something within me.

At first it was like a sense of lightness in the weight that had settled in my chest. The longer I sat with it the stronger it became, soon taking on a feeling of resolve and warmth. Like a pepper seed—smaller than a fingertip—that grows into a great flowering plant with roots that embrace the ground.

The feeling grew and though I still felt tentative with it, I knew that there was something here at my center that was *me*, in a way that I hadn't felt before. From my damp face, I let my fingers trail back through my hair, combing my tangle of curls until I had a fist-full in each hand.

Later, as Mother sobbed and raged, my father asked me why I had decided to do it.

The truth is I don't think I ever decided. I only know that I was breathing calmly as I fished my pocketknife from my pocket. My shoulders were relaxed as I unfolded it in my hands. My heart felt light and free as I carefully pinched handfuls of hair and cut them away, watching the cold wind carry the loose tufts off into the woods.

Two

"What are *you*, then?"

I froze where I stood, hand reaching into the cart for the next sack of barley. The words were innocuous enough, if not particularly polite, but the tone of voice caught me short. It was a sneering, deliberate sort of voice. Smooth on the surface but roiling with something unidentifiable underneath. "Dunno what you mean," I muttered finally.

At ten years old, my bones had grown long and gangly. I was already nearly taller than Mother, and giving Ranji a run to reach Father's height. But where my brother was starting to form a dense muscled build from endless farm work, my body was already showing a tendency towards wire and string. Since last year I kept my hair as short as possible, trimming it back every few days with my pocketknife to Mother's ongoing despair.

As I pulled out the sack and turned, I saw a face to put to the voice. I'd seen him before: the son of a farmer who held a large homestead between Meers and Maplewood. He was only a little older than Ranji, but where my brother had the same compact build that ran through our family, this boy was all hulking shoulders and heavy brows.

He towered over me with nearly his full man's growth. He stepped closer and I tried to step backwards but I was against the cart. Only the sack of barley was between us, and he looked down on me with blank eyes that ran up and down once, taking me in.

He wore the same woolens common throughout the Freelands, but his family were well-off enough for dyed yarn. His dull green shirt looked rich and wonderful. He wore brown leather boots instead of shoes, and clearly took great pride in them—they were cleaner than his clothes and well-oiled. His olive skin, darker than mine, was burned by recent sun.

I stood there, backed against the cart and clutching the sack to my chest and staring into his face. I wish I could say I was calm, but it was fear that held me. He was trying for intimidation and he was well versed in it. I couldn't think why he should take any interest in me.

"C'mon Arin, keep moving," my brother said as he came back for another sack. He deftly stepped up to the cart at an angle that forced the bigger boy backwards and freed me to move. "Whacha doing here Royen?" he said. "Ain't your folks under the tents?"

In a daze, I slipped away and trudged along the path to our market stall with the sack over my shoulder. We had a small spot roped off on the edge of the mass of stalls in the Maplewood public market, well away from the large permanent tent at the center. There, the largest farms sold and traded their wares in the cool shade. Our little stand was meager and poor by comparison.

Weaving through the milling mass of market day shoppers, the anonymity comforted me after being singled out by the older boy. No one looked at me strangely. No one noticed my close-shorn hair against my long eyelashes and delicate features, or my coarse clothing and hardy shoes.

When I arrived at our stall, I dropped the sack into the trough on the table. Father was already off arranging possible trades with holders in other stalls, leaving Mother alone to manage the stall and greet anyone who walked by. She wore her feast-day finest, a dress of cream-colored wool trimmed in pink ribbons and embroidered lilacs.

I still had the one she had given me last year. I still hated it, and she had long since despaired of forcing me into the thing.

She eyed me, her lips pressed into a tight line. We both knew she wanted to say something about my clothes, my hair. We both also knew she would not.

"There's still three more," I said. "And some veg."

"Well, get on, then. Cart won't empty itself."

I turned and walked back to the cart, taking my time. I was in no rush to finish the work and be stuck in the stall with Mother for the afternoon. Any market day was nearly a festival in its own right. Neighbors and distant family whose farms might be separated by a walk of a day or more rarely could afford to spend those days visiting. It gave them an excuse to gather, while still seeing to the needs of the farm. Produce, livestock, tools, and other goods were exchanged, but the air rang with friendly banter and family reunions.

I passed a pair of aunties cooing over a newborn baby, "Those eyes! Oh, he'll be a heartbreaker!"

"This 'un'll tear him up, he will. Just look at his talons!" Three young boys—surely cousins by their noses—bragging and arguing over a pair of gamecocks they had in wicker cages.

Two grizzled men leaning on a fence shaking their heads over the weather, the harvest, and children running off from the farm. "She just up and disappears, without a by-your-leave, can you imagine? Run off to her sweetheart, no doubt, and you just see if they don't come crawling back."

"No, five, I think. These're younger still than the kids." The voice carried through an odd lull in the din. It was Father's, unmistakable. In curiosity, I turned off the path and sought him out. Three stalls over from the fence, I found him with another man, both knee-deep in a drift of hogs. He saw me over the other fellow's shoulder and winked at me. They bartered a few moments more, then he waved me over.

I came up shyly. In those days I mostly tried to avoid the direct notice of grownups, but the man was already turning away, crouching down to some task. Father handed me a rope lead as I waded into the mass of squealing animals, and told me to lead them back to the cart.

As I moved away holding the lead, it drew taut and before long I was pulling five small piglets from the milling pen. They were strung to the lead in a line, and though they squealed, they came docilely enough. Halfway back to the cart, Father caught up with me.

"How do you think, Pips? Five piglets to start our own little bacon line."

"You traded the new kids for them?"

"Only three," he said, full of himself. "Old Bran'll send his oldest down tomorrow to take 'em home. These'll take some feeding, and we'll be well into next harvest before any can litter and we can think about slaughter, but oh my! Bacon and eggs every morning!"

As he reached out and ruffled my hair, I grinned wide, both at the thought of daily bacon and at his infectious enthusiasm.

Two things could always put Father in a good mood: fine rich soil, and food.

As we towed the piglets through the crowd, Father chased his favorite topic.

"We'll build a pen and wallow alongside the goats. Come spring, I'll cut back the woods a bit and we can set up a curing shed by the springhouse. I've been thinking, suppose we start laying by cheese from the goats? Met a fellow who comes down by Voort far up north. He does a spritely spin in it. Gave me a taste, oh my! The most delicious thing you ever tasted, Pips. I'm sure we could make it work. The springhouse would make a perfect grotto.

"Just imagine, Pips. We roll into market with our barley, vegetables, cheese, bacon, sausage. Maybe a few fat hogs. Set up under the tents, we will. We'll go home on market day with wheat flour, sugar, anything you like! Beef! What about fine linen for Mother's dresses? Just think of it!" Nothing could rein Father in when he began dreaming. All I could do was laugh with him and share his excitement.

He continued on like this all the way to the cart. When we reached it, Ranji was just hauling a grain sack up onto his shoulder. He turned as we came up behind him and started off to the stall, not even stopping. I grabbed his arm and held up the piglet's lead.

"Ranji, we got pigs now!"

"Nice, nice," he said stiffly, pulling away. "Still gotta unload the cart. You gonna help?"

I looked after him for a moment. Father hadn't noticed anything odd, and was already lifting a pair of sacks from the cart. It wasn't like Ranji to be cold.

I pulled the line of pigs to the head of the cart and tied them fast to the tongue beside Milly. She seemed done with her feedbag, so I pulled it off over her head and dropped it in the cart.

Father had taken the last of the barley, leaving only a few sacks of vegetables. I grabbed the closest to the edge, grimacing at the feel of the contents. Peppers.

I lifted the sack and started back to the stall. I passed Father coming back as I went. There were few enough sacks left to haul that he likely would bring them all together, making this my last trip.

Only after I reached the stall and emptied the peppers into a basket, I realized I hadn't passed my brother. I nearly asked Mother where he had gone, but the distance that seemed always between us held me back. I stood for a while, trying to will myself to break the cold silence. I lost my chance as a shopper came up to inspect the produce, engaging Mother in conversation. I turned and left, wandering the market. Ranji couldn't have gone far.

I found him leaning against the fence at the horse paddock, staring into the distance. Men stood around in pairs, discussing this horse or that, proposing trades, arguing and haggling over horseflesh or barter, shaking hands or walking away. I didn't think he was watching any particular deal. His eyes were unfocused, his face slack. I leaned next to him, arms crossed on the fence like his.

"What do you see?" I asked.

He said nothing for many moments. Long enough that I wondered whether or not he had heard. The space between us stretched out, breaths in and out, endlessly. The horses trotted and showed away. Twice I opened my mouth to say something more, or repeat my question, and twice I closed it again.

"I want to go home," he said, finally, exhausted.

"Tonight," I said. "Market closes at sundown, don't it?"

"No. Now. I wish we could go now. It doesn't matter

though. It wouldn't matter." He sounded so tired.

"What's got into you, Ranji?" I whispered.

He was silent again. An interminable silence, all the clearer for the din around us. I waited. Somehow I knew that speaking now would be the worst thing I could do.

He watched the horses a while longer, saying nothing. Then he turned to me, and I saw the side of his face that he had hidden with the sack of grain. A dark purple ring around his eye and down the side of his jaw. His lip was split and puffy, blood on the shoulder of his shirt, and I realized at once that his hunched lean against the paddock fence was not him taking his ease, but him bent in pain. He had been beaten.

"What... who?" I stammered. But I knew.

"What are you, Arin? Really? Are you a girl, or a boy? Or..." he turned away then, hiding tears, I thought.

It was my turn to stare into the distance. My turn to lose myself in thought. I don't know how long I was silent. To my brother's credit he didn't push me to answer. He didn't repeat his question, or demand more than I could say. He didn't take it back, though—his plea that I didn't know how to answer.

"I—I don't know," I said.

It took me even longer to whisper, "I'm not a girl." And having said it aloud, I was certain.

When we returned to the stall, there was no time for recriminations. Father noted Ranji's injuries while haggling over a trade of barley for salt. Mother made a fuss over his lip and the blood on his clothes, but soon was drawn away to talk peppers and onions.

Throughout the day, the produce dwindled. Now and then,

Mother or Father took a turn to shop while the other oversaw the trading, and bundles of their acquisitions were stacked under the table. Ranji and I spent the day helping whichever was in the stall at the time, carrying, counting, bundling. Mother kept us both back away from customers as much as she could. Ranji because of his purple-splotched face, and me because—I assume she was ashamed of my habits of hair and dress.

Just past noon, as the morning crush began to wane, Father gave us each a pair of coppers and sent us out to find lunch and a market-day treat. We separated, in no mood to talk or even to be silent with each other. My admission hung heavy between us.

I wandered through the crowds, keeping to myself and lost in my head. I bought a skewer of chicken meat roasted over fire, and a honey cake after. I barely tasted either. Having said the words, I realized now how long they had been taking up space in my head. Now I was free of them, and I felt lightheaded as if the thoughts had been physically crowding my brain. I can't say what I felt then, or what I thought. Just that I felt free in a way that I didn't even understand.

I found my way back to the stall and slipped back into the tasks that awaited me. I did them, not even noticing what I did. Ranji came back some time after I did, and *that* I did notice. He seemed even more subdued, and there was a tension between the four of us throughout the rest of the afternoon.

Some hours later, Father let out a big sigh of exhaustion. I looked around, startled to realize that we had sold or traded all of our produce. That we did so earlier than expected would have been reason to celebrate on any other market day, but today we all felt the oppressive weight of the explanation that would happen when we were away from the market, on the road home.

Even so, there was a pleasure in hauling all of our market day prizes from the stall back to the cart where Milly and the piglets waited. There were skeins of woolen yarn and bolts of woven wool for new clothes, a small bundle of good knife-steel wrapped in oiled canvas, a scrap of leather pierced with three fine steel needles, a small clay pot of honey, a bag of salt, and a few small pouches of seeds that Mother wanted to try planting in next year's vegetable field. A small roll of tanned leather for tack and shoes and what-not, a sack of tea leaves, and a very small cask of brandy came out last. Father hefted his purse, looking satisfied as he looked over all we had come away with. Between his shrewd haggling and all the produce we brought for trade, we spent very little hard coin.

As Mother, Ranji, and I brought the last items from the stall, Father packed them into the cart with care, making sure the load was balanced and stable. I untied the pigs and un-hitched Milly from the tongue and led them to the water trough for a drink before the trip home. Once watered, Milly went back on the tongue and I tied the pigs' lead to the rear of the cart.

With Ranji leading, we walked out of the market along the Meers road, and on to home.

"Fighting!" Father said. Disappointment and sadness filled his voice. "Fighting in the market like—like rats in the cellar. I know the Geoff boys are dumber than a sack of rocks, and have half a wit to share between the three of them, but son... what were you thinking?"

Ranji said nothing. We were just out of Maplewood, having all walked the first half hour with no one speaking. We would reach Meers in another hour and a half, then the same again or so to our farm. We would arrive just as night was falling, with no daylight left but no shortage of chores needing doing.

I wanted to say something to Father, to beg him to stop berating Ranji. But I couldn't see any way to do so without also explaining what had caused the fight in the first place. Surely, my brother kept his silence for the same reasons. We all marched along the road, silent but for Father's occasional objections.

"What could possibly have happened that was worth it? I suppose I'll be hearing from Royen's folks about this. You know, his father is one of the wealthiest farmers in the area. If you hurt his son, and he decides to take a complaint to the Freeholders' Circle..."

I winced at this. I knew we were not so well off that we could afford to pay a judgment from the Circle. As we walked, a tension was rising in my body. My shoulders ached with it. Soon, I recognized the same must be true of Ranji who walked hunched over and tense, and even Father's angered nagging seemed to have a similar source. A glance back at Mother's face, lined with worry showed that we all felt it.

We were nearing the fork in the road that would lead to the Geoff's farm. As we topped the rise and the lane came into view, so too did the three waiting, seeming at their ease. Royen was there of course, and his two brothers, one older, one younger.

Father's pace faltered for a step or two, then he continued with his head high. Some fifty yards from the Geoffs, he called out to the eldest.

"Ho, Ollin. How's Market treating you?"

The eldest Geoff said nothing, only looked us all over. I saw his eyes note Ranji's bruises, and then linger on me for longer than was needed to take me in. Ollin was big enough that Royen was diminished by comparison. His shoulders were as wide across as the wheels on our cart, and he looked like he could lift Milly off the ground with little effort. He had almost a foot of height over Father. He and his two brothers were dressed much alike: Fine feast-day woolens dyed in green or blue, and shiny oiled leather boots nearly to their knees. All three were built like oxen. The youngest brother was closer to my age, yet had some inches on Ranji.

Royen had a light bruise on his cheek and the younger boy had a puffy lip. I felt a little burst of pride that Ranji had stood up to them both. If he had been beaten, it hadn't been without cost to them.

As we drew nearer, the three spread out as if to block our path. Father slowed the cart and pulled to the left to pass wide around them, but did not stop.

"Is there something you need, Ollin?"

"Aye. I'd like to know why your boy attacked my brother today."

"Seems to me that whatever happened, if you'd have been there, we'd have heard of it sooner than now. And by the bruises, looks to me that like for like was traded, and two to one. You know differently? If so, I'd sure like to know how, and why you decided that a public street is the place to have it out."

This calm reasoning seemed to catch Ollin off guard, and he stood there with his mouth hanging open long enough for us to walk by. Father made it through their gauntlet, and Ranji just ahead of me. I was walking at the front corner of the cart, on the side where the three boys stood. Just as I passed Royen I saw something vicious in his look. He reached out in a flash and had a hold of my arm.

"This one thinks she's a boy, but that don't hold with us,

does it?"

I froze. Things began to happen faster than I could track, and yet it seemed that time stretched into forever. Someone shouted behind me: Mother. Ranji spun in front of me, cocking his arm back to throw a punch. Father, not realizing that Royen had seized me, reached out to stop the fight, while Ollin stepped in and thrust his elbow against Ranji's chest.

Royen was still moving and had me pinned, his body looming over me and bending me backwards against the cart. His face was too close and ugly with rage. I could feel his breath against my cheek. Bent back as I was, I couldn't breathe, and tears welled uncontrolled and blurred my vision so I couldn't see anything but clouds and unformed chaos.

But I could still hear. Ranji and Father and Ollin struggled to my left near Milly. Father's bellows called for the madness to stop. Mother was crying and yelling for someone to get out of the way. The five piglets were squealing. Blackness started to creep in from the edges of my tear-blurred vision. Horrible laughter, sniggering and lewd from my right. And a coarse whisper very close and full of cruelty.

"I can tell if you're a girl."

I felt his hand at the ties of my trousers. His calloused fingers slipped underneath, against my skin.

Something inside me broke.

At once, there were three voices screaming. The sound itself was painful to hear. It might have been death, or worse than death. Endless suffering. I could breathe, and I could move, and I was no longer pinned down, and there were no hands on me. I wiped my sleeve across my face to clear the tears and I could see.

Royen was on the ground at my feet, his back arched in agony and heels drumming on the dusty road. Ollin crouched down on hands and knees, eyes wide open and staring at nothing, his jaw locked open. The younger brother held himself tightly and curled against his own body as if trying to disappear altogether. They all three were screaming with every last drop of breath they had inside them.

I looked at them, wide-eyed. I had no idea what was happening.

It might have been hours or seconds, but the screams eventually rattled to a halt. They took in ragged breaths, still where they had fallen. Whatever semblance of humanity had been there before slowly returned to their eyes, now gripped with naked fear.

Two of the boys crept back away from us. They withdrew to their branch of the road, still breathing like wounded animals. The younger one sobbed softly. They didn't look up from the ground.

Royen stayed a moment longer, and he did raise his eyes to meet mine. The rage hadn't abated at all, though now the terror drowned it. Terror of me. When he did move, it was in shaky, spastic bursts. First scuttling back from me, then to his knees, then back to his brothers. Each move punctuated with vulgar curses.

"Fucking Mixie! You're dead you goddamn witch! Mixie fucking witch!"

I stood still, looking at nothing until Mother took my arm and guided me along the road beside the cart, which Father had started rolling again by nudging Milly. Ranji had my other arm, walking between me and the three crouched boys until they were lost in the distance.

I don't remember much of anything else of that day or night. I suppose we all walked home from there, though all I remember is being held and guided, and soft murmurs of reassurance and calm.

I remember walking by a gathering of people—the square at Meers, I'm sure—who chattered and murmured and were never close enough for me to see them.

I remember being unable to climb the pegs into my bed—my legs seemed to have turned to jelly. I remember hearing my father call me Pips, and being tucked into Mother and Father's bed instead. I remember the quiet of the house, as the three of them went out into the night to see to the chores that needed doing. I remember the smell of the fire warming the house, its gentle crackling the only sound over my breathing.

At some point I awoke and felt Mother slide into bed behind me. I felt her arms wrap around me and hold me close, and I remember thinking that this was the closest we had been in years. I felt her breath on me, and our breathing seemed to merge into a single rhythm. Ranji climbed into his bed, and I saw Father shadowed in the firelight, seated at the table facing the door and the window, a stout cudgel of firewood across his knees.

And I slept.

Three

I woke alone. I don't know how long I slept. The sun shone through the window, well past sunrise, and birds were chattering in the wood.

I lay in bed for some time, trying to figure out what had happened. There were holes in my memory, but I remembered Royen's fingers reaching out to touch me. My mind seemed to skitter over that moment. Then I remembered he and his brothers screaming. I thought back and forth across that gap, and I couldn't understand what was missing. I lay still for a few minutes more, then forced myself to get up.

I shed my nightshirt and dressed. By the time I had my socks on and shoes laced up, I noticed a mug of tea and a plate under cloth on the table. I was too hungry to care that the tea was tepid, the eggs cold, and the mash jellied. I devoured it all, scooping the barley and pepper mash into my mouth with my fingers and gulping the tea.

My legs still wobbled as I stood, but I made it to the door

without falling. Holding the latch, I hesitated. The previous night was still in bits and crumbs in my memory. But I remembered enough that I didn't think I could face them.

Mother had held me last night. Her touch had been warm and comforting, reminding me of when I was six years old. The speckled fever ran through the Freelands then, and I had caught a mild case. Several days and nights of chills and shaking and fever dreams, and I was terrified, sure I was going to die. I didn't even really understand death at the time, but I knew it came for me. Mother held me and hummed lullabies, and told me that all things would be right in time. I had believed her then. I didn't anymore. I knew things would not be right again.

Ranji's battered face came to me, pleading with me to be his little sister, even while we both knew I wasn't. Exhaustion and pain and fear showing in his eyes. Ranji had always looked out for me, taught me, stood between me and the pains of the world. He was too young to have such weary eyes. Too young to carry the burden of worrying over me.

Father's infectious laugh rang in my ears. When I heard him laugh—always unguarded and full of joy, no matter the worry that loomed—I knew everything would be fine. It was the sound of unconditional love. Even his nickname for me, Pips, that no one else ever used and that I didn't know the origin of, meant love and comfort to me. But how could he love what I was now?

How could any of them? It didn't occur to me that they all already knew what I was; what I always had been. All I felt was that they had had a daughter, a sister, and I had betrayed them somehow by taking her away. I took two steps from the door and sank down to the floor, my back against the wall under the window with my knees drawn up to my chest. The room swayed and tears welled in my eyes.

I sat there, not thinking, not feeling for some time. I heard a stranger's voice calling out Father's name from down the path, and it drew me out of my mood.

"Ho, Bran," came Father's reply. "I thought Jaem was to come down."

"Ah well. 'Bout time he had a try at running things if he's going to make himself a farm one o' these days. Besides, I needed to move my feet." The voice rumbled in a low, gravelly bass, and I recognized it from the market. But there was also something odd in it, a strained, cautious quality, pretending to carelessness.

"Well," Father said, "as well you came, you can take your pick of the goats. You always had an eye, if I remember right."

I heard them moving to the edge of the yard, shoes crunching on the hard packed soil.

"It's a good flock you've got here. Overgrowing your yard a bit, though." They must have stood just the other side of the window.

"Aye," Father said. "It's crowded now, with the pigs added. We'll build them a pen over there soon. You'll want one of the bucklings. That one there's got good growth already. Looks to be a solid sire."

"Mmm. He's one, for sure. Those two gray doelings seem healthy enough."

I heard Father call Ranji and direct him to round up the chosen animals. Father and Bran stood a while longer in silence. Watching my brother, I imagine.

"Good, good," old Bran said absently. I heard Ranji's steps lead back away, and silence for a time. "You ought to know, I came down through Meers this morning. There's a right fuss brewing."

Father was silent a while before speaking. Then he said only, "Geoffs."

"Aye. Geoffs. They're raising ire in the Circle. Saying things. I don't much hold with them, you know. Too much think they's the *Lords of the Freelands*, that family. But, they speak and people listen. There's lots being said, and none good."

Neither said anything more for a long time. I held my breath and watched a small brown ant crawling across the floor.

"Now I'm not standing in one place or another, you know. A man's family is his family, and nobody should say this or that if it's not public business. But a thing comes out, and there's no penning it back up, if you take my meaning."

"I do," said Father.

Old Bran sighed, long and sorrowful. "I been farming these hills damn near fifty years. Seen a lot to come and go, and time was, something like this would quietly fade away. There's no shame to put to it, exactly. But come what comes, there might be trouble, and no mistake. The trouble they're stirring up right now isn't the kind that'll leave your little one alone."

The ant found a gap between the boards and paused, perhaps deciding whether to go around or through.

"You're not my son for me to give advice. But if you think on it, and find you might want to move on more than see what comes... well, my Jaem's near old enough for his own holding, and we've been setting by some to get him started.

"It's a fine home you've made here, and you're a fine neighbor. Least I can do is see you off as right as can be made. Me or Jaem'll be round the 'Hawk next few evenings or so. If you come into Meers to test the wind, come find us and have a pint. Think on it."

I heard footsteps crunch away down our path, followed by

the bleating of goats. The ant entered the crevice and disappeared.

I cried myself dry, then rose and scrubbed clean my plate and mug in the wooden washtub and stacked them on the shelf. I straightened the blankets on the bed and hung my nightshirt on its peg. When Mother came in carrying the egg basket, she found me sitting at the table staring at nothing, my face composed but blank.

"Up you come, Arin. Chores need doing," she said. I stood and let her drag me out into the sunlight. "I already took care of the egging for you, thank you very much. You can repay me by fetching wash water, then weed the vegetable patch. Ranji's already in the barley."

I said nothing, but took the water bucket and walked out to the rain barrel. In and out I went carrying bucketful after bucketful of water until the large washtub was about half full. Two buckets more went into the great kettle Mother had hung over the fire. I watched her for a moment as she busied herself stoking the fire and then began gathering all of our clothing changes to wash.

As I walked out the door once more, I grabbed a hoe leaning against the house and made my way to the smaller field. There I set to work, up one row and down the next. The repetition was comforting and the day ran away from me. I was vaguely aware of Ranji some hundred yards over in the barley field, harrowing the stubble and preparing the field for an off-crop of clover we could use as feed for the goats and pigs.

I worked through to the late afternoon, when I saw Father walking down the path with a small sack over his shoulder, towards the house. I hadn't seen him leave, and that path led only to the road to Meers. He went inside and closed the door. Some time later, he came out and went round the yard, feeding the animals. I paused and watched as he gave Milly an extra measure of feed and a large carrot.

A couple of hours or so later, Mother called us in for supper. I had spent the whole day by myself, and after my morning bout of crying and misery, I had found peace in the solitude. Now, having to face my family—to sit before them at table like nothing had changed—filled me with new anxiety.

I propped my hoe against the side of the house and dipped some water from the rain barrel into the washing bucket. I was scrubbing dirt from my hands and face when I felt Ranji step up behind me, waiting his turn. When I finished, I stepped aside and let him wash. Still saying nothing, we went inside together.

Mother intercepted us at the door and made us change into the clothes she had washed in the morning, putting our work-soiled clothes straight into the washing tub. Ranji and I looked at each other, wondering. This was enough of a break from routine that we both knew something was happening.

Father sat at the table. Before him on the largest dish was a chicken, beautifully roasted, surrounded by carrots, onions, and potatoes. The crispy, brown skin glistened with salt. It was a feast to rival Midwinter, and I wondered at it. We all sat and waited as Mother carved and parceled it out to our plates.

"Well," Father said, "It *is* a feast, and no mistake. You'll wonder what's the occasion, and I'll tell you. I've made us a pretty bundle today, and tomorrow we set off on a great new adventure!"

Father paused as if expecting cheers. Ranji and I sat, mouths chewing but otherwise too shocked to move. Mother poured a mug of cider for each of us.

"Set off?" Ranji asked.

"Oh yes!" Father replied, digging into his food. "We're going to pack our cart, hitch up Milly, and drive off over the mountain to great new things! We'll start off to Rock Hill, or Oakroot, or hell, maybe we'll buy us a townhouse in Anbress! What do you think of that?

"No more hardscrabble farming if we don't like it! We can do what we want. I've built most everything here—maybe I'll be a carpenter and make fancy chests and furniture for the Anbress Governor himself."

"We're... leaving the farm?" Ranji asked again, still puzzled. He lifted a forkful of chicken to his mouth, and his eyes darted to me then away.

"Sold it, to Jaem Win. You've never seen so much coin, lad. We're rich. We can go wherever we like, Arin, ain't it grand?"

When he said my name, the food tasted like ashes in my mouth. Thinking about what had brought us to this moment made both my head and belly hurt. I looked around at our cozy home that I had grown up in. Realizing that I would likely never see it again after tomorrow was too much to bear.

We finished the meal with an apple each for dessert, and Father and Ranji started packing even as Mother and I cleaned up supper. I went through the chores without thinking or feeling.

In the morning, even before the sun was up, Father rose and butchered the piglets and two of the goats, salting the meat and packing it into a cask for the trip through the mountains. Mother packed up the house in two neat chests, while Ranji and I spent the morning hauling tools and barley from the shed and stores from the springhouse to the cart. When Father finished with the butchering, he washed up and started his careful packing of the cart, the third time in as many days.

Before the sun stood far past noon, Milly was hitched, two each of chickens and nannies were tied up to the back of the cart, we were dressed and shod and each carried a good walking stick. Father started off and I led Milly, with Mother walking beside the cart and Ranji taking up the rear.

The road from Maplewood to Anbress ran through Meers and along the South Fork through the mountains, but Father meant to cut southwest cross-country to meet it. We set a steady pace through the foothills and rocky gullies.

As he walked, Father started singing a marching song in his terrible froggy voice, and soon enough Mother and Ranji joined in. I opened and closed my mouth in time, pretending to sing along. Nobody seemed to notice that I made no sound. I had my hand in the pocket of my trousers, my fingers wrapped around the pocketknife Father had given me, and the small purple stone I still secretly cherished.

"No, this won't do," Ranji said, coming back down the game trail to us "It ends in a gully, a full six feet down and up. The goats could make it, but the cart won't."

We had reached the Anbress road without incident and followed it through The Finger, a long narrow spit of mountains that ran for some dozens of miles separating the northern Freelands from the southern. The road should have cut a clean path through from Meers to Rock Hill, but deep in the stony wilderness we had found the road blocked by a rockfall. We lost a day backtracking and exploring, trying to find a way around or through.

Father sighed, looking at the scrap of paper that held his

ongoing sketches of a map of the hills. We'd have to drive back an hour to the last track wide enough for the cart.

"I used to crawl all over these hills when I was a boy. There's a way through, I know there is. We just have to find it. We'll head back to the spring and camp for the night."

It was the third time we'd been forced to turn around, and the hardships of travel were chafing after two days and little progress. He marked off the trail we had found, and Mother and Ranji and I worked to turn the cart around. Nearly a quarter of an hour later we had it facing the other way. Milly rolled her eyes and huffed as we worked, surely amazed at our foolishness.

The spring was a narrow crack in some rocks that bubbled with ice-cold water and ran on to form a creek just wide enough to be troublesome to step across. This was the source of the South Fork, the small spit of a stream that formed a tributary to the Sommíre. The river stone Father had used for our hearth and springhouse had been tumbled and smoothed by this water. The hearth that we'd been forced to leave because of me.

No one had said it, but I knew we were here on my account. If I hadn't been a mixie, we'd be building the pig wallow today. If I'd died in birthing, Father would be starting to think about expanding the house with another room for Ranji's bed. If I'd never come about, Mother and Father might have had another child who wouldn't have steered their lives into a journey through wilderness, to an uncertain future trying to rebuild their lives anew.

By the edge of the spring was a cluster of broad flat stones, large enough for all four of us to spread our blankets, and still warmed from the afternoon sun. A rough circle stained black by soot showed where a campfire had burned sometime in the last few months. It was this evidence, newer than the rockfall, that Father had seized on to confirm that a path wound through the hills. We only had to find it.

Ranji unhitched Milly and hobbled her to graze the scrubby weeds and shrubs, then retied the goats' lead to give them more freedom to feed. Father had his hatchet out and was splitting the fallen logs he and Ranji had collected along the trail for firewood. Mother unpacked the large pot and foodstuffs to get dinner cooking before the light faded to twilight and the Autumn chill came on.

I had little enough to do, so I unpacked the blankets and then took the small shovel from the cart. Walking downstream a ways, I found a likely spot for a privy and dug a short trench. It had been a camp job for Ranji at first, but I had watched Father instruct him on how deep and how long to dig, and how far from camp and water it needed to be. After the second day, I had silently taken over the task. After squatting over the trench, I retied my trousers and covered over the end with a shovel-full of dirt.

I heard a voice as I headed back to the camp. I knew right away from the pitch and rhythm that this was not Father or Mother or Ranji. Slowly and as quietly as I could, I approached. The fire crackled, and though the pot sat in its heat, Mother wasn't tending it.

She stood some distance away, with Father nearest the fire, hatchet in one hand and a length of split log in the other. Ranji was by the cart, and I saw his hand grasping the handle of the spade hanging tied along the side.

The two strangers, a man and a young woman, stood between me and the fire. They must have come across the creek just after I passed by. She wore typical Freelands homespun: a wool dress and stout shoes. She wore her hair in braids, but it was messy with pulls and tangles.

The man wore an odd mix of woolen trousers and a leather vest. He had on a crumpled straw hat with a wide brim and scuffed boots. He carried a large pack on his back with an unstrung bow and handful of arrows tied to the side, and at his waist on the left side was a very large knife, its blade the length of his forearm. He raised his right hand in greeting, and his left gripped the woman's arm, to steady her.

"Ho, traveler," Father said. "You're welcome to join our fire, in peace." I could see Father eyeing the two, trying to figure out if they were a threat.

"Right kind, sir. Right kind," the man said. "Didn't I say, Beaty? That looks like a welcoming and kindly fire, I said." He spoke in a wheedling sort of voice that set my teeth on edge. She said nothing.

They stepped closer to the fire and sat, the man first helping the woman to the ground. She moved slowly and a little unsteadily, as if hurt. The man set down his pack next to her and untied a tin cup, carrying it over to the spring for a dip of water. As he did, he traded introductions with Father. He called himself Cal, and the woman Beaty. Father introduced himself and Mother, but didn't name Ranji, or mention me at all.

He sat down, leaning back against his pack and took a deep drink, then offered the cup to Beaty, who grasped it with both hands and sipped, never lifting her eyes.

"Yes, sir, I said to Beaty, I said: Yon fire looks mighty welcoming. Let's go see if it's a kind traveler what sets it. And here you are.

"We's up from Rock Hill, come visiting distant relations in Maplewood, you know the Veres? No? Have a little homestead just north o' Maplewood, raise sheep? Ah well. We's up from Rock Hill, Beaty and me, and now we're heading on home, ain't we."

"Long way to go afoot for a visit," Father said.

"Ah, well... as to that. Ye see, Beaty and me, we was hoping my ol' uncle Veres might see his way to a little starter for us, bein' newlyweds and all. An' he did, right kindly old man, he is. But that's why we was cautious coming up to your camp, you know. Can't be too careful 'round here," he held his hands up, palms outward in a gesture of peace.

"But I seen right away you was a good family on your own travels, and I said to Beaty, I said: That's a good righteous family to share a fire with come a lonely evening. Didn't I say so, Beaty? But where's yon little one? There was four of you we saw setting up camp, weren't there?"

Seeing no point in staying hidden, I came up out of the darkness, skirting around the circle of firelight to stand with Ranji who still stood at the cart.

"Ah, there she is. Greetings, young'un," Cal said to me. I said nothing.

"You being from Rock Hill," Father said, "you know the way through the hills?"

"Oh, aye, we know it, don't we Beaty? Oh yea, we can help you through. Goin' to Rock Hill? I always say 'a good change is a good change.' The road was blocked last winter, an' last I heard the Elders at Rock Hill sent off to Anbress to ask for help in clearing it, but blocked it stands," he shook his head. "Afoot, we'd normally go right on through an' around on the game trail, but with your cart an' all we'll need to show you the Old Road that goes by that ruined fort. That's a longer road, but nice and easy, ain't it Beaty?"

I watched them as he spoke, and now I noticed that Beaty just stared idly into the flames. She was much younger than Cal—perhaps sixteen. Her look was glassy and vague, and while she nodded without enthusiasm whenever he prompted her, she didn't seem to have any attention to give the conversation, and had not uttered a single word.

Cal picked up a small thin stick from the wood pile beside the fire and prodded the coals a bit. The stick caught, and he left it in the flames, leaning back again. He unbuckled his belt, and tucked it and the knife under his pack, then dug into the pack and withdrew a small clay flask. He sat back down and sprawled against his pack. Uncorking the flask, he dumped out the remaining water from his cup and poured a small measure, then offered the flask to Father.

"Aye, it's a fine night for a fire. 'Good fire and good company,' as they say, right? A little touch to warm the insides 'fore a good meal is just the thing."

I watched Father consider a moment, then he set down the hatchet and took the flask, "'Good fire and good company.'" He took up his cup and poured a few drops, handing back the flask. They both drank together.

At Father's gesture, we all relaxed a bit. Mother resumed her dinner preparation. Ranji and I approached the fire and sat. The evening chill was already settling and the warmth was welcome on our faces and hands. We all sat in comfortable silence while Mother added some cut carrots and onions to the pot, where salt pork simmered.

The fire settled, throwing out sparks. Cal stood and took up a pair of split logs from the woodpile. He fed them into the coals one by one, nestling them gently to avoid raising ash into the cook pot. He stood there a moment, then picked up a third.

With a brutal, fast swing he brought it down against Father's face. Father crumpled, falling flat backwards, unmoving.

I screamed and scrambled to my feet. Ranji yelled in a

wordless rage and took up the hatchet, raising it to strike Cal from behind, and then there was an arrow in his chest, and he fell like a pile of rags. Mother cried out and tried to stand, and an arrow took her in the throat. I turned to run and something tangled my feet and I fell, striking my face against the rocks. All became bright light and ringing, and it felt like the ground was spinning.

"Damnitall!" I heard Cal yell, "Why'd you kill the boy?"

I sobbed, trying to roll over to find Ranji, but my legs were still tangled. I watched Cal step over to Father who was struggling to rouse himself, and cut his throat with the long knife in a single, careless motion.

I didn't understand. This couldn't be happening. Desperate to see anything but the fountain of Father's lifeblood and seizing limbs, my eyes fell on Beaty, who still stared placidly into the fire with empty, dull eyes and no expression on her face.

"At least we got another girl. She'll fetch a fat purse, this one will," a new voice said. I heard boots step up behind me, then everything exploded in stars and darkness and I knew no more.

Part Two

THERE ARE SOME memories which seem veiled, draped in black silk. I can reach for them as often as I like, but only achieve the vaguest sense of their shape. Even somatic memory has failed me in recovering these. Grope as I might, they remain insubstantial and ill-formed.

My captors kept me drugged for my time with them. I believe there were four men who held us, though I wouldn't swear it wasn't more. The only name I recall beyond any doubt is Cal, because that is a name I will never forget.

I can't say how long we were held, but it must have been some weeks. Days and nights all run together, but I remember foggy glimpses of the structure they held us in—some ancient fort, ruined and crumbling, half burned and the other half full of rot. We were somewhere deep in the mountains. The darkness of our prison was cold and full of damp echoes.

While I was otherwise ignored for the most part, my co-captive Beaty suffered periodic attention from the four. She went to their bedding, unresisting in the vague blissful stupor of whatever herb it was they laced our food with.

I recall that at first I rolled over at these times, ashamed for her, and afraid of what might happen to me if my body began to mature. But at some point in the endless time they held us, hiding from it no longer held any meaning.

I watched them rape her because looking away would mean deciding to look away. I had no decisions left in me.

Four

Some time past winter, the routine changed. I have vague memories of arguments and councils among the men, and of activity in and out of the crumbling shelter. And then light and walking, and camping under the stars.

It must have been nearing spring, for the snows and chill were easing as they marched us down the rocky hills. Beaty and I rode in the cart that Cal had stolen from my family, with Milly pulling us out of the mountain pass, indifferent to her new masters and to my fate.

The journey down from the fort is as lost to me as the time locked in darkness, an endless repetition of creaking cart rides and campsites. I recall a fuzzy sight of a village in the distance, a tight cluster of narrow wooden buildings with unfamiliar peaked roofs of tile instead of thatch. The men steered well wide of it.

There was a point where they rejoined a road, as the juddering shake and bounce of the cart over rough ground eased into a more regular rocking. And still the hazy cycle of our days wound on.

Beaty and I huddled together in the bed of the cart, wrapped in scraps of woolen blanket and our ruined clothing. When the rain soaked us we held each other for warmth, and when the sun baked us we covered our faces and lost ourselves in the rocking sway of the cart and the fog of the herb the men dosed us with. The best that could be said of that journey is that the rapes ceased. Our captors had too much to do each night setting up camp.

My first firm memory of my time with them sticks in my mind: Milly pulled us over a rise and we saw a large expanse of a city in the distance. A broad river sparkling like beads seemed to cut right through the buildings, silver granite and whitewashed cladding glinting in the sunlight, with tall peaked roofs of slate and tile. There was an arching bridge in the midst of the crowded structures I could see even from this distance. It looked like a paradise.

I was sitting up in the cart, more clear-headed than I had been in uncountable days. Cal and his men must have been reducing our dose over the last several days, for I could think and remember again. Beaty's response to this sobriety was to withdraw further into herself. She curled her legs to her chest, wrapped herself in her arms, tucked herself against me, and sobbed softly. Now that she could think properly and understood that her nightmare was real, she had reached a point of perfect desolation. I tried to comfort her, murmuring empty words of reassurance in her ear.

I couldn't feel so deeply. I hadn't been subjected to the abuse she had suffered. I hadn't been ripped away from my home and family—my losses were of my own doing. I knew nothing of our eventual fate, but I also had no fear of it, since

I deserved whatever came.

A half day's ride from that city and with daylight still to make it, the men pulled off the road to a pond under a small copse of pine and began setting up camp. Cal took up his pack and walked on, trading a few words with his partners.

With the herbs wearing off, one of the remaining men stood watch over us while the others did the camp chores. He was tall and thin, with sunken cheeks and a nose that had been broken more than twice. Of all the men, he looked the most out of place. His skin was lighter than anyone else's in our party, sallow and patchy with sunburn. His balding head had a fringe of dusty hair and his chin covered in a scraggly short stubble of the same.

He had been somewhat kind to us on the journey—his attentions were more indifferent than violent, and when he spoke to us he was less likely to shout or sneer.

As the fog in my mind cleared and our management changed, I found both a curiosity and a voice that I hadn't used in longer than I could recall. I didn't meet his eyes, for that was still well beyond me, but I spoke, my unused voice cracking like dry leaves. Beaty tensed at my side.

"Where did he go?"

He didn't reply at first. I wasn't sure he would, and I wasn't prepared to ask again. I had no wish to be struck or beaten now that I could remember it. When he did speak, his voice was quiet and flat, and had an odd lilting accent.

"Down into Anbress to arrange your sale. Your journey's nearly done little one. You and the tart have arrived at your new home."

They let us sleep under the cart. In the morning, Cal was back, chivvying us all up with a bundle of cloth under his arm.

Beaty and I were stripped of our rags and made to wash in the pond. To our great surprise he produced a lump of soap that smelled of flowers. We were by then long since inured to the lack of privacy or modesty, not having any energy to feel embarrassment at being naked in the midst of the men. The luxury of the scented lather and the feeling of clean skin and hair was enough to draw a fragile half-smile from Beaty, even in spite of the open leers and comments of our captors and the bone-chilling cold of the pond.

When we emerged, we were surprised again with clean clothes and sandals. Not new, but neither hard-used. For the first time in my life I wore color. Never mind that it was a dress, or that the bodice was too loose and the skirts too long—I reveled in the feeling of clean fine-spun wool dyed a deep violet. Beaty pulled on a similar dress, though hers was red, and fit much better: snug in the bodice with a deep scooped neck.

Without speaking, she turned me and began plaiting my hair. Over the weeks or months we were captive, it had grown longer than I could bear, but I had no way to cut it. As her fingers worked through my curls working out the tangles, I felt an intense conflict. I hated the feel of my long hair. If I was given a knife, I would cut back my hair before I thought to turn the blade on my captors. Despite that, it was soothing, feeling her hands run through it, gentle tugs of dividing and crossing. She had been so passive since the first moment I had seen her at my family's camp, this new energy she showed gave me hope that she wasn't utterly broken. I didn't understand much of our situation, but I knew I needed a friend and ally. So I let her work my hair into a short braid and said nothing.

When she was done, at a loss for a bit of ribbon or string,

she pulled up a length of ivy that was growing beside the pond and tied off the end, twining the remaining vine back into the plait. This was a piece of ingenuity that I would not have guessed of her. I realized then that I knew nothing at all of my fellow captive. Not even if her name was really Beaty; this could have been an invention of Cal's. I didn't know what family she had been taken from, and if they still lived. I wasn't sure what her voice sounded like, as she hadn't spoken beyond murmurs and sobs since I had been held with her.

She turned her own back to me, and I realized that she wanted me to do the same for her. Tentatively, I ran my fingers from her scalp to the ends, working out tangles and knots. I had never touched someone else's hair so intimately before, and I felt hints of odd and disquieting emotions stirring within me.

"Alright, lovelies, time enough! Stop yer primping and into the cart. It's to the big city with you." Whatever I was feeling, the moment was broken by Cal's sneering voice, and Beaty froze and folded in on herself again. The brief glimpse of who she was was lost again. She climbed into the cart, which one of the men had swept out with a pine branch while we were bathing. I followed, pausing for a moment to kneel and pull up another strand of ivy for her hair.

The other men had broken camp while we bathed and dressed, and as soon as we were settled in the cart, we started off. With the cart rolling and our captors spread out along the road before and behind, we had some measure of privacy.

Beaty sat against the side, eyes downcast and arms wrapped around her knees. I moved beside her so that I could speak to her without raising my voice over the creak of the wheels.

"My name is Arin," I said after a moment. I couldn't think of anything else.

After several moments, she spoke, almost a whisper, "Beatrice. But everyone calls me Beaty. 'Cept my Da. He always said 'Beaty sounds like a mule's name.'"

I could feel her tremble at the mention of her family. Trying to keep her talking, I pointed to the front of the cart, "That's Milly. She always was more obedient than clever. They took her too, when..." and then I couldn't speak. Tears welled in my eyes and I lost control.

Some time later I had done all the crying I could manage. My face was buried in her lap, her dress soaked with my tears. Beaty was stroking my head and murmuring to me. "We'll take care of each other. We can be sisters."

Whatever ease I had felt in her arms was gone. I sat up, my eyes wide. "I'm not—" I began. But I caught myself in time. I needed her. Wherever they were going to sell us, I needed a friend. I couldn't afford to alienate her, or push her away, or inspire in her the fear or disgust that seemed to follow from what I am. She was looking at me, surprise and hurt and curiosity in her face. I realized that as much as I needed a friend, she needed me too. She needed someone to be brave for, to protect and look out for. She needed a little sister. If we were both to survive what came, I would have to lie to her. I would have to be her sister. I would have to be a girl.

My fingers found the length of ivy I had pulled. I held it up to her. "I've never had a sister," I said. "I don't know how to..." and at a loss, I gently tugged on her hair. She accepted this and gave me a small smile.

"I'll show you." She turned her back to me and began working her own hair, dividing into threes and weaving it into a braid, much longer than mine.

Before we crossed the bridge into the city, the men pulled to a halt by the road. Cal loomed over us, admonishing us to stay silent. "Either of you lovelies get the notion to call out, for help maybe? Know that Jandry here or Wilts is right beside you with a ready knife. You won't get a second word out. You play it nice and calm, and you'll be rid of us all in a couple of shakes." We eyed the two men he indicated. Jandry was the tall, pale-skinned man I had spoken to earlier. Wilts was short and stocky. Their names might have been different, I don't recall. They both looked at us, their eyes empty and disinterested. As we set off towards the bridge into Anbress, the two walked on either side of the cart, watching ahead but each keeping an eye on us.

Beaty and I rocked backwards as Milly pulled us across the bridge. The stone footings on the northern bank of the Bresnin were rooted among a tight cluster of small stone buildings lining the river. This northern extension of Anbress was all small houses and taverns too mean and new to be considered a part of the city. They clung like barnacles to the edge of the river, spreading out only grudgingly.

The bridge was just wide enough for two carts side by side, the arching planks smooth and grooved by countless travelers and the low wall framed in monstrous timbers gray with years of lime whitewash. From my position in the cart, I could see over the edge to the rushing, churning wash beneath us.

A handler dressed in the red-on-black city livery came the other way, leading a pair of horses. Cal steered Milly closer to the edge to make way. Wilts was walking on that side, and stepped up to the front of the cart to clear the space between the wheels and the railing. As we continued towards the peak of the bridge, I felt a rising urge—a pull and a longing that was almost physical. I could see myself with the slightest effort pitching over the edge of the cart and off of the bridge railing. No more than a short leap to oblivion. The water called to me, cold and dark and violent. It tumbled far below and folded in on itself forming shadowed valleys and white froth. It would take only seconds of cold and pain and then I could be free of Cal, free of the men's leers, free of whatever fate awaited me. This was my last chance, and all it would take was that single step and I would never have to fear again.

I heard a low moaning wail, and it was only a hand gripping my ankle that brought me back to myself. I realized the moan was escaping my own throat and I stopped. I was half standing and leaning over the cart rail. I looked back at Beaty who held onto me, her face white and eyes wide with terror. I sat back on my knees, and she embraced me.

"You can't leave me like that. You can't just leave," she whispered into my ear.

Seconds later, we reached the bottom of the bridge and the moment was gone. A quick glance to either side showed that neither of our watchers had seen.

The city-side of the bridge opened into a broad central square paved in great cuts of the same silvery granite that had been quarried for the buildings. There were veins of pink and sulfurous yellow running through each, forming branching and intersecting networks that made the streets seem the skin of a living thing. It would have been beautiful if not for the milling crowds and drab refuse of the city itself.

There were people everywhere. Most looked much the same as I was used to: olive skin in varying shades, dark curls—worn short and loose by the men and in long tight braids by the women. But there were others who stood out, and these Beaty and I made a game of pointing out to each other. Here: a man and woman, both standing out as much for their height as for their pale sallow skin and smooth long hair the color of hay. There: a broad imposing man with the darkest skin I had ever seen, almost the color of over-brewed tea. He wore his hair in a multitude of tight braids which combined into a single queue pulled over his shoulder. A grizzled old hedge-witch, battered and scarred, leaned against a fountain drawing an ewer of water. As the witch limped through the crowd, a wide open circle moved with them, other people almost instinctively keeping their distance.

There was more variety in clothing than I had ever seen. Woolens and linen in every shade of dye I might have ever imagined, but also a cacophony of styles and cuts. As we continued through the streets of Anbress we saw women in long flowing dresses, in billowing robes, and even in what I took for skirts at first but soon saw were trousers formed of myriad pleats so that they flared like a bell. There were men dressed in trousers and familiar shirts and tunics, but also long coats that buttoned from under the chin to just above the knees, and a man wearing what looked to me like a single bolt of ivory cloth, wrapped many times over around his body so that it formed a garment that covered him from shoulder to ankle, with the last measure folded over his shoulder to drape like a sash across his broad chest. The man with the dark skin and complicated braids wore *three* coats over a crisp linen shirt, each coat open wider than the one beneath, and each the same rich blue.

Hawkers and shopkeepers called their wares, and conversations and haggling filled the air, nothing much audible to us over the creak of the cart and the surrounding chaos.

As we rolled out of the central square, a pair of city guards in glittering mail of thousands of metal rings entered on the same street on patrol. They wore open helms and carried stout staves banded in steel. Beaty and I saw them at the same time, and we both tensed, but a deliberate cough from Jandry drew our eyes to him, and he shook his head slowly, pulling an inch of his knife from its sheath. The guards walked by us without incident.

At each turning, we rode deeper and deeper into the narrow streets. The broad paving stones became smaller and duller— the quarry cast offs, then cracked flagstone, then dirty cobble. The buildings on either side of the street were just as tall, but built of less impressive stone and timber and with fewer and fewer windows as we went, so that before long we were in a dark warren. Only a narrow strip of sky was visible above us. The people we passed reflected the same sort of descent, their clothing meaner, their faces more guarded.

I started to wonder in which of these dilapidated buildings we would meet our fate, when we exited the alley into a wider street. Not the brilliant bright paving of the main square, but still a far cry from the filthy cobblestone and greasy walls we had passed through. The buildings here were handsome, well-dressed block and silvered whitewashed timbers. There were windows in the second and third stories looking over the relatively clean street, and even a narrow flagstoned sidewalk divided the carriage road from the buildings.

Cal halted beside a wide door, painted bright purple and hung with a large brass knocker. Jandry motioned us out of the cart, and Beaty and I complied, holding each other for support. I felt a distinct chill, whether from the shadows or from finally finding my fate, I couldn't say. We were brought up to stand beside Cal at the door. He pounded with his fist three times, and a small window opened in the top of the door with a pair of dark eyes peering out at us.

"Here to see your Ma'am with some new sweets," Cal said.

After a moment, the window closed again. There was the

sound of latches and the great purple door swung wide open. The eyes belonged to a huge brute of a man. Tall enough that his bald head must scrape the ceilings. He had several scars on his face, and his nose had been broken more than once.

Cal entered and Jandry came behind, half driving us, half following. The others stayed with the cart. I felt a brief pang that I was leaving Milly behind, the last connection to my previous life. I started to turn, but the large man was already closing the door behind us. His fists seemed larger than my head, yet he closed the various door latches with deft efficiency. He turned to lead us deeper into the building, gesturing without words to Cal to follow. A second man had risen from a chair located beside the door, holding a stout cudgel in one hand. Seeing us off with our escort, he sat down again, losing interest.

We walked behind the giant deeper into the building, and I was startled to notice the rich opulence surrounding us. The polished flagstone floor of the entryway gave way to a hallway carpeted in a lush pile of wool, dyed in swirling patterns of deep reds and purples. The walls were paneled in dark wood waxed to a luster that shimmered in the light of myriad lamps, and above was opened to the second floor. We passed closed doors on either side, and an open parlor where three girls lounged in embroidered dressing gowns. They took no notice of us.

At the end of the hallway, our escort turned and led us up a grand staircase which Beaty and I navigated with some care, holding hands. We had been off the herbs for days now, but were still occasionally gripped by a certain unsteadiness. The top of the stairs opened onto a landing which split into a gallery with railings overlooking the hall below. Each side ran past several more doors and then joined back together at the far end in front of a pair of carved doors set with great copper handles. The man knocked, waited for some command which I didn't hear, and then led us into the room.

I let out an involuntary gasp as I stepped through the doorway. The room itself was several times the size of the home I grew up in. It was rectangular, with a huge fireplace at either end. The windows were leaded in diamond-shaped panes looking out over the street. We walked in facing a polished wooden table surrounded by chairs, a great vase of flowers and greenery on a woven cloth in its center. On the far wall under the windows was a sideboard covered with platters of some variety of delicate biscuits and cakes, two silver pitchers and several cups, and two large oil lamps.

To our left was an arrangement of couches and upholstered chairs around a low table facing a cheery fire.

To the right, before the second crackling hearth were two more plump chairs facing a heavy wooden table. A most impressive woman was seated behind the table, her back to the windows.

She picked up a stack of papers she had been annotating with a silver pen, and placed them in a black lacquered box on the edge of the table, the lid closing with a soft click. She did not stand as we approached, but nonetheless seemed to loom over us. I did not miss that Cal's demeanor changed in her presence, becoming somehow smaller and more obsequious, while at the same time gaining a thin veneer of formality and class to his speech.

"Lovely as ever to see you, Ma'am. It's been too long."

She said nothing, and didn't deign to look at him, raising a crystal glass in a silver-chased holder to take a sip of steaming tea. I saw her eyes flick across me and rest on Beaty for a moment, taking our measure. She was old, perhaps fifty years, but her green eyes were sharp and intense, set in a pinched, bird-like face. Her long silver hair was unbraided, tied back with a single black ribbon to fall in a fan of tight curls across her back. She wore a gown of crisp linen, black and hot-ironed into a multitude of sharp pleats, with spills of white lace at her wrists and neck.

As my gaze came back to her face, I realized that she was watching me examine her. Our eyes met for a moment, and I looked down at my sandals before she took offense. I felt unclean and rude in my too-big second-hand clothes. I gripped Beaty's hand more tightly, and felt her answering squeeze.

"I brought you two nice little pies, Ma'am," Cal said, trying to fill the ongoing silence. Ma'am seemed comfortable to let the silence continue.

"You brought?" she said, after several uncomfortable minutes. Her voice was light and sounded as if she wore a smile when she said it. I risked a quick glance under my lashes then, but her face hadn't changed. It was impassive, like cold stone. "You happened upon them I suppose? Were they thrilled to learn you were traveling in my direction?" I saw her eyes flick to the door guard, and then back to Cal.

"Oh, well, you know how things are up north. Winter bleak, farms failing... we found what we could," Cal whined. His attempt at polish slipped as he spoke and I could sense him beginning to flail for a new topic, "There was a nice young'n I wanted to bring for you, but he up and got himself killed, sorry to say. And his mother, well... I knew you'd think she was too old..."

As I realized he was speaking of Ranji and Mother, my eyes filled with tears, and I noticed my breathing was becoming ragged. I felt like I must be breaking bones in Beaty's hand. Trying to ignore his words, I glanced at the door guard who, at Ma'am's look had stepped behind us to the wall opposite the windows to open a small door I hadn't noticed earlier. It was trimmed to fade into the wall paneling. He was leaning into the doorway, whispering to someone, and then shut the door and returned to stand just behind us.

"...and she's right good, even doped as she was. Soft in all the right places and willing as anything." Beaty's hand was shaking. I closed my eyes, trying silently to will him to stop talking.

"Enough," Ma'am said. Now, her voice had changed. Still cold as ice, but the undercurrent had gone from stone to fire. "Benjin, please get these... gentlemen... some tea."

The door guard, Benjin, placed a huge hand on Cal and Jandry's shoulders and turned them towards the sideboard, half leading, half shoving them.

The small door opened again and a woman came out, carrying a folded white sheet over her arm. She went to Ma'am's side and bent to whisper to her, eyeing us as she did.

She was small and slight, perhaps thirty years old. Her skin was a dark brown and she wore her black hair in a long thick braid almost down to her waist. She moved with a limp and when she turned to us, I saw that she had suffered a terrible injury in her past. The right side of her face was scarred and misshapen, her nose broken and crooked, and her right cheekbone sunken.

She straightened and limped around the table to us as Ma'am spoke, "Neme here is going to take you both over to those couches and examine you to make sure you are healthy. She'll be very gentle and take good care of you. You cooperate with her and you can have some sweets after, yes?"

As neither of them seemed to want any answer from us, Beaty and I turned and followed Neme to the other end of the room. Her limp did not seem to slow her much, and when she reached the seating at the far end, she spread her sheet over the largest of the couches and indicated that I should sit upon it. While I settled myself, she walked to the hearth, moving one of the lamps from the mantle to the small table in front of me.

When she spoke, her speech was touched by an accent I had never heard before. Her A's and O's were rounder, her R's nearly disappeared, and her consonants were softened, almost slurred.

"What are you called, and how old are you?"

"Arin," I croaked. I was still not practiced with my voice since our long ordeal in the mountains. "I'm ten," I said. Then I realized that in our long hazy captivity, if winter had come and gone, so had my birthday. "Sorry. Eleven."

She looked at me with a critical eye, perhaps deciding if I was lying or slow-witted. "Has your bleeding started?"

"No," I said, quietly. I hadn't thought of that in some time, and now the idea left me nauseous.

She felt my neck, pressing her fingers along my throat. She made me open my mouth and peered inside, even sniffing my breath. She felt my chest with her fingertips, seeking the earliest budding of breasts. She made me turn and pressed her ear against my back, listening to my breathing. And finally she made me lie back and spread my legs, lifting my skirts and peering closely, adjusting the lamp for better light and prodding with her fingertips. I complied with it all and stared at the ceiling, which was plastered in twenty-seven intricate rosettes.

After a few moments, she emerged and when I stood, repeated the process with Beaty, who reported she would turn sixteen in the summer, and had been bleeding for a year and a half, but wasn't sure when her last was.

When Neme finished with Beaty, she wiped her hands on her apron, led us around and seated us at the table in the middle of the room, facing the windows. She brought us one of the platters of sweets and two cups. Beaty stared for a moment before plucking a miniature cake and stuffing it in her mouth. I chose a short biscuit decorated with green sugar. The cups held a chilled wine, which I had never tasted before. I wasn't sure if I liked it. Beaty took another sweet, and a gulp of the wine.

I was watching the room. Cal and Jandry were back to standing before Ma'am's desk, with Benjin a pace behind them. Cal's eyes danced from floor to walls, avoiding Ma'am's icy gaze. Jandry was eying Cal, and I could sense calculation and something more. He had not known what he had walked into here. I wondered what lies Cal had told to his band of men. Neme limped up to Ma'am, bending to her ear once more. Then she straightened and departed through the door. There was silence for a moment before Ma'am spoke.

"Twelve."

I saw Jandry close his eyes slowly, as if he had found confirmation of something expected.

"Twelve?" Cal objected, "they're worth at least fifty!"

"One is barely a woman, and hard used. The other a child and no more than a scullery for years yet. Neither asked to be brought here. I'll be generous and give you fourteen."

Cal looked apoplectic, "Forty."

"Fifteen. Consider the shorting your repayment to them for your violence and cruelty, if you like. I have no desire to encourage such tactics."

Cal clenched his fists, "Thirty-five."

Ma'am said nothing and looked directly into his eyes. The silence stretched. Ma'am blinked once and looked to Benjin, opening her mouth to speak.

"Aye. Yes, fifteen," Cal said abruptly, sighing.

Ma'am lifted her hand to a small wooden box on her desk and withdrew a purse, dropping it on the table in front of Cal. It clinked with coin, and he snatched it up. It occurred to me that she had not needed to count out the coin, having already decided what she would pay. She looked past him to Benjin, "Please escort our guests back to their carriage," she said. She didn't wait for them to exit, retrieving her papers from the lacquerware box and picking up her silver pen.

As they walked out under guard, I saw the expression on Jandry's face, walking behind Cal. I did not think that Cal would be leading his little band very much longer.

Five

We waited at the table for some minutes before the side door opened once more and a girl about Beaty's age came. She stopped for a moment of private discussion at Ma'am's side before walking over to retrieve us. Her name was Elyse, and she was short and buxom. She had dark, almost black hair in dozens of tight braids almost to her shoulders that made her skin look even paler. Her bright green eyes were framed in startlingly long lashes. She was draped in a pale pink linen robe that hung down to mid-calf with impossibly wide sleeves that fluttered behind her as she walked.

She came and took us back to stand before Ma'am's desk. The daunting woman looked us each over for a moment, then spoke. "Whatever you have suffered, you are here now. Unless either of you have family here in Anbress to take you in, you may as well make the most you can of your lives with us. If it helps you to know, those men will never enter here again, and I'll be writing to the other houses to ensure they have no other welcome." She paused for a moment, as if waiting to see if either of us objected. "In my house everyone works their share, and everyone is taken care of. Elyse will take you upstairs to your rooms and then instruct you on where to go."

We were dismissed.

The girl led us through the small door which opened into a cramped servants passage. There was a narrow flight of stairs up immediately to our right, and all the walls were lined with cupboards from floor to ceiling. Around the corner I saw another doorway that must open into the second-floor hallway. A small lamp mounted beside the door gave light to the room. Between the open treads of the stairs, I could see a second flight going downward.

When Elyse spoke, her voice was soft and deep and rang with a vaguely artificial tenor, as if she was practicing. "Down the stairs is the laundry, then through the dining room to the kitchen, an' that's all for Cook. Stay outta her way if you know what's what, but if she says jump you jump for it. These is for linens for the whole house," she said, waving to the cupboards. "That door goes out to the main gallery."

She led us up the stairs to a narrow hallway which ran the length of the house, with doors opening along one side every few paces. There was a large door opposite the staircase, and a second smaller one on the same side to the right. She touched the door in front of us and then gestured to the other further down, "This one opens to the roof, where we set the laundry out, and that's to the attic."

She turned right and stopped at the first door on the right long enough for two rapid knocks. She hardly waited a breath before opening the door, and gesturing me inside, "You're here with Ardenne. She's down in the lounge I think, but once you're settled, run down to see Cook, who has some work for you." She turned about and walked the other direction with Beaty in tow, and I could hear her continue, "You'll be with me down at this end. Ma'am says I should show you the ropes."

I stood a moment in shock. I wasn't expecting to be separated from Beaty so soon, nor to be put to work so casually or carelessly. I paused in the doorway, taking in the room. It was small and spare, but clean enough. A narrow hearth was banked with coals producing a meager warmth. Over the small fireplace was a wooden shelf holding a lamp and flanked on either side by two small narrow beds. A serviceable rug filled the floor between the beds. Beside the door was a washstand with a large mirror and basin, and along the walls at the foot of each bed on either side was a series of pegs and shelves. One side was empty, but the other held various gowns, dresses, and robes on the pegs, and the shelves were strewn with small jars, a tiny glass bottle, and several brushes for hair and various smaller, softer brushes.

I didn't have anything to settle, but I took a moment to pour some water from the pitcher into the washbasin and splash it on my face. I washed my hands using the small lump of scented soap that sat on the shelf beside the pitcher.

I had been peering at myself in the mirror for some time, focused on the drops of water quivering on my eyelashes, when I realized I was crying. Tears flowed down my cheeks and dripped into the basin. I was lost, like the sailors in the bedtime stories Father used to tell us, whose ships were wrecked in storms and who washed up on distant shores. Here I was, bereft of family, of home, of history. I was nobody now, just the latest addition to Ma'am's house. Even at eleven I had no illusions of what this place was, and yet I was too young to be more than a maid to the others. In Father's stories, the sailor always found his way... discovered new lands, or hidden treasures, or became a pirate captain. Became something.

I was on my knees now, my forehead almost touching the floor, taking ragged breaths between sobs and shaking with grief. I cried for Father and his lost dreams. I cried for Mother and her lost daughter. I cried for Ranji and his lost future. I cried for Beaty and her lost childhood. I didn't cry for myself. I didn't deserve tears.

Even the smallest thing I could cling to here—being Beaty's little sister—was a lie twice over. I could not find it in me to believe that Ma'am, or Neme, or Elyse, or even Beaty would treat me kindly if they discovered my secret. I had spoken it aloud once to Ranji, and he had died for it, an arrow through his heart. Mother and Father had likewise died for it. I would speak it to no one else, no matter what died inside me each and every time I embraced the lie.

I'm not sure how long I cried, but eventually I was spent. I resolved myself to be this lie. I would be Arin, Beaty's little sister. Ma'am's new maid girl. I would grow up here in this new life, a new person, and bury myself deep in the cold, hard rocky soil of the mountains alongside my family's bones. I stood with this new determination and washed my face once more.

Having little else to do, I retraced my steps back down the stairs, and now circled the landing and continued down the second flight. These ended in a narrow laundry, with a great stove and kettle at one end, and washing tubs and baskets stacked on shelves along one wall. One door was closed, and I guessed this opened into the lower hallway. Another stood open and through it I could see a large dining table with two chairs each at head and foot and half a dozen down each side. Through another door on the other side of the table, there was a short passage leading to the kitchen.

The kitchen must have taken up an entire corner of the house. The largest hearth I had ever seen ran along one wall with two separate fires set in it. A large kettle simmered over one, and the other burned cheerily under an empty spit. A great brick oven above the fires glowed with heat. The center of the room held an enormous work table and there, working a great mound of dough, was Cook.

She was older than Ma'am, with dull gray hair pulled into a severe bun. She wasn't tall, but stick-thin and bony, with a pinched face with a permanent scowl. She wore an ill-fitting black dress and a white apron covered in flour. Her bare arms and face were weathered and lined with wrinkles. I stood for a moment watching her knead the dough as if she had a personal animosity to bread.

I don't know how she knew for I was not in her line of sight, but I wasn't standing there for more than a few breaths before she barked, "Oy there, new child! Get yerself here, I won't stand for dawdling."

Remembering Elyse's warning, I jumped, making my way to the work table beside her.

"You know what an onion is?" When I assured her that I did, I was sent to the larder—a broad expanse of shelves and baskets in the far corner of the kitchen—to retrieve five onions. "Know how to chop? You take that knife and chop those onions. Not too small, mind! I want to be able to *see* them in the soup. And no skins or I'll skin *you*." She pointed to the other side of the table, which was scarred with years of chopping. There was a large knife on the table, too big for me really, but the only one I saw. Taking comfort in the familiar work, I was soon deep into the onions.

I could describe the hours spent preparing that evening's meal in endless detail, but the eating of it is much more interesting.

Just before mealtime, Cook sent me to my room to wash and put on a clean dress, which I did not know I had. When I entered my room, hanging on the pegs by my bed were two clean white dresses, both a much better fit than what I was wearing. Below them was a pair of new slippers in a soft cream color. I pulled off the dress Cal had given me and dropped it to the floor. I stared at it for a moment, then kicked it into the corner, vowing never to let it touch my skin again. A moment later, I did the same with the sandals.

After a quick scrub in fresh water from the pitcher, I donned one of the new dresses, slipped my feet into the new slippers, and looked at myself in the mirror. Not much had changed in my condition, but it was a start.

I went back down the stairs to find Cook to ask what my next task was, but as I passed through the door to the dining room, I found it occupied. At the head of the large table with their backs to the fireplace, sat two young women side by side.

The one on the right corner of the table was oldest. She had long braided hair, so dark it was almost black, and plaited so tightly that the curls were barely visible. Her skin was a deep tan, and she had striking green almond-shaped eyes. Even sitting at table, I could tell that she was taller than most. She was beautiful and stately. Had I not seen Ma'am first, I would have assumed that this woman owned the house. She held herself with poise and polish, and her gown seemed an extension of this, crisp and shimmering emerald with myriad tiny pleats and a spill of bright white lace at the cuffs and bodice.

Sitting at her left was Beaty, who looked small and lost in the large room. She smiled when our eyes met, though. We were sisters at sea together. She also had changed into a new dress, this one a pale rose.

"You are Arin, yes? I am Korenne," said the woman beside Beaty. She gestured to the empty seat to the right of her table-mate. "You will come sit beside Hannah."

To her right was another girl, somewhat younger. In star-tling contrast to Korenne, Hannah had the palest skin I had ever seen, like fresh cream. Her hair was golden and she wore it in a loose fall to her shoulders, straight and smooth. This was set off by a dress in deep blue, sewn in crisp, clean lines that contrasted with her ample bosom displayed in a deeply scooped bodice. She had large round eyes, blue like a clear summer sky, and plump lips that seemed to want to smile at the slightest provocation.

She did so now. "Come Arin, sit by me and I'll introduce you around to the other girls."

I stood, numbly taking in this welcome, and more girls en-tered from the hall door, finding their places along the table and filling the room with banter and giggles. Realizing my mouth was open, I closed it and did as she said, taking the of-fered seat and taking up as little space as I could manage as the room filled with the flutter of robes and gowns and laughter.

As it did, Hannah was true to her word, pointing out each in turn with a name and some small piece of gossip or a story, so that when all were seated I felt like these were not entirely strangers to me. I overheard bits of Korenne giving similar in-troductions to Beaty across the table from me.

Lane, sitting beside me was about the same age as Hannah, and spent her free time drawing and painting, and had even sold one or two of her works to patrons. Torre was the daughter of a banker in the city, and though she had grown up at his side learning his trade, he passed her over to employ her younger male cousin who had no head for numbers but a cock between his legs, and so she had left home and bought her way into the House. Silfy was an orphan, her dead mother some distant relation to Ma'am and so had been taken in to save her from the streets. Teela shared a room with Bess on the third floor, and was a master hand at sewing and embroidery—if I needed anything altered she was the one to speak to. Jinn wasn't at table tonight, but having made a prior engagement with a favorite patron, was cavorting upstairs and unlikely to emerge for some hours yet.

The introductions continued like this until we were all seated, but two. Elyse and Bess were sharing the serving duties today, and they began bringing out the feast. When everything was on the table the two girls took their seats and the dishes were passed around. There was my soup, half a dozen loaves of warm crusty bread, crocks of soft butter and herbs, baked partridge with golden crispy skin, roasted potatoes and carrots, a dish of spinach stewed in a spicy cream, two fruit pies in laced shells of flakey pastry... more food in more variety than I had ever seen. I was tempted to eat everything, but limited myself to little more than a taste of each. With dinner we each had a cup of wine, and even though mine was watered it took only a few sips before the room took on a warm and happy glow.

When everyone had settled into their seats around the table and we were working through our plates, Korenne tapped the side of her plate with her table knife until they all took note and a quiet gradually spread amongst us. She raised her goblet and when she spoke, her voice was clear and carrying.

"Tonight, we welcome Beaty and Arin. They've had a difficult road to us, but now they're here, let us bring them into the embrace of the House. May they both find life, joy, and fortune." She took a drink from her cup, and the rest of the table followed.

Forgetting myself, I took a deep swallow and my head swam from the wine despite the food in my belly. I looked across and saw Beaty, her eyes shiny and face flushed from her wine, looking adoringly at Korenne.

That night as we ate and I listened to the babble of near a dozen voices, my perspective shifted. This place was not a prison. It was not a place for me to find the abject punishments or torture that I worried I deserved. The girls here were not slaves, not chattel. They were whores, yes. But they were something else. Something I had lost and never thought to have again.

They were a family.

Over the next several days, I learned the patterns of the house.

Benjin and Doan were the house guards, and they spent their days at the front door, or in the suite of rooms they shared off of the entry. Benjin was a huge hulk of a man, but before long I realized that he was quite aware of his strength and used it sparingly if at all. Doan was a wiry man, light and quick, but no less intimidating. They interacted with the denizens of the house very little, even taking most meals in their small shared apartment. Their job was not to keep us contained, but to keep us safe. Their presence alone seemed to ensure in most cases that the patrons behaved themselves and took only those liberties that they had paid for.

Neme had a room on the third floor on the other side of the staircase from mine. She saw to the medical needs of the house, dispensing herbs and remedies to the girls to keep them working, free of babes and fevers and other inconveniences.

Cook was a power unto herself. I never saw her take any direction from anyone, including Ma'am, and she ran her kitchen, the dining room, and the laundry as if they were her own private fiefdom, belonging to and peopled by her and her alone. She had a small room—no bigger than the garret I had shared with Ranji—directly off the kitchen, and I'm not sure she ever set foot outside those rooms.

If Cook and Neme and the guards kept the house running, it was Ma'am that *was* the house. It was as if her indomitable will took hold of the world and forced her vision into existence. Her's was the foremost house of pleasure in Anbress. Her patrons, men and occasionally women, were the wealthy, the well-regarded in society, and the powerful. Ma'am approved every patron, every assignation. She largely kept to her apartments and yet somehow still knew every movement in her house.

And then there were the girls.

Korenne was the oldest, and informally Ma'am's lieutenant in the house. She shared rooms and a bed with Hannah on the second floor at the top of the main stairs. Also around the second floor gallery was Lane, Silfy, Torre, and Jinn.

I say "girls", and that's how we all referred to each other, but most were young women, and Jinn was a man. A year younger than Korenne, he was lithe and graceful and beautiful to look at, and knew it well. He looked so much like Ranji in face and coloring that it would have been painful for me to look on him, except that I had put my old life behind me. Like all the girls, he served both male and female patrons, but even when not with a patron, he rarely slept in his own room, preferring instead to make the rounds of the other girls' beds whenever unoccupied.

There was a stark hierarchy between the senior girls whose rooms were on the second floor, and those of us on the third-floor. Each of the second floor rooms was its own private parlor, furnished by patron gifts and the monthly stipend that Ma'am doled out based on their various efforts. They were trusted to make their own arrangements with patrons, to leave the house for assignations and shopping, and were exempted from all house chores.

On the third floor with Elyse, Beaty, and I were Ardenne, and Teela and Bess who roomed together. Whereas I exclusively served the house, helping in the kitchens, doing laundry, cleaning the first and second floor rooms, and other domestic chores, the other third-floor girls divided their time between entertaining patrons in the first-floor parlors and occasionally joining a senior girl in her rooms, and taking their turns alongside me with the household work. Each day a different girl served the house along with me. They were allowed to keep any patron gifts, but otherwise our room and board was our only payment. They all yearned for the day they earned enough in gifts to buy their way out of chores. This was their way out of the drudgery of cleaning and serving, and into the glamorous life of patronage.

Into these dynamics, Beaty and I were introduced.

Ma'am had taken us each aside for a private word. To me, she said that my work would be daily house chores as assigned by Cook, until such time as I came of age and chose to move to the parlors.

Everyone seemed to appreciate my addition to the house. The third-floor girls because I relieved them each of a full day of household duties—that they could focus all the more on earning a place in the main gallery. I believe the other members of the house appreciated the consistency that I offered. That each and every day, Cook knew who would be at her side in the kitchen or doing the washing just so. And if Cook was meticulous, Ma'am was even more particular about how and when trays were brought and taken, how her rooms were cleaned and linens washed. And as she set the values of the house, so the girls along the gallery took her as their model.

So I haunted the service corridors, laundry, and kitchen. I was ever aware of the line of bells in the service stairwell that would ring and pivot the small wooden flag from black to red whenever one of the bell ropes was pulled through the house, each flag indicating a request from a different chamber. I took trays, refreshed pitchers, fetched baths, retrieved laundry, and all the thousand things that kept the girls' lives moving along smoothly.

For Beaty's part, she seemed to immediately take to her new life. For all her talk of our being sisters, she drifted away from me. The realities of life in the house meant that as she shared her room with Elyse, she spent most of her time with her and the other girls learning the techniques of seduction and sex. The intimacy that sustained us through captivity and deprivation had gone stale now that we had comforts and futures.

That's not to say that she abandoned me. On the days we were partners in housework, she shared endless gossip with me about the other girls, about Jinn, about the patrons she had seen. And about sex. We had both grown up on farms, so the realities of sex was nothing new to us. And even if not for that, I would have thought her treatment under Cal's captivity would have rendered her utterly incurious.

Instead, she seemed to revel in it, finding endless pleasure even in discussing theoretical acts she had only heard tell of. She spoke tirelessly and in jubilant detail about this technique or that sensation, and I had difficulty at first distinguishing what she had known first-hand and what she knew only by rumor. Some four weeks after our arrival, that difficulty disappeared.

Five days before, I had finally shed the name of "new child" in Cook's eyes. It was the early afternoon, and I was working in the laundry stoking the fire under the great washing kettle. Every few minutes, I dipped fingers in the water. When it began to boil, I would tip it into the large wooden washing tub and mix the bucking. In would go the next batch of linens, shifts, hose, and all the other laundry for soaking. Each tub-full would soak, be churned with the great wooden paddle, and then be hauled trip after exhausting trip up the narrow service stairs all the way to the rooftop, to be stretched out and beaten with the paddle, left to bleach, rinsed in the barrels of rain water, hung to dry in the sun and wind, and finally brought back down to the second floor in another endless repetition of steps to be folded and put away or redistributed throughout the household. I had been at it since dawn.

The washing day procedure took the entire day to finish—I would be folding until well past dark—and left muscles aching and hands and arms raw and burned by the lye soap. I think it was primarily this which motivated the third-floor girls to escape the drudgery of chores. I was working this day with Bess, who was helping Cook prepare for supper. I usually volunteered for the bulk of the laundry duties—a move calculated both to spare the other girls the chore which I knew helped them to love me, and to give me a great deal of solitude which otherwise was difficult to come by in such a crowded house.

While I waited for the water to heat, I took an empty basket and went up the stairs to the third floor. The girls there were meant to bring their own washing down to the laundry, but I had made it my habit to collect it from them as I did with everyone else in the house. Having already brought mine and Ardenne's earlier, I turned left at the top of the staircase and knocked first on Neme's door.

She opened it after a moment and smiled at me, the damage of her face turning what I knew to be meant as a friendly, gentle smile into a severe twist of a smirk. "Laundry day?" I nodded to her, and she made way for me to enter her narrow room and collect the items she indicated.

The next door was Teela and Bess's room, and I knew that Bess had brought down their washing that morning, so I moved on to knock at Elyse and Beaty's door. When there was no answer, I pushed it open and entered, thinking it to be empty.

Instead, I found Beaty curled up on her side upon her bed, knees drawn to her chest and staring at nothing, face slack. Her right hand was a fist, knuckles nearly white.

I sat on her bed beside her foot, and saw her flinch back from me. After a moment, her eyes drifted towards me and focused, and she relaxed slightly, her fist slackening so that I could see she held something in her hand. We both said nothing for some time, just sat in silence, listening to our own breathing.

When she spoke, it was a small, fragile voice, halting and uncertain, "I thought... I thought it would be fun. They said... It didn't feel good... He... Silfy was kind... did most of... but she... said I should..." She sighed, then took several deep breaths, seeming to take strength from the weight of air. When she spoke again, her voice was firmer and more assured but still quiet, "It wasn't like I was expecting."

I leaned down and hugged her, my sister, and she hugged back. We embraced for just a moment, and then she moved to sit up, full of manic energy. She dropped a heavy silver coin on the shelf beside her bed.

"You're collecting laundry. Can't waste time with me. There," she pointed, "those, and the stockings, and..." here she bounded up and stripped her shift off, and scooped up the bed linens and several more items to drop into my basket. "Off with you, can't let Cook catch you dawdling!"

She chased me out, my basket now overflowing with washing. As I passed Neme's door I knocked again. When she opened it, I lost my voice for a moment. She looked at me with a questioning expression marred by her broken face. Finally, I said softly, "Beaty is in her room. She just... I think she needs to talk." I didn't know what more to say, and so I turned and descended the stairs.

Two years of my life passed in much the same way. The routines of the House were as ingrained in me as the routines of the farm had been in my previous life. Changes were mostly small and subtle, though some were more notable.

Torre had left us, having so enthralled one of her patrons the previous year that he had come one warm August day with a leather and brass-bound coffer under his arm and spent an hour or so alone with Torre and Ma'am in Ma'am's sitting room. When he left again, Torre left with him upon the same arm, and she carried the coffer.

In celebration of Torre's new circumstances, she left gifts to us all to be distributed by Ma'am. The girls on the second floor were given only a symbolic pittance. Cook, Neme, and the guards all received some small sum as a gift of appreciation. We on the third floor each received ten silver coins. For me, this was the most money I had ever held in my hand.

By December, Bess had bought her way into the main

gallery, taking Torre's old room. She could now earn real money, taking a share of her every lay and assignation. She joined the other senior girls in the lavish lifestyle of the second floor.

The day that she moved down into her new room, she left the house to shop for various needful things for her debut on the main gallery, and asked Ma'am for permission to take me along to help carry. I followed behind her in a plain woolen dress and slippers. I had been on such trips now and again, to carry for the older girls, or to help Cook or Neme collect some ingredient for their respective arts. But this trip I was with Bess, and we had essentially grown up together these last years. We were close as cousins, and she hadn't yet grown into her change in circumstances.

And so, as she stepped into this shop or that boutique to browse gowns and shoes, scents and makeup, she held my arm, pointing out this fabric or that slipper. She spent some time in a small shop picking over perfumes, asking to smell this one or that one, occasionally trying a drop on one wrist or the other, and once grasped my hand and dabbed one scent against my skin. I will admit that I liked the smell.

But at another, she poured over innumerable tiny jars of color. The subtlety and variations were lost on me... one red looked very much like the next. But she kept up a chatter with the woman who prepared the various creams and powders, and at some point I realized they were speaking of me.

"Oh, yes, our Arin... she has *such* eyes, doesn't she?"

"Them's what we call storm eyes, m'dear. Change color like the sky as a winter storm rolls over the land—now bright blue, now dark gray, now black, now a hint of violet," she held up a small pot of something dark and leaned close to me, still talking to Bess as if I was a clothing dummy. "Now watch this," she said, as she dipped her thumb into the pot and so quickly that I didn't have a chance to react beyond closing my eyes, she swiped her thumb against my eyelids. She exchanged the pot for something else as I blinked rapidly, trying to understand why my eyes felt different. Then there was a brush against my lips, and she stepped back. "Oh, now *that* I call a picture. You'll tear their hearts out you will, m'dear."

Bess made an O of her mouth and her eyes widened. "You look *so* beautiful Arin," she said, turning me to face the mirror in the corner. What I saw there made me deeply uncomfortable.

It was me—but wrong. It was as if my mind were split into two.

There was my mind looking on at another person who looked just like me; she *was* pretty, and the makeup made her glow. Her storm eyes shimmered under shadowed lids like the glowing sky under storm clouds, and her lips were glossy and just touched with enough color that they seemed to draw the eye, and I wouldn't have minded kissing them.

There was also another mind, and she was looking down on *me* in the mirror. I could feel her grim disgust at my garishly painted face; sense her sneer of derision at the grotesquerie that she saw. Smears of thick dark paste stained my eyelids, collecting in the corners and folds when I blinked and sure to drip down my cheeks at the first provocation. My lips were coated in a sticky wetness, as if with rancid, congealed blood.

For the remainder of the outing, I wandered in a senseless daze. I replied to Bess's prompts and made conversation. I oohed over her purchases as expected, and managed her baggage as needed. But I did these things with no sense of reality. I was holding on to the edge of a cliff with my fingertips, thinking of nothing at all except: when would I find the first moment that I could wash my face clean of the makeup and feel my face once more. That time did not come for several more hours.

When we finally made the house, I was almost breathless with the need to wash. I carried her new things to her room, thanked her for the outing, and received a silver penny as thanks. I scrambled up the stairs to my room and scrubbed my face until the washbowl was a murky gray and my skin was nearly raw. I never allowed any kind of cosmetics on my skin again.

If the time hadn't changed the house much beyond Torre's leaving and Bess's promotion, these two years had brought some more subtle changes to me. I had grown taller, my hips were wider, and my body was becoming rounder. Not softer, for the endless tramping up and down stairs hauling trays of food, buckets of water, tubs of laundry, and all other manner of sundry necessities of a house of almost twenty people meant that I could not be soft. But my hips had a new shape, and my gait a new roll, and the first buds of breasts were visible now under my shift. This last alarmed me. Wider hips made me feel more grounded, more settled into myself and the earth. Even though I was taller by some inches, I felt more stable and less gangly. But every sight I caught in the mirror of enlarged nipples, of the protruding curve of breast beneath my clothing filled me with disquiet.

That my body was changing as I grew was a given, but to be betrayed in this way... to be forced by the stuff of myself to embody the lie that I was telling the world, was too much to bear. Every day that I found myself alone in my room, I stood naked and stared into the mirror, feeling the churning emotions—unnameable, but just short of revulsion—at the subtle hints of curving breast that probably only I could even see. But to me, they were grotesque growths that simply didn't belong on my body. I strained with every ounce of will I could muster for them to stop. I bargained with my body that I would find a way to accept what had grown so far if only they would grow no further.

And then my bleeding started. Much was made of it at the time by the other girls, but to me, it was more a nuisance than anything else, especially as it started in the night, so laundry day came half a week early. Neme examined me, and started me on the same daily regimen of a bitter tisane brewed from herbs and bark that the other girls took. This didn't stop my period altogether, but reduced it to bearable inconvenience and according to her, also would prevent me from getting a child if I drank it consistently. This last was not in my mind—I was content with my duties and had not the slightest interest in joining in the House profession—until some weeks later, I was summoned to Ma'am's study.

The years did not seem to touch her beyond perhaps a new wrinkle or two at her eyes and mouth. She was as impressive and commanding as when I first came to the house.

"I hear from Neme that you can join the other girls when you think you're ready."

I sat still, looking into her face trying to tell if she could see my discomfort. I already knew all about the girls' work by now of course. I could hardly live in the house for two years and not know all the ins-and-outs, as it were. A house of pleasure is not a place where mincing formality and modesty can survive long.

I had seen the girls with their patrons, bringing wine and morsels from the kitchens, or fresh linens, or whatever was needful, before and after the deeds, and sometimes during. I had seen cocks aplenty in various acts, and the inevitable aftermath of sex. When they weren't actively engaged in it, it was the primary topic of conversation much of the time.

No, my discomfort came from a very different place. As much as I had felt my own desires growing as my body did, as much as I had played the part of Beaty's sister and girl-of-the-house, I knew that I could not bring myself to be counted with the girls. And in this house, there was no room for the ambiguity and ambivalence that I felt. For me to lay with a man here would be to lay as a woman. And as much as I had pretended and lied to myself and everyone else these years, I was not a woman. The more I felt my body shifting in that direction, the more I knew the lie for what it was. I couldn't make sense of this in my own mind, but my reactions to the makeup, to my growing breasts could not be denied.

I opened my mouth to speak, but nothing came to my tongue.

She eyed me, weighing, considering, "You need not if you don't like. I normally would not stint the House, and would seek another situation for you, but I will admit you are something I have not seen before now."

I held my breath. Had she understood? Had she seen through my lie?

"Most girls groan and complain of the drudgery of housework. You know most of them came to me willingly, yes? To escape pain or abuse or the monotony of their proscribed futures. The men who brought you were not meant to take you unwilling, and they will never see coin from me—or any of the other houses—again for it."

She leaned forward, eyes still fixed on me, "But you came to us nonetheless, and instead of shirking, instead of grumping, you've taken to the housework. You are well liked by the other girls and even Cook has told me, 'she doesn't always burn the bread,' which I must assure you is high praise indeed. You know that not everyone here serves in the same way. If you wish to keep to the service rooms, or simply to wait and bide until you feel the desire to do more, no one here will force you."

Taking my continued silence as understanding, she took her eyes from mine and turned back to her papers. "I'll have a bath in half an hour," she said, dismissing me.

I stood numbly, still churning over her words as I left through the service door, and started up the stairs to the roof to bring down one of the two hammered copper bath tubs that were kept there.

And so my life continued. I took more responsibilities in the kitchen, I doubled my efforts in serving the girls and the rest of the house, and I tried to avoid the parlors except when there was no one else to take a tray or wine pitcher. I was as content serving as I think I would have been farming. I would have stayed so, likely eventually taking over entirely from Cook and living out my days there. But the world is not complacent when people like us are at peace.

It happened some months on. In late spring, there were occasional nights of a damp warmth in Anbress. It was uncomfortable enough that we opened all the windows to try to catch every breeze and most of the girls went about in light fluttering dressing robes and little else. I had a robe of fine brushed linen that was a gift from Ardenne, who had outgrown it. It was the nicest thing I owned, and I normally wore it only as a cover over my plain working dress if I needed to enter one of the finer public spaces of the house, or interact with a patron.

This day, I had worn it all on its own. The lavender-dyed linen was thin and light and cooling against my skin, but even this much was sticky and uncomfortable on such a humid night. The hearths were all cold, and even the kitchen fires were banked. No one wanted hot food. I spent much of the evening circulating through the house replenishing pitchers of chilled wine and mint-and-cucumber-steeped water, and platters of delicate cakes and pastries.

The House wasn't busy this night. I suppose there is being *driven* to heat and fervor by passion, and then there is *beginning* in swelter and discomfort. Few patrons were out this night, and most that were were more inclined to lounge and sip wine and *look* at young, beautiful flesh than to join theirs with it. Still, some were led upstairs from the parlors into private rooms: Korenne and Hannah had taken one of their regulars to their bed, while Lane was deep in negotiation with a man I had not seen before.

I made rounds of the parlors, pouring for some and removing empty trays and discarded cups. I wound my way around the rooms and backed into the kitchen with a stack of empties carefully balanced against my hip. The wash water was still warm enough, and it took little time to scrub out the pitchers and cups and wipe down the trays before stacking them neatly on their shelves. Avoiding Cook's ire was second nature to me now, and it took no more than a steady effort.

When I returned to the laundry, I saw one of the bell flags was showing, indicating that Lane had pulled the rope in her room, probably while I was collecting dishes. I had no desire to attend her while she entertained a patron, but tonight I was serving alone.

I climbed the stairs and before stepping out into the main gallery, I tied my robe closed, making sure that I was well covered. I circled the gallery to Lane's door and knocked twice.

"Come in," she said.

I opened the door enough to see Lane and her patron naked in a tangle of arms, legs, and bedclothes. They were both flushed with lovemaking, the man I had seen earlier lying back against the pillows with eyes closed and breathing deeply.

"Arin, can you please bring up some more wine, and also a pitcher of chilled water? Mine has gone warm."

I said nothing, but nodded my head and withdrew, descending the service stairs and into the kitchen to set a tray. A pitcher each of wine and water, two cups, and a small plate of sweet cakes went on the tray, and I was heading back up the stairs in only a few minutes. As I passed the bells, I reached up and reset the flag for Lane's room.

I wound back around again, rapped twice to announce myself and entered with the tray. I was well into the room and setting down the tray on the small table beside the bed before I realized that the patron was no longer taking his ease in the bed, but standing naked at the washstand by the door.

As I straightened, my eyes met his for a brief moment in the tall standing mirror in the corner. I did not like the way they measured me, and I self-consciously drew my robe tighter around my body.

"Anything else?" I asked Lane, willing her to dismiss me.

"No, thank you Arin," she said.

I nodded and turned to the door, keeping my eyes down and making myself as small as possible as I neared him.

"Come back to bed," Lane cooed to him from behind me.

But before I could reach the door, he was standing before me, one hand gripping his cock—rousing himself—and the other reaching out to the shoulder of my robe. I stepped back out of his reach, but he followed.

"Oh now, why do you run little one? Join us. I have strength enough for the both of you." His eyes were lined in red and glistening with too much drink, and his speech slurred. He weighed easily three of me, his body ropey and muscular. He took another step towards me. I backed again towards the corner.

Lane rose from her bed and her voice had a tension that wasn't there before, "Jakob, she was no part of our negotiation. Leave her be."

He looked at her, but he did not stop his advance, a sly smile creeping across his face. She tried to step between us, but he brushed her aside angrily. She struck the bedpost as she fell with enough force to shift the bed and jostle the tray, and porcelain pitchers, cups, and all tipped over to shatter against the floor in a terrific crash. Cold wine and sharp splinters were strewn across the room.

It seemed for a moment that everything stopped and the room was still and silent. His eyes widened, and Lane lifted herself from the floor, her hands bleeding from pitcher shards.

And then, time seemed to condense into a single moment, too many things happening all at once.

His hand grasped my shoulder. I stumbled backwards and fell against the mirror. My robe was torn open and he slipped, broken dishes crunching under his bare feet. He lunged towards me reaching with both hands. His erect cock was inches from my face and he loomed over me. I heard Lane calling for help. My head struck the mirror, cracking the glass.

I was so small beneath his looming hulk. His nakedness above me was a grim and violent threat, his rigid tool like a great knife held to my throat, ready to tear my body and spill my lifeblood. His eyes were wild with an animal fury that would not be sated short of desperate violence. I could smell sour wine sweat and animal musk and stale sex. I felt my thighs and buttocks wet with ice-cold wine and the back of my head matted with hot sticky blood, and I knew that if he touched me again I would die.

I felt some delicate balance within me teetering under a great weight.

I was towering above a small quivering creature who shrank beneath my great strength. I was death itself and knew I could reach out to snap this poor thing's neck with almost no effort. I could plunge my iron rod deep into that young flesh and take my pleasure and the terror I saw in those eyes would only add spice to the savor. I could imagine those soft lips wrapped around me and drawing forth the waves of ecstasy that were only my due.

The balance shifted slightly.

I was crouched beneath a lumbering giant, so drunk and unsteady and overbalanced that he would topple at any moment. So fragile in his mind and poisoned in his thoughts that the slightest provocation drove him to lash out in unfocused violence at the world that he understood only enough to see that others navigated it easily where he stumbled and failed. He stole from his employer because his limp efforts gained him little pay. He gambled in the taverns because no one would share society with him for free. He paid for women because none would have him otherwise.

My mind tensed like a cat preparing to pounce, and the balance swayed.

I was staring down at a small, compact, dangerous creature crouched before me. Tearing my gaze away from those narrowed storm-gray eyes was difficult, but worse still was what I saw then in the crazed mirror above them. I saw a grotesque and pathetic monster, bulging red veined eyes shining with fury and pain set in a face full of hatred and self-loathing. A body covered in patchy coarse hair like a beast riddled with mange. Hands contorted into arthritic caricatures of vicious claws. And a prick hanging half-hard, misshapen and roped with tangled veins, dripping disgusting slime from its pink tip like a slug mired in its own glistening trail.

Without thought, without knowing what I did, I tipped the balance a hairsbreadth.

I heard a desperate wail of agony and despair. It tore through the room, shocking and terrifying. A crash sounded from above my head and fragments and splinters of glass rained down on me and I saw him clutching a long shard of the mirror in a bloody fist. He was sobbing and screaming and thrashing his head all at once, but there was no hesitation in his actions.

I watched him grasp his softening cock in one hand, and saw through it with the glass knife in the other. His face was full of horror and madness as he tossed the shriveled lump of bloody flesh to the floor beside me.

He staggered back a pace, blood pulsing from his ruined groin and flowing down his naked thighs, his face locked in a rictus of pain. In one last convulsion of agony and fury he advanced on me and I saw the glass glinting in the lamplight. I felt a flash of white-hot heat against my face and then there was shouting and a struggle and Benjin and Doan were pulling him away. Lane was at my side pressing something to my cheek. Silfy and Jinn stood in the hallway, peeking in from either side of the doorframe, their faces aghast and trembling in horror. And between them stood Ma'am. Her narrow frame was wrapped in a dressing gown and her hair in a tight bun, but her eyes shone with a cold fury.

She swept into the room, taking us in and issuing commands. "Take this filth out!" Ma'am said in a quiet rage, biting each word. "And Benjin," she said, catching his arm, "the back way—and see that you are not noted. And then send for Orban of the Guard. Jinn, run and fetch Neme. Silfy, wake Ardenne, Elyse, and Teela. Have Teela start water boiling and bring—"

I lost whatever else she said. The room was starting to sway and blur, and I felt ice running from my chest up to the top of my head. The world spun, and I heard Lane beside me call out, "Ma'am, she's..." and then I was pillowed in a deep, dark gray, drowning in featureless goose down. My face was afire and my body was shaking with chills. Time and sense disappeared into a spiraling, nauseating tumble of darkness, light, ringing, and silence, punctuated by moments of intense pain and clarity.

"...so much blood..."

"...needle and thread..."

"...keep her warm..."

My eyes fluttered open at a searing pain and I could see nothing but a dark and twisted face only inches from my own.

"...terrible scar..."

"...if the fever doesn't break..."

Now the bright hot room was gone and I was swathed in darkness. A cooling breeze flowed over me but part of my face felt of both fire and ice at once. There were others in the room with me, and they whispered and muttered too quietly to follow.

There were still voices wavering in and out of my head, but quieter, muffled and echoed so that I couldn't say if I heard them or felt them through my body.

...Orban reports no...

...steady, no change...

...nothing you did wrong...

"Drink this."

Sunlight streamed through an open window nearby and a cup was at my lips. I sipped the warm liquid, bitter and herbaceous. I drifted away again, too vague and unformed to care that opening my mouth to drink felt unfamiliar.

Seven

I was a giant picking through thousands of tiny pebbles, pinching each one with ungainly fingers too large to control, but desperate to sift through them all to find the one that I was searching for. It was futile, as they all looked identical and they kept shifting beneath me, but I knew that if I didn't find the right one, I was doomed.

I was running across an infinite expanse of stone, crumbling flagstone alternating with areas of treacherous cobble, all lying in wait to turn my ankle and slow me down. A viscous, slippery gray fluid was slowly, ever so slowly, rising from between the stones. The liquid was now around my thighs, and I was slogging forward, slowed to an agonizing walk. And still it rose.

I was standing on a grand balcony overlooking a great valley below. Immense stone columns fluted in spirals wound from the balcony edge upwards to vanish into the clouds. I was not alone there. Dozens of elegant people dressed in a multitude of rich styles stood in groups of three and four, sipping drinks from crystal goblets and chattering happily. The sky beyond the columns glowed in variegated hues from bright blue to blazing orange to deep purple. And through that sky flew fantastic creatures. They were bright purple and flew with slow beats of great leathery wings and with their bodies upright. Each one trailed a long fluttering tendril behind them from a crest upon their heads. I called out to the people below to look, to see these beasts. I was desperate to get their attention, but the people milled and smiled and gossiped. Not one of them looked up to see the majestic creatures just above them. I was filled with an agonizing, abject fear. Not terror of the dragons in the sky, but fear that they were flying past us—that soon they would be gone and that no one else but me would ever bear witness to their beauty.

I had many more fevered dreams before I woke.

I cannot say how many nights it was before I regained lucidity and opened my eyes. I knew this was cold reality by the squalor of the dusty furniture piled in the corner of the room. By the dull gray light coming through bleached wooden shutters, illuminating dust motes floating in the air. And I knew by the large wad of a bandage wrapping the right side of my face. I could open my left eye, and by turning my head I could take in my surroundings. I was in one of the unused rooms on the third floor. By the position of the small window, I could tell it was the last on the hall, the next door from the one I shared with Ardenne. I reached up with my right hand to explore the wrappings on my face.

It hurt. There was a diffuse and radiating pain from my jaw to my scalp, and I couldn't think well enough through it to recall what it meant. A thick padding of linen covered that portion of my face, and a thinner gauze was wrapped under my chin and around over my crown to hold it in place so that both of my ears were somewhat muffled and I felt hot under it all. Something was wrong with what I felt through the bandage, but I couldn't understand it.

The door opened, and Neme limped into my field of view.

"You're awake. How do you feel?"

I looked at her with my left eye, trying with nothing but the steadiness of my gaze to convey the futility of that question.

"Wumm mmpned?" I asked.

She pulled a chair beside the bed and sat, looking at me for a moment. "I need to check your dressing." She began unwinding the gauze from my face. As she did, she spoke almost absently, her slurring accent softening the clinical words. "Lots of minor cuts on your thighs and bottom, but you'll hardly have noticed those. Mostly healed already. The lacerations to your scalp from the mirror are scabbed over and healing nicely."

The long loosely-woven strip of fabric came away and my right eye opened. In the sudden change in light, I blinked my eyes several times. A moment later my eyes focused and I could see normally. I could feel tears on my cheeks. She gently peeled away the thick wadded linen.

"He cut you deeply from your right temple to your chin. I had to sew your cheek closed. I'm sorry, but you are going to be scarred." I looked up at her. My eyes focused on the right side of her face, her sunken cheekbone and the brutal twisting of bone and muscle that deformed her face. Her lips quirked into a sardonic smile. "You won't look as bad as I do. But you're not going to be pretty anymore."

I was startled at these words. Both at the thought that I had been pretty, and also that I would care that I no longer was. My hand moved to my cheek, almost of its own accord, but hers reached out to bat it away.

"Don't. Right now the most important thing is to keep the stitches clean. No touching. Now let me look." She leaned over to peer closely at my cheek. She held a lamp close to my face. She put her nose close enough to sniff twice. "No infection. Healing cleanly."

She lifted a small clay bowl, dipped a small brush into it, and I felt a thick paste being dabbed onto my face. It smelled foul.

"Hurts," I said.

She finished swabbing my face, and traded the bowl for a cup. "Drink this." As I parted my lips I could feel the awkward tugging of my cheek all the way to the top of my head. It was disconcerting. I sipped the barely warm tisane. It tasted about as bad as the paste smelled, but the sharp edges of the pain seemed to soften. Everything in my vision took on a comfortable glow.

"If I leave off the bandage, can I trust you to not touch your face?"

I had to think for a moment. My mind wasn't moving as fast as I was used to. "You can."

She nodded, and began gathering her things. There was a knock at the door as she stood, and the door opened before she had fully left her chair.

Ma'am entered and without saying anything, she took the seat Neme had just vacated. She took a moment to settle herself, looking at me. Her eyes were sunken, and she looked tired, as if she had not slept enough lately. But if her eyes were red-limned, they were as sharp as ever. She leaned forward, taking my measure. Her eyes traced the scar on my face, down the sheet-covered form of my body, then back up to my face for a moment. She glanced over her shoulder at Neme, who left the room without a word, closing the door behind her. Ma'am looked back to me.

"You remember what we spoke of some months ago? That you need not serve the way others here do?"

I nodded.

"Your options have been diminished by the acts of a man who should never have set foot in this house. For that I must apologize."

I opened my mouth to speak, and her eyes sharpened. But she paused, and I found some courage a moment later. "Is that what happened to Neme?"

She regarded me for a time. "If you mean, 'was she abused under my roof?', the answer is no. She was not. Neme was trained in the arts of healing in her homeland, in the capital of Somiere. The story of how she was scarred is her tale to tell, not mine. But when she came to Anbress, seeking an escape, a fresh start, and above all anonymity, I saw in her the value that a woman of science and healing could provide to us here, and I made her an offer of home and of purpose." Ma'am shifted slightly in her seat, before continuing.

"I make now the same offer to you. Cook is aging, and while she is likely to reside yet for several years in her rooms by the kitchen, her joints are beginning to resist the virtue in Neme's tinctures and potions. In a year, maybe two, she will retire from her duties. And she herself has recommended you to continue in them."

My eyes widened at this news. Cook never gave so much as a compliment, let alone indicated that another was worthy of her kitchen.

"Yes," Ma'am smiled ruefully, "a remarkable testimonial. This offer stands, assuming no further... incidents occur. Think on it. You have time yet to heal, and nothing will be asked of you for at least a week. More will depend on Neme's judgment."

She paused then, and I looked away, thinking the interview over. But after a minute, I looked back and she was still sitting, still looking at me intently. She opened her mouth to speak, then closed it, considering. I had never known Ma'am to be unsure of anything, and so I knew that what she might say next was something vital.

"Do you," she trailed off, then started again, "Do you know what made him do what he did?" Her eyes narrowed slightly. I would have thought I imagined it but for her hesitancy. "The girls talk, you know. There is always gossip. And despite the ordeal those men put you through so many years ago, Beaty remembered meeting you, and has wondered aloud at how you looked to her."

My breath caught and my eyes shifted, down, to the door, the window, then back to Ma'am. There was no escape from what she would say next, and my reaction seemed to confirm something for her. She proceeded with more confidence.

"You needn't fear. The girls talk, but they don't understand most of what they have seen or heard, and would never think to guess your secret. But... well, I have resources to make delicate inquiries. There is a... patron of sorts. Not the kind we usually entertain here, mind. But let us say, he has an interest in... unique individuals. I think we both know that your story is not as common as you wish it were."

She stood, still watching me. "Think on it. My first offer stands. You can be a cook here in this house for as long as you keep the rules and care for this family. Or you can be something... else. The choice is yours."

Her eyes met mine briefly, then she nodded to herself and left the room.

Later that evening, Neme entered again carrying a tray piled with bandages and other items of her craft, and a bowl and mug under cloth. The smell of food made my empty stomach lurch, but I wasn't sure I could bring myself to eat. She set the tray aside and sat beside me, lifting the lamp from the bedside table to my face.

"Let me look at it."

Again I suffered her impersonal gaze as she examined me. She probed gently around the scar, asking how much it hurt. She had me open my mouth and peered inside. Finally, she sat back in her chair and moved the tray beside me.

"Eat."

"I... don't want to," I said. Even those few words pulled at my cheek and irritated the stitches inside and out.

"You have to eat. There are two reasons. One, your body needs food to rebuild itself and heal the damage. Two, I know that you are feeling pain, and I cannot give you more medicine to dull it unless you have food in your stomach." She made this speech with no emotional plea. She simply stated it as facts that could not be argued with. She looked at me steadily, unmoving.

I realized that if I did not eat something, she may well feed me like an infant, so I removed the cloth covering the food to find a earthenware bowl of dark soup. It smelled delicious and I was suddenly lightheaded with hunger. There was a small silver spoon beside the bowl, and I smiled to myself as I realized that against her inclinations, Cook had minced the vegetables—including the onions—as finely as possible so that I had no need to chew. The broth was stewed rich and fatty from ham bones, salty and spiced with mild peppers, garlic, and onions. Once I started, I couldn't stop myself lifting spoon after spoon of it to my lips. I didn't need to open my mouth wide and could just sip a small mouthful at a time. Despite this pace, I soon emptied the bowl.

Neme watched me as I ate, and now she moved the bowl to the side table and handed me a small warm mug. I could smell the same bitter brew as before. I sipped it and the pain and heat eased a little. I found I preferred to let my head rest back on the pillow than to hold it up.

"You'll want to sleep a great deal more than normal for a few days. You're excused from any chores until I say otherwise, but tomorrow, I'll want you up and walking around. I'm going to bandage you each night so that you don't bother the wound in your sleep."

As she spoke, she moistened a small hand towel with scented water from a kettle and began dabbing my skin. The warmth felt good, and her touch was gentle and delicate. With warmth radiating from my belly and the warm smell of medicinal herbs hanging over my face, I began to feel myself floating. Before I could stop myself, my fingers were stroking her ruined face.

"How did this happen?" I asked.

She didn't reply at once, but she gently and firmly moved my hand back down to the bed. I thought she would ignore me, but as she continued to wash my wound, she spoke, "It was an accident. In Somiere. I was visiting a patient as part of my apprenticeship. Just a pre-birth visit to check on her, but she was feeling ill, so it took longer than expected. By the time I was done, I was late to meet my fiancé, so instead of walking, I hailed a carriage."

She put down the damp cloth and the small pot and brush came out again, and she once more delicately dabbed the foul-smelling paste onto my face. "The driver took a turn too quickly. Something in the hitching gave way, and the carriage ran away down the *Voulange*—a great road on a steep hill in...in the city. The carriage rolled over, and I woke up much as you have, in the care of a physician of the *Gruende*."

She leaned close and thumbed my right eyelid open, peering closely into my eye. "When I could walk again, there was too much for me. Too much pain, too much care, too much pity. Mostly too much pity. My fiancé was full of it. My teacher was full of it. And so I had to leave and start anew."

She placed a clean bandage against my cheek and began winding my head in gauze once more. "When a person sees the likes of us, they will react in one of two ways. They will draw back in horror, or they will draw back in pity." She trailed off in her tale, but continued winding the bandage. I was asleep before she finished.

This time, I can't say if I dreamed. There were moments I felt that I was floating in darkness, and moments where I was carried in a stream of cold light. I saw glimpses of worry and shadows of pain. There were voices now and then, echoing through endless layers of gauze and drugs and pain and sleep and darkness.

... have... called me here? You know... none of...

Calm yourself. I... to ask—Ask you... deliver a message to your master. I may have... something he seeks.

May? You know that the Viscount will not be... have his time wasted.

I say may. *I do not know for sure, but I do... what he seeks is rare—and valuable enough—that "may" is worth the message... choose himself what he does with it. I have written down the particulars here... only that you see it delivered, and bring me his response. ...terms of sale if... interested...*

Eight

In the days that followed, Neme was in my room each morning to chivvy me up and make me walk up and down the service stairs. I was slow at first, as she still made me drink her bitter tisane that left me unsteady but eased the pain of my face. But having regained my feet, I began to recover quickly. By the fourth day I could ascend and descend from my dusty corner room to the laundry on the first floor just as quickly as I had before the attack, and the bandages had come off for the last time.

By the fifth day, I was ready to do something more than sleep and eat and walk, but Neme insisted I needed more time before returning to service. To keep myself occupied, I began to clean the room. I began by dragging old crates and disused furniture out, across the hallway and into the cramped attic space.

Neme clucked at me that night, for whether due to my exertions or simply because I was no longer lying abed, my pain had returned and my injuries were inflamed. An extra-strong dose left me drowsy and insensate, but I was at it again the next day. I brought a bucket of warm wash water and a fistful of rags up from the laundry, and began scrubbing the dust and cobwebs from the remaining surfaces.

The latch for the window shutters was rusted closed, but I managed to force it with the fire poker from the room's hearth. Further along the same wall there was another, smaller window, and this I forced open as well. With two windows open and fresh air and sunlight flowing through the room, it seemed suddenly an inviting space full of potential.

As no one had said otherwise, I decided that I would move my things here and take the room for myself. The bed was comfortable enough, and in the attic across the hall I found a serviceable washstand, a small table and an extra chair, and an old hatstand which I stood in one corner to hang clothes on. With a stiff brush, a rag, and a pot of wax, I worked and polished the neglected wood of the furniture, the floor, and an old clothes chest until it all shone with a warm golden glow.

Now and then as I went back and forth between the room and the laundry or elsewhere through the house, I passed one of the other girls. If I needed a reminder of my injuries on top of Neme's story, their flinching away from me gave it to me each time. It had never been my habit to use a mirror, and I still hadn't looked on my own face since my injury. But now I was starting to become impatient with the furtive grimaces and silence that greeted me each time I passed them. I waited until I heard Ardenne leave the room we had shared and went in.

Now in my former room, I could sense Ardenne's mirror like a presence in the corner. I avoided looking, instead moving here and there gathering my few belongings into a basket. It took almost no time, and then I had no more excuses. I moved to the mirror, still staring at my feet. I steeled myself for a moment, then with a deep gasp of breath as if inflating myself to raise my head, I looked up and stared my reflection in the eyes.

Or I tried to. My eyes had always been my most striking feature. "Storm eyes" they had been called. No longer did they draw the eye. Instead it was the scar. It was pink and raw and angry, and despite Neme's efforts, the tight even stitching puckered and creased the skin, especially near my eye and lips. It started at my temple, perhaps two fingers back from the corner of my eye, and ran in a perfect, gently curving line down nearly to the tip of my chin. If a lover were to caress my face and lean in for a kiss, their thumb would trace that same line just so.

I stared for some time, forcing myself not to look away. To memorize my face anew. This is who I was. I was not pretty anymore. So said Neme, and so thought all the other girls if their wincing looks spoke for them. So be it. I had never wanted to be. Perhaps now that I was free of it, others might cease to pursue it on my behalf.

I carried my basket back to my new room and began arranging things to my liking. Clothes hanging on the hatstand. Bed and chest along one side of the fireplace, table and chairs at the other. A shallow shelf along the wall beneath the far window held my hairbrush and other assorted items beside the washstand which I placed directly under the small window. Instead of a mirror, I could look out onto the street in front of the house. I was directly above Ma'am's desk, and the view I had was the same as from the windows behind her as she worked.

There was a knock at the door, and I called out cheerfully, "Come in!"

The door opened, and there standing just outside was Lane, her head down and tears already pooling in her eyes. "Arin...

I'm—I'm so sorry."

She looked devastated on my behalf. She couldn't look at me, couldn't lift her eyes from the floor. Her shoulders were hunched in guilt and it looked as if she had barely had a thought for her hair or face or clothes since that night. Her shoulders were shaking, and I realized she was sobbing softly.

"Lane," I said.

She didn't respond.

"Lane!" more sharply this time. Her head jerked up and I watched her eyes dart to mine, to the scar, to the floor, then back to lock on my eyes by whatever will she had left. "Lane, it's okay. It is not your fault and there is no blame here. I am *okay*."

She took several deep breaths, her eyes still locked to mine. "But... you can't..."

"I never wanted to. Do you understand? The life you have, I never wanted. I'm happy enough here. In this room. In the kitchen. Doing your laundry."

She laughed and by reflex, I joined her, the laughter making my face hurt. "Ow!" I gasped, bringing my hand to cup my cheek. Her eyes widened as she looked down at me. I grasped her hands in mine, and put my head against her breast. "There is nothing for you to be sorry for."

We stood like that for several minutes until I felt her breathing ease, and her crying reduced to a few sniffles. I drew back and turned her hands over in mine to look at her palms where there were still several cuts scabbing over.

"How are your hands healing? I saw that you cut them that night."

"Only cuts," she said. "Neme says to wash them all the time." Freed from my gaze, I saw her look around the room in surprise. "I've never seen this room look so nice. It's been just... storage for as long as I can remember. Just dust." She wandered slowly around the room, pausing at the table. Then her head came up suddenly. "I just realized, I have something perfect!"

Before I could ask what she meant, she dashed out of the room and down the stairs. I stood for several minutes, wondering, and then I heard feet stomping back up, taking the narrow steps two at a time. She had a great roll of fabric clutched in her hands, and several pins held in her lips.

"Uh rmmbrmmd thd Uh ud thzz n mmm rmmm," she said.

"What?"

She handed me one corner of the fabric and took the pins from her mouth. "I remembered I still had it in my room. I painted this last year."

Not waiting to explain, she began pinning the fabric to the wall above my table, starting with her corner and moving towards me. As she unrolled it, I could see it was a beautiful swathe of fine linen painted in wide stripes of astonishing colors, purple and orange and blue. The edges of the color blocks ran together, so the whole was one ethereal blend of color that glowed in the sunlight.

"What do you think?" she said, stepping back to admire it.

They were the same vibrant colors as the sky I saw from the stone balcony in my fever dream. I realized my mouth was hanging open.

"Well?" she bit her lip.

"Dragons," I said.

After that, the other girls visited me in my new room, and if there was still discomfort about my scar, they tried harder to hide it. I did not hold it against them. I could easily forgive them a flinch or a wince here or there. A tenth of what I had suffered would have destroyed their ability to earn for themselves and for the house.

Beaty came more than once, but we found that we were awkward together. She had recently turned eighteen, and while she had taken to the routines of the house, it was no secret that her heart wasn't in the work. She had taken Torre as her model, and when she took patrons now it was with an eye to an exit from the life. I wished her luck with it.

As the days passed, the girls began to fully make their peace with my new status. Part of this was my own self-understanding. No longer was I a junior girl, waiting to take my place in the parlors. If anything, I was waiting to take my place as part of the foundations of the house. To be the strength that held them up, and let their efforts rest against my shoulders.

If my new social status within the house left me somewhat isolated, I can at least say that a discovery I made kept me from dwelling on it overmuch.

It was the ninth morning since my injury, and Neme had recently begun talking of removing my stitches. I was anxious for this as the scar had begun to itch fiercely, and I was growing to hate the damn things with a passion.

This morning, I was lying abed, still lacking the permission I waited on to resume my duties. The house was quiet, the girls from the third floor had all gone down the stairs like a tramp of oxen to their various chores and assignments, and I thought I had the whole upper level to myself.

It was then that I heard the voices. For a moment, I wondered how I had fallen asleep without noticing and if my fever was back, but raising my head, I realized I was quite conscious. I closed my eyes and willed my body to silence.

...think she's well enough?

...pull... stitches today... can keep it clean... reason to wait... light work.

This was no fever dream. The voices were weak and muffled, echoing as if from a great distance, but it was Ma'am and Neme, talking of me.

I got out of bed, and looked carefully at the wall beside my pillow. I got on my hands and knees and crawled under the bed. In the corner just by the heavy wooden leg of the bed frame was a narrow opening in the wall. It looked like a channel running vertically through the wall, perhaps for a bell rope. Long since unused, it was full of cobwebs and dust, and had been boarded over with the wall paneling, but there was enough of an opening from a missing board. Wary of my stitches, I eased myself further into the corner so that my ear was close to the opening.

"... about Lane's injuries?" It was Ma'am's voice.

"Healing well. If she can keep her hands and feet clean, and stay out of her stylish shoes long enough for her feet to stop bleeding, she should heal with no issues. Emotionally, she's been much better since visiting with Arin. I believe she has moved past that foolish notion of blaming herself," Neme said.

I reluctantly pulled myself away, not wanting to eavesdrop further, but at the same time, finding it difficult to resist. As I backed out from under the bed, I realized that my sleeping shift was now covered in dust, and I stripped it off, changing it for one of my work dresses.

Giving in to a sudden urge, I pulled the bed several inches from the wall, far enough that I could examine the paneling in the corner from the floor up to above the mattress. I could see there were two boards making up the bulk of the panel which covered the old rope chase. I could just fit my fingers under the lower of the two, and by bracing my bare feet against the wall and pulling with all the strength I could muster, the nails gave way suddenly with a squeal. As the board let go, I fell back onto the bed and narrowly avoided rolling off onto the floor.

I lay there for a moment, feeling lightheaded, the shorter of the two boards now in my hand, and the rope chase exposed up to just below my pillow. I wondered if anyone had marked the screeching of the nails coming loose, but by then, the whole house had become used to strange sounds coming from my room as I dragged furniture back and forth from the attic. I put my ear to the open chase, but heard nothing.

I placed the board now with its lower end against the floor, and left a hand's-width gap in the rope chase at a level that my pillow would cover. Using the butt of the fire poker handle, I hammered the old nails into this new position, and then pushed the bed back into place. Lying down now, I could uncover the opening by shifting the pillow. I would have to wait to know if it worked as I hoped.

I can't say exactly why I did this. I could claim boredom as an excuse. But before long, I would be glad of my efforts.

Later that afternoon, well after I had cleaned up any evidence of my morning project, Neme came into my room, bearing a tray with her usual mug, pot and brush smelling foul as ever, and a miniature pair of scissors and a pair of tweezers like the girls used to pluck errant eyebrows. She set these down on my table and took a chair.

"Ready to be rid of the stitches?"

"Yes!" I practically bounced from the bed into the other chair facing her.

She smiled her crooked smile and handed me the mug. "Drink up. This is going to be very uncomfortable. It's a strong dose, so don't move or fidget. I'll help you back into bed after."

Desperate to be rid of the horrible threads, I downed the brew in one great gulp and settled back, ignoring her stern look.

"Lean forward and place your head on the table. Left side down."

I did as she ordered, and she moved the lamp close to my face and took up the scissors. She was entirely right—it was immensely uncomfortable. Endless tugging and short, painful jerks commenced, and it seemed like this would go on forever. I began to tire of seeing the sharp points of the scissors so near my eye, and the room was slowly spinning. I closed my eyes and sighed.

"Almost there. Hold steady."

This continued for what seemed like hours. I may have dozed. I certainly wandered in my mind.

"We're done," Neme said, drawing back and setting her tools down. I lifted my head and overbalanced, and she reached out to steady me. She cleaned my face, applied the usual paste, helped me to my bed, and tucked me in.

After she left I lay still in bed, floating on a fuzzy cushion of vertigo. I have no idea how much time passed. I watched the ceiling sway and ripple. I closed my eyes and felt myself rocking back and forth.

I came alert again as I heard Neme's muffled voice through my spy-hole.

"She'll sleep the whole afternoon and night with the dose I gave her, but the stitches are out and she's healing nicely."

"Good," said Ma'am. "You think she can resume her duties tomorrow? Well done."

I closed my eyes once more and smiled as I drifted off to sleep.

I did resume my duties the next day. It felt energizing to be amongst the girls once more and not banished to my room and the staircase. I helped Cook prepare the mid-day meal: great platters of olives, cheese, figs and other fruit, pots of jam and cream, great spills of seedy crackers, and endless slices of cured meat and coarse day-old bread toasted on the fire grate. I took these platters throughout the house, two to the dining room, one to Ma'am's quarters, one to Benjin & Doan's sitting room, and the rest distributed between the parlors.

I spent much of the afternoon tidying the service hall. Laundry day had come and gone while I was bedridden, and while it had all been accomplished, the aftermath was something to witness. Lye bucking residue had settled into the crevices between the stones of the laundry floor, only three of the five wooden washtubs were present, and the baskets hung on the wall in a great higgledy-piggledy mess.

I poured water over the stone floor and swept the resulting lather into the drain in the corner. I took all the baskets down from their pegs and rearranged them by size so that they hung flat against the wall, the smaller nesting neatly within the larger. I went hunting for the errant washtubs, and found them on the roof, where one sat with a finger of gray, days-old wash water still in the bottom. I carried this to the gutter in the corner and carefully poured it down the spout—I had no desire to see what days of concentration of the lye washing solution might do to my skin. I flushed the tub with several dippers of rainwater and repeatedly poured them out.

Just as I was satisfied that the washtub was usable again, I heard a sharp knocking from below. I leaned over the stone edge and peered down.

Below, I could see someone at the kitchen door. As I watched, they rapped again sharply with what looked like a lacquered wooden stick as thick as my wrist. I looked for a moment longer trying to work out if there were any deliveries today, and if this person could be a delivery boy. They were of middling height and stout, not the build of a child. There was no cart or other goods beside them. What skin I could see from directly above was dark, like Neme's, and the hair was black streaked with silver. They wore a coarse jacket with short sleeves that bared thick arms, ropey with a multitude of scars. The knocks continued.

This was no delivery.

I left the washtubs and raced back down the stairs to the first floor. Cook had retired to her room for her afternoon nap before beginning dinner preparations, so it was likely no one had heard the knocking. As I stepped out of the laundry into the main hall, the lack of any activity confirmed this. Benjin and Doan were at their ease in their sitting room, having finished their lunch. They kept the door open to hear if visitors came to the front door, but they would never hear the knocking at the back from here.

I leaned my head in and they looked up at me from the couch where they sat together, Doan leaning comfortably against his partner. Benjin smiled. He, more than any in all the house, had been the easiest with my scar, perhaps having so many of his own. Where before he had largely ignored me, now he doted as an older brother or uncle might.

"There's someone at the back door," I said. "Not a delivery... I don't know what. But they've been knocking and seem happy to keep at it 'till the sun goes down."

Benjin traded a look with Doan, and rose to his feet. Doan rose and picked up his cudgel from the corner before taking a place at the front door. Benjin followed me as far as the door to the laundry, where he stopped and looked at me pointedly.

"Whatever he is, you go in here an' don't come out, hear? It's my job to deal with strangers at the door."

I was not going to argue then, but I also would not meekly leave it be. I don't know why, but I *had* to know what this visitor wanted. I stepped into the laundry and closed the door behind me. Then, as quickly and quietly as I could, I went through the dining room to the shallow alcove in the corner of the kitchen we used as a larder. There were shelves full of vegetables and sacks of grain and flour and eggs and all the other goods that kept the kitchen running. The lowest shelf was placed to allow for small barrels underneath, and there was just enough room for me to squeeze myself in beside a large basket of potatoes against the short wall that separated the shelves from the kitchen door.

I was just settling into my hiding place when Benjin moved through the doorway to my right, just inches away from me. The knocking came again once more before he reached the back door and opened the small viewport.

"What do you want? No deliveries today. Respectable visitors should come to the *front* door."

I didn't hear what was said in return, but there was a long pause before Benjin spoke again. When he did, his voice was grim.

"Wait here. Stop marring the door with your cursed banging."

I heard him walk back through the kitchen at a steady pace and ascend the main staircase. I waited some minutes, and was just debating whether or not to extricate myself and run up the stairs to my room to listen in from there—he must be reporting to Ma'am—when I heard his heavy tread returning down the stairs. He made his way back to the door, more slowly this time, as if regretting his next task.

The door latch was undone, and the door opened.

"You give me those swords. You'll not go armed in this house. You'll get them back when you're done with your interview." There was the sound of an exchange, then, "come."

I heard them both walking through the kitchen now. Benjin's heavy boots and an unfamiliar hollow clapping sound. As they passed me, I couldn't resist anymore. I leaned out of my hiding place and around the short stub of wall just in time to see a flare of cloth as they turned the corner towards the staircase.

The visitor was wearing a coarse gray jacket with sleeves cut short, tucked into broad dark pleated trousers, travel-worn and stained, and tied with a wide leather belt. The legs of the flowing garment stopped just below heavily muscled and scarred calves, and I saw a brief flash of rough, dark-skinned feet wrapped in sandals made of a simple plank of wood and cotton straps to tie them in place.

When I could hear them on the stairs, I darted from my corner, back to the laundry and up the stairs to my room where I closed the door and rolled onto my bed, pulling the pillow under my chest and placing my ear up to my spy-hole. And I waited.

I knew from previous experience that I would not hear anything unless they were speaking at Ma'am's desk, but I also thought that given the unpleasant welcome the visitor had received she was unlikely to be anywhere else—Ma'am's desk was like her throne, a place of power.

Sure enough, after several minutes I could hear soft movements, and words slowly resolved out of the muffled sounds.

"I will know why you would come here again, and what you

expect," Ma'am said.

"The child does not belong here," said another voice. From my brief glimpses of the stout body and muscled arms and feet, I had expected a deep, heavy voice, more like Benjin's than Cook's. The visitor spoke with a thin, almost reedy timbre, so that I could not guess either their age or gender. Their accent made me think of Neme. "First you ignore my missives, then you turn me away when I ask according to your protocols. I *will* see the child."

"She does belong here. This is her home and we are her family. If you asked her, she would say the same to you."

"Let them say so to me, then."

"You have no claim here. What are you? A wanderer and a vagrant. You have not even a hedge to your name. Why should the girl belong to you?"

"*They are no girl*," came the voice, fierce and angry. My heart stopped and I felt it rise into my throat. "And they do not belong to me. They belong in *Reft*. It is my call to take them there, nothing more."

There was a pause, then Ma'am spoke, and from her voice, I could imagine her shaking her head, "Reft..." Then softly, "You would have her scarred beyond recognition like you? Her body nothing more than... an engine of power?"

"You speak of things you don't understand. Are they not scarred under your care? I don't mean their face, though I know of that incident—is their body not now an engine of other peoples' pleasure? What scars are left by your *patrons*? Can you count them?"

"*You* know nothing of what you speak. She has not served thus, and I would not force her."

"If you care as much as you say, then you should want them to understand their potential."

"We are done here," Ma'am said, angry. "She stays. You leave."

There was a pause, then, so softly that I almost missed it, "I will return."

Nothing more was said, and the silence stretched on, so I assumed the interview was finished. I realized my breathing had slowed to shallow gasps, and I forced myself to breathe deeply. They had been speaking of me, but I understood almost nothing.

Almost nothing.

They both knew that I wasn't a girl. Ma'am knew, and still wanted to keep me here. Called me family. And this other... knew and wanted to take me to... Reft? I didn't know the name, wasn't even sure I had heard it correctly. They had spoken with the same accent as Neme, and so they were from Somiere? Maybe Neme had heard of this Reft.

I was still reeling from these thoughts when I heard voices again.

"I've sent the filth away," I heard Benjin say. "How do you think they knew? Savat's man let something slip, maybe?"

"It doesn't matter. We need only hold off until I receive a reply." There was a long pause before I heard Ma'am's voice again, and when she spoke, it was softly, with an odd undercurrent. "Benjin, lock down the house. Return any patron's payments and see them out immediately. Are all the girls in? Good. No one comes or goes, and no deliveries. Except... your cousin is still at the Cock And Barn? Once you and Doan have the house locked down, go to him and offer him double wages and two percent on anyone he can recruit for the next... week. I want at least ten more guarding the house, inside and out. Armed, mind you."

"Ten? Ma'am... I don't understand. They're a witch, okay.

A club to the head will still bash it in."

"They're not just a witch, Benjin. They're a *grim*. Have you never heard the stories?"

"Stories is stories." I could almost hear him shrug. "I don't pay much attention to what someone *says*."

"Go see to it. And Benjin... make it twenty. Hire at the river docks if you need to."

Again there was silence as Benjin left. But in those last words I recognized the current in Ma'am's voice. It was fear.

Nine

Nerves were taut and frayed throughout the house over the next few days. Ma'am spent time with each of the girls in twos and threes, presumably explaining the situation or placating their fears. Unfortunately, these conferences took place in their rooms, so my spy-hole was useless.

While Beaty and I were working with Cook in the kitchen the next day, she pulled the three of us together, saying only, "A threat of violence has been made against members of this house. Until I hear from my sources that the danger has passed, I'm sorry but there will be no deliveries, patrons, or departures." Cook only grumbled caustically about fools and their muscles and returned to her work.

Within the house, there was little sign of the heightened danger. Benjin's cousin and a fourth man took up residence in the front sitting room. The rest were positioned in the streets front and back, which I knew only through my covert listening.

And so we waited.

A normal house would rapidly face difficulty and discomfort under such siege conditions. Food, at least would be running short before many days had passed. But we were accustomed to feeding not only the sixteen residents, but also at least as many patrons on a daily basis. And because "feeding" usually involved multiple removes of elegant and luxurious foods to restore energy and vitality after multiple sexual escapades, now that we were sheltering in place and exercising all manner of restraint, our provisions would easily last some time,

I continued my regular activities as we all still needed to eat and wear clean clothes, but I also kept my eyes and ears open to the movements of the house, ensuring that I was nearly always able to get to my room to spy on Benjin's regular status reports. Unfortunately, the reports were largely empty of any real news. He had had the foresight to circulate a description of the visitor through the lower-status haunts of the city, and now received occasional reports of sightings, but even he admitted that these were likely spurious.

With all the disruptions to our routine, it was a comfort that Neme still sought me out each morning and each evening to check on my healing scar. Each visit, she pronounced my progress satisfactory, and if she still made me drink bitter concoctions and wear a greasy paste of herbs and lanolin on my face like a grotesque parody of the girls' makeup, it was a small price to be rid of the stitches.

Ma'am's conversations on the day of the visitor were still rattling in my mind, and on the fifth day of the siege, I built the courage to test my theory with Neme.

"Do you know of a place called Reft in Somiere?"

She only blinked at me, and said nothing for a moment. When she did speak, it was absently and without meeting my eyes, "There is no place called Reft in Somiere."

This was an odd answer, but I did not pursue it further. Instead, I asked another question that had my curiosity up, "Do you know the name 'Savat?'"

She looked at me now, confusion clear on her face. "No. I've never heard it before."

Before I could ask more, a sharp, hollow clapping sound echoed through the open windows and my veins filled with ice. Neme hadn't witnessed the visitor's arrival as I had, and so watched with amusement as I leapt to my feet and rushed to the window, leaning out for a view of the street.

The visitor stood in the street facing the front door, and as I watched, a dozen men emerged from the surrounding alleys and doorways, making a ring around them.

Neme's head peeked from the other window and took in the scene. I heard her mutter an oath and she left my room and descended the stairs as quickly as her limp allowed. My eyes stayed locked on the tableau below.

Five men separated from the ring and closed with the visitor. They brandished a mix of clubs and short swords, spreading out to encircle. The visitor drew the shorter of their two swords with the sharp edge of the blade lying backwards against their own forearm. With the other hand, they pulled the longer sword entirely free from their belt, scabbard and all. They held it from the middle like a short staff. For a moment, everyone was still.

Then the five advanced in a sudden rush, yelling throaty cries to give themselves courage. In an odd shuffling hop, the dark-skinned visitor closed the distance with one of the swordsmen, crouched low in a wide stance, their elbow bent to angle their blade outwards to the man's face. His war cry cut off sharply and he staggered as he flinched back from the sword point, and the visitor ducked under the attacker's sword arm, hooking it with the sword scabbard and spinning the man around and into the path of his onrushing companions. They all five went down in a heap in the center of the ring, and the visitor took a calm step to the side, turning slowly to face the others.

Again no one made a move, though the five slowly pulled themselves up and disentangled their weapons. They formed themselves in an arc now within the larger circle. The double ring of guards looked back and forth to each other, then in a ragged consensus they each took a cautious step forward. The ring contracted.

The visitor took several small steps, their odd sandals clacking on the paving stones. They turned through half a circle, eyeing the encircling guards, but leaving their back to the five behind them. I had the sense that they knew precisely the angle and distance to everyone on the street.

The ring contracted again as the guards stepped forward. The five in the middle were now within striking distance, but they held as the visitor turned to face them. In a silent rush the seven men in the outer ring closed suddenly, and it seemed that with eight swords and four heavy clubs, the visitor must be overwhelmed almost immediately.

In the three strides it took for the men behind to close the distance, the visitor drew their short sword against their own opposite forearm, and even from my window above I could see a bright red line of blood against their dark skin and a fierce grimace spread across their face.

And from one breath to the next, the swordsmen reached the visitor in a snarl of violence and confusion. Two of the guards went down almost immediately in a welter of blood. A third tripped and smashed his face against the pavement.

The visitor's movements were uncanny; unnaturally fast. They scored five strikes to every one of their attackers', every one of which they caught on their scabbarded sword. They weaved in and amongst the guardsmen, catching this sword, turning that, spinning away and dodging. Every few strikes, the short sword in their right hand would flash out like a viper, and one of the men would fall.

Only a few seconds after the rush, there were only four guardsmen left standing, and the only mark the visitor had taken was that first deliberate cut. I could see now that it was no mere scratch. The blood flowed freely down their arm and they favored the arm, pain in their expression with each parry.

The eight men down were crawling or pulling themselves away from the melee, and I realized with a start that none of them were dead. They all had injuries that were painful, perhaps crippling, but all of them were conscious and moving. Some were crying out or whimpering in pain.

As the remaining four reorganized themselves in a line in front of the purple door, the visitor slowly paced among the injured. Sandals clacking, they made a full circle through the street and finally turned once more to face the guards. As they did so, I saw that their arm was no longer bleeding. With their right wrist, they wiped away the blood—the wound was gone.

One of the four ran, unwilling to face pain or death for mere coin. The visitor took slow steps toward the door. Only a few paces away, the other three looked at each other, and bolted.

The visitor raised the still-scabbarded sword and knocked on the front door.

Three sharp knocks echoed down the street. Then silence. I could see nothing more from here without leaning fully out, so I left my room and descended the stairs to the laundry. I could hear a great tromp of booted feet running through the hallway. Benjin had brought the guards from the back alley through the house as a second line of defense.

I could hear them milling about now, and before I could decide what to do, the hall door opened, and a stranger stepped in, taking a position in the open doorway, a broad long knife in each hand. He glanced back at me, and said in a terse, ugly voice, "Get ye' gone. Fight ain't no place for a child!"

I retreated back up to the second level and peeked out into the main gallery. The doors were all closed here, and no one was about, so I flattened myself to the carpet and crept out silently until I could see over the edge to the hall below.

The men had formed several ranks of defense, taking advantage of the doorways into the parlors along the hallway. From my vantage, I could see across to the two main parlors and at least two men crouched in each. They held their weapons at the ready, but I wondered whether they stood any chance against what I had seen outside.

Once more the knocks rang out, and it seemed I could feel the house tremble. Then with a tremendous crash, an explosion of purple splinters spilled through the entry hall. As the dust settled, I saw lamps and vases in the hallway below knocked over and the carpet peppered with fragments of the front door. I could see one of the hired guards down and writhing in agony, his arms, chest, and face lacerated and pincushioned with splinters.

There was the sound of a brief scuffle at the door and moments later, I saw the visitor step calmly into the hall below. They had a neat diagonal slice across their chest, deep and angry, blood running down and staining their jacket. I had no doubts about whose hand had done it.

They stood still, and the word took on a new depth of meaning. I had never seen someone so utterly calm, even with such a wound and an expression of pain on their face, they were calm. Benjin had called them "witch" and I finally understood. Ma'am had used the word "grim" and this too was clear. It seemed as if they stood slightly apart from the world.

They were shorter than I had expected, five feet at most. The voluminous jacket and flowing trousers gave them a sense of bulk and softness both, but I could tell that underneath this they were not as thick in body as they appeared. Their hair was a heavy cabling of black braids shot with strands of gray and silver, each joining together into a single wrist-thick plait that was tucked down the back of their jacket.

This they wore shirtless, and the short sleeves and open V in the front exposed the dark skin of their arms, chest, and neck. They had neither the protruding throat or stubble of a man, nor the narrow jaw and breasts of a woman—I could put no gender to them at all. I was shocked to see from their face that they could easily be fifty years old.

But if there was anything that earned the name *grim* it was the scars. Every bit of visible skin—from their scalp to their face to their chest and arms and hands—was crossed and re-crossed with scars. Fine and narrow, thick and ropey, jagged, ancient, recent, and the still-bleeding chest. I didn't think that I could touch their skin anywhere with a single finger and not place it upon a scar. My cheek itched in sympathy.

Two men rushed out from opposite doorways, swords and knives already swinging. With an almost dance-like pivot that ended on one knee, the visitor evaded the strikes and somehow tangled both of their legs at the same time, bringing them to the floor. With a flash of the short sword in one hand, and a sharp rap of the scabbard in the other, the pair were immobilized. One had dropped both knives to clutch desperately at his bleeding throat, and the other gasping and doubled over, both legs broken.

The visitor stood calmly once more. This time, I could *see* the wound on their chest closing. The blood slowed to a trickle, and while the gash did not disappear completely, it looked as if it had been healing for some days.

Below and to my left, Benjin stepped out from the kitchen doorway to stand at the foot of the stairs.

The visitor glanced at him, and also to the doorways to either side. Several men were visible, clearly unwilling to engage this whirlwind of violence and pain. "Is this all worth it to you?" came the small, oddly accented voice. "All I want is the child."

They took several more steps, their wooden sandals crunching on the shattered glass and porcelain.

They called out again, louder, "Can *you* teach them what they are and how to reach their potential? Can *you* teach them to survive the blades and the hate and the violence that the world will hurl at them when they stop pretending to be what they are not? When they cannot live this lie any longer?"

The door to my right opened, and Ma'am stepped out. She saw me lying on the floor watching, and our eyes met. She said nothing, but I sensed that she was willing me to understand something. My eyes darted around the gallery to each door and I imagined the girls behind each. Lane curled up in her bed, her arms wrapped around her knees and biting her lower lip, waiting for the worst to be over. Bess raging with fury at this intrusion into her home. Jinn leaning against the door, wondering whether to stay hidden or risk himself to gather the others in safety. Korenne, pacing her sitting room in worry while Hannah watched wide-eyed from the couch. Silfy crying softly in the corner, but never wanting anyone to see her being weak. Cook holed up in her room below, and Ardenne, Elyse, and

Teela above, maybe taking shelter together in Neme's room or in the attic. Doan somewhere in the wreckage of the front door. Benjin, willing to make a last stand at the stairs. And Beaty, my sister.

They knew that I lied about being a girl. They knew about the terrible, inexplicable things that happened around me. Ma'am knew and wanted to... send me off to some patron. This stranger knew and wanted to take me to... *Reft*? I seethed inside. What about what *I* wanted?

The visitor took a step forward.

"*Stop!*"

The voice carried through the gallery and the floor below, and they stopped their advance. I realized I was standing now at the railing. And I realized that it had been my voice.

They looked up at me, and I looked down at them.

"No more," I said. "I will go with you." I turned to Ma'am, who was still looking at me, her gaze unreadable. "I am sorry to have brought this upon you all," I said, almost a whisper.

I turned and descended the service stairs for the last time.

At the bottom, Neme was waiting. I couldn't pull my eyes away from the ruin that was the hallway, and part of me didn't want to look at her. I felt her hand rest on my shoulder for a moment, drawing me into her arms. Then she stepped back and pressed a satchel into my arms. "Your coin and clothes, and a pouch of the herbs for your monthly bleeding, and a pot of ointment for your scar. Every day, mind! And keep it clean!"

She embraced me once more, and I realized that she was crying. We both were. She held me a moment longer, and then left me and limped up the stairs.

I stepped out into the hall. The visitor stood only a few steps away. They turned to me and wiped their sword clean upon their own jacket, sheathing it and tucking the longsword back into their belt. They seemed to have forgotten Benjin and the other guards surrounding them.

"I am Sem," they said. "I will take you to Reft." Sem extended their hand towards the door, and we walked out silently together, wooden sandals and soft house slippers crunching on the carpet. As we reached the remains of the entryway, I looked back, hoping to see Beaty, or Neme, or Lane, or any of the others one last time. I saw only the ruins of the house. Benjin was leaning over Doan, tending his wounds, and didn't look up to see me leave.

Sem led me out of the house, past the carnage in the street, through the central square, and over the bridge. We retraced in reverse the path that had brought me into Anbress. Then, I was making my way towards a new family, though I didn't know it at the time. Now, I left that family and headed back into the unknown. I felt as if my life was unwinding.

Across the bridge we turned west, taking the road to Branmoor. We traveled in silence. I couldn't bring myself to speak to them after the destruction I had witnessed, and they seemed comfortable not speaking. After some hours of walking, they turned off the road onto a narrow trail and followed this to a small shack.

It could barely be called a house. Not much larger than the springhouse had been, this was built of a seemingly random assortment of materials. Some stones piled together here and there, some knotty boards nailed and leaning, here the wall was a lattice of sticks, still covered in bark and tied with dirty twine, there it was a ragged cob of mud and straw. Somehow, it held up a thinly thatched roof which must leak terribly in the rain.

Other than two fine mules—one sorrel, one gray—tied to a low branch, the yard around the hovel looked equally unpleasant. A rangy nanny chewed happily at a shrub, and there were bits of broken pottery and other trash scattered around. Two headless chickens hung by their feet from a rafter, half-plucked, and there was a filthy pile of small bones and half-cleaned carcasses of small animals some few paces away, buzzing with flies.

I almost asked if this place was "Reft," but remembered that I wasn't speaking.

They knocked at the doorway and called out, "Honfry!" There was no response, so they stepped inside, emerging with a large pack which they slung on their back. They saw my face, and their lips twitched a little, almost as if to smile. "Honfry is a witch in these parts. They held my pack and mules for me while I was in Anbress fetching you. Probably out birthing something. I've left them some coin inside."

Sem pulled a ragged straw hat out of the pack and stuffed it on their head, then took two leather water flasks, handing one to me and taking a deep drink from the other. They tied the pack to the back of the sorrel mule and climbed onto the gray, riding bareback. They held the lead rope for the sorrel towards me. When I didn't take it from them, they said simply, "It's four months, walking to Reft on your own feet."

I took the rope. They nudged their mule, and she began walking slowly back down the path towards the road. I looked at my mule uncertainly, but realized I had no other option. I climbed up, ungainly and uncomfortable, hiking my skirts up to my thighs to get my leg over. It had been years since I rode bareback, and I was smaller then. I settled my satchel over Sem's pack, hung the flask from a knot in the strap, and nudged the mule with my heels. She set off at a steady pace and seemed to know the way.

I was glad one of us did.

Part Three

THERE ARE LIES that we wear so long that they settle into our bones. We think they have become part of us, and that we have become the lie. But the truth is that they are always still a foreign presence. They inhabit us not like the breath of life, but like a rot that slowly eats away at our foundations. When the lie is ripped from us, torn from our bones in violence and necessity, it leaves us brittle and hollow. Fragile things requiring the utmost care to survive.

I watched blackened wood settle into coals as the fire crackled, a rabbit roasting on a wooden spit stuck in the soil beside it. I looked around at the darkening clearing where Sem had brought us. The mules grazed happily, but the woods around us felt ominous, oppressive.

We had skirted around Branmoor and were camped north of the town. After seeing to the mules, Sem had left me. They walked a great circle slowly around the camp just within the tree-line before disappearing. With no instruction from them,

I spent the time alone cleaning the rabbit they'd taken earlier on the road with a sling, splitting wood for the fire with the small hatchet I found in their heavy pack, and starting the fire and dinner.

We still had not spoken since leaving Anbress.

After a few hours of solitude, I heard the snap of a branch and Sem entered the clearing with a bundle under their arm and a sack across their shoulder. They set the sack by their pack and dropped the bundle in front of me, then squatted down on their heels a pace away. I untied the cloth and found clothes, used but sturdy. Two pairs of brown trousers and a wide leather belt, two tunics and a shirt, underwear, thick woolen socks and a stout pair of shoes, all wrapped in a dark-dyed cloak.

"Those harem clothes you've got will fall apart before we reach the mountains."

I said nothing as I picked through the things, but I was acutely aware of the holes already worn in the soles of my slippers. I continued to unpack and sort through the clothes, and there was not a ruche, bit of embroidery, or piece of lace to be seen. My hands trembled slightly. Tucked inside one of the shoes was a whetstone and small folding knife, similar to the pocketknife Father had given me.

"From now on, you go *nowhere* without a blade," they said, watching me intently.

My hands were shaking as I unfolded the knife.

Sometimes, to evict the lie, you have to be ruthless.

I looked into the crackling fire, probing my feelings carefully, finding every edge and corner of it in my mind. I reached up with my left hand and grasped my braided hair, and began sawing through it with the knife close to my scalp. Tears were streaming down my cheeks, and I did not care that Sem was still watching. When the braid came away in my hand, I held it for a moment, feeling the weight. My head felt lighter. I felt lighter. But I still wept.

Tearing out the lie is sometimes violent. It is always painful. Grief doesn't mean that it wasn't a lie.

I tossed the braided hair into the darkness.

Ten

I woke to find Sem sitting up, watching me. I pulled myself up stiffly and tried to shake off the morning chill.

They looked me up and down, noting my hair newly shorn close to my scalp, and nodded to the fire pit where fresh logs and kindling were already set, waiting, the small iron kettle just outside the ring of ash from last night's fire.

"You need to make your moon tea, yes? Light the fire."

My eyes narrowed. "How do you know about that?"

They shrugged, wincing when the gesture pulled at the still-raw wound on their chest, "I looked through your bag last night while you were asleep. That herb is commonly known in Somiere."

"You went through...?" I sputtered, outraged.

They shrugged again. "I needed to learn about you, and you were not speaking to me. I presume you did the same with mine yesterday while I was gone."

I sat sullenly, unable to argue that fact. Finally, I couldn't resist asking, "And what did you learn?"

"That you have little attachment to material things. That you are acquainted with Somiri medicine. That you care for your health. That is all to the good. Light the fire."

I moved to fetch the flint and steel from their pack.

"No. Use your knife."

"My... knife?"

They drew a finger down one of the fine, short scars on their forearm. "Light the fire."

I recoiled, and I'm sure my face showed my horror. "You want me to...?"

They sighed and closed their eyes. I could hear them mutter some short words to themself. It sounded like they were counting. They looked at me again. "You are very powerful, Arin. What you did to that poor man in Anbress demonstrates that." Their eyes flickered to my scar. "But it also shows what you will do to those around you if you do not take control of your power."

"What I did? He did this to me!" I cried, turning my face to show the scar.

They nodded. "Do you think that man spent his coin at a house of pleasure *intending* to ruin his manhood? Yes, you did it. You didn't know what you were doing, and I daresay he deserved punishment for his actions and intent. But if *you* are not in control of your power, then who is? And who will you unleash it on next? Once your power breaks, it will continue to do so more and more frequently, and for less and less reason. Unless you can control it."

I slouched back, stunned and afraid.

"I heard you crying out in your dreams at night. You are not to blame for what happened. When our power *breaks*, we have no control. But now that yours has, you must learn. Light the fire."

"I don't know what you mean!" I said, frustrated.

"Pain is the source of our power. It refines thought, it intensifies focus, and it amplifies the will. Do you want the fire?"

"Yes," I said, shivering.

"Then ignite it. Use your knife, draw on the pain, and *will* the fire to be."

I looked at their face, then at their chest. I remembered the explosive violence of their assault on the house, and saw the angry wound, the pain on their face with each breath.

I took my knife from my pocket and opened it. As if in a dream, I brought the short, sharp blade to my forearm. There was a finger-width of space between the tip of the blade and my skin, and I couldn't seem to move. I looked at my hand holding the knife. I looked at my arm. I could feel in my mind the action of joining them together, and yet my arm held still, refusing. I don't know how long I sat there, staring at my hand and willing it to move. The knife point quivered.

"It's difficult, isn't it?" Sem asked.

I nodded. "It's going to hurt," I said.

"Yes," they replied simply. There was an odd tone in their voice. Somewhere between compassion and sadness.

"How... how much... do I need to...?" My hand still wavered.

"How much do you want the fire?" They asked softly. "Just that much."

I touched the tip of the knife to my skin, still hesitant to actually cut myself.

"I *can't!* I... why do I have to?"

"In Reft, they will teach you a different way—a more subtle way. But a longer way. There is a kind of pain that can still fuel your power long after it is inflicted, if you can learn to access it.

Those hurts that overwhelmed you—that broke down your mind in the moment. Those memories hold a deep well of pain that you can dip into. But it isn't easy... you may find you prefer the more direct, simpler power of the blade. But right now, in *this* moment, you need to find some measure of control, and I don't have the skills to teach the other way."

I looked back up at Sem, at their scar-covered arms. I looked at the kindling piled neatly just so, awaiting a spark. I looked at the knife against my arm. I closed my eyes.

And pressed.

A flare of stars exploded behind my eyelids, and a high-pitched ringing flared between my ears. White-hot pain radiated from my arm. I think I dropped the knife.

I gasped, a half-voiced cry as I squeezed my eyes shut against the pain.

"Open your eyes and look," Sem said gently.

I took a deep breath and looked. My arm was still there. A bead of blood flowed from the small cut, barely half an inch long. I watched the drops welling there in my flesh, and I felt the pain—a sharp crest and a deep well, both fire and ice. I gritted my teeth and tried to ignore it.

"Relax," they said. "Don't fight the pain, don't flee from it. Embrace it. *Feel* it." The voice was steady, soft; a calm chant. It resonated in their light, reedy pitch.

I found my shoulders were tensed and hunched. I tried to relax them. The pain flared and I felt it, tears welling in my eyes.

"Relax."

I was breathing in short gasps. I tried to slow them.

"Feel it."

It hurt. The pain was real, the blood was real. There was no fire.

"I can't do it. I don't even understand," I cried.

"I can't lead you through it. I can't even help you. All I can do is be here for you."

I looked them in the eyes and saw an endless well of feeling in them. I shook my head. I didn't want this.

Sem nodded to themself, and took a deep breath. I felt... *something*... shift, and then I heard the fire crackling to life.

"How? I didn't do anything," I protested.

"It is possible to use someone else's pain, if you can open yourself to it," they said. "That is something that comes much later."

I sighed, still clutching my arm. They stood up, picked up my knife from the ground and took one of my dresses from my bag. They cut a strip of linen from the hem and tied it around the wound.

"It still hurts," I complained, surprised.

"It will never *not* hurt." They moved back to their own bedding, leaving me to my thoughts. I opened my bag and took out the small pouch of leaves. Neme had given me a small clay mortar, little more than a cup, and a pestle the size of my thumb. I took three leaves as she had taught me and ground them into a paste with a splash of water from my flask, losing myself in the repetition and the rising astringent scent. By the time the fire had settled into coals, I had a smooth dark green paste in the bottom of the mortar. I kneeled by the fire and saw that the kettle was steaming. I filled the mortar and returned to my cloak, waiting for the tisane to cool enough to drink.

"What did you mean?"

Sem looked at me for a moment. "What do *you* mean?"

"In Anbress. You said, 'Can you teach them what they are?' What did you mean?"

"Your family raised you as a girl, but that didn't feel right to you, did it? So what are you?"

I spoke with certainty, "I'm a mixie."

"No," Sem said, "you're not."

I looked at them in shock. I opened my mouth to speak, to argue, but I couldn't think what to say.

"Most babies are born, the midwife looks between their legs and sees little girl or boy parts, and she says, 'it's a boy' or 'it's a girl.' But sometimes, now and then, a baby is born, and the midwife looks and... *can't tell*. In the *Gruende*, the House of Medicine in Somiere, they call these children *Midsée Evont*— 'Mixed Expression.'

"And because people feel the need to diminish what they do not understand, some shortened this to 'mixie,' and then they used it for everyone that didn't fit their ideas of what people should be, because it makes those who don't fit sound small and silly and makes the people who say it feel superior."

They focused for a moment on the fire. "You're not a 'mixie,' because your body isn't mixed. The use of that word is... unpleasant to those whose are." Their gaze wandered back to me before continuing. "The word that you'll hear more where you're going is *nyssa*. It's also Somiri, and it means 'neither one nor the other.' That's what you are."

"How do you know all this about me? How did you even know to find me in Anbress?"

Sem shrugged. "It's what I do. The witch that birthed you sent a message that eventually reached me. Took its time getting to me. I was busy elsewhere for a long time. There are other children like you that are not so lucky with the families they're born into. By the time I got back to your part of the world, you and your family were gone. I had to track you down all these years later. But I don't give up."

I had seen ample evidence of this. I cradled my forearm,

still radiating pain from the wound I had inflicted on myself. I stared into the fire, feeling defeated.

"This was not a failure," Sem said, quietly but firmly. "Yesterday, did you think you could attempt what you just did?"

I looked at them and shook my head.

"Take one hundred steps forward and ninety-nine steps back—you still have made progress."

I looked away and my eyes found Sem's two swords by their pack.

"Teach me to use the sword," I said. I couldn't tell if my voice was a plea or a command.

Sem looked me over for a moment. Their only reply was a soft grunt.

Sem rocked back and forth atop their gray mule, swaying with the rhythm of her hooves. They held a piece of unused firewood in one hand and the hatchet in the other, held close to the head and whittling with short, careful strokes.

A few paces beside them, on the sorrel I had named Beatrice, I was rediscovering the comfort I felt in short hair and sturdy clothing. The cloak was packed away in my satchel as the days were still warm, but I wore my shoes and trousers, and a sleeveless tunic. I had spent a little time each evening working my hair with the knife, so that now it was little more than a short fuzz over my head. As Beatrice plodded along, I sometimes closed my eyes and felt the breeze ruffle through it.

My left arm was throbbing under a long strip of linen, wound three times around. I bore multiple cuts now. The first was scabbed over. The latest from this morning, still throbbed painfully. Sem made me try to light the fire each morning. I was still failing. The best that could be said was that I was perhaps hesitating less with the blade. One hundred steps forward and ninety-nine back.

We were moving as close to north as I could figure from the arc of the sun, and were now well into the wild moors of the Freelands. Branmoor was the nearest town and it was days behind us. We were likely days more from the nearest farm. The first obstacle on the way to Reft lay some weeks ahead: the Sommíre, the broad, strong river that all the rivers in the Freelands fed. It cut across the moors west to the sea, dividing Somiere and Torfall, and formed both a natural political division and a daunting military border between the two nations.

The soil was becoming clay and rocks as we gradually descended to the lowlands. Off to the east we could see The Finger trailing out from the purple arcs of the Ontarch mountains on the distant horizon. With The Finger hard to our right, we were a third of the way to the great river which would mark the midpoint of our journey. There, the challenge would be finding our way across.

North of the Sommíre, we would follow the Red River, a tributary that tumbled down from the Thorénsielle, the great mountain range north of the Freelands that divided Somiere from the vast lifeless expanse known as the Far Arids. Sem planned a stop for rest and supplies at a common waypoint known to them, and then we would strike out on the hard trek deep into the mountains to reach Reft.

All this I knew by Sem's intermittent lecturing. Their subjects rambled from history to geography to herbalism to philosophy, and often began with an innocuous question from me.

"How long..." I tried to ask. "How long before I get... accustomed to the pain?"

"You're really asking when will you be able to draw your

power without pain. The truth you don't want to hear is that you never will." They focused for a moment on a knot in the wood, smoothing it carefully with the hatchet head.

"Pain itself is the source of our power. You want to use the pain, and expect it to diminish as the water you drink from a flask. You couldn't light the fire because you want to consume your own pain. You seek to master it."

"Isn't that what I'm supposed to be trying to do?"

Sem shook their head, "There's no power in attempting to master pain. Pain is its own master—it can't be conquered. When we speak of controlling our pain, what we really describe is controlling our response to it." They put their hand over the angry wound on their chest, grimacing.

"When you try to light the fire, pain is not the firewood, fuel to be burned up in the process of making heat. But neither is our body consumed by the pain. It may feel like it burns us down to ash, but when it does finally fade, we find we are still here."

We rode on for some time more.

It was early for camp, but shortly we came to an odd lake. It was narrow and long, straight as a line drawn on vellum. Its water was crystal clear but so deep that staring into it, it seemed I could see forever into darkness. Sem said that it was an ancient quarry, cut deep into the stone foundations of the mountains to the east by people long ago who wished to build a great fortress in the Ontarch. That fortress was gone now, long since devastated by war and fire and ruin.

I asked them the name of that fortress, wondering if it was the same that Cal and his men had held us in.

"No one I know still remembers. It may be that it is marked still on an old map somewhere in the great Library of Somiere. The Freelands has a long and fractured history and many powers have peaked and fallen over the ages. Anbress is not the first city to hold that river crossing, and probably won't be the last. Time rolls on, and if there is a constant truth to this world, it is that people strive for more power than they have, and take that power from others when they can."

We made camp on a broad flat stone beside the lake. I laid out my cloak for something to sit upon. The stone was still warm from the afternoon sun and for a brief moment I remembered that last campsite with my family. I thought I had cried enough over the loss, but my eyes filled once more.

Sem said nothing, but I'm sure they saw.

When I had cried myself out, I rose and walked to the edge of the water. Sem was swimming easily through the water a few feet from the stone bank. They had left their clothes piled on the ledge, and I sat down next to the still bloodstained jacket.

With nothing to do, and not wanting to interrupt them, I took the jacket and soaked it in the water, scrubbing the cloth against itself to release as much of their dried blood as I could. I couldn't light the fire, but I was skilled with laundry. I lost myself in the labor, and when I had done all that I thought was possible with the jacket, I spread it out on the stone beside the fire to dry and then repeated the process with the odd flaring trousers.

I was tending the fire, stoking it to start water boiling for porridge, when I saw Sem pull their naked body out from the water. I couldn't help but look.

Their arms and legs, their face and chest were rippled and finely textured with scars, and I had assumed the same was true beneath their clothes. The scarring diminished in intricacy along the trunk of their body, but that skin was not unmarked. Several larger scars crisscrossed their chest, thighs, and abdomen. These had a different character—less controlled, more ragged. Battle wounds.

And there was another scar, even older. I forced myself to look away and focus on the fire as they moved to put on their still-damp clothes.

Sem sat by the fire, saying nothing for a long moment. I thought perhaps they hadn't noticed my spying on them, but eventually they spoke.

"There was a time in the *Gruende* when it was thought a kindness to 'repair' mixie babies through surgery."

I prepared the meal, and we said nothing more to each other that evening.

In the morning, I cut myself again. I failed to light the fire again. Sem drew on my pain again to do what I could not. I was becoming tired of this ritual.

As I drank down my bitter tea, Sem finished their whittling, tied on their wooden sandals, and stood, walking far enough from the lake to reach softer sandy soil. They took the stick they had been working for two days, now a reasonable facsimile of their short sword, and planted it point down into the ground. They stepped back two paces.

"Come, Arin. Take the sword and strike me."

I stood, walking warily towards the wooden sword. "Why don't I get two?" I asked, eyeing the pair of swords tucked into their belt.

"Do you know how to use a sword?"

I admitted I did not.

"First one. *Then* two," they said.

I walked up to the sword, reaching out to take it.

They moved like a viper, their long sword coming out—still

in its scabbard—to bat my hand away faster than I could blink. I stumbled back, easing my stinging knuckles and scowling.

I reset my feet and tried again, this time trying to mimic their footwork, pouncing to reach it. I came away with my forearm stinging, and no sword.

I ran towards the sword, raising my left arm to defend myself from their strike and reaching out with my right. They moved past me with a sliding step, and their scabbard fouled my feet. I went sprawling in the dirt. I screamed a wordless cry of frustration.

"How am I supposed to learn to use the sword if you won't let me pick it up?" I asked in anger, standing.

"First *one*," they repeated. "*Then* two."

Eleven

I woke up the next morning and my whole body was sore. Sem's training had left me with new aches and exhausted muscles, and following this with hours sitting bareback atop a swaying mule was a new experience of physical exhaustion. Now after sleeping the night on the cold hard ground, I felt like I could barely move.

I groaned as I straightened from the ground and struggled to stand. Still wrapped in their cloak, Sem opened one eye and watched me for a moment, then rolled over. I didn't want to move, I wanted a fire. I stuck out my tongue and made a face at Sem's back, and limped over to the privy trench.

By the time I returned, Sem was awake and rubbing their chest through their jacket to warm up. I sighed to myself and thought *first one, then two*. I made a pyramid of firewood over a small pile of bark for kindling. I sat back down on my cloak and took out my knife and set it to my skin.

I closed my eyes.

I could feel the pain in my arm, but I could also feel the response to it in my body, in my mind. My mind *was* retreating from it, holding it off, trying to contain the sensation to my limb. What happened next, happened by instinct. I opened myself to the pain and it filled me. I looked at the kindling. I felt the pain in my mind and held it in the center of my being. It expanded and contracted with my heartbeat. I focused on nothing else—the pain, the kindling. From one beat to the next, the pain was everything, and then it was condensed to a point so small that it had no measure. I was the pain. I was the fire. The fire was the pain.

I opened my eyes to the crackle and heat of a cheery campfire, and to Sem looking at me with an odd expression.

"I did it!" I said. "Ow!" My arm still hurt fiercely.

Sem looked at the fire silently.

"What's wrong?" I asked.

"Bind that before you bleed all over your clothes." They moved to the fire and poked it with a stick from the small woodpile. "I was hoping for some smoke. Or enough of a spark to light the kindling," they said softly. "You... just willed the fire fully into being from nothing. With a little nick."

I looked down at my arm, already crossed in a neat line of scars, some all but healed, some scabbed over, one hot and flowing. "Feels like more than a 'little nick,'" I said sullenly.

"What you just did is... very impressive for a first conscious feat."

I felt an odd feeling in my chest—a fullness. Pride, I realized. I sat for a moment, staring into the fire that I had made from nothing. After a moment, though, I frowned to myself.

My arm still *hurt*.

Over the next several days as we continued our steady progress north, I lit the fire each morning. Embracing the pain was becoming second-nature. As was ignoring it afterwards. The other lesson however, was not proceeding so well.

In addition to my growing decoration of scars, I was collecting an impressive bouquet of mild bruises as well. My attempts to take the sword, planted each morning or afternoon in the soil nearby our campsite, were met with defeat after humiliating defeat. I was tripped to fall in the dirt more often than I can count. I was struck, deflected, and tangled.

I tried dashing in a random series of feints, doubling back and spinning. Sem moved in a calm, even flow, stepping here then there, and all I took that time was a sharp rap to the top of my head from their scabbard that left me seeing stars and hearing a ringing bell for a few moments.

I tried tossing a fistful of dust into the air in front of Sem as a distraction. They simply closed their eyes, and managed to trip me up by the sound of my movements.

I spent afternoons jumping, hopping forwards and backwards and sideways, trying to strengthen my legs. I succeeded in tiring myself so that I was slower than ever, and they didn't even bother to strike me when I tried for the sword.

It became a fixation. Not "first one, then two" any longer. Only "one". Everything I had was focused on *one*. I entirely forgot why I was trying for it. Only that I wanted to hold the wooden sword in my hand, just once.

I dove for the sword from two paces away, resigning myself to scrapes and bruises from hitting the ground in exchange for the chance at grabbing the sword. They slid their foot out and kicked it out of my reach before I could.

I tried to slide beneath the swing of their scabbarded sword and was deflected by their knee.

I tried rolling across their reach and had my wind knocked out when they planted their scabbard firmly in my path.

I jumped and dodged and dashed, and was always too slow.

After a week of failures, I was sitting up late one night staring into the last coals of the evening fire. The stars were arrayed in a magnificent dusting of tiny lights above me, and the darkness surrounded us in an unrelieved expanse.

Sem was curled up in their cloak to my left. I eyed them for some time, watching their chest rise and fall. The last coals faded from bright orange to dull bronze to shimmering gray ash, and finally went dark. I sat still until my eyes adapted to the light of the stars. Still the only movement from Sem was their slow, steady breathing.

In that silence and darkness, I was struck with a moment of perfect clarity. *First* one, *then* two. I rose from my cloak and walked carefully, silently to the small stack of belongings beside them, unfolding my pocketknife as I went. After a few moments, I returned to my bedding and slept soundly.

The next morning I woke as usual. I lit the fire, having only a little trouble with dexterity. Sem had insisted that I use my other arm now that I was easy cutting on my left. They woke and stretched, walking away some distance to squat over the privy trench I had dug the evening before. As I prepared my moon tea, they brewed a kettle of regular tea and warmed up the leftovers of porridge and beans from last night's meal. We ate breakfast, and I asked a question that had been in my mind for some time, but somehow hadn't thought to ask until now.

"What is it? Reft. A... school?"

"No," Sem said, simply. Then, "Yes."

I sighed, letting my exasperation show.

They shrugged their shoulders. "Do you need a teacher to tell you to breathe? To eat?" They sighed this time. "There are some there who may help you learn things. Certainly they can help you learn mastery, and nuance. But most of all, it's a haven. A place to gather. A place of safety. A place for many to work together to one end."

"Is that why you spend your life wandering, instead of residing there?"

They looked at me sharply. "Oh yes, you're going to fit in *just fine* in Reft. Come!" They said, reaching over to tie on their sandals. They stood and tucked their swords into their belt and hefted the wooden short sword. "Practice!"

I watched as they walked out into the moorland and planted the sword once more. I stood and followed, trying to not let my tension show in my shoulders or in my stride. They took their position behind the sword, and I took mine some paces away.

I wanted this to work. I wanted the sword. It had taken me days of consideration to understand. First one, then two.

I set my feet and leaned forward. I saw them quirk a little smile, and I knew now how to spot the tension as they prepared themself.

I started forward with an easy couple of steps, then changed directions suddenly, running outward in a wide spiral, circling around. Sem only turned slowly in place, keeping between me and the sword. As I reached almost halfway around, I changed directions again, dashing straight in to the sword, just to their left. I saw their movement begin, and I immediately darted back, running out from the sword.

As they performed a sliding sideways hop to catch me in my flight, their longsword came out in its scabbard and they planted their left foot... and both of their sandals came apart beneath them.

Sem sprawled, falling flat on their back as the sandal straps that I had cut *almost* all the way through in the night tore loose.

I changed direction again, running back to the sword, and this time, I reached it, wrapped my hands around it and yanked it up. I turned to face Sem who was still lying on the ground. I stepped carefully to them and lightly tapped them on the forehead.

"Two." I said.

They looked at me for a moment and then sat up. Then they saw the broken straps of their sandals. Picking up one end, Sem looked closely, and I saw their eyes widen in realization. I bit my lip, waiting for anger.

Their laughter rang out across the moorlands. I wondered if they could hear it all the way back in Anbress. Sem rolled back onto their back again, laughing with visible joy and rocking side to side.

"Well done, Arin!" They gasped, and continued laughing.

We topped a rise and began descending the hill towards the bank of the Sommíre. It had been a little over a week since I took the sword. Sem had grumbled the remainder of that afternoon about their ruined sandals, until I shared Neme's ointment for the angry cut across their chest. After that the grumbles had subsided considerably, though they did cut up my last dress to make new straps for their sandals.

They had been training me every day since. We rode most of each day, but spent a good hour or more in camp each night and again each morning practicing a complicated series of patterns, moving my body and sword just so in endless repetition. The purpose, they said, was not to learn to fight—that would take far longer to teach than the journey to Reft, and my muscles were not nearly strong enough for real sword practice—the purpose was to learn my body, its senses, its balance, and its motion, and to build strength and endurance in my body and limbs. First one, then two.

We reached the bank, and I pulled Beatrice to a stop. I swung my leg over, feeling the muscles tighten and release, flex *this* much, rotate *so*, relax and extend to *there*. I was intimately aware of each movement, and just how each part of my body moved to execute that movement. I thought now I moved with no wasted effort, no extraneous action. I felt like I could repeat the motions exactly, mounting and dismounting.

"Stay here, let the mules forage, but don't make camp yet."

"Where are you going?" I asked. This was not our usual procedure.

"I'll be back," they said.

I stood for a moment, watching Sem walk away upriver. The Sommíre was broad here, wide enough that I knew I could not swim it. Sem had assured me that it was too deep to ford as well.

The soft rushing sound of the water and gentle lapping of ripples against the rocky bank belied the river's violence. I scanned the near and far banks, trying to discern where a likely crossing might be managed, but all I could see was a small mudflat protruding from the near bank a few dozen feet away. That would let us wade into the river, but we wouldn't make it across on our own.

Some time later, I startled to see a small boat floating downstream from the east. As it drew closer, I could see Sem guiding it with a paddle, and a line of casks floating behind on a trailing rope. As they neared, they called out to me, and pointed to the mudflat with the paddle. I picked my way over, getting there in time to help pull the boat up onto the bank.

"I stashed this up there on the way south," they said, pointing with the paddle. "Hoped it would still be waiting."

They turned and began winding the rope up, pulling in the four casks from the water before the river dragged them and the boat away. "The mules can swim, but there's no reason to tire them out overmuch. They'll be happier on the other side if they can float a little like us."

It took us about an hour to get the two mules down to the bank, get two casks strapped to either side, both of them tethered to the boat, and our baggage and ourselves settled. Sem sat in the front of the shallow boat and I took the rear position, making sure their pack and my bag stayed put.

When all was ready, they pushed off of the mudflat with the oar and started across. There was a moment of concern when we reached the extent of the tether and both mules stood firm, not appreciating being dragged into the river behind us.

With a good bit of gentle clucking and tugging, we eventually succeeded in getting them into the water, and then it was a relatively easy paddle across. I worried over Beatrice and the gray, but whenever I looked back, they were swimming well, buoyed by their wooden floats. If they looked at me with special reproach, they at least didn't seem to be drowning. Sem allowed the current to carry us a fair bit west for every stroke north. After a half hour on the water, I could see a large sandy bank ahead to our right.

They grounded the boat and I hopped out, pulling on the bow line while they pushed with the paddle, until the boat was firmly ashore. Sem stayed in the boat, their weight keeping it from being dragged downriver while I pulled the mules up one by one.

They climbed out and pulled the boat further up the bank, turning it over. "Someone else might find it useful."

Finally, we were settled again. I mounted Beatrice, and with Sem astride the gray we set off. The land on this side was much rockier. I could see we were well into the low mountains, and it was now passes and valleys we looked to for our path.

I was close to asking when we would stop, when Sem pulled the gray to a halt and pointed. It took me some time to understand what I was seeing—one fall of stone looked much like the next. But suddenly, in what I had thought was a shadow cast by a boulder, I saw an archway. A pile of stones became a crumbling wall, and a fallen log was a rough-hewn and weathered roof beam, partially exposed by time.

We had arrived at a ruined fort.

My arm throbbed. This time, they had lit the fire with flint and steel, instructing me to *prevent* the fire from starting. This had proved much more difficult than it seemed.

"Will you be staying in Reft?" I asked over the small fire.

Sem didn't answer immediately, instead staring silently into the crackling fire. The smoke from our fire seeped slowly through the rotting and half-collapsed roof beams and out into the night.

"I don't mix well with other people," they said, quietly and finally.

I looked at them in the flickering orange light. The scar on their chest had scabbed over, but was still ugly, more than two weeks on. The pot of ointment Neme had given me had run out days ago.

"Why don't you heal that?"

"It doesn't work that way. Could you light a fire now, with your arm hurting from earlier?"

I hadn't considered that, but I thought about it now. My arm hurt just as much now, but the pain was dull, lacking the sharp focus and acute intensity of the initial cut. I thought back to the sensation of the blade parting my skin, setting the nerves on fire. The animal panic that rose in my throat every time I caused myself a new injury.

"No," I said slowly. "It's..." I struggled for a word, "...empty."

Sem nodded. "When we draw power from physical pain, it's like... digging a hole. You dig and you dig and you dig, and by the time you've reached the depth you want, you're exhausted from the effort. If you leave it be, eventually wind and rain will wash dirt and debris back into the hole, fill it in. If you don't want to wait, want to fill it in again *now*, that takes even more effort."

They shifted, getting more comfortable. "Our power is that way. It doesn't come for nothing. The pain always will take its due, and so the power we have to spend is that much smaller for it. If I wanted to heal this cut, I'd have to cut myself just that much worse to get enough power, and then where would I be?"

"But, I saw you do it," I wiggled my fingers to the south, indicating the direction of Anbress.

They sighed, looking into the fire. "I drew on the pain of those who attacked me. I didn't want to hurt them. I tried to avoid it. But they chose to fight, and so I had a choice. I could kill them, or I could cause them pain and forge myself a way out of the mess *they* created."

They were quiet for a time. "It's a thing not well looked upon by many *nyssén*. They call it *dire*. The way they see it, I hurt others and draw power from it. Power from someone else's pain, unwilling... it's weaker, wasteful. They're fighting the pain, trying to hold it at bay." They looked up at me, and I nodded. Before I knew to embrace it, I had done the same. "Their efforts to hold back the pain... there's less power to be had from that. So it takes more. Much more. They call me *grim*, the other *nyssén*. But it's never an easy choice, and I avoid it when I can."

Twelve

The next morning, the true hardships of our journey began. It seemed for every mile we moved north, there were three we had to move this way and that to get over or around another mountain. We climbed, and climbed. We went up endless switchbacks to reach a pass, then down another set to reach the valley on the other side. The mules did most of the work, but there was only so far we could push them at a time. We lost hours each day letting them rest and graze.

Each time we crested a rise, I caught sight of the Red River to the west, a tributary that marked the border with Somiere. It was well named, for it seemed to catch fire in the sun. Sem said that this was partly due to the minerals in the stone it washed through. The clay in its basin was a deep rust color.

On the third day, we reached the top of a trail and a great vista opened before us to the northeast. There was a wide, deep valley, sparsely wooded and green. The short, stunted trees blended one with the next so that it was difficult to get a sense of scale. It might be a day's walk or a week's through to the far hill. That hill was an impressive and daunting piling of fissured stone, full of sheer cliffs and sharp spires. At the highest point, a great butte rose from the surrounding stone. And atop this was a narrow faceted tower which rose several stories further. Its top was ragged, and even from this distance, it looked like a ruin.

Sem nodded to the tower. "Redwatch. Built over five hundred years ago as part of a chain of fortifications through these mountains. It's a common stop for travelers to and from Reft."

I felt a wind rise up from my back and flow down into the valley. The treetops caught the current and began to sway so that the valley looked like a great roiling sea. I turned to look the way we had come, and saw a dark strip of ominous clouds on the horizon.

"We should move on," Sem said beside me. I saw they too were looking to the looming storm. "There's no shelter between here and Redwatch. Come."

We nudged our mules and began the slow descent into the forested valley. We were well into the depths of the trees when the storm caught us.

The rain sheeted down, drenching us and making the ground treacherous, even underneath the low forest canopy. The summer storms further south could be fierce, but I was not prepared for the violence of it. A sudden chill set in as the temperature dropped, and I could hear lightning crackling in the distance, not far enough away for comfort. Between the trees and the dark clouds and the rain, we lost nearly all of our light in moments as the storm covered us.

The mules rolled their eyes and brayed, frantic at the thunderclaps and sound of dislodged foliage from above. I tried to calm Beatrice, but she was having none of it—she took to bucking and nearly unseated me.

"How can you tell where we're going?" I shouted over the din.

Sem replied with something, but their voice disappeared in the gusts of rain. They pointed, and we kept moving. We were both forced to dismount and lead the mules, as they were becoming too fractious to ride.

I can't say for how long we trudged like this. It was miserable. We were sodden and cold, the mules were irritable and prone to bolt at each clap of thunder. I lost one of my shoes in the sticky muck churned up by Sem and their gray, and it was too dark to try to find it. I had to press on.

I was exhausted and sore, and there came a point in the raging torrent that I wanted to just sit down in the mud and quit. I could feel Beatrice becoming more and more resistant to my tugs, and began to think that maybe we could shelter against each other and weather the worst of the storm.

I was now simply moving, in the grip of an animal drive to stay alive and conscious, but without thought. The only things I was aware of: the constant trudge through the mud, my hand on Beatrice's lead, the shapes of Sem and the gray marching some feet ahead of me. I lost all sense of time and space and reason.

I startled alert as I walked into the gray's rump. Sem had stopped, and as I blinked and wiped the stream of water from my eyes, I suddenly realized the forest around me had thinned. In front of us was a gray wall of rock.

Sem led us along this sheer face until a small fold of stone turned into a narrow crevasse that doubled back into the rock.

From one step to the next, the pressure and noise of the rain abated, and we were suddenly under the shelter of a narrow cave.

I looked at Sem, and receiving no immediate indication of worry, I stepped over to the wall and slid down to the rough stone floor, utterly spent. I might have sat there for hours. I might have slept. But some time later, I saw them standing before me, reaching out a hand to pull me up. As I grasped it, I noticed a fresh cut on the inside of their forearm.

The rain still fell in all its violence and rage. To my surprise, we turned not out into the deluge, but deeper into the cave. Beatrice and the gray were tied to a stout wooden beam mounted with iron ties nailed deep into the stone wall, and were happily munching in their feedbags. Beside them, a narrow arch led to a tight stair cut into the rock, winding upwards.

"This is the only way into or out of the tower. Elsewhere, there is a system of pulleys and baskets for lifting supplies," Sem said.

I knelt down to remove my other shoe, tying the laces to my satchel. They pulled a torch from a small basket beside the archway and lit it with their flint and steel, and we ascended. I began counting the steps, but lost count and gave up long before we reached the first landing.

I began to despair of ever feeling the open air again, but three landings and innumerable steps later, we arrived at Redwatch.

Through another arch, I stepped into a wide octagonal room. The walls were built of large stone blocks, and there were narrow windows in the center of each side. A staircase wound partway around the perimeter to disappear into the floor above. Outside, the storm continued to rage.

On a shelf built into the wall, Sem found a pair of oil lamps and lit them from the torch. They noticed me peering at the space, and nodded to the stairs. "Go ahead and explore. We're safe here. I've Delved all the way to the top and we're the only ones here." My eyes flickered to the cut on their arm, and they nodded. "There's supplies laid by for travelers on the next floor. See if there's anything we need."

Sem looked now at my feet shod only in mud, then to the one shoe tied to my bag. "When did you lose that?"

I sighed. "Sometime in the forest. The mud took it."

They twisted their mouth in thought. "Unlikely to find new shoes up there." They walked over and sat down before me, gesturing me to sit. "We'll do a Finding."

I sat in front of them and waited. They sat for a moment and thought before speaking.

"Normally, this would take a full Circle, and all practiced. But the loss is both recent, and near."

They took out a small belt knife, and indicated I should open my pocketknife. "Since you know what you lost and where, you will have to contribute. Bring yourself to the moment you felt the shoe slip from your foot. You must hold that moment, the sensations exactly as you experienced them, in your mind and in your body. Put yourself there and embody the memory. When you cut, allow the pain to wash over and through that memory. I will draw both from you."

I closed my eyes. I remembered the feeling of cold sticky mud squelching into my shoe, soaking my sock. Somehow I thought that merely remembering would not be enough. I breathed deeply, trying to reach a point where the memory became more than a thought.

I was sitting on the cold stone in the dim light of the tower room. The storm churned only feet away, but the stout walls kept its fury at bay. Sem sat before me. I could hear their breathing in time with mine, echoing through the space.

There was a thin barrier between myself and my memory, like a caul between reality and the impressions it had left behind. My breathing steadied and matched its rhythm to my heartbeat. I *pushed* through the boundary.

Water trickled down the back of my shirt, its cold touch running down my spine. My feet were sodden and each step felt like I carried a mountain on my back. My legs ached and I only wanted to stop, to rest, even if I drowned from it. I could briefly see before me the shadowy shape of the gray's rump and Sem, bent and trudging resolutely through the driving rain. I couldn't keep my eyes up for the rain that filled them. In chill and misery, I lowered my eyes again to the morass of mud and leaf litter that dragged at my feet. I was focused only on each step, lifting one foot, then the other. I lifted my right foot, and felt something give—mud pulled at me and then my foot was cold and wet and slime, and I realized that my shoe was gone.

I cut.

The pain radiated across my arm, and I let it fill my center. I embraced it and let it perfuse me as I stood in the mud, rain washing over my body and driving thought away. The pain was a heat and a light roiling my being and I allowed it to contest with the cold and wet. I felt a pulling, and the pain and memory both seemed to attenuate, like a branch being drawn away downriver by a powerful current.

I was there in the rain and mud, foot half raised and leaning forward into the squall. I was also sitting on cold dry stone just beside myself, watching. Sem was there too, trudging in front of me, yes, but also sitting calmly on the other side of my drenched self. They opened their eyes and looked at me across the memory of me. Our eyes moved together down to the lone shoe, abandoned and half buried in the muck.

And then we were sitting in the tower room once more. With a start, I realized I knew exactly where the shoe was. I could point right to it from where I sat. I thought that I could feel a draw from it, tugging at my mind. I turned my head to stare at a spot on the floor near the wall. I knew that I was looking in a straight line directly to the shoe, out there in the mud on the forest floor.

I glanced at Sem, and they were looking at the same spot.

"Well," they said, "It's not far. You explore the tower as I said. I will go fetch it." They looked at me a moment, an odd look on their face. "Well done, Arin."

In moments, they were heading down the stairs, and I was alone in the tower. I took one of the two lamps and started up the stairs to the next floor. This floor was much the same, only the walls between the windows were filled with wooden shelves stacked with supplies, and the center of the room taken by barrels and chests. On the wall near the stairs was a pile of split firewood. One of the eight windows was larger than the others, and beside it stood a great wooden contraption of beams, ropes and pulleys. It seemed this was the method used to lift provisions into the tower.

I wandered through the stores, inspecting this and that, opening boxes and barrels and chests. In one chest I found a pack, similar to Sem's but smaller, a better fit for my frame. My satchel was near overflowing, so I transferred my clothes into the pack, and continued my search.

I found a box of rolled bandages, and took one to wind round my arm, shedding the soaked and dingy linen strips. I pulled out several more and stuffed them into my satchel, now near empty. Beside these was a small jar of ointment that smelled similar to Neme's. I took this too.

I found a trim little tinder box with a flint and steel that fit into the lid. There was a stack of thick woolen blankets, and I took one for my pack. I found a straw hat. A sack of dried beans, another of mushrooms, and a third of some grain that I was not familiar with but smelled wholesome. These I stacked at the top of the stairs.

Satisfied with my haul, I went up another flight. On this floor the staircase opened onto a small landing, and the floor was subdivided into three rooms. Any doors were long-since rotted away, but in the light of the small lamp I could see these rooms were likely meant as sleeping chambers. I went further up the stairs.

This floor was the most impressive so far. The windows were large, so wide that the stone walls between them were little more than pillars holding up the ceiling. A raised stone circle in the center of the room was recently used as a fire pit. One corner of the ceiling had fallen in, and between the great windows and the crumbling ceiling, this floor would be uncomfortable in the storm, but the rains were weakening to a drizzle, and though the sky was still dark with clouds, I could see glimmers of light from the south and west. The storm was passing.

I could still feel the pull of my shoe, and I moved to the edge of the window where I could look out on the forest below. The view was dizzying. I thought I had never been so high in my life. I could see all the way past the other edge of the valley. Suddenly, the pull was gone. I'm not sure why I knew, but I realized then Sem had found it.

I moved to the western-facing window, and could see the long rusty ribbon of the Red River cutting through the landscape. This view must be the origin of the tower's name. I walked a slow circuit around the room, looking out at the view in each direction. The world was so vast. I had never thought there was so much to be seen. The horizon pulled at me in every direction, and I wondered how many lifetimes it would take to see everything.

After some time to my thoughts, I took the stairs back down to the storeroom and began hauling up firewood. By the time Sem arrived back with my shoe, they found me sitting on my blanket in the great observation room with a crackling fire and a pot of mushroom and bean porridge bubbling happily.

In the morning, Sem pointed out our path from the great north-facing window. From our spire perch, it looked all broken rock and scrub. North-northeast through a series of valleys and rises towards the highest peak visible in any direction. It was daunting.

We repacked our packs in the storeroom, and Sem looked over my choices, approving. They tied two bundles of firewood and with these in hand and packs on our backs, we descended the twisting stair to our mules. We settled our baggage, each mule carrying a bundle of firewood in addition to their previous load, and set out. Sem led us out of the cave and along the cliffs until we reached a narrow trail leading up.

The road we traveled was an endless series of treacherous switchbacks and crumbling trails. I think that without the surefooted mules we would not have made it through. Each night, Sem continued my lessons in movement, balance, and concentration. Each morning, I tried to prevent the fire from igniting.

When I finally succeeded in this, they smiled, and allowed me to light the fire with flint and steel. It was an odd reward, but welcome. Both of my arms were by now a mass of cuts and scars, and I was struggling to find new places to cut that wouldn't hinder my movements.

This time was exhausting, but I realized one morning that I was happy. I felt free, and unburdened by expectations. I had no idea what to expect in Reft, but there was no fear in me.

Thirteen

We had been two weeks traveling from Redwatch, and the day before we had finally wound through a pass and the view opened up to us. From a distance, Reft was a marvel. A sprawling construction, something between a city and a palace; wood and stone wrought in an intricate lattice spider-webbing across the sheer face of the broad ridge. Portions of the structure penetrated the natural formations so that there were places that looked as if the mountainside had windows and balconies, and other places where the human structures had grown mountainous stone from their midsts.

We approached Reft from the east, the only passable road. There was precious little to see from this direction, most of Reft being arrayed on the sheer side of the mountain. From the road, we saw nothing more than a few small cottages and an open-sided covered structure clustered around a large wooden hall like a barn, built up against the rock face. There was a rocky yard between these structures, and on a low bench beside the largest door, someone sat, idly whittling a stick in the shade.

The smell of wood smoke wafted in the air. Sem dismounted and lifted down my pack, slinging it over their shoulder. I followed and we walked towards the barn doors.

Off to the right, I could see several tall horses stabled in the open structure. Five soldiers sat at a table playing some kind of game with dice. They paid us no mind. As we passed, the wind caught the corner of a standard they had propped against a post, and it partially unfurled. Orange and lavender with a device like a hawk in dark purple. It matched the colors on the men's livery.

"Ho, Sem," the door warden said, not looking our way—their eyes were fixed on the five soldiers. "Brought in another stray for us?"

"Theni," Sem said in greeting. Their eyes darted to the right. "That one back again? What's he want this time?"

Theni looked much like any middle-aged man I had ever seen, hair thinning, middle gone slightly to paunch. Their face was weathered a little less than a farmer, and their body a little softer, but otherwise this could be any freeholder from Meers.

"Oh, you know *him*," Theni said. "He came 'seeking wisdom' or somesuch. Why the Council puts up with him, or his pet..." Theni spat into the dirt.

Sem grunted. "The ways here are not for everyone, Theni. I don't begrudge you your comforts, why begrudge others their path?"

Theni's face turned sour. "Oh, you know I don't blame you for wandering. But *you* don't take service with some lord and wear his colors."

Sem nodded to Theni and opened the door. Theni made no move to stop us.

We entered what I had thought of as a barn and I stumbled in surprise. The inside was appointed more like Ma'am's entry and main hall—flagstone floor and thick, polished wood paneling. The walls were layered here and there with tapestries and patterned hangings in rich wool, and there were several tables and chairs along the walls, with lamps providing good light. Across from us was another door, set in stone post and lintel.

At the far end of the room was a broad fireplace and several chairs and couches arrayed before it on thick layered carpets. Sem turned to these and I began to follow, but they gestured me to wait. As they approached, I realized one of the seats was occupied.

Sem began speaking with the person in the chair, who closed a book they were reading. I followed, but at a long expressionless look from Sem, I backed away, leaving them to speak in privacy. I walked slowly around the room. The tables held a variety of books. There was a wooden sculpture in the corner, some animal I could not identify.

Along the wall by the door was a great parchment framed in dark wood, and inscribed upon it a vast map. The Freelands were labeled in a large, clear hand, as were Somiere, and Torfall, and the Far Arids. I found Reft, nestled in an expanse of mountains, and Anbress towards the bottom. I marveled at the distance Sem and I had traveled. I traced the Sommíre to the Seeber and found Maplewood marked, though Meers was not. Still, I stared for some time at the small corner of the mountains where my parents' farm was.

Sem called out to me, drawing me away from the map. I walked over to stand beside them.

"Turin," Sem said, "this is Arin, out of the Freelands, lately of Anbress."

Turin leaned forward in their seat, looking me over. Their

eyes hesitated a moment on my scar, then returned to my face. They were perhaps the same age as Sem, but in every other way, seemingly opposite. Where Sem was lean and muscled, Turin was round and fleshy. They were tall and large-boned where Sem was compact, and pale-skinned instead of dark. Where Sem wore a long thick braid, Turin was bald.

Sem's body was covered in scars. Turin's face and hands at least, were not. I had expected everyone in Reft to be as scarred as Sem, but so far, they seemed to be the outlier. *I* had more visible scars than Theni or Turin. They were wearing a rich blouse and overwrap in soft, brushed wool over their pronounced belly.

They met my gaze placidly, and I could see their eyes were calm and peaceful. "Hello, Arin. Welcome to Reft."

I took a deep breath, and felt a tension I hadn't been aware of ease. Turin's voice was deep and calm, much like Father's. But it had a quality of stability and assuredness that Father had never had. Their voice sounded like the mountain.

"Whatever you have experienced before now, Arin, you are safe here." Their voice carried such a deep well of kindness and care that I felt my eyes moisten.

"Thank you," I said, and suddenly felt foolish.

"What do you know of Reft?" they asked.

I looked to Sem, then back to Turin. They both looked at me blankly. "It's... you live here? And it is sort of a school, and a town? And everyone works together... and everyone is... witches?" I struggled over these words, drawing out everything from my memory, and stumbled over the last word.

Turin waited a moment, as if expecting me to dredge up more. Then smiled gently. "Well, you might say that we are a town. And we certainly work together to common ends." They leaned forward and their face became more serious.

"We are mostly *nyssén*, though not all. You know that word?"

I nodded.

"Some who live here have family with them, others came to us alone like you. And some of us have embraced our powers, though not all. Reft is a fellowship. We are a community of people who together strive to a vision of life at peace, free from the pain and violence of the outside world, and free from the fear and hatreds of those who will not see us as people worthy of life." They looked now to me intently, waiting for a sign of understanding. I nodded.

"You may certainly learn some skills here, as we are many and all here commit to sharing everything we have. Indeed, *you* may have skills to teach *us*, young as you are. From what Sem has told me, your power at least will be a welcome addition." I blinked at this.

"Now, there are rules you must abide by. You must be an active member of our community, learning, working, and sharing. You may not draw power from another's pain without consent." My eyes flickered to Sem. "You may not use your powers to harm another except in coordinated defense of Reft. You will protect and hold sacred first the lives, and second the confidences of those around you. Do you understand these rules, Arin? Can you accept and live by them?"

I nodded.

"You must say so."

It took me a moment to recall them. "I will be an active member of the community. I swear to not draw power from another's pain without their consent. I will not use my power to harm others, unless I'm told to defend Reft. I will protect the lives around me, and I will protect their secrets."

"Good. We ask all that come to live here to give over their

possessions towards the common good. We live together, we work together, we dine together, we hurt together, and we heal together. What will you contribute to our community? "

"I have to pay you to stay here? Sem said nothing to me about this. I have... almost nothing."

"Let us see," they said, and gently took my pack, untying the cords and laying the things out on the low table between us. My blanket and cloak came out first. Spare clothes, my water flask, tinder box, whetstone, and the tiny purse and its few coins. The bandages, pot of poultice, my dwindling pouch of herbs, and the small mortar and pestle that were all in my satchel. They even lifted the straw hat from my head and drew the wooden sword from my belt. All that I owned but what I wore was laid carefully out across the table.

"Is that everything?"

Slowly, I took the folding knife from my pocket and showed it to them, but I did not let it go. "Sem told me to always keep a blade with me."

Turin grunted, but did not insist I put it down. We looked over all the things I had carried through my travels with Sem.

"We do not ask that you pauper yourself. Only that you give what you can. What can you part with?"

I looked over the things still on the table. There was very little that held any value to me. I took back the mortar and pestle that Neme had given me. I took the wooden sword Sem had carved.

Turin looked up at me. "Do you still wish to join us?"

I nodded.

Sem had watched this exchange in silence, but now they rested their hand on my shoulder, and I turned to them. Their look wavered between sadness, relief, and appraisal.

"So you really are leaving me here?" I asked, a little sullenness creeping into my voice.

"Arin, it is time for me to go, this is not my place. What I could teach you, I have taught. What I could give you I have given. It is now time for those here to help you find yourself."

I struggled with various emotions for a long moment. I couldn't say they were abandoning me. They had never made any pretense of their task. That I might wish that I could stay with them, that they would stay with me, was obvious. We had traveled together for weeks—of course I wanted to hold onto the familiar.

But I also felt a pull, a longing to find out what might be waiting for me here.

I nodded. "Thank you for bringing me here," I said. They reached out and lifted the wooden sword from my hands and tucked it into my belt.

"First one, then two," I whispered.

They nodded their head solemnly. "You will see me again." Sem smiled, and without saying another word, turned and moved to the door.

I watched them for a moment until the tears welling in my eyes dried, then turned to face Turin. They stood, and gestured for me to follow them towards the doorway set into the face of the stone. We walked together into the mountain.

"Can you read? Write?" Turin asked as we walked through a stone passage. Candle lamps along the walls every dozen feet gave sufficient light to see.

"A little. My parents taught me some."

"Hm, Freelander though. No Somiri, I suppose?" I shook my head. "Well, It's a start—enough for a farm—but you will learn more here. Knowledge is passed down in books. We will teach you to access it. Sem tells me you are thirteen?"

"What month is it?"

"It is August."

"I'll be fourteen in four months."

"I will arrange classes for you. Once you are competent with what we feel all here should learn you may choose your own skills to master, but reading and writing comes first. Language is the root of knowledge and thought, and Somiri is the language of scholarship."

The stone, beginning rough-hewn, took on a smoother, more refined texture. We continued down the tunnel, and it opened up on the left side into a wide hall that opened out of the side of the mountain. Great timber balconies extended out from thick arches and overlooked the valley below. I lost what else they said as I stepped out into the afternoon sun.

Below, I could see several layered terraces richly planted with gardens. I heard a dog barking somewhere below, and could see several people moving about among the greenery.

Turin stepped out beside me. "We grow almost all we need here, in terrace gardens like those and in the Vale, though you cannot see that from here. Anything we can't grow or make ourselves, we get in trade with caravans which come to us, mainly from Somiere."

"How many?" I was still stunned at the view.

"Some thousand of us altogether, I suppose. You spoke truly when you called us a town. We have farmers, weavers, millers, bakers and cooks; tailors, smiths, artists, healers, and scholars; we have a system of councils for adjudicating disputes."

I glanced at Turin, hearing something like pride in their voice. After a moment, they drew me back inside and we continued. Soon we were walking through comfortable halls sculpted in living rock. There was too much for me to take in. As Turin continued to walk, I caught sight of wonders in stone and wood, but I was too distracted trying to follow their quick steps, the winding halls, and their continuous descriptions and periodic questions.

"Everyone here divides their time between work they have chosen, and working towards their own healing and power. Sem said that they taught you some control. Here you will learn more of that control, and less... brutal... ways of achieving peace with your power. Did they talk to you about your breaking?"

We turned a corner to a wide spiral of stone steps, descending and ascending, winding around a great column of open air and light. We descended.

"They said that I did... something. I still don't understand though."

"We will help you understand."

By now I had lost track of the turnings and descents. I could sense we were deep within the mountain, but between the lamps on the walls and occasional shafts bringing in air and light, it did not feel oppressive. We turned down a narrow hall and passed several doors before Turin stopped and knocked at one. The door was opened by a youth about my age.

"Kari," Turin said, "this is Arin. Please help them get settled, and introduce them to your housemates. Arin, Kari will show you what you need tonight. Tomorrow morning after you've eaten, come to my chambers for first lessons. Kari can tell you how to find it." With a smile for me and nod to Kari, they turned and left.

Kari was of a height with me, though thicker of body. They had the same dark Somiri skin and hair as Sem and Neme, though they wore their hair in a multitude of short, fine braids that framed their lovely face. Their exposed forearms were lined with short scars, which I found oddly reassuring—the first hint that there were people like me here.

They took my hand and pulled me into the room. I saw their eyes flicker to my scar for a brief moment, then back to my face. Then they gave me a wide, easy smile.

"Welcome Arin. I'm Kari, and you'll meet Migs and Chan later. They're still at their chores or lessons." Kari's speech was more strongly tinted with the Somiri accent than Neme's had been.

The room we entered was near enough the size of one of the parlors in Ma'am's house. It was furnished with several comfortable chairs, couches, and low tables arrayed around a hearth where a cheerful fire crackled. The two walls to either side had two doors each.

"Here is your room," they said, opening the first door on the left.

I stepped into a snug room with a bed, a small table, chest, and washstand. A curtain hid a nook with pegs and shelving for clothes. I set my few belongings on the table.

"Old Turin took the reckoning, eh? We can go next to collect clothing and other things you'll need." They eyed me up and down and laughed, "Truth, you need some new cloth."

I felt conscious of my travel-stained rough clothing. Kari was wearing a green knitted tunic fitted to the skin and long cream-colored flowing trousers. I followed them back into the main room.

"If you need it, there is a privy and bathing room further down the hall, shared by all rooms on this hallway..."

I was drawn towards a wooden panel beside the hearth that was set with squares of parchment glowing with afternoon light. I saw that it was made to slide in tracks in the floor and ceiling, and as I slid it open my breath caught. I stepped out onto a small balcony, and it felt as if I had stepped out of the mountain into the sky. The stone above and to either side was worked such that I could see no sign of another room or balcony, yet I felt certain we had passed many rooms like this one. Far below and to the right was a large platform extending from the mountain planted in lush greenery.

I'm not sure how long I goggled at the view. I turned to Kari, who was leaning against the doorframe. "You live here?" I marveled.

"No Arin," they said, laughter and joy in their voice. "*We* live here."

Kari took me to the nearest storeroom to choose out clothing, bed linens, and various other sundries. I found clothes in soft brushed wool, finer than I had worn on the journey. There were some trousers cut to lie more snug against the skin than the baggy homespun I wore, and a pair that was wide and pleated like those that Sem favored. I picked out three shirts that fit loosely at the shoulders and back to allow freer movement. By the time I had underwear, socks, a pair of slippers and a pair of sandals, I needed a basket to carry it all.

They pointed out the laundry room next to the clothing storage and showed me where to drop soiled clothing, explaining that the laundering teams would return clean clothes to the common stores to be claimed again by me or anyone else. If I wanted to keep what I had chosen out for myself, then they were mine to launder.

On the way back, they showed me other parts of Reft, and

taught me the system of way-finding symbols etched into the walls that made the warren of passages navigable. They pointed out several rooms where we would meet for lessons, and the hall leading to the library where there were more books than I had ever seen in one place.

After dropping off my basket of clothes, Kari led the way to the nearest eating hall for dinner. There were four eating halls in total, they said, and three kitchens. As we walked, they pointed out one of the garden tiers which I thought would be a good place for my morning movement exercises.

The sound and chaos of the eating hall was staggering. I had never seen so many people gathered together in one room. It was early for dinner, Kari said, so it would be even more crowded in an hour or so.

The hall was nearly square with a high ceiling of rough stone. The middle was filled with long tables with benches on either side, and people seemed to sit wherever they wished. It looked like the main square at Anbress had all descended on the room at once. There were Somiri and Freelanders and some with the pale skin and hair that I had learned came from Torfall in the southwest. They sat and talked and ate in small groups more often formed of like age than origin.

Kari drew me to the far wall which was pierced with a long, deep window. Along the ledge this formed were tureens, bowls, and platters of myriad foods, baskets of bread and fruit, and great pitchers of teas and wines and water. Across the ledge I could see through to the bustle of a large kitchen full of cooks and helpers.

We took trays and filled them with food, Kari advising me on what was good and what to avoid. They chose the free end of a table for us to sit, and while we ate they explained the hours that hot meals were served, that beverages and cold food were always available, that the hall on level five had the best pastries for breakfast but the one on two made the best roasts, and that a white enameled ewer at the end of the serving line always held Somiri moon tea.

The food was good and satisfying, especially after weeks of camp porridge, but I thought that Cook made better. My mind wandered for a moment back to the house in Anbress, and those I had abandoned there.

"Arin? You okay?"

I looked up at them, and forced a smile to my face. "Yes, sorry. Just thinking."

"Thinking can be hard on you when you first get here," they said quietly.

"How long have you been here?" I asked.

"Oh, four years now? My parents sent me when I was eleven."

Kari continued speaking, but I was somewhere dangerous in my mind. To my surprise, I found the scars of loss and pain were still tender. My thoughts wandered into tangents. The smell of Milly's coat. The squeak and rattle of cart and harness. The feel of my fingers through rich soil, and the rough texture of the hoe handle on my palms.

"Ho Kari!"

My dark reverie was broken by a piping voice, and I looked up to see two new youths bearing trays and taking seats beside us.

The one who had spoken was my age and had the coloring of a Freelander. Their hair was a cloud of reddish curls and they were short, plump, and full of curves. The other was a Torfallin, taller than any of us though they looked younger. Their body was thin and straight as a fence post. Their hair fell over their face, and I got the impression they were hiding even as they sat beside me.

"Arin, this is Migs and Chan," Kari said, indicating first the short Freelander then the tall Torfallin. "Arin is our new housemate."

Migs smiled at me, their grin warm and happy. "Welcome Arin!" Their eyes danced between my face and my scar.

"Seen the visitors yet?" Chan muttered quietly—to whom, I couldn't guess.

"Aye," Kari said, "some far-off lord and his followers came in to see Council." They shrugged. "What's it to us?"

Migs leaned forward. "What it *is*, is that one of those followers is Eelie."

Kari's eyes widened, but their voice went cold, "You sure?"

"Saw them myself coming out of Deme's rooms. That Torfallin lord, and Eelie at his heels *in livery*."

I looked at each in turn, wondering if they would explain. Migs saw my confusion.

"Eelie was one of us. Older. Two?" they looked at Kari for confirmation, "Two years older than Kari. They were here for a couple of years, but left last year all in a huff."

"Why?"

"They didn't like the rules. Or didn't like living by the same rules as everyone else." Migs shrugged. "Anyway, it was a big thing and they left. Now they're back, in service to this Viscount Tamar Something, wearing his orange and purple." They paused, waiting for my reaction. I just shrugged, shaking my head in confusion. Kari took up the story. There was something tight in their voice.

"He's some minor lord from Torfall—"

"Fall, not Torfall," Chan broke in, quietly.

"—minor lord from Fall. Infamous in the west for being open about asking help of witches in his political maneuverings. I mean, most of those lords do, but they keep it secret like they're dirty for talking to us. But he comes here at least once a year, and he says openly that witches are always welcome in his lands."

"So, he's good then?" I was struggling to follow.

Kari's mouth twisted and Migs shrugged, but it was Chan who spoke. "Good? Bad? Who knows? He has a use for us."

Fourteen

I stood for a few moments facing east, letting my bare feet feel the soft soil of the garden terrace and enjoying the early morning chill on my skin. The sun was just peeking over the crests of the nearby mountains, so the sky was turning bright while the landscape below still held on to twilight.

I breathed slowly filling my chest and belly, then let it out in a great burst, as Sem had taught me.

My left foot slid forward while my right knee bent, pivoting onto the ball of my right foot until my heel touched my haunches. My right hand went to the hilt of my wooden sword in my belt; my left arm extended northeast, thumb-side down and palm out. Keeping my spine straight, I shifted my weight forward, using both knees to bring my torso over my left foot. As I moved, I drew my sword, rotating my shoulders and hips so that my sword hand stayed fixed relative to the ground, and I moved around it, facing south.

The evening had passed in a blur. Migs and Chan returned

with us to our rooms, and we spent hours in the common space between our rooms, each taking it in turns to tell stories about our lives in and before Reft.

With my hips now over my left heel, I drew my right foot in a great arc through the dirt, pivoting as I rotated to face west. The wide pleated legs of my trousers flared as I moved. My sword followed a similar arc to the east, and my left arm rose palm up into a guard position.

Migs had told of their childhood in the southern coastal town of Grant in the Freelands. How they always felt an outsider in their own life, set apart from other children thanks to a tendency to say inappropriate things, their difficulty understanding social niceties, and their perfect memory.

I rose on my left leg, turning to face south while my sword pivoted into a vertical guard in front of my chest and my left hand met the flat of the blade to strengthen the stance. I pushed back with my left foot, sliding backwards on my right and bringing the sword down and to the right in a great sweeping arc as I bent both knees and lowered my hips.

I turned through the sweep, sword now coming up and over across my body into a downward strike as I rotated through a full circle, rising into standing with both knees slightly bent, right foot forward.

Kari had talked freely about their journey with a caravan their uncle led between A'liérre and Reft twice a year. They had helped with the bookkeeping on the journey and had such a head for figures that they now spent part of their time tutoring others in mathematics.

I made several forward strikes as fast as I could manage, shifting my feet with each one so that I finished several paces ahead with my left foot back and pointed to the side.

Chan had said little, but over the course of the night, I

learned that they were twelve, had been born in western Torfall along the Somiri border, and had been raised a boy before being beaten by their father—and ultimately seeking refuge in a hedge-witch's shack—when they told their parents they weren't.

Reversing direction suddenly, I bent forward and swept back my left foot. My arms swept outwards to either side and I reversed my grip on the sword so that it now lay backwards along my arm.

I had told them about traveling with Sem from Anbress. About lighting the fires and about taking the sword. They winced at parts of my story, and they all laughed at my victory-by-sabotaged-sandals. I could tell they were curious about my past, but they didn't press, which I appreciated. Some wounds remain raw long after you believe them healed.

I spun on the ball of my right foot, sweeping my left foot out and around. My sword arm on the opposite side came around to guard my face through the turn, and I came back up into a resting stance with the blade pointing up at my side. I stood, letting breath into my center and finding a stillness of mind and body.

A soft clapping came from behind me. "An admirable demonstration." The voice was calm and assured. Masculine in tenor, and polished. When my breathing and heartbeat had returned to normal, I turned my head to find the voice. My eyes widened when I saw livery in lavender, orange, and dark purple.

I suddenly felt small and foolish, a child playing with a wooden sword. I tucked it into my belt and turned to face two people standing several paces away. This must be the visiting lord and his follower.

He was not what I had expected. He was young, perhaps

younger than Neme, and tall and lithe with hair darker than usual for a Torfallin. He wore his hair trimmed short and had a short beard and mustache just around his mouth. His eyes were the same color as mine, and his face seemed kind and held a touch of humor, as if he were about to smile or laugh.

He wore sleek black trousers and a black coat over a crisp white shirt. A pin enameled in purple and orange worn on the lapel of his jacket was his only concession to his colors—a hawk in profile, standing upright on one foot with wings outstretched.

Beside and slightly ahead of him stood a scowling person a few years older than me. They were dressed in snug black trousers and a tight-fitting black sleeveless blouse slashed diagonally with narrow stripes in the lord's colors. The clothing showed off their slender and well-muscled build, narrow hips and flat chest. The fair skin on their arms was crisscrossed with fine scars.

Eelie.

Their face would be beautiful—large striking blue eyes and delicate chin and cheekbones, all framed in a fall of fine straight hair, so pale it was almost white—but their lips were set in a sneer and their eyes were cold as they looked me over. They rested a hand on the hilt of a short sword at their hip and stared openly at the scar on my face.

The lord stepped slowly up to me, watching my face as he moved. My eyes locked on his and I wondered what he was thinking. When he was less than a pace away, his hand came up and his fingers moved as if to caress my cheek, but he did not touch me.

"You must be very dedicated to practice so early in the morning. Please forgive my intrusion, it is my habit to take the morning air each day, and I couldn't resist watching when I saw you."

His eyes left mine for a moment to take me in. My short fuzz of hair. My clothes. My scar. They came back to my eyes.

"What is your name, young warrior?"

I was tongue-tied for a moment, lost in his storm-gray eyes. I cleared my throat. "Arin, of Anbress." I wondered suddenly why I had said more than my name, and was embarrassed.

He let out a small, satisfied sigh and smiled.

"I am very pleased to meet you, Arin of Anbress. The Council here call me Viscount of Fall, but I would be delighted if you called me Tamar. Tamar Savat," he said, with a little gesture like a bow, "at your service. Perhaps we shall meet again."

With that, he turned and continued on through the garden. Eelie glared at me for a moment as he passed, then pivoted sharply and followed him away.

The sun was up and just starting to burn off the morning dew as I made my way back through the gardens to my room. There were other people about now, and some were already coming out to tend the plants or take benches along the perimeter. It seemed Tamar Savat was not the only one who liked to take the morning air.

The main hall led from the garden tier to the great spiral staircases that I thought of as the heart of the mountain. I ascended two floors and worked my way through the winding halls following the numbers and symbols Kari had taught me until I found the triplet that marked our rooms. I eased myself through the door quietly. I did not want to wake my housemates.

The common room was dark and empty, so I went to my

room and shed the pleated trousers and tunic that I thought of as my sword-work clothes. I went out to the common bathing room at the end of the hall to wash off the sweat and dirt. My mind was still spinning at meeting Savat, and so unexpectedly. I had not thought on the name I had overheard between Benjin and Ma'am since Sem's arrival at the house, and now I struggled to understand what this fine lord—Viscount?—of a distant nation might have to do with Ma'am's social maneuverings. Was he a patron of the house? I had never seen him before.

Kari had said that he was known for associating with the witches of Reft. Ma'am would surely have been aware of this gossip, then. Could this be the patron that Ma'am had suggested she could introduce me to? I struggled to remember what she had said—my memories of the time were somewhat clouded by pain and Neme's potions. He had an interest in "unique" individuals? Eelie surely fit that description.

I felt my heartbeat rise as I thought of Eelie. My lips quirked ruefully thinking about them. Their face so full of disdain and... something else. I tried to recall their expression and couldn't tease out the emotion I had felt from them.

I finished scrubbing and was back in the common room wrapped in a thick towel just as Chan was up and lighting the lamps. By the time I was dressed, the others were up and about as well, Migs cracking their jaw in a monstrous yawn.

As we made our way together to the eating hall, I thought of telling them about my encounter, but was suddenly shy of explaining the feelings that meeting Savat and Eelie had awoken. I said nothing to them about either.

I was silent and withdrawn through breakfast, but the others were still sleepy-headed, so my mood wasn't noticed. As we took our trays back to the deposit shelf, Kari waved to Migs and Chan and pulled me away.

"I've got to take Arin to Turin's rooms this morning. We'll see you later!"

We wound through the stone halls and down the stairs and I tried my best to remember the way-finding symbols we passed. I was starting to form a vague understanding of the layout of the mountain, but it still felt that I knew only a handful of paths through an unimaginable labyrinth.

Soon enough, we reached a closed door and Kari knocked twice.

"Come in," came Turin's voice.

Kari opened the door, waved hello to Turin and goodbye to me, and walked away down the hall.

I stepped inside and found something about the room disconcerting. They were sitting in a large upholstered chair by a small fire crackling in the hearth, reading. It took me a few moments to realize that it was laid out on the same pattern as our common room. The same fireplace and sliding panel onto a balcony. The same open common room, with doors to either side, but where our's had four rooms off the central space, Turin's had only two doors.

They stood and moved towards the office door, and ushered me inside. I could see now how my bedroom and curtained clothing nook would account for half of this space. The rooms seemed to be built on a common model. Turin's office was set with a writing table at one end where Kari's bed would be, bookshelves lining one long wall, and a pair of comfortable chairs at the other end, where my bed would be. They took one of these, leaning forward, and I sat in the other.

"I will introduce you later to Deme, who will be tutoring you in speaking, reading, and writing Somiri. You'll meet with them every day in the afternoons, at first. You'll see me before for an hour or so on the same schedule, until we can assess where you stand and how you'll fit in."

I nodded.

"We don't expect you to be a productive member of our little society at first, but it would be good to start thinking about what you might wish to do with your time when you are not studying. Even the young in Reft work to the common good. Much of that is study, but you'll have chores as well."

They settled back into the chair now, and were silent a moment. "For now, if you're willing, let's just talk a little about you and your path here to Reft."

At Turin's prompting, I began talking of my childhood. They nodded and made calm noises of encouragement as I spoke, broke in with questions occasionally, and urged me on when I faltered. I told about the farm, about Mother and Father and Ranji. They asked if I was raised a boy or a girl, and when I told them, if I was bleeding yet, and when I started, and if I was taking moon tea.

Then they brought me back to the incident at market with Royen, and his fight with Ranji, and later the altercation with the Geoffs on the road home.

"Was that the first time something strange happened around you?"

I told them about the red day.

"What did you think about that at the time?"

"I didn't. I..." It was hard to sort out feelings from so long ago. "It feels like a different life."

"Did you know, at the time, anything about your powers?"

I talked about the time Ranji called me a mixie. I told about Sem's explanation of why I wasn't. I somehow found myself talking about their explanation of our powers. About pain, and about cutting myself. I wondered aloud that I had seen many at Reft who were unscarred.

"They're not... wrong, exactly," Turin began, by way of explanation. "But *grims* like Sem have a... singular... relationship with pain. It colors their experience. They are so focussed on the direct usage of their power that they are driven to take very... practical steps." I could tell they were being very careful to avoid disparagement.

"We can teach you different ways to access your power, for different means. In many ways, what you can learn here is more powerful."

I asked of them, "What do *you* think about what happened to me that day? Is that... common?"

"Our abilities manifest in times of extreme emotional or physical stress. Dig deep enough into any *nyssa's* past, and they'll tell of a moment in time where they felt such fear or pain or strain that they thought it would break them. In these moments, our power breaks through and we wield it instinctively—uncontrolled and often unknowing."

I thought of the attack in Lane's room and my scar itched. I thought of Royen and his brothers on the road home from Maplewood. I nodded. This sounded much like what Sem had told me.

"Before this *breaking*, we sometimes experience small trickles of that power, like... water leaking through a dam before a flood. Our mind knows some unconscious level of control even if we don't. That's what your 'red day' was."

"So, how do I do it consciously?"

"We'll get to that in time. What did Sem show you?"

I told about lighting the fire, and preventing it. I described the finding of my shoe, and what I had seen Sem do at the house.

They asked about my hair, and when I started trimming it

short, and why. This led to me talking about the afternoon out with Bess and my reaction to the eye and lip coloring.

I kept waiting for them to ask about my scar. They eyed it for a time, and I watched them watching me. But it seemed that subject could wait. Whenever I began on a topic they moved on to another, pushing me on and on, skimming the surface of my life until we reached my time with Sem.

"What did you think of Sem?"

I hesitated to answer. I still was unsure what relationship they had to this place and people like Turin. "I hated them at first," I said quietly. "They... hurt people and... stormed the house and broke things. They threatened... They didn't *ask* me. *No one* asked me."

"You wanted them to ask what *you* wanted."

I nodded.

"You wanted both Sem and... Ma'am?... to ask you."

I nodded.

"Do you know what you might have chosen if they had?"

I sighed, looking at the floor. At the time, given the choice, I knew I would have stayed. I had just figured out how I fit there. Who wouldn't choose a home and family over wilderness and a battle-scarred stranger? If I had stayed, I would be cooking and cleaning and serving, and... content.

But I would not be happy. I knew that now. I had known it the moment I cut off my braid and trimmed back my hair. I knew it again when I lit the fire for the first time. I knew it once more when I finally took up the sword. I looked up at Turin.

"I would have chosen to stay. But that would have been a mistake. I wouldn't have regretted it, I think, because I wouldn't have known. It still would have been a mistake."

Over the course of the next several days, I was integrated into the life of Reft in truth.

Each morning, I woke before my housemates and made my way to the garden where I did my movement exercises. The four of us took our breakfasts together, then went our separate ways. I continued seeing Turin each day, where we talked in greater depth about moments in my life. I thought at first that we would begin with the breaking of my power, but they seemed in no rush at all to delve into that, instead asking me questions about my life growing up, about Father and Mother and Ranji, and about my relationships with them. It seemed Turin was content to review my life over again in as much depth as they could dredge.

After the sessions with them, I would spend some hours in various chores about the mountain. Turin introduced me in turn to the local group leaders of the launderers, cooks, and farmers. I spent a few days working under the purview of each, increasing my sense of how the society of Reft functioned. Few enough of the citizens of Reft were witches in practice, most choosing instead to spend their lives in peace and, as I saw it, mundanity. But even in these pursuits there were sparks of the witchery I was excited to see. I watched one old *nyssa* in the laundry humming to themself as they stirred a great vat of bucking over a cold stone hearth. They closed their eyes and tensed, and in moments the water was roiling in a steaming froth.

In addition to the work I knew, I also spent time with the carpenters and stoneworkers. These last were of great interest to me, as many of their profession also used their powers directly in their work, shaping and smoothing the living stone of the mountain to their needs.

Late one morning I was helping haul temporary scaffolding

for the crew and saw twelve stoneworkers sitting together by a blank wall as they *grew* a new tunnel into the mountain. The wall simply moved further away as if it was mud being washed off a boot. I noted that some of the twelve had used small knives to reach their pain, some seemed to prefer long needles, and still others used nothing at all, seeming to bring their power forth through concentration only, their expressions hinting at the pain they drew on.

This pooling of the power of many to direct to a single task was a common theme I saw. Rare was the single witch acting on their own. Something in me yearned to take up my power and join them, but Turin was in no hurry, and I was held to the pace they set.

Each afternoon after these chores, I was learning Somiri. My teacher Deme was an impressive person. Large, with broad shoulders, they towered over me in their sitting room. Their hair was worked in a thick rope of a braid and their skin and hair was dark as night.

Their voice was deep and resonant, and when they spoke their native tongue they did so with a rich, rolling accent. But when they switched to Freelander—which they did sometimes mid-sentence while explaining some nuance of their language—their accent disappeared entirely. If I had heard their voice alone, I would be hard-pressed to tell their nationality.

Despite their size and build, they were a gentle, patient teacher.

Learning a new language was a grueling experience. After the first meeting, I met them with Chan and two other younger students. We began with words for common things and progressed rapidly to building simple sentences. After the first few meetings, Deme would not allow us to speak Freelander within their rooms, forcing us to stumble through the simplest of thoughts and explanations in Somiri.

Even though I struggled early with memorizing words and the rules for their modifications, I found I had a knack for the sounds and the feel of the language. Where Chan, Fabri, and Leema all spoke like they had blocks of wood in their mouths, for me the round, rolling vowels and soft consonants felt natural and almost musical, now that the sounds were paired with their native words. More than once, Deme complimented my pronunciation, even if the words I had chosen were entirely wrong.

But if speaking the language was a manageable, even exciting challenge, reading and writing it made me feel like I had stumbled into a raging river, crashing against rocks and being swept over rapids.

It was not a skill I had ever needed—even in Freelander—beyond the odd street name or label on a sack or barrel. I could pick out the names of towns I knew on a map, and I could tell ale from brandy in the larder. I could work out a recipe and I could make sense of Cook's account book. But *reading a book*? Reading page after page after page of *words*... It made me nearly despair.

I'm sure I wouldn't have managed to keep up without Kari's help. They sat with me most nights patiently correcting me as I picked through the pages Deme had assigned, word by excruciating word.

I still remember the first night I read an entire passage by myself. It was late at night and the others had long since gone to their beds. I was sitting on our small balcony with a lamp to work by and a blanket to hold back the cooling breeze.

The passage had been written long ago by a Somiri scholar, summarizing the popular debates of the time over what actions should be taken about the pale foreigners who were landing their ships on the unpopulated southern shores. Should they be allowed to build fortifications and cities? Or be driven back into the sea?

After painstaking hours piecing the words together and struggling through, I gradually was gaining fluency. The words began to come one after another and form themselves seamlessly into thoughts that I had never had myself before. Through this writing, the long dead author gave them into my mind.

It felt like a kind of magic.

Fifteen

"If you can think back to that moment on the road, heading home from market... tell me what you were feeling."

I struggled to remember—not the feelings, but the moment Turin was asking about. My memory was fractured, scattered through my mind like shattered fragments of a porcelain ewer. Each was its own shape, seemingly unrelated. I could find one here in this crevice, one there under that table, another partly wedged in a groove of the floor, ready to sink deep into an unwary foot. Even finding the pieces in my memory didn't really help, as they resisted assembly into any coherent whole. And each was sharp enough to draw blood.

"I... was confused." This was an easy answer, and Turin didn't leave it alone.

"You were walking with your family and the Geoff boys tried to block your way..." they prompted.

"I was proud of Ranji," my throat was tight here. "Two of them had bruises."

"You felt pride in your brother, for standing up to them on your behalf?"

"Yes. And Father," I paused, "was so calm. I... sensed... something was wrong, but he was already working to control the situation." I realized this even as I said it.

"You were comforted that he was acting to protect you, even though you weren't sure what from?"

"Yes," I said. "Then Royen... he came at me... he was so full of hate... why? Why couldn't he just let me be?"

"You wanted to be left in peace."

"I wanted them to go away. They were... hurting Ranji again—the older one. And the younger one held Mother back— she was trying to come to me to help." My breathing was coming in short gasps.

"Tell me what you were feeling."

"Scared," my voice was small. "So scared."

"You were afraid for yourself? For Ranji? And your mother?"

"Yes," I whispered. "I couldn't breathe." And now I couldn't, here in this calm room. "He... he held me against the cart." I was gasping for air and I hunched over slightly in my chair.

"What are you feeling? Not just in your mind. In your body, now."

"My stomach hurts." It was a child's plea.

"Your stomach, like you're feeling physically sick?"

"Yes. And... and my shoulders are aching."

"Feel that ache. That pain. Focus there, and breathe. Try to relax your shoulders. Breathe with me slowly." They began breathing deeply, slowly.

I tried to match them. My breaths were so short that I couldn't get enough air to get to the long, slow pace they were setting. My stomach was cramped and my body tense.

First one, I thought in Sem's voice. I closed my eyes and imagined moving my body now here, now there, broad sweeping strokes. Precise, controlled movements. *Then two.*

The cramps eased and I was able to slow my breathing.

The pieces started fitting together...

...I can tell if you're a girl.

I felt his hand at the ties of my trousers. His calloused fingers slipped underneath, against my skin. He was pulling them down.

He held me pressed back against the cart, and I could feel his breath against my face. His face was twisted with hate and fear and raw anger. Anger that such a monster should exist.

I couldn't breathe bent back as I was. And yet I was also there, breathing calmly, observing.

His eyes locked on mine, drinking in the fear I showed. He was relishing my fear. It stoked his hatred and rage.

I blinked, and my face calmed. My eyes cleared and there was no fear. No pain. No weakness.

He recoiled, as if the loss of my fear drew the fuel from his anger, turning the tide between us. Now I was not giving life to his fury, it was powerless—the sad, broken whimper of a fragile animal.

I could sense in his mind his story of power built brick upon brick. Each was an act of heroism, of power, of strength. At the very top was this moment. I could read the brick like I could read each below it. A person like me didn't belong. This land belonged to the likes of him. His brothers. His father. His grandfathers and soon his sons. He would defend these rights heroically from other men. He would defend their claims on the women in his life. His mother and grandmothers. The wife he would have one day, and the children that she would make for him. His sons, to whom he would pass on this righteous mantle. His daughters whom he would gift to others to grow his family and expand his legacy ever onward.

And if I was neither boy to be fought nor girl to be mastered? If I could be what I was and be allowed to exist, if my existence was *right*... then his history of victory and strength; his mastery of other boys and competition for girls, this *simple* story was flawed. Because the likes of me couldn't fit into such a story. I was neither a trophy to be sought, nor a challenge to his rights.

So, I must not be allowed.

I smiled. A grim, sad smile full of pity.

His eyes widened in horror, as the acts in his self-story began to tremble. Without knowing how or what I did, I shifted the stories, pivoting them on some axis. Each act was unchanged, but now each act was framed differently. Instead of stories of bravery, conquest, and victory, they were acts of a small bully, scared and threatened at every turn, lashing out in abuse and fear whenever possible.

I was a young person trying to figure out how I might fit in the world, and trying my best to understand feelings that were as frightening to me as they were to others, and he—near enough twice my weight—thought it fitting to hurt me because he was scared of what I represented.

His strength and power over younger boys—meted out when warranted by their deviance from what it meant to be a man— was a legacy of the same abuse and constraint placed on him by *his* elders. Any deviations must be punished because they posed the same threat to their fragile social structures that *I* did.

The stack teetered under the weight of these poorly framed acts. Cracks began to form in them spreading downwards, and the whole of his self began to crumble and collapse.

He started to back away from me. To flee; to escape.

I pushed harder and the cracks accelerated. I saw in his stories the interdependencies, the web of power from generation to generation and from old to young; a through-line from him up to his older brother and father, and down to his younger brother.

I saw the abuse he had received from his brother who now was hurting Ranji. I could see the same story mirrored in his older brother's mind, only from his perspective. I did the same thing to Ollin's stories and his bricks began to crumble.

The younger was holding Mother back and laughing, showing his older brothers how well he could follow their model. This was not his first taste of this sort of power, and he enjoyed it. He had been on the receiving end of his brothers' actions before now, and he knew well his place they had shown him in the order of things. I began crushing his stack of bricks also.

I was over and done with the fear and pain these boys had caused. I wanted nothing more than to destroy them. I watched with pleasure as the three minds crumbled under the weight of their own shattered self-stories.

They were all trying to crawl away now as their very selves collapsed within them, and all that was left was their anguish and their tears and their screams.

We screamed in peals of laughter, losing all control of ourselves as we rolled on the floor of our sitting room. It was late at night, but we'd had a difficult enough day that Kari had suggested a tutorial that had rapidly devolved into our current game.

"Oh, no no, please, it *can't possibly* mean that!" pleaded Chan as they caught their breath. They wiped tears from their eyes and struggled to sit up. They were half on top of me and I gave them a firm shove so that I could breathe again.

"I promise you it does!" Kari said with a wide grin. They had been regaling us with the most impressive curses they had learned in their time with their uncle's caravan. *Nobody*, it seemed, could curse quite as eloquently as a Somiri caravaner.

"Tell us another, please?" said Migs from the couch. They had shared it with Chan, but in the fits of laughter after the latest translation had managed to shove them off the edge of the couch onto me.

I sat up, finally free of Chan's weight, and leaned on their back, wrapping my arms around them. "Yes please," I said. "Another."

Kari made a show of deciding if they could think of another impressive curse. We all knew they would not have started this game if they only knew three.

"Ok, how about this one: *Al paliérre amidone tallí ponche bucc don guenté malmacré*"

I mouthed the words as they spoke them, trying to commit them to memory as I had with the others, but I knew it was futile. I had already forgotten the last. Chan probably remembered them. They had a fine head for vocabulary.

"And?" Chan begged. We had given up guessing. The fun wasn't in guessing in any case, it was in the absurdity and filth of Kari's translations.

"Well, so the first part means something like 'an eternity of endless wanting and never finding,'" they bit their lower lip as they tried to work out the literal meaning, "and the second part is referring to this rare vegetable that grows up around Nor'Salande that's considered a real delicacy, and about how you can't ever get enough of it to make a proper meal..."

"And?" Migs and Chan said together, already laughing. Kari was drawing this one out for all it was worth.

"And... well, you know the last part, it's already been in two of the others... so the whole thing together basically means, 'Go fuck yourself forever with this delicious vegetable so far up the ass that you can taste it, but that you'll still never be satisfied.'" Kari grinned at us, daring us to challenge them on it.

All four of us broke down together into fits of giggles, Migs laughing so hard that they fell off the couch on top of Chan, and somehow managed to tangle us all up together.

"When our power breaks—especially for the first time—it is usually followed by a period of dissociation," Turin said. "The mind stops functioning consciously in the normal way. Your feelings of unreality, your inability to remember details following the attack on the road... That's perfectly normal."

"And what I did?" I asked tentatively. The memory of not only breaking those boys' minds, but the satisfaction I had taken in their destruction... it frightened me.

"That is... less common. It would seem you have a gift for Mind Magic. It is something for us to work on. Altering others' perceptions is difficult enough for most trained *nyssén*. Doing so untutored and instinctively is very impressive."

I sat up straighter. This was the first suggestion from Turin that I was ready to try magic here in Reft.

"You say I'm especially gifted. Sem said I was very powerful. Where was that power, that *gift*, when..." tears welled in my eyes as I realized I was about to say the words, "when Father and Mother and Ranji were... murdered? Why didn't I *do* something then? When it mattered?"

Turin sighed, and composed themself before answering. "It is especially difficult now, understanding that this power was inside you, now knowing a little of how to control it, and thinking that maybe you might have changed your fate, and the fates of your family. But remember, you weren't in control of that power, and when it surfaced, that was only in your own reflexive defense. You were untrained, unprepared for violence, and from what you've said, it was a carefully coordinated attack. You had almost no time to react before you were knocked down."

"So I'm selfish? It only came out to protect me and not my family?"

"Those kinds of reflexes are always somewhat selfish, by their very nature. But moreover Arin, you were a child. A small child holding a knife might flail around if attacked by a soldier, and might even cause some harm. Would you expect that same child to take up a blade in battle, even in defense of their family?"

I shook my head. It was clear enough, put that way. I didn't like it though.

"The second time... I remember it more clearly than I did the first. I *know* what I did. But I don't understand *how*. I was there in... myself and... I was also... him. I could see from both sides..." I shook my head—*both* was wrong. "From all the sides... there were so many different ways of seeing. Was that... Mind Magic again?"

"I believe so. From what you've told me, much like with your first breaking, you found a place of... fragility in his mind, and you leveraged it. You pried it wide open, cracking his 'self.' What he did after that... well, who can say what desperation a mind broken may be driven to?"

"Is that all I can do? Break people?" It seemed a dubious gift.

"A blade can kill. But it can also whittle, cut leather, shave, trim fingernails, and carve a roast. If you're skilled and the blade is sharp enough, it can be used in surgery—to heal. And Mind Magic can be an especially subtle blade." They leaned forward in their chair. "Let us try something. What is the earliest moment of your life you can remember?"

I thought for a moment, casting back for the earliest memory that came to mind, then tried to reach further. I closed my eyes trying to recall enough details to describe what was little more than a feeling. "Ranji was tending goats. One of them escaped the pen. I was laughing because I thought it was funny seeing it jump. I... I must have been no more than three. He was chasing it and trying to catch it, and I just kept laughing. It made him mad."

Turin nodded. "Now, in a moment, we're going to try to go back further, but first, I want to tell you what to do. You remember how you cut yourself, and accessed the pain? And you used that pain to ignite the fire?"

I nodded.

"I'm going to talk you through a painful memory. You won't like it. But I want you to try to embrace the pain we find there in the same way. Instead of lighting a fire, you are going to reach into yourself. Your mind observes and records everything you see, hear, smell, and feel over your entire life, even if you don't realize it. It is there. Every sound you've ever heard is engraved into your flesh as surely as an ax marks wood. I want you to reach into your mind and find the earliest experience you can recall. Use the pain to bring it forth."

I braced myself.

"Ready? Then we begin. I want you to remember your father's death. Think back to that night, around the fire."

I felt a hollowness in my chest. *This* was where we began? My eyes filled with tears. But then I realized I wanted—*needed*—to learn this. I would not turn away.

"Tell me," they said softly.

"We... we were camping. We were having trouble finding the way through the mountains... the road was blocked, and we couldn't get the cart through any of the passes we could find."

"Yes. And then?"

"And... he came into our campsite. *Cal*," I sobbed. "And Beaty. I didn't know then that she was... captive."

"They shared your fire..."

I nodded. "He seemed harmless enough. Father was cautious, but," I shook my head. But he had trusted in the end. "Cal hit him... with the firewood... knocked him down. I..." I was crying now, I didn't want to continue, but I needed to. "Ranji... he..."

"Your father, focus on him. What happened next?"

"I... tried to run but... something tripped me. I turned and I saw him standing over Father..."

"Your father was still down, and Cal was standing over him?"

I nodded. No words. I felt the moment coming and could no longer speak. Turin seemed to sense this, and didn't say any more. I knew what I needed to do.

I let the memory play out against the inside of my eyelids, clenched shut. Cal bending over with his long knife in his hand. I felt such horror and disbelief in that moment.

Father struggling to rise, his nose broken and face covered in blood. My reality was coming apart.

Cal's knife casually slicing across Father's throat; the fountain of blood. Father's blood. Father's life, spraying out into the air in droplets to fall back upon the stone.

The very center of my being was gouged by the pain. I wanted to cry but there was no source of tears wide or deep enough for the weight of such pain. I couldn't hold it back any longer.

And so, I did not.

I embraced it, sliding into the pain. I opened myself to the panic and fear and the feelings of horror at my life sliding into chaos and calamity. I became one with pain. The pain was everything. It was all of me and I grew beyond it in every unmeasurable dimension.

And I cast backwards in my memory...

...It was four months since my second name-day. I was standing outside the house on legs only lately stable enough to walk so far. There was still a lingering winter chill in the morning air. My brother was in the goat pen separating the new kids from the rest. One of the kids was energetic and full of mischief. It kept butting the others, and Ranji had to keep pulling it aside. It managed in a frenetic moment of spirit to trip one of the larger goats and climb upon it, and in two bounds it was atop the wall of the pen. It looked at me, and I laughed, finding the large eyes set in its small baby's face endearing. It jumped down outside the pen just as Ranji tried to grapple it, and feeling its energy it jumped twice more for sport. I laughed again even as it closed the distance with me. I held out my arms to it in joy...

...*Further back*...

...I was bound to Mother's body, slung under her breasts in a fabric womb, tied twice around and over her shoulders so that she could move freely through the forest. I remembered that this was part of my daily routine. I felt Mother's warmth and the easy sway of her body as she moved, now striding through the trees reaching up into the morning sky, now crouching beside a wild herb or mushroom. Some of these she plucked and laid carefully into the bag slung across her back, others she examined and discarded. As she worked she sang to me, a half-humming, half-singing stream of nonsense words and wandering melody. It was the sound of contentment...

...*Further*...

...I sat naked in a wooden tub as Mother poured water over me. The water was warm, and reminded me of a time when all I knew was warmth and wet and the slow shushing flow of Mother's blood. It calmed me, this feeling, and reminded me that it had not been long since I was one with Mother. I looked up at her now, my wide eyes locking on hers instinctively, and my mouth opened in a broad smile of peace and love...

...*Still further...further*...

...There had always been the warm throbbing weightlessness around me. That warmth was everything within me and around me and my whole universe.

But lately, the weightlessness had begun to fail and a great pulsing pressure had intruded into my existence. It was pressure before I understood pressure. It was painful, and I didn't know what pain was. There was the voice of my universe which echoed and reverberated around me and was always the voice of love, and it had changed lately to become the voice of pain, calling out over and over, calling to bring the pain. There were other voices, hard to make out.

One said, *Soon, soon, but I must leave you now. I can't stay.*

And the universe said, *No, you can't leave me, please!* And then there was calling to the pain. Calling to the pain forever.

And then, after forever, another voice—one that meant comfort—one I had heard often before: *I'm here. I'm back. Where did she go Ranji, she just left?* And, *Come in, please,*

please hurry.

A new voice, wise and wizened, *Oh, ah. Aye, it's twisted wrong just as you said. No fear, no fear. Aye, it hurts, and well it should. The pain is the power, and it takes its due.*

And then there was something new. Something more than warmth and more than pain. There was a gentle force that turned me and held me and then the pressure with no pain and the warmth was close so close so close so close so close so close.

And then light.

And *cold.*

And then air.

And I breathed.

And I cried, short little squawks in a tiny piping voice that reached my ears as a chirping sound.

"She pips just like a little hatchling bird," said a voice. It sounded different with ears, but the voice still meant comfort...

Sixteen

Migs arrived late to breakfast, having had some morning er-
rand with their work leader. They had recently begun applying
their prodigious memory to working in the library.

Chan, Kari, and I had been conducting our meal in Somiri
as extra practice. Or at least we had been trying. I was still
struggling with certain verb forms, so everything I tried to say
came out as a word-soup.

"It's not *falinde*, it's *failínde*," Chan corrected me casually.
"'I'd like to have seen,' not 'I'll like to be seeing.'"

I sighed and tried again, just as Migs sat down with their
tray. They had taken an extra confection—a pink concoction of
whipped egg whites and berry juice that they knew I adored—
and as they sat they moved the extra to my plate.

"You deserve this for working so hard."

"You know I do," I replied even as I stuffed the sweet fluff
into my mouth. I looked at Chan, and recited very carefully
with my mouth full of sticky egg, "*mmawh meeff*-failín-

dehm."

Kari and Chan broke down in giggles.

As I swallowed the morsel, Kari asked Migs, "How's the work in the library going?"

"It's fine," they shrugged. "Moving books here, moving them there. 'Where is the *Brene* Migs?', 'Have you seen the *Almede* folio Migs?', 'Did you move the *Grunéndalle* text Migs?' I swear I don't know how they ever found anything before me."

Chan shared a private little smile with me and Kari. Migs had a perfect memory, but was also the least organized person I had ever known, and absent-minded to a fault. They could remember everything they ever saw, read, heard, or encountered, but perhaps because of this, rarely paid any mind to what they were doing, trusting they could always rely on their recall. I wondered if anyone besides them would be able to find any book at all by the year's end.

We sat for some time, sharing company while Migs finished their breakfast. As we all began to stand to take our trays to the deposit shelf, I caught a flurry of movement from the corner of my eye. I turned just in time to see Savat walking casually up to our table, Eelie trailing behind him.

To my consternation, he walked directly to me, and gave the same little sketch of a bow.

"Arin, I am taking my leave of Reft for now, but I hope that we might find time to speak again the next time I am here. I am grateful to have made your acquaintance, brief though it was. I have heard much of your power and talents, and hope that you might consider me at your service in any way I can be."

He briefly took in the others with a gracious smile, then met my eyes and gave another small bow before turning. As he walked away, I could feel Eelie's cold gaze on us. They lingered, their eyes taking us each in turn before settling on me.

"Don't take what he says too much to heart. You're not that special."

I gaped, but it was Migs who stepped between us, their voice trembling with anger. "What? You worried he's got his eyes on a new pet? Don't be; Arin's not dumb enough to go chasing the likes of *him*."

Eelie smirked at Migs' bristling outrage, rolling their eyes in scorn, "You're going to defend your friend? You? You're barely strong enough to light a candle."

Migs shied back, face white.

Eelie glanced at Chan, lips quirking into a knowing grin and their voice took on an exaggerated tone of care, "I wonder if there's a hedge-witch nearby to hold a sad little child's hand?" Chan bowed their head, hiding behind their hair. Eelie turned next on Kari, who was just stepping forward. "Just like a caravaner's brat, always following the herd."

"And you," They stepped so close to me that I could smell them—they smelled of lilac and spice. Their face took on a considering expression and they shook their head slowly in wonder, "you're sharp enough... but your aim is terrible."

My brow wrinkled, perplexed. "What's that even supposed to mean?"

"It means: You destroyed the wrong man," they said, glancing at my scar. Their hand came up absently and they delicately traced it with their fingers. I shivered at their touch. "If it had been me, *I* would have gone after the one who murdered my family and sold me into slavery, not some poor drunk bastard who was too horny for his own good."

I recoiled in shock.

Eelie showed a small satisfied smile, and turned away to follow after their lord. I stumbled backwards until I sat down hard on the bench behind me, still not quite believing what had just been spoken out loud. My hand rose of its own accord and cupped my cheek where they had touched me.

It was several moments before I realized that the others were looking at me, silent. Only then did I remember that I had never told them of my encounter on the terrace.

"Seems you made an impression on the Viscount." Kari's face was flat and their voice expressionless.

I looked up at them and suddenly wanted to apologize. To explain. "I... it was..." I shook my head. How could I tell them that I had met both Savat and Eelie days ago, and chosen to say nothing? I dropped my eyes to the floor.

Migs stood and carried her tray away, speaking to Kari as they passed, "Seems to me there's a lot they haven't told us. It must be nice to have 'power and talents' and to hobnob with his lordship."

I felt all three of them leave. I remained staring downwards at nothing for some time, trying to understand what had just happened.

I was withdrawn the rest of that day, especially in my regular meeting with Turin. They noticed, and tried to draw me out, but I was too deep in my own thoughts to engage. I didn't want to talk about my friends shunning me. I wanted more than anything to crawl into my bed and hide.

"Your mind seems to be elsewhere, Arin. Is there something you want to talk about?"

"No, not really."

It was an unproductive session to say the least. They sat with me in silence for a time, sensitive enough to leave me to my thoughts and not push me to speak.

After some time, they asked simply, "Perhaps some of your movement exercises will help?"

I took them at their word and went back to my room to change and retrieve my wooden sword.

Feeling self-conscious about my encounters with Savat and Eelie, I avoided my usual practice grounds. Never mind that they were gone from Reft, my mind was running to the irrational. I chose instead a broad open platform on the sixth level. It was little more than a raw field, unplowed and unplanted. The loose sandy soil and few weedy plants made the footing slippery, which gave me something practical to concentrate on. Keeping my stance solid and my movements controlled was enough of a challenge that I thought I would be able to distance myself from the worries and weight that was plaguing my mind.

Even with my daily practice, even accounting for the loose soil and bad footing, my patterns were imprecise and sloppy. My left foot slid too far on this movement, my right arm wooden and stiff on that sweep. Where I tried to hold still, my limbs trembled, when I strove for fluidity, my muscles bound and jerked.

I simply couldn't focus. My mind was dwelling on the events of the morning. In frustration, I threw down the sword and fell to my haunches in the dirt. I pulled my knees to my chest and rested my chin on them, staring absently out into the distance.

First one, then two.

I could do nothing about changing what I had or hadn't said to my friends. Their responses were their own. Even if they chose to avoid me at meals, we would see each other this evening, and I could apologize and try to explain then. So, I set that problem aside. It was not something to stew over now.

With that out of the way, I could consider the problem that—now that I could think on it—was hurting me more.

How had Eelie known?

Of course it had been Ma'am. Hadn't I overheard her sending word to someone about me, after my breaking? She knew all the details of that event, enough to relate them at any rate. She had dealt with Cal, and knew about the attack on my family—he had *told* her as much! She had made inquiries into my past. And she had told me of a patron for someone like me and I had even overheard Benjin using Savat's name.

She had corresponded with Savat. There was no reason to think Ma'am hadn't provided these details. Eelie could easily have learned them through their work with him—either in handling that correspondence, in overhearing the report from the courier, or in any number of other underhanded ways.

I rose to my feet and began my exercises again. This time, with my mind free of the weight of dark emotions, my movements were smoother and more controlled.

As I left the platform in search of my next work assignment, a tall broad-shouldered *nyssa* found me in the hall and introduced themself as Marki. Their face was masculine and lined with weather and worry, but their voice had a tenor of playfulness, as if they liked to laugh.

"Arin, yes? I am pleased to meet you. Welcome to Reft. I was watching you practice, and wanted to speak with you. I am Marshal of the Mountain Watch. I am somewhat aware of your story, and that you are still exploring the various Fellowships you might join. I thought you might like to try out the Watch as a work worthy of your talents. I am on my way now to meet with the watch leader of the Second Watch. Would you join me?"

I nodded, and they led me down the hall to the large spiral stair, descending. As we walked, they continued their explanation.

"The Mountain Watch is neither a militia nor a garrison force. We are classed as a professional Fellowship by the Council, just like the stonemasons, clothiers, and all the others. We do train in military skills, and we serve as sentries and guards over the various mountain approaches and the Vale. But we are neither large enough in membership to stand against invaders nor inclined to police our own people."

We stepped off the stairs on the second level and proceeded down Leaf hall.

"The mission of our Fellowship is three-fold. One: to serve the people of Reft, providing whatever manner of aid is needed, and to respond quickly in emergencies. Two: to watch for threats to Reft both immediate and distant. Three: to lead the people of Reft in defense of our home should the need arise." They paused and seemed to wait for some response.

"That sounds like... a lot," I said.

"Indeed it is. In truth, the first is where we spend most of our efforts. When all is going right, most of us actually *do* very little besides studying and training. When something goes wrong though, we help as we are needed. It is through training that we are able to provide that help with speed and skill. Members of the Watch train in everything from healing accidental injuries and quenching fires to intervening in crises and to military strategy and tactics. And some of our membership does their work abroad, following political currents, bringing us news of the outside world, and facilitating the journeys of those seeking refuge here."

A thought caught in my mind, and I spoke it without thinking. "You maintain the stores at Redwatch?"

Marki smiled. "Indeed we do, and some other caches and forts throughout the mountains. You have a quick mind."

We paused at a wide door off the main hall. They pushed it open and we entered. To the right were two doors, and to the left a single door and a desk. As they led me into the room, another *nyssa* entered from one of the doors to sit at the desk.

"Ah, Marki. I was just gathering my report."

"It can wait. I'd like you to meet Arin." Marki gestured me forwards. "Arin, this is Ciala, watch leader of the Second."

Ciala was younger than I expected to find as leader of a watch. They were perhaps twenty-five years old. They kept their hair short like mine, but for a long thin tail at the back that hung part-way down their back. They had the coloring of a Freelander and a slim, narrow-shouldered build and delicate cheeks and jaw.

"Well-met, Arin. Interested in the Watch?"

Not knowing how to answer, I shrugged my shoulders slightly. "There is a lot here to learn."

Ciala nodded. "There is. There is a lifework in the Watch, in service to all those here in Reft."

My gaze wandered, and I noted a wooden rack against the wall by the platform, holding several scabbarded swords and wooden practice swords. My feet carried me to the rack, and Marki and Ciala followed.

"You train in the sword?" I asked.

Marki answered, "We do." They looked aside for a moment, and asked, almost shyly, "Was it Sem who taught you?"

I looked up sharply. "How did you know?"

Marki smiled. "I recognized the forms. Sem is a legend in the Watch, and several of us trace our mastery of the sword to their coaching."

"Sem was in the Watch?" I asked, bewildered. I tried to imagine Sem here, in Reft, living amongst all these people and working to build this community. I couldn't make the image fit. It was like imagining a wolf herding goats, or a falcon hitched to a plow.

Marki's smile softened, "Sem *was* the Watch. Reft was still young then. It was Sem who convinced the Council that it was not enough that we be separate from the world. That we needed to be of it, and aware of the movements of other nations. That there may come a point when their envy of our power overcame their disinterest in our existence."

As I processed this new information, a question begged to be asked. "Are they still of the Watch, then?"

Marki frowned slightly before answering. "No. Sem chose to leave Reft some years ago. Our Fellowship stays in contact to some degree, but no, they are no longer of Reft." They brightened, shifting the subject, "It was the Watch that brought word to Turin of your pending arrival, so they were able to meet you the day you came to us."

"How?" I thought of couriers, but the difficulty of the journey made that seem implausible, or at least wildly inefficient, and I had seen no use of pigeons in my time here.

It was Ciala who answered, "When one of our number leaves on a mission into the world, they first form a bond with another who stays. It is a thing we call Pairing. With the link established, the watch member here can communicate directives to the member in the field, and receive intelligence."

Marki nodded. "Sem met with one of our members in Branmoor after leaving Anbress with you, and left written word for another in Redwatch when you stopped there."

I took this in, realizing how little of the world and of Sem's actions I had been aware of in our journey. Though in all fairness to myself, I had been preoccupied, especially at the start.

Marki seemed to take my introspection for hesitation, "But as I said, there is more to the Watch than swords and spies. We practice healing and crisis response and leadership. There is a lot to learn and to become in our Fellowship. You need not make any decisions now, but I wanted you to know of our work here."

They placed a hand on one of the practice swords on the rack. "And you are always welcome to train with us. From what I have seen, you are actually well ahead of the novice training class, and given your time with Sem, that is no surprise. There is a spot in the second class any time you wish to try. Ciala is the training master for the second."

I looked at Ciala now with curiosity. They met my gaze with confidence and a slight smile.

"I think I would like that," I said.

When I entered the eating hall for dinner, I could see Kari, Migs, and Chan seated together at the end of our usual table. A knot of worry formed in my stomach and my shoulders hunched. I skirted the perimeter of the room to the serving line and picked up a tray and plate. I took food from this platter and that, not even knowing what it was I served myself. My eyes looked at the food but my mind was elsewhere.

I reached the end of the line and I could delay no longer. I made my way back to the table, and stood for a moment beside the end of the table, waiting for my friends to acknowledge me. Their silence told me they saw me, but no one looked up for a long moment. When Kari finally did, they must have seen something in my face, for their look softened and they slid over to make room for me.

I sat, murmuring my thanks.

The three continued to say nothing, and I stared unseeing at my tray for several heartbeats. Finally, without looking up, I steeled myself and spoke all in a rush, "I'm sorry. I'm sorry I didn't tell you about meeting them. I'm sorry I didn't tell you about how I felt about meeting them—I was so confused about it. I'm..." I swallowed hard. "I'm sorry I didn't tell you about myself. I..."

My voice broke and I could say no more.

They were still silent, and I couldn't bring myself to look up.

"What..." Migs said, their voice dripping with disbelief and disgust. "What *in the world* are you eating, Arin?" Chan snorted a laugh.

I was confused for a moment, but then my eyes focused, and I could finally see what was in front of me. My plate was filled with a bed of wilted salad greens drenched in a thick brown gravy that had been meant for a roast. Floating in this was a serving of trout I had topped with a large dollop of sweet custard. My stomach lurched at the sight and smell, and I nearly retched.

"I can't..." I said, trying to speak through tears, "I can't believe..." I didn't know if I was laughing or crying. I had to look away from my plate now, and saw that they all three were fighting back grins. Kari came to my rescue.

"You take that... meal... to the return shelf and I'll grab some food and we'll go somewhere we can talk more easily."

Migs and Chan kept their distance until I had disposed of the offensive slop, and I can't blame them. Afterwards, they joined me, one to either side and we waited outside the eating hall. Even though it was only this morning that Eelie had confronted us and we had been apart as long most days, it still felt good to have them beside me again. Kari caught up with us carrying a tray covered with a napkin, and led us off with a conspiratorial grin.

We wound through the halls to an unfamiliar side passage which led to a tightly spiraling stair. Kari led us upwards. Up and up we went until suddenly we emerged into a wide circular platform. The stone was all of a piece: floor, walls, and smooth ceiling.

There was something unaccountably *new* feeling about it.

Kari turned in a circle looking out over the mountain. I followed their gaze, startled to see how high we were and how much we could see. To the west the whole backbone of the mountain trailed away beneath. To the south we could see far into the valleys and over the smaller mountains diminishing into the horizon. Over the north lip was the Vale, the great level valley divided into fields and farmland that produced most of our food.

And the eastern overlook perched directly over the entrance to Reft. I could see not far below us the wooden buildings and stables that I had passed with Sem and the lonely trail descending the ridge that had brought me to Reft. Most of the yard was bathed in the lengthening shadows.

"I didn't know this was here," said Chan.

"It wasn't." Kari grinned. "I saw a report from the masons. They just finished growing this tower yesterday, and it won't have a watch posted until it opens officially tomorrow." Kari had recently begun work as a clerk in the Council Office, and was privy to all manner of low-level information that passed through their hands.

Kari sat and placed the tray between us as we formed a circle on the bare stone, still warm from the late afternoon sun. They uncovered the tray and served out a cup of watered wine to each of us from a small decanter. At the first sip, my stomach grumbled, and I reached out to take a slice of cold chicken and stuffed it into my mouth. I followed this with another slice of chicken dipped in mustard, and a thick slice of hard cheese.

Thus fortified, I told them my story starting with my family's farm, and left nothing out. When I reached the confrontation with the Geoffs and my first breaking, they were still and silent. When I came to the attack in the mountain pass, and Cal murdering my family Migs reached out to hold my hand, and Chan on the other side, wrapped their arms around me.

I drank more of the wine and kept going, the horrors of captivity with Beaty, the journey to Anbress and being sold into Ma'am's house. The peace and the place I had found there.

My hand went to my face involuntarily when I told them of my second breaking, and the injury I had taken. They listened with rapt attention and gasped appropriately. When I reached Sem's assault on the house and my departure, I could see by their faces that they were able to finally assemble the pieces I had told previously into a coherent whole.

The sky was starting to blush into deep pinks and purples and oranges by the time I reached my encounter with Savat and Eelie on the garden platform. I held nothing back, struggling to describe the odd feelings that had stirred at meeting Eelie.

"They are striking," Kari said carefully. "And they are very strong. Like you, apparently." They ducked their head slightly and watched me from under their lashes. "If they weren't so foul of heart, I'd wish you well of them."

A chill breeze cut through the watchtower and I shivered, but it was Chan who spoke for us. "Why are we up here? It's pretty, but it would be a lot more comfortable in our rooms."

Kari grinned. "I wanted to watch something." They stood and moved over to the eastern view. "Any minute now."

We all stood and gathered around the opening. I folded my arms on the low wall and leaned my chin on them. The sky was darkening and the streaks of color deepening as the sun set.

Below us, a burst of activity arose in the stables, and when I saw the soldiers in purple and orange livery assembling with their mounts in the stony yard, I straightened. Presently, two figures emerged from the building below us. Savat and Eelie.

I turned to Kari in surprise. "I thought they were gone."

"They had one more meeting with the Council this afternoon."

I watched the entourage begin to form up. Savat's guardsmen each led a horse, and two held lead lines for an extra mount each, presumably for Eelie and their lord. It took me a moment to understand what was wrong in what I was seeing. There were no pack animals and no spare mounts, and none of them had more than a light pack. And why would they be setting off down the mountain at sunset?

I saw Eelie consult briefly with Savat, and then step slowly—almost hesitantly—away from the group. I felt a tension rising in me, and I couldn't say why. They drew something small from their belt, and my shoulders tensed in anticipation.

"No way," I heard Migs mutter beside me.

I started to turn to them and opened my mouth to ask what was happening, but I was cut off by a sound of abject agony echoing from below. My head turned of its own accord to look on at the tableau.

Eelie was on their knees, head bowed and right hand raised to their left shoulder. I could not tell exactly what they did, but they seemed to move in some subtle way, and the gesture tore another gut-wrenching cry from them that reverberated off the distant mountains. The sound made me sick to hear it, and I was not the only one. To my left Chan uttered an inarticulate sob, and I heard Kari swearing softly in Somiri under their breath.

Once more a nearly inhuman cry of pain and harrowing anguish broke from Eelie's crumpled form, and they bowed their head nearly to the ground. I wanted to vomit. My body was hunched and tensed as if I could feel a blow coming. I wanted to squeeze my eyes shut, but I couldn't look away.

Eelie stretched out their right hand along the rocky soil as if trying in desperation to grasp something just beyond their reach.

I realized then that I could feel something, a tension that was forming—not just in my shoulders or in Eelie's prone body—it was as if the world itself was tensing, clenching down like a towel wrung over-tight. The horses whickered and danced.

The whole world held its breath.

Just in front of Eelie, the air came alive—became *angry*. There was a moment where looking at that spot felt vertiginous, as if I might be pulled from the tower high above and fall forever into the space just before them. A shape like an arched doorway formed before them, and for a dizzying, terrifying moment, I thought that doorway was *down*, and I was slipping inexorably towards it. I felt Migs grab my shoulder, and Kari braced themself against the stone wall.

Then like a rock striking a pool, the tension broke and two things a universe apart snapped together. I felt a gasp escape my chest.

The doorway was still there, a hazy shimmer in the air. Through it I could see as if through flawed glass to a rolling hillside leading down to a gray sea with white breakers crashing against dark rocks. It was brighter on the other side, still late-afternoon. The edges of the opening coruscated and jittered as if it were something alive and untamed.

Savat raced up to Eelie's side, and bent to them. One of his guardsmen came forward too, but he waved him off absently. I could see Eelie shuddering as Savat helped them up, first to their knees, then almost to standing. The Viscount bent protectively and gently took something from their hand. Some words were spoken, their faces close together, almost intimate. They must have been whispering. Eelie nodded.

Then Savat bent and lifted them up, cradling Eelie in his arms. Even from the tower I could see their face sickly pale and streaked with tears. He waved his guardsmen through, and they went single file leading the horses. There seemed to be no resistance to moving through the cloudy, shimmering arch. The lord of Fall carried Eelie through the uncanny archway last, and a moment after he stepped through, it was gone as if popped like a soap bubble. It might well have been as tenuous.

Slowly, I realized that I could breathe again and turned away, sliding my back down the parapet wall until I was on the floor, my knees drawn up. The others looked similarly deflated. I thought my hands would shake if they weren't clutching my legs.

"What..." I looked at Kari. "What was *that?*"

"A *Bridge*," Migs answered, wonderingly. "They made a Bridge. I've read of it, but I've never seen anything like."

"I overheard Deme and Filla coming out of Council chambers," Kari said slowly, solemnly, "and they were not overly happy that Eelie had Bridged here. Or that they would return the same way. I wanted to see it, but..." they swallowed. "I was *not* expecting that."

"What's a Bridge?" I asked, feeling foolish. "What did they do?"

Migs answered. "Its... you find the similarities between two places, and you concentrate massive amounts of power into them and you *make* the two places become the *same place* for a time. *Almede* wrote of it extensively. It's said to be a little easier the more similar the two places actually are, but it's still rarely done—you have to know both places *very* well, and it takes so much power that it needs a Circle." They gulped. "Well, usually."

We were still for a time, simply breathing together. The sun had dipped below the distant peaks and the stone was taking on a distinct chill. In silent consensus we gathered the tray and cups and descended back into the mountain to the comfort of our rooms.

Seventeen

After that, my days and weeks in Reft blended into a happy, comfortable routine. I had close friends and kind teachers. I was reading Somiri—competently, if not fluently—and twice a week I met with Ciala's training class and began learning real swordwork.

One morning some weeks on, I waved to Migs, Chan, and Kari as I left the eating hall. They were still at their breakfast, having a lazy morning with no tasks between them for an hour yet. I was heading towards my session, when I saw Turin walking my way.

"Good morning Arin," Turin said. "I was coming to find you. Today, we're going to do something different, if you're willing. Your presence and participation has been requested."

"Requested by whom? For what?"

"By my colleague on the Council, Atua. As for what, it is a work that requires a great deal of power and control. I'll let them tell you more."

I followed Turin down the hallway and we wound our way through the halls and passages of Reft towards their rooms. Down a side passage to an older section of hall, they led us to a door that stood slightly ajar. Turin knocked twice, and a soft, fragile voice spoke.

"Come."

Turin gestured that I should enter first, and they stopped just in the doorway. "I have brought Arin. I will see to preparations." Atua nodded from a chair in the corner of the small room, and Turin left.

I stepped further inside and looked around. This room was different from Turin's; from mine. Instead of a clean modular pattern, the cramped space seemed haphazard, with books and loose parchments piled on shelves and floor and furniture, and bookshelves and furniture arranged with seemingly little reason or intent. A single door in the stone wall to the right stood half-open and I could see the contents of a small bed chamber through it, just as messy.

"Arin, come and sit."

I moved forward carefully, trying to avoid tumbling any of the precarious stacks of books and papers. Where they had gestured was a narrow bench with thread-bare upholstery, but it too was covered in books. I stood before it instead, and Atua seemed not to notice.

"Has Turin told you anything of today?"

I shook my head. "Only that you requested my presence."

Atua nodded absently. "I will be helping a sister in need. Are you willing to aid me?"

"I am," I said slowly, "But I don't know what that means..."

"Ah. Well, we are *nyssén*, yes? Neither man nor woman."

I nodded.

"Some, our brothers and sisters, are like us: their minds at odds with the shape of their bodies. *Aiyssén*. Their body says 'boy' when their mind says 'girl' or the other way around."

I thought this through, and it made some sense that if I could be sure I was not a girl, someone else might be equally certain that she was not a boy. I nodded.

"They face much the same difficulties we face in the world out there. Some manage well enough, regardless, but some come to live here with us for respite. Some come to us for assistance. Not being *between* as we are, they have not been able to access power as we do. Some wish nothing more than to live their lives as they are. But some desire to inhabit bodies which are not at odds with their self. Those that come to us, we aid in this. What I ask your assistance with today is a Reshaping. A little sister, near enough your age, has come to us from Torfall to be made whole."

I worked my mouth for a moment, trying to speak the anxiety in my mind, "I... what do you want me for?"

Atua smiled kindly. "Oh, you need *do* very little. I have been meeting with Anoma and her parents over these last weeks and know what she desires. I will perform the work. I will change her body—from its overall shape down to the smallest details of life. I have been studying the mind and the body for more than three times your years. But such a work requires a great outpouring of power. To do this, we form a Circle—many working together to provide the power that I will draw on. Do you understand?"

I nodded, relieved that I would not be asked to do more than that. "I did a Finding once, with another directing. Will it be like that?"

"In part. You will be part of a larger Circle, and the experience can be a heady one. You will feel all the power flowing. I daresay it will be more than you've ever experienced, strong as you are." They eyed me critically for a moment. "The most important thing for you will be to hold to yourself, and avoid the temptation to wrest control. My concentration will be entirely on Anoma and the work. The power you can contribute will be a welcome addition to the Circle, but I will have no time or concentration left aside to help you when we begin. Turin assures me you are ready for this, child. I hope you are. Is this something you still are willing to try?"

I was all nerves, but I wanted to learn my power. "Yes, I am."

Atua leaned forward, their eyes suddenly intense and sharp. "Now, focus. When you draw on your power, where do you go?"

I thought I understood, and answered without thinking, almost a whisper. "My father's death."

Atua grunted. "Show me. Seek that pain and hold it in your mind, but do not draw. Hold yourself at the moment where you feel the pain in full, let it flood your senses and saturate your being."

My breath quickened and I closed my eyes, tensing. I could feel my shoulders and my stomach clench. I returned once again to that place in my memory where I dreaded to visit. Where I ever dwelled.

Father lying on his back, face bloodied. Cal and his knife. The spray of blood. My world collapsing in horror and agony.

I felt it in my bones—the pain and the loss. I felt sick and my body slumped inwards, trying to curl in upon itself and seek the floor.

And then I felt a lightness as it was drawn from me as if pulled by a river's current. I heard a soft gasp as my pain rushed from my mind and dissipated.

"Good," Atua murmured. "Very good."

I released a pent up breath and sank to my knees, shaking slightly. I opened my eyes and tried to reassure myself I was no longer mired in that pass, that my father's body was not before me. I recalled the exercises that I had practiced with Turin.

I locked my gaze onto Atua's eyes and forced myself to name their color, a deep green tinged with gold.

I placed my hands flat against the woolen carpet under my knees and splayed my fingers, feeling the coarse fibers.

I took a deep breath, savoring the odor of musty pages and leather bindings.

I could feel my heartbeat slowing. I breathed and I counted, focusing on my body's tension as it relaxed. After some moments, I was able to stand once more.

They poured a cup of steaming tea from a porcelain service on a small table beside their chair and handed it to me. It was strong and sweet.

Atua nodded decisively. "You *are* very strong. And you have excellent control. Turin was right. I am sorry to have pushed you so, but I needed to know. Anoma's future rests on the work we do today. Come."

Atua rose from their seat and began towards the door, gesturing me out ahead of them. Once clear of the overstuffed room, they led me down the hallway, further from Turin's quarters and the more familiar parts of the mountain. Not far down the narrow hall we entered a room so peaceful, it was the opposite of Atua's chaotic chambers.

It was half a room, really. The walls opened at gentle angles away from the door onto a broad balcony, open to the bright blue sky. The balcony narrowed again until it formed a blunt side directly opposite the door. Grass from the balcony spread in patches into the room, and stepping stones punctuated the grass. It was as if a strange mirror divided the room, reflecting lush green life and endless sky instead of cold stone, and a little of each spilled across the mirror to the opposite side.

In the very center, lying right along the boundary between the two half spaces was a block of polished stone large enough for a grown man to lie upon. It rose up from the floor, a vertical thrust of mountain rock about waist-high. The top surface looked almost soft, gently dished inward and polished to an inviting luster.

I was still taking in this strange space when several others entered the room. First was Turin and a Somiri *nyssa*. They were not much older than me and had an appealing, open face. They were dressed in a strangely beautiful garment—skin-tight dark leggings that showed every muscle and curve of their long legs, with a soft, billowing blouse in a pale pink that held only loosely to their upper body, open widely at the neck and coming down to points to trail diaphanously below their waist. It was like a feast-day gown in reverse.

Behind them came a young Torfallin who was my height, dressed in a simple flowing white dress. My instincts told me this must be Anoma, confirmed when Atua approached and greeted her by name. Turin and Atua led Anoma and her two adult companions who I took for her parents out onto the balcony to confer quietly, leaving me and the young Somiri by the door.

Too aware of their presence beside me, I tried to focus instead on Anoma and her parents. Her mother and father seemed deeply uncomfortable, visibly at odds between deference to Atua's power, fear at being surrounded by witches, protective of their child, desperate to see her healthy and at peace, and grieving the loss of what they imagined her life to be.

Anoma herself was almost a specter, pale and silent and taking up far less space than seemed possible. Her dark hair was long, and it looked to be her habit to hold her head downwards, letting it cover her face. Even with her face hidden, I couldn't help but see that her body was showing distinctly masculine development in her arms and chest—I felt an unexpected pang, realizing that her build reminded me of Ranji. Puberty was well underway, and it was pushing her body in every wrong way—a brutal, pitiless war with her mind.

I knew some of what that felt like. I worried daily over my still-developing body. My breasts showed no inclination to stop their slow, steady growth. I had taken to wrapping a scarf tightly about my chest whenever I could, trying to reduce my awareness of them, and their visibility to others. Unfortunately, I had found that doing so only made me *more* aware, and the intermittent growth pains I felt from them was another ongoing reminder.

If I understood rightly what was about to happen here, perhaps this was the answer for me as well.

"I am Fanti," the Somiri *nyssa* said quietly to me in their round accent. They had a broad, easy smile. "Arin, right? Is this your first Circle?"

I looked up at Fanti, who had stepped closer and was leaning down to speak to me quietly.

I nodded. "First Reshaping, too."

Fanti nodded. "Don't worry. Turin asked me to guide you in this. It is a beautiful experience."

Soon, more *nyssén* began to enter, and Fanti and I moved further from the door to make room. It was a varied group totaling nine, and Fanti and I were the youngest.

Presently, Atua led Anoma forward to the stone table, and Turin helped her to climb upon it. Her parents came to either side to hold her hands as she laid down. A hush descended and the Circle began to form around the table, each of us standing about two paces back. Turin stepped back to join the Circle, while Atua stayed by Anoma's head.

Atua bent down to whisper something in Anoma's ear.

From across the room Turin nodded to me. Beside me, Fanti whispered, "embrace your pain now."

It was my intention to find my way back to the moment of agony of Father's death, but I found Ranji instead. Maybe it was Anoma's resemblance. Maybe it was my hope for some kind of transformation, for some good memory to be born of his death. My mind went to the moment where my world had fallen apart.

Tears welled in my eyes and my throat clamped down on the memory of my scream as Father collapsed. In my mind I saw the scene playing out again. Tears were streaming down my cheeks now.

"Breathe," Fanti intoned softly beside me.

I saw Ranji bolt to his feet, eyes wide in pain and fury.

"Accept the pain," they whispered

I watched him take up the hatchet, his face contorting in rage. Ranji raised the hatchet over his head, and I felt my stomach clench. I knew what happened next. I knew it, but I was shaking my head in tiny jerks side to side. I wanted to deny it with everything I had within me.

"Let it be. Let it go," Fanti's calm steady voice matched the drumbeat of my heart.

Time in my memory slowed and I could feel each infinitesimal moment as a lifetime. I could see the arrow, loosed from somewhere behind me inching ever closer to Ranji's chest. My heart was dying in this moment. My shoulders curled inward and I knew I could not change things. I was about to die there with my brother.

The arrow struck his chest and I could see the life leave him from one heartbeat to the next, and the pain of his death, of his loss forever rolled over me and crushed the breath from my breast.

A new voice joined Fanti's now. They seemed to be speaking to my thoughts. A part of me recognized Atua's reedy timber. "Now open yourself. The pain is not yours alone to bear. It does not belong to you."

My breath escaped with a gasp as I felt the weight upon my shoulders lighten by the smallest bit. Keeping myself open, I stretched my mind out towards Atua and offered them the pain. They breathed in quietly as they took it, their eyes widening at the strength of the flow of power. It was a response that I felt more than heard. Even as I felt my pain and power flow to them, a massive surge fell back upon me, like a great crest of water sloshed over the edge of a washtub.

The pain flooded me. Not just my own, but the collective pain of the whole Circle. It was too much. It was devastating and unbearable.

It was enough to drown, but I released myself to it, and it buoyed me up like a cork bobbing on the surface of a river. I had no control—desired none. The pain was an embrace and I could feel its power surging through me. I felt it flow and weave through me and through Fanti and Turin and all the others. I felt Atua's presence like a hand on a tiller, steering the flows.

I was in their minds and they were all within me, and yet we were each ourselves. There was not one and another, there was only this: I *knew* what it felt like to be old and *remembered* being raised to the Council of Reft. I felt the *memory* of receiving a young *nyssa* named Arin into the embrace of Reft. I *knew* the play of fabric under shears and needle and thread to craft a garment of surpassing beauty.

I *knew* what it was to lose Father and Mother and Ranji in violence and I also remembered burying my mother in a beautiful ceremony with the loving support of my village, after her long years of illness. I knew the shape of stone and feelings of mastery over it after long decades of practice. I felt the beatings my father subjected me to when I told him I was not a boy.

I remembered growing up in Somiere and also growing up in Torfall and also in the Freelands. I was orphaned in a border skirmish and I was brought to Reft by two loving parents who knew they needed to travel to Reft so that I could live my best life. I had run away from home and was taken in by a hedgewitch. I also grew up with only a mother. And I was raised by only my father.

I remembered giving birth, and I remembered becoming a father. I recalled fondly my love of a husband and of a wife and of several *nyssén*.

And I was Anoma. I *knew* what it was to be born with a boy's body and I *knew* what it was to *know* I was a girl. I was terrified of what was about to happen and relieved and felt apprehension and grief at what I would lose and also filled with overwhelming joy at what I could finally become.

And Atua began to Shape.

It was movement and it was sculpture and it was art and music and dance.

It was light and sound and touch and awareness and I was finally able to discern myself from the others.

The Shaping washed over Anoma and I could feel its caress and the changes we wrought in her. Millions of pricks of needles and sweeping hands and flesh and pain melded together and melted away.

Her brows softened and receded. Her nose and ears refined. The budding protuberance at her throat disappeared and her jaw took on a more feminine shape. The muscles in her shoulders and chest softened and her body seemed to flow and adjust like soft clay.

The very fiber of her being was reformed by Atua's precise control. Uncountable and unmeasurable parts of life that I had never known existed were changed and rewritten in a wave that tore through her body with enough violence that she cried out suddenly as it passed, leaving a flush of heat on her skin.

I could feel the change myself and gasped in shock with her, and I was not the only one.

Her hips widened and her shoulders narrowed. Breasts budded within her gown even as we looked on. The very scale of her body—her height and her hands and feet—contracted. I felt the physical evidence of her manhood recede and reshape and become the new mark of her womanhood, even to the source of life as her womb quickened and her first blood flowed, staining her dress.

And then it was done, and I felt myself diminish as Atua, Anoma, Turin, Fanti, everyone receded from my sense of self and the Circle was broken.

I sobbed and my body collapsed with the loss, and someone caught me under my shoulder. I curled towards them, burying my face in the firm chest and soft fabric.

Distantly, I could hear Anoma and her parents softly weeping in catharsis, her father's deep warm voice giving thanks and laughter to anyone he could reach. The room was filled with joyous tears and hearty gratitude and congratulations. It sounded like a gathering of old friends, and it felt like a birth celebration.

Firm comforting hands guided me. I was still insensate and unsteady on my feet, and I followed without awareness into a place of quiet and peace. When my eyes began to focus and I was aware of myself again, I was seated on a low couch in a small room. A single lamp gave a dim light.

Fanti sat across from me and offered me a mug of water. "Are you okay? I have heard that the greater the contribution you give to a Circle, the worse the severing is."

I took the water and sipped slowly, finding my voice. I was still disoriented and not fully in myself. A sharp pain was beginning at the base of my skull.

"I was not expecting that," I said finally.

Fanti broke into a wide smile, their teeth bright white against their dark face. "You were amazing. Atua said you were strong, but I had no idea. I am glad to know you, Arin."

I was suddenly shy, remembering that I had huddled against their chest as the Circle broke. They were beautiful, I suddenly realized, and holding them had been relaxing and intriguing at once. Casting for some way to change the subject, I latched on to something they had just said. "I was asked because of my strength. Atua did the work, and Turin is on the Council. What brought you?"

As soon as the words were out of my mouth, I worried that it sounded as if I was boasting, but Fanti only shrugged.

"Atua is my counsellor. They thought it would be a good experience for me to participate. I have joined Circles before, but this was surely the most impressive work I have participated in."

"Have you never done a Reshaping, then?"

"Not like this," Fanti said, thoughtfully. "A friend of mine here, I was in the Circle for them, but it was only minor changes compared to this. What Atua did..." They shivered slightly. "It was truly a blessing that we helped bring to that family. Something profound."

I nodded. I didn't have any more words than that, but I understood the sentiment. I gave them a small smile, and they gave me their bright grin once more.

I ducked my head, the pain in my head blooming now into a full headache, rolling over me in waves and I clenched my eyes shut.

I felt more than heard Fanti moving around in the small room, and shortly they pressed a small warm mug into my hands.

"Drink this tea. It will help."

I took the mug with one hand and clutched their hand with the other, sipping the bitter brew slowly. I could feel the warmth of the tea filling me, but I also felt their hand on my shoulder. I reflexively leaned into their touch.

Eighteen

I raised the practice sword over my head, hilt grasped in both hands and sword-point upright to the sky. My right foot slid forward and swept in an arc to the side as I brought the sword sweeping downwards and to the right, my hips turning into the movement to lend the cut power.

Two years had passed in a blur of contented moments with my friends, of quiet thoughtful sessions with Turin, and of training with the Watch. I still practiced on my own each morning, but now I incorporated techniques learned and refined under Ciala's critical eye.

I turned my body through the move and brought my hands back high above my head, the sword now curving downwards to my left, blade facing outwards in a defensive stance, my right foot swept back and to the side. Quick as thought, I pushed off with the back foot and my left slid forward as I descended into a tight crouch and brought the sword hilt down to my chest, point outwards—the blade turned horizontally to slide more easily between ribs—and the force of my whole body's momentum behind the thrust to drive it home.

Training in the Watch was indeed a life-long endeavor, as Ciala had said. I was learning, and reveling in the feelings of competence and purpose I gained. I was learning the sword properly now to be sure, but more: I was learning the depths of my own capabilities in ways I couldn't have imagined. I was practiced in Pairing and had joined more Circles than I could count. I was learning strategy and leadership. And I was learning healing.

I drew my weight back over my right foot, pulling the sword back along the same line of the previous thrust so as to not bind on the flesh of my imagined foe. Back through a deep curving arc, I turned my body to pause for a moment defending in the opposite direction—the hilt once more above my head and blade point down guarding the length of my body.

Healing was a skill I had not thought I would be drawn to. It seemed I excelled at it and that talent was blossoming into a passion that surprised me. I was taking every opportunity to shadow those already approved to heal injury, whether among the Watch, or in the Healer's fellowship. I watched as they sewed wounds with needle and thread, listened intently to their explanations of anatomy, of the faults of broken bone and torn sinew, and of how to best mend them. I joined them in Circles with their patients so that I could perceive their every delicate application of power to the worst of the injuries. I spent every moment I was allowed with Atua, their wisdom and decades of experience with the finer points of healing too precious to miss.

I retreated four steps—not directly backwards: I avoided tripping over the imaginary fallen foe I had just run through— pivoting and resetting my guard with each measured pace. On the last step, I crouched low with my left leg extended backwards and brought the sword point up, chin-level on the advancing opponent in my imagination. Half a breath for them to flinch back, and my sword flashed down cutting across their thigh. I used the tension in my right leg and the momentum of my arms to swing myself back up into a high stance, the blade sweeping out and across my chest as I pivoted into a turn.

I was reading now, not for practice or mastery of language, but for learning. The Library of Reft had become a second home. There were inspiring books on strategy, exciting books on tactics and accounts of battle, dreadfully dry books on theories of supply and logistics, and there were books on healing. The head librarian claimed with no little pride that Reft had the largest collection on Somiri medicine outside the *Gruende* itself. I devoured these with the same passion I applied to the whipped egg confections in the eating hall.

I still struggled with Somiri, especially the intricate and complicated rules that altered the most common words to their context, but I found reading it easier than speaking. If I couldn't remember the correct conjugations and variations half of the time, at least I could absorb the ideas, and I could learn. I sometimes marveled at the thought of ideas put down by a master of their art and picked up again by a novice more than a lifetime later. That I could be taught to treat an invisible and fatal weakness of the heart through careful preparation of specific herbs, and be taught it by Grunéndalle who had died in his dotage over a hundred years ago... I understood now why it was worth so much time and agony to learn the language of scholarship.

It had become something of a joke among Kari, Chan, Migs, and Heiu—a new member of our circle, and suddenly inseparable from Migs—that I spent every waking moment with either a sword in hand or a book.

I brought my left foot forward and out in a sliding arc, dropping my hips into a low stance with the sword tip forward, blade up, hilt held beside my head. In a single fluid movement, I turned my body and head, my feet pivoting on their balls so that I was facing nearly the other direction, and without a pause I stepped forward, bringing my left leg and hip into motion as the sword swept down in an overhand cut to end with the point downward and extended to my right.

"That move was pretty sloppy."

I froze. I knew that voice, always with a sharp edge of mockery. I turned slowly, still holding my stance, sword point tracing through a broad sweep as if I was guarding myself against an attack.

Eelie stood some paces away, pale skin and cold, blue eyes; their hair glowed in the morning sun. A small private smile quirked on their lips.

"What are you doing here?" was all I could think of to say.

Eelie turned and moved in a wide arc. Their face was casual, calm as if out for a morning stroll, but their body was taut and each step precise. They paced a slow half circle around me, the distance between us narrowing ever so slightly with each step. They were a cat stalking a mouse, sure and confident; lithe and deadly. The smile never left their lips.

They shrugged. "My lord has some business with the Council."

I turned with them slowly, trying to not seem as tense as I was. I felt off balance. I felt a child and a fool and something more. My awareness was bound up in that narrowing distance. My breathing was becoming shallow.

Their gaze on me was cold and assessing and predatory. Their eyes swept me up and down noting my tension and my unease, and their smile changed very subtly. They looked on me with satisfaction and possession. A cat who knew its mouse had nowhere to run.

I blushed and their smile deepened.

Their pacing brought them nearly around in a full circle now. They were only two paces away and turned to face me. For a moment I thought they would take the four steps towards me. The tension in the distance between us was becoming uncomfortably close. Part of me wanted to step back. Part of me wanted to raise my sword. I shivered despite the warm morning sun. Part of me wanted to step forward.

"I thought it might be fun to spar," Eelie said, and for the first time, I realized they carried their own practice sword at their side. My face heated as I realized how unaware I was, and I glanced around, wondering what else I had missed while focused on their sharp features.

I brought my eyes back to them in time to see their smile turn up at the corner as if they could read my thoughts. They were taking pleasure in my unease. Well, I had sparred with the best of the second watch, and had bested Ciala more than once. This mouse had teeth.

I settled myself back into my defensive stance—more a matter of relaxing my muscles than anything else—and nodded.

Eelie closed the distance between us in half a breath and our swords met, their cut sliding against my sword raised in defense and away from my body as I pivoted, bringing my sword back down in the classic counter-stroke. They let their momentum carry them just far enough to avoid a strike at their flank and turned. Their sword cut a low sweep that would have taken my ankle if I didn't pull my right foot back just in time.

We both stepped back a pace and reset ourselves. Eelie had a slight imbalance to their stance. They were favoring their left shoulder, and I could see it affected their technique just enough to annoy them. I waited calmly, my awareness expanding to take in the whole of their body. I was aware of their breathing, the shifts in muscle as their weight wavered ever so slightly from side to side.

When they moved again, I knew it before their stance had shifted. Their shoulders rose into position for an overhead cut—right slightly higher than left—but their feet were set too wide. "Feet are the key to every strike," Ciala had taught me. Their body posture was a feint—they were moving to strike low.

Even as they dropped their hips to bring their sword in for the low sweep they had tried to hide, I closed the distance and crouched low, my wooden sword driven point-down at a steep angle into the ground before me, anchored and solid. Their stroke hit the back of my blade with a startling crack and a shock that traveled up their arm, loosening their grip and setting them entirely off balance.

I pressed forward, springing up with all the tension of my legs and placing my left palm flat against their chest. I pushed them backwards and brought my sword down hard against their blade with my right hand. Eelie fell backwards upon the grass and their practice sword fell at my feet. I stood over them, sword pointed casually at their throat.

"*That* was very, very clever of you," they said. Somehow, disarmed and lying on their back in the grass and with me standing armed above them, they were calm and in control. The cat at its ease, never mind the mouse was alive and just out of reach.

Eelie's lips twitched into that same secret little smile, as if my mind was open to them once more. I blushed again.

"Help me up," they said.

I reached down and they grasped my forearm as I pulled

them to their feet. They didn't let go. They stood too close. I was suddenly aware of their body, taller than me still though I had grown since the last time we met. Lithe and tense and strong.

"How did you know that I was going low?" They spoke quietly, an intimate whisper. Their face was only inches away from mine. My eyes were locked on theirs and I realized with another blush that I was breathing in time with them.

"Your feet," I said. "Your stance was widening—too wide for an overhead strike."

Their eyes measured me and their face turned somber for a moment. "I'll remember that."

I knew I should step away, I should let go of their wrist and pull my arm out of their grasp, but that same heat and potential was filling the short distance between us. I could smell lilacs and sharp spice. My left hand trembled slightly—I wanted to touch them again.

Eelie shifted, pulling me even closer with their hand still gripping my forearm. They could bend forward and their long hair would drape over my face, curtaining us off from the world. All I could do was look into their eyes. Their smile returned.

"I knew you would be a fun workout," they said.

My face was hot and my heart was racing.

Their left hand rose to touch my face, their thumb tracing the scar from my temple to my chin.

"For what it's worth, I'm sorry for the things I said to you and your friends last time we met," they said. I could feel their breath against my lips.

Their touch was possessive and their eyes cold and hard. I wanted to turn my face away. I wanted to lean into their touch. Then their lips were on mine, firm and forceful, and I felt the heat lighting break between us, its thunder rolling through my body in waves. I was lost in the storm of myself and shivering. I would be shaking except that Eelie still held my arm in an iron grip, and I was powerless to break it.

The kiss lasted hours, an age, a lifetime. It was over in a blink of the eye and then Eelie let me go and was walking away. I stumbled backwards and nearly fell onto the grass. They scooped up the fallen practice sword as they passed it, and walked away from me. I was trying to catch my breath, trying to steady myself.

"I'd like to spar with you again while I'm here," they said to me as they left, without looking back.

I stood still for a time after they had gone, wondering how to name what it was I was feeling. I licked my lips. The storm still churned in me. My stomach was unsettled, and my head felt light.

I was late to my lessons with Ciala. I had lingered overlong in the heat of the washroom. I wish I could say I was luxuriating in the warmth and relaxing in the steam, but in truth I didn't even remember it. I cleaned the sweat of practice from my skin and scrubbed my short fuzz of hair, but more than anything, I stewed over the feelings that writhed within me.

Eelie.

They were cold and cruel and sharp—a finely honed blade with a barbed spine. I couldn't forget what they had said to my friends the last time they were in Reft, and the pain they had sown among us. By all rights, I should be offended, horrified that they presumed to kiss me, even after the apology.

Something fluttered in my chest, and for a moment I wondered if my heart had developed a murmur.

But they were beautiful and they were strong and they were... menacing. I remembered the predatory look in their eyes. It was thrilling and terrifying and unsettling and dizzying. I thought I could smell lilacs and spice. I could still feel their hand on my face. My hand wanted to touch them again.

When I reached the rooms the Watch had set aside for the messier aspects of training, Ciala looked me over with worry. I was never late, especially to healing studies.

"All okay, Arin?"

"Yes, sorry," I said.

They studied me, weighing me with their eyes.

"Well, come in then. Our patient is waiting."

I smelled the rich metallic odor of fresh blood then. Behind Ciala on a heavy wooden table was the carcass of an enormous hog, lying in a welter of its own blood and gore with its abdomen open and viscera exposed and several patches of skin carefully cut and peeled back to expose muscle. It must weigh more than me, even partly flayed and carved as it was. Panri, Ciala's other student, stood beside the table. Despite having studied five years longer than me, their Torfallin coloring had gone faintly green at the sight and smell.

"We're going to do some practical study of anatomy today," Ciala began in their lecturing voice. "You've read the books, you've studied drawings, you've watched as others worked, but nothing substitutes for getting your own hands wet and covered in gore, and setting your own eyes and fingers on the inside of a patient while they're bleeding all over you." They stepped around to stand beside Panri at the table and slapped the haunch of meat, making a horridly wet smack and sending a spatter of blood to speckle Panri's chest and face. I involuntarily took a step back, and Panri gulped and looked like they would be sick at any moment.

"Obviously we can't let you go cutting up a person yet," Ciala smiled grimly, "And we aren't going to wait until someone is dying to try to teach you. So this is the best we can do. It turns out that pigs aren't so different from people once you start cutting into them."

My eyes darted to the constellation of blood on Panri's shirt and I was suddenly aware that I was wearing clean trousers and my favorite shirt. I moved to the corner of the room where baskets held a variety of old tunics and trousers, too worn and threadbare to be wanted for the common stores. I stripped off my clothes and folded them neatly on the bench beside the baskets, and pulled on some of the worn scraps before joining Ciala and Panri at the table.

"Now Panri, you'll work here at the front leg, and Arin you'll be at the back. I want you both to begin by feeling for the primary ball joint—shoulder or hip. Once you've identified it, I want you to begin carefully dissecting the joint. I want you to locate—but not sever!—the primary veins, arteries, and nerve bundles. After that, dissect enough tissue to expose and visualize the joint. Pay attention to the various layers of fascia and muscle fibers: I expect you to be able to point them out to me. Do as little damage as you can while you go—once you've found the structures I've named, you're going to put the poor fellow all back together!"

Panri and I looked at each other, and I expect I wore the same expression of tension and anxiety and anticipation that they did, even if their eyes were tighter and their lips were tense and white under their beard. I was nervous and excited at being able to learn, but luckily I didn't seem to be bothered by blood or carnage.

Ciala was watching us, waiting for us to begin, so I put my

hands on the animal's flank and started pressing with my fingers, trying to locate the thigh bone and hip by feel. The muscle was still pliable and warm—this hog was recently butchered. Idly I wondered if it had been brought straight up from the butcher's hall at the base of the mountain by the Vale. Still, even fresh, the thigh muscles were thick and dense, and finding any bone, let alone the one deep inside the hip, was difficult. I spent several minutes futilely feeling the hog's rump in growing frustration.

Then I remembered: "Feet are the key to every strike."

I grasped the hoof and began flexing the leg back and forth with one hand while I felt for the telltale movements with the other. Satisfied that I had found the joint, I placed the first two fingers of my left hand to mark the spot, and picked up the surgical knife with my right and began to cut.

I thought I remembered the general layout of muscle and tissue from the illustration plates I had studied, but those were human, and this was a pig. And I wasn't even sure I remembered them correctly. In that moment I longed for Migs's perfect recall. Ciala hadn't said that this was a test, but it had the feeling of one. I did not want to fail regardless.

My first cut only parted the outer layer of the thick, tough skin. Despite the keen edge of the tiny knife, it took far more force than I had expected to make it through. After a second cut, I was through the skin into the muscle.

"If you're cutting into a person, the skin will be much thinner and not nearly as tough. Remember that," Ciala said from behind me.

I nodded as I continued cutting.

Moving through the bundles of muscle, my mind started to wander. Eelie was back, and that meant Savat needed something from the Council. I could ask Kari, they might have heard the reason for the visit.

The major blood vessels would be along the inward side of the bone, I thought, more protected there from accidental laceration. I worked my way through, finding the silvery fascia, and fine nerve fibers, noting each as I went.

I had to tell my friends what had happened this morning—I had learned my lesson and there would be no secrets for Eelie to leverage this time—but that meant telling how I felt about what had happened, and I still wasn't sure. My face warmed as I remembered their touch, their lips.

"Arin, you've severed his artery," Ciala said calmly behind me.

I turned to look over my shoulder to find them, puzzled. They met my eyes, then looked down, and suddenly their words reached my mind.

"*Faila i la!*" I cursed, looking down. Sure enough I had cut right through and sliced diagonally along the artery running through the groin. Not quite severed, but if this were a person, Ciala's calm warning wouldn't have come before a violent spray of blood as they bled out. Even now, there was a well of blood in the incision, rapidly occluding the damage I had done. I reached in with my left hand, trying to find the edges and pinch them closed while I dropped the knife and hunted with my right for the curved needle and thread.

"If this was a person you were trying to save, you may have just killed them," Ciala echoed my thoughts. Panri glanced up from their work to watch, and Ciala continued, speaking to both of us. "What Arin is trying to do now has a chance, but if you're ever in this situation for real, you're going to be panicking and there will be so much blood loss so fast that it's a slim chance. Your fingers get slippery, you can't see what you're doing, and every breath you take to calm yourself is a breath less you have to work a miracle. If you're intent on saving them, better to take a step back and draw on your pain to close the artery."

I looked up at them, a question in my eyes.

"No, continue, Arin. I want to see if you can do it this way. I know you can do the other."

It seemed like forever before I had the two edges pinched together with slippery fingers, and the first stitch started. From there it got slightly easier, my world contracting to a half-inch length of tissue and the movements of an inch-long needle.

Finally, sweating, panting, and forearms and shirt covered in blood, I stepped away from the carcass. I had the presence of mind not to try to wipe the sweat back from my forehead with my soiled hands.

"So, not so easy as it sounds in the books, is it?" Ciala asked grimly.

"No. No it is not," I said.

"In a real situation, they'll be screaming, crying, thrashing. You may have seen it when you've shadowed watch-members, yes?"

I nodded, feeling the weight of my mistake.

"You cannot afford distraction, Arin. Whatever it is that is taking space in your mind, see it taken care of before our next lesson," They looked me over for a moment longer, then took pity. "Go on now. Get cleaned up and get to lunch. Don't be unkind to yourself about this mistake. This is why we train. You'll make many more mistakes as you learn."

I nodded, breathing slowly to calm myself. Ciala turned back to observe Panri's work while I stripped down to the skin, tossing the bloody clothes into a basket reserved for soiled rags. Beside the bench and spare clothing was a small bathing cubicle, which I used to clean off the blood before dressing in my own clothes again. I decided as I left that I would stop by the full bathing chamber by my apartments on the way to lunch. My hands still smelled of blood and raw meat, and I wanted the hot soapy water to scrub myself clean.

I also needed more time to think before facing my friends.

Nineteen

When I found my friends in the eating hall, I had no need to turn the conversation. Kari greeted me with the news they were desperate to share.

"They're back. They arrived by Bridge last night."

The others looked at me, perhaps expecting me to ask *who* was back. "I know," I said. "Eelie found me this morning while I was practicing." I sat down with my tray: a bowl of steamed barley and a plate of raw greens tossed with sweet red berries and a tart vinegary relish. I had no stomach for anything richer after the morning's lessons.

Kari and Migs leaned forward, and Heiu's eyes widened. Chan was less animated as usual, their long hair draped to hide their face, but I thought I saw their head cock slightly to the side—as much as a gasp of surprise from anyone else.

"And?" Migs asked.

I took a spoonful of barley and chewed for a moment. My feelings were still raw and unformed. Instead of answering, I turned to Kari.

"Any clues on why they're here?"

I saw a flicker of something in Kari's eyes, but they didn't press me yet. "All I know is that the Viscount met with Deme and Purun, and whatever they said, it's not over. They're meeting again day after tomorrow, this time with Atua and Gesh as well."

I sighed. That told me nothing, except that Eelie would be around at least another two days. It seemed they would have their chance to make good on their promise. I could see Kari was waiting, knowing that I had something to tell, but they were not willing to ask.

"They found me this morning while I was practicing," I began again, starting with facts that were easy to name. "They brought a practice sword, and asked to spar with me."

Heiu leaned forward, "Did you? Were they any good? I wonder with them always following the Viscount, and carrying that—I guess it's a short sword? I don't know one kind from another, but it looks like they know what they're doing..."

Heiu had a tendency to nervously fill silences with a torrent of thoughts and questions. Migs covered their hand in a subtle gesture, almost absently, and they quieted.

"They were good," I said into the silence. Then I grinned. "But I was better."

Kari's eyes snapped up to meet mine.

"You beat them?" asked Migs.

I nodded. "Two exchanges in, I had them disarmed and flat on their back." The others whooped their satisfaction at this. Kari was still watching me. They seemed to know there was more coming, and that they wouldn't like it.

"How'd they take it," Chan asked quietly, speaking for the first time since I had sat.

"Cool as a cat." I sighed. "I don't know if there's a way to beat them where they wouldn't make it seem like it was their plan all along."

"Oh, there's a way," Kari whispered grimly. I'm not sure if anyone else heard.

I steeled myself, and let the rest of the story out.

"I helped them up," I said. I looked down at my tray, not seeing anything. Seeing Eelie. "They held on... didn't let go. They... kissed me."

My friends were silent. I risked glancing up and my eyes locked with Kari's. Their face had gone cold, their eyes tinged with concern and shock and something more I couldn't identify. I had guessed that there was some kind of history between Kari and Eelie from when they were younger, but they had never shared what had actually happened.

"Was it a good kiss? How did it feel? Did you kiss them back?" Heiu was breathless, oblivious to the chill that had settled between us.

Kari dropped their eyes from mine and looked away. I willed them to look at me again, but after a moment I turned to Heiu.

"It was... It felt..." I shuddered, and I could feel their thumb stroking my face again, felt the firm hard planes of their chest under my fingers. I could smell them. I knew I was blushing, and wanted to shrink in on myself and slink away from the table.

"*Satá wei ette!*" Kari said suddenly, their voice full of venom. The caravaner's expression meant "Think of fleas and start itching."

I looked up and followed their gaze, and my breath caught. Eelie was there, stalking gracefully into the eating hall, their eyes fixed on me, and that secretive little half-smile on their lips. I felt my stomach flutter.

They were in their usual livery, black slashed with purple and orange stripes. The sleeveless shirt showed off their pale skin and densely muscled narrow shoulders to magnificent effect. Their hair was pulled back into a severe tail, making their delicate features even more sharp and predatory. This morning, they had looked a cat—now they brought to mind one of the foxes that prowled the southern mountains, their silver fur sleek in the summer months.

Eelie stopped some paces from our table. A look crossed their face that seemed out of place: uncertainty. I could see them taking in my friends, and their eyes darted to Kari for the briefest moment before sliding away and finding mine again. They did not come closer.

When they spoke, it was as if they spoke to everyone, though they still held my eyes. "I apologized to Arin already, but I want to say the same to all of you. I'm sorry for the way I spoke to you the last time I was here."

It felt like we all were still for an age. I was keenly aware of Kari beside me, of Migs, Heiu, and Chan behind me. And of Eelie, their presence and their speech creating ripples of discomfort through us for very different reasons. There was an empty seat beside me, but I knew they wouldn't ask permission to take it. I looked at Kari, a question in my eyes.

Their face lost its stoney demeanor and they turned back to the table smiling blandly. "So, Heiu, you were telling us that story about how Migs has all the librarians frothing over this new organizational system?"

Heiu looked at Kari wide-eyed, turning briefly to Migs and glancing at me. They looked at once lost and stricken. I had never seen Heiu speechless before.

"Go on," Kari prompted. "They reorganized the whole history section by binding color or something, right?"

"Kari," I said softly. I gently reached out to touch their hand.

They tensed, and I could tell they were seething with rage. I drew back. When they spoke it was quiet and cold, and they still did not look at me.

"If you want to drown yourself in that rotting mire, you go ahead Arin, but go do it somewhere else. They're not welcome here."

I flinched as if slapped. I looked to the others, but no one was willing to step into the fray, certainly not on Eelie's behalf. I glanced at Migs, who only shrugged slightly and looked down at the table. Chan wouldn't meet my eyes.

Eelie still stood, waiting patiently as a stone would wait, still and expressionless.

Unwilling to sit in silence and discomfort through the rest of my lunch, I stood, throwing a glance over my friends and shook my head. I didn't want to abandon them, but I wouldn't be a part of Kari's vendetta if they wouldn't give me more reason than umbrage.

I walked over to Eelie who turned smoothly as I joined them and matched my pace. We strode out of the hall together.

"It's not their fault, you know," Eelie said as we moved through the wide stone hallway. The smile was gone from their face now, their lips pressed together into a line as they thought over what they were saying. "Kari, I mean. It's not their fault that they're full of hate towards me. Have they told you what happened between us?"

I shook my head but said nothing, unwilling to interrupt

this unexpected candor.

"It's this place. *Reft* and their rules and their... *oaths*. My skin crawls every time he brings us here. Every time he has to bow and scrape and pretend that he's less than them, just to get them to condescend to help."

We emerged onto a sunny platform, planted as a lush garden with a narrow shaded path of paving stones winding between low spreading shrubs and flowers. The Vale grew all the food that was needed for Reft. These platforms were meant for peace and to bring a sense of nature and connection to life into daily reach of those who dwelt inside the mountain.

"What does he want help with from the Council?" I asked, genuine curiosity overcoming my self-control.

Eelie didn't seem to hear. "The last time, I was so mad. So angry at them for refusing—It's why I said what I said to you all. I really am sorry."

We arrived at a wooden bench, secluded in a little copse of low trees and flowering shrubs. I didn't know the ornamental plants that were tended here: tiny pink and yellow flowers nestled among dark green leaves. Eelie sat and pulled me down beside them.

I became deeply aware of their hand on my arm as I sat on the bench. They didn't seem to notice that they had moved me into place, but I noticed. They moved their hand to my thigh possessively. My cheeks warmed.

"Kari... well, we were friends. Back when I lived here. We were young. I had arrived just a year before they did, and we roomed together."

They were looking at me intently, as if wanting me to acknowledge their words.

I nodded.

"I was... I wasn't happy with myself then." They looked

away, staring into the empty sky. "I was really struggling. I didn't fit. I didn't feel *right*." Their eyes flickered back to mine, seeking understanding.

I nodded again. I knew this feeling.

"I watched *them*—Atua and their precious Council—time after time give everyone what they wanted. Heal their minds for them, fix their bodies for them. They even had me join their Circles to feed off my power. Oh, they wanted my power. Every damn time, it was Eelie this, and Eelie that when they wanted to use my power. I'm sure they're doing the same with you, right?"

I nodded.

They paused for a moment, seeking something in the sky again. "But whenever I asked their help for *me*, it was always: 'Oh, you're not ready yet, Eelie,' 'Give yourself time, Eelie,' 'Let's talk some more about how you *feel*, Eelie.'" They shook their head angrily. "I knew what I wanted. I knew exactly what I wanted for myself. Why couldn't they understand?"

They looked at me and smiled that secret little smile. "Tamar understands. He came to me there at the end, when they were deciding what to do with me. *They* were deciding whether to ask me to leave their precious *Reft*, and he asked me to join him. They were going to cast me aside like a used up milk cow. He took me in and saw me for what I could be. He doesn't tell me what I should be or what I shouldn't do. The only oath he asked of me was to be true to him and support his goals."

Eelie was moving their fingers, rubbing my thigh in short little strokes so that I had to concentrate to catch their words. I could feel the warmth of their body close to mine. They still didn't seem to realize what they were doing.

"I finally decided to do it myself, you know? My Reshaping.

I had watched *them* do it enough times for others, hadn't I? But I made the mistake of trusting Kari."

"How old were you?" I asked. I wanted to ask more: How they had done it. What had they needed to change so badly that they would reject Atua's counsel. The Reshaping I had seen had used *so much* power. Could Eelie truly have done that themself?

They shrugged and continued as if I hadn't spoken, "I thought our friendship meant more... but they were young, and they had been taught the damn *Oaths* too well, hadn't they? 'Protect and hold sacred *first* the lives, and *second* the confidences...' right? First one, *then* the other."

Their eyes returned to the horizon, tracing the mountain ridges. "Well, I knew what I was doing, but they got worried and thought I'd hurt myself and so they decided they had to tell—had to stop me." Eelie went quiet then for several moments.

They shook their head. "Anyway, I thought you deserved to know." Finally, they looked at me again, that little smile returning. Their thoughts seemed to jump like drops of water on a hot skillet. "You're *so powerful* Arin. Like me. They're holding you back here." Their fingers clamped down on my thigh, squeezing nearly to the point of pain. "You asked what Tamar wants... He wants *us*. He wants to lift us up, to bring the *nyssén* into the light of day so that we don't have to slink around and hide in this wretched little mountain. The world should be ours."

As I opened my mouth to speak, they seemed to realize their fingers were digging into my thigh and relaxed them, turning the grip into a gentle, slow stroking with their hand. The contrast drove all words and thought from my mind.

Their lips turned up at the corner and their eyes narrowed,

their face taking on that feline look. They languidly let their hand slide up my hip and waist, tracing slowly up the side of my chest to that hollow between shoulder and breast and on up my neck to cup my chin, never losing contact. My eyes closed involuntarily as they leaned close and their fingers brushed my cheek.

Then the heat of their body and the touch of their fingers were gone, and my eyes snapped open to find them standing. I felt unstable, like I might fall from the bench if I didn't concentrate on my balance.

"I have to go now. I *do* enjoy our sparring, Arin," they said with their secret little smile.

Luckily my training that afternoon was study, not surgery. Without Ciala's careful attention, there was no one to note that I turned the pages of my book more slowly than usual, or to count the number of times I had to turn back again, realizing after half an hour that I had been looking at the words without reading, my mind elsewhere. In my own defense, there's only so much attention that Ferental's *Essays on the Provision of Communities at Peace and War* can hold even were I not preoccupied with Eelie. When my stomach began grumbling, I left the watch post for dinner, nodding to Panri as I left.

I found my friends again at our usual table. As I sat, I noted the tension, though the company was not as cold as I feared it might be. Chan was in the middle of explaining their current study under Deme, some complicated research involving the earliest forms of written Somiri, and how the interactions with the Torfallin seafarers had changed the two languages. I did not understand the details—or truly even the purpose—they discussed with so much excitement. Their pronunciation and facility with language had improved dramatically since we studied basic Somiri together, so that while I still stumbled over simple conversational vocabulary, they could pass as a native speaker—if one relied on ears alone—and had begun studying earlier forms of that language as well as the ancient precursor to Freelander that they called *Fin-an*.

When Chan wound down, Heiu filled the silence as usual. "Arin, you going to tell us what happened this afternoon? What did you talk about with Eelie? *Did* you talk?"

I looked down at my tray, though I felt Kari's eyes on me—even as I knew they all were waiting for me to speak, I felt the weight of theirs more than any others. I wished I could turn the conversation with some clever joke, but I had waited too long and the silence was heavy now.

"We talked," I said. "That's all. They told me a little about Savat and what he wants." I looked up towards Kari, not quite meeting their eyes. "They also told me about when they were here at Reft, and a little of why they left."

Kari seemed to flinch and their eyes darted to the side. Their shoulders hunched as if they wanted to withdraw, though when they spoke their voice held the same cold rancor as it had during lunch.

"They did, did they? They told you what they did, and you're fine with that?"

I opened my mouth, unsure what I would say, but Migs filled the space before I could speak.

"What *does* Savat want?"

Caught between Kari's expression—halfway between hurt and hatred—and Migs's sudden question, my mind seemed to stutter over the memory. Kari's face held my eyes even as I turned my head to answer Migs, though I didn't quite understand what I was relating.

"Something about lifting the *nyssén* up into the light? Gathering strong *nyssa* together so we don't have to hide here anymore?" I shrugged.

"We're not hiding here," Kari said with some heat.

Chan spoke almost on top of them, "Reft is a sanctuary, not a hole. They don't *want* us out there."

"Is that all they said? That doesn't really make much sense," Migs said with confusion on their face. "It's no wonder that the Council refuses him if that's what he's promoting. Strong as we may be, there are too many of *them* out in the world." They didn't need to explain what 'them' meant. We all had some experience with those who hated us for what we were—for what we *weren't*—or for what we could do.

"It doesn't matter what they said, Arin," Kari said with a sudden quiet intensity. It was almost a whisper. "It doesn't matter what Savat wants. Eelie is a snake! You're being stupid if you think they give a damn about you. Don't fall for their act."

It was my turn to flinch. Their words stung worse than I thought possible. Whatever history stood between Kari and Eelie, whatever Kari felt about what they had done, I didn't deserve this anger and disdain. I thought that they trusted me more than that.

I turned away.

At a distant table, along the other side of the hall, I spotted a familiar face. We hadn't spent much time in each others' company since that first Circle we shared two years ago, but through a brief encounter in a hallway, or in quick chats before or after group sessions, Fanti and I had maintained our casual acquaintance.

And then there was the laundry.

My habit of seeking solitude in laundering clothes was an oddity, though my housemates appreciated the free personalized laundry service I provided them. We kept a basket by the door of items that they liked enough to want to keep out of common stores, and once a week I carried the basket down to the laundry rooms and lost myself in the process. It reminded me of a simpler time in Ma'am's house, when my world was small and included only the two dozen rooms and seventeen members of the household. When my responsibilities were counted on the fingers of one hand and getting a wine stain out of a fine linen dressing gown was my goal in life.

Fanti also preferred to do their own laundry. As far as I knew, everything they wore had been made with their own deft hands. Their skills with fabric and needle and thread were peerless, and having spent so much time and effort to tailor each item to their physique, it would be a shame to lose them to the common stores.

It wasn't every week that we saw each other over laundry, but it was often enough. We rarely spoke even so, but there was a peace and joy and camaraderie we found in the simple practice of seeing garments cleaned and folded.

Fanti smiled at me from across the room and it lit their face with joy. I couldn't help but smile back. I watched as they stood, picking their tray up and walking it towards the return shelf. They moved with a grace that I hadn't really ever noticed. The wide flowing trousers they wore—almost a skirt—accentuated every move of their hips so they seemed to dance their way to the stack of used dinner trays. I didn't notice until they were almost at our table that those hips were dancing my way.

I became aware again of the talk around me only as Heiu drew down to an uncharacteristic silence. Fanti stopped a pace away and greeted us.

"Arin. Kari," they said with a nod for each of us. Their Somiri accent lent Kari's name a subtle lilt that I hadn't appreciated before. "And friends," they said, including the others, "How has everyone passed this lovely day?"

"Hi Fanti," I said. "These are my friends Migs, Chan, and Heiu."

"Ah, hello friends," their smile took in the whole table and seemed to be meant personally for each of us in turn.

Heiu broke into the momentary silence, "Fanti, very nice to meet you. I've heard your name, I think. You make clothes? Do you take special requests? I've had my eye on something I think you made for someone else I know, but I was thinking the color isn't right for me, and maybe something a little lighter would work better, what do you think?"

Fanti grinned their beaming smile and showed only a little tightness around the eyes at this onslaught. "I do indeed make clothes, and yes, I'm happy to consult with you. I think a soft yellow would do wonders. But, you must promise me that you will never allow a garment I make for you to enter the common stores, yes? I make what I make for one person. These are not meant to fit every body."

The rest of us watched, bemused, as the two negotiated to meet at Fanti's rooms to pick out cloth and for Fanti to take Heiu's measurements. The consultation arranged, Fanti gave us each a broad smile and wished us well, departing in good spirits. I'm not sure I had ever seen Fanti less than content.

We all watched their flowing trousers dance away upon their hips and disappear from the eating hall.

"Now, there's a *nyssa* you should be pursuing, Arin," Kari said. The heat in their voice pulled my eyes to them, and the look I saw there told me that they intended to continue the argument over Eelie.

Migs brightened up at this idea, missing the tension as they were still watching the doorway as if waiting for Fanti to return. "Oh, yes. That would be grand, Arin. They're lovely!"

"Who I speak to, and who I spend time with, and who I *pursue* is none of your concern," I said. I surprised myself with my anger. I didn't understand where it came from, but the idea grated that Kari would choose to decide on my behalf who I should talk to.

"Maybe it should be our concern," Kari countered. "You clearly aren't thinking right if you choose to spend time with Eelie!"

I was standing calmly, lifting my tray, but this was like a glowing coal dropped into a kettle of heated water. My fury immediately leapt to a froth and I slammed the tray back down with such violence that my teacup jumped, spilling tepid tea over the remaining food. I caught movement all around me and saw that those at the tables nearby had all paused in their conversation to stare.

I dropped my gaze to Kari and leaned down so that I could speak quietly. Even so, there could be no mistaking the rage in my words. I bit each word out through clenched teeth.

"You are *not* me. I am *not* your ward or your child. You made *your own mistakes.* I'll make mine, thanks."

Feeling spent, I straightened and picked up my tray. I didn't want to see the looks on my friends' faces. I especially didn't want to look at Kari.

I dropped off my tray and walked out of the eating hall, realizing belatedly that storming away from the table alone was becoming a habit. So be it. Friends were supposed to support each other, not stand in the way.

Twenty

That evening, our apartment was thick with tension and a chill that seemed to spite the warm night air outside. It hung heavy in our common room, and each of us felt it. Chan and Kari and I stayed in our bedrooms in unvoiced agreement, ceding the common area as a neutral space. Migs avoided the apartment altogether, staying the night with Heiu.

Staying closed up in my bedroom, I felt the walls close and wished more than once that I had a window out into the open sky. The air felt stale and I was restless through the night. I normally sleep well, if lightly—except for the nightmares that come on me sometimes: besides the recurring dreams of my family's deaths, the endless murky memory of my days of captivity comes to me now and then like a heavy blanket drawn over my face, thick and smothering.

That night though, it was neither violence nor languid suffocation that bothered my sleep. Instead I worried over the words and fury that Kari and I had hurled at each other. I stewed over their presumption to shield me from actions they deemed foolish, and my own rising anger over their protectiveness. I considered going to them, to try to talk through the argument. In my mind, I rehearsed my position and conjectured their responses, trying to find a script that led us out of the mire we found ourselves in. But each approach I took with the Kari in my mind was foiled by one common theme: Eelie.

I was unwilling to quit their presence, unable to consider that they were the caustic danger that Kari asserted. I didn't understand why I was so enamored of them, but I could see that I was. I didn't doubt Kari's belief that they were a danger to me—wasn't the undercurrent of menace part of the attraction? They were almost three years older. They were strikingly beautiful in the way that a finely crafted sword was beautiful— elegant and gleaming and wickedly sharp—the very potential for harm was part of what drew the eye.

And they were free. It wasn't that I chafed at the guidance and tutelage of Turin and Ciala and Atua. I was learning so much in Reft, and I loved learning. But there was an undeniable romance in the idea of being able to *do* instead of only *learning to do*. The part of my mind that knew reason from romance knew that Eelie was less free in many ways—they were in service to Savat and must follow his orders for one, whereas I could study whatever I wished, at least until I formally joined the Watch. But the part of my mind that looked at clouds and saw fanciful beasts thought of the places that Eelie traveled and imagined color and passion and adventure out there under the endless sky beyond the mountains.

Hours of spiraling thought and worry alone in my bed had left me tense and irritable, and I came to no conclusions. When I finally reached sleep it was fitful and unquiet.

The following morning I had no worries of running into either housemate as I always woke first. I dressed and slipped out to my usual practice space. I fully expected Eelie to appear at my morning exercise, but I saw no sign of them. The unfulfilled expectation on top of poor sleep left me unbalanced and clumsy, too intent on watching the entry to the mountain—looking for Eelie—to focus on my own movements.

After the events at dinner, I didn't want to face my friends. I was still fuming, and didn't want to be presented with an apology from Kari, or attempts at peacemaking from Migs and Chan. I knew we would make up eventually; that Kari would accept that I knew what I was doing and could make my own choices. They needed time, and I could give them that. But today, I was reveling in my anger and it felt good to give it space.

I walked down to a different eating hall for breakfast, deliberately avoiding any of our usual spaces. My anger made for a poor mealtime companion though, and I chewed my food mechanically, feeling especially lonely at the end of a table surrounded by the oppressive noise of other people's social chatter.

Today was a free day for me, so I could avoid disappointing Ciala for one more day as I tried to figure out where I stood with Eelie. I checked in at the watch post anyway to pick up a book to read, and made my way out to the secluded bench I had shared with Eelie the previous afternoon. No one had claimed it yet today, so I curled up in the corner against the armrest and lost myself in the book.

Today, it was Artem's life's work, *The Tides of Plain and Mountain*: A catalog of famous historical battles and the stratagems employed by the generals on each side, with a deep examination of personal histories of the winners and losers. More importantly, he explored *why* each had gone the way it did. I lost myself in Artem's intricate descriptions of conflicts fought so long ago that some were waged with weapons of iron and bronze instead of steel.

As I read, I imagined the ebb and flow of the battles, letting them play out in my mind. I transposed the maneuvers to the terrain I knew, weighing an imaginary entrenchment over a flanking pincer in the moors west of the Finger, or considering the best positions to take to control the Vale.

"It haunts you, doesn't it?"

I startled, eyes darting up from my book to find Eelie standing over me. They were dressed in slim black trousers and a snug tunic—sleeveless and scooped at the neck and dyed in a rich, dark purple. The contrast between the dark rich cloth and their pale skin made their bare arms and exposed neck glow in the late morning sun. Whether by accident or by art, they were standing in the right spot to cast no shadow over me, and where the light would catch them just so.

For a moment, I couldn't speak, my mind gone blank at their stark beauty. When I regained my tongue, it was only to ask in confusion, "What?"

"What happened to your family," they said as they sat down beside me. They were so close that our hips touched. "That you couldn't save them."

I closed the book and balanced it on the armrest. I looked into their bright blue eyes. "What do you mean?" I shook my head in denial. "It wasn't my fault. I was a child."

"And yet... you spend your time practicing the sword. You learn emergency surgery and healing, and," they leaned across me to look at the book I had set down, "you bury yourself in the study of strategy and tactics." They brought their gaze back to my eyes leaning close. I could feel their breath against my cheek and the warmth of their body. "I'm not saying you could have—you're right, you were only a child. But there's something inside you that believes that if you only knew enough, if you had been just a little bit quicker, just a little bit more... ruthless... you might have saved them."

I closed my eyes and took a deep breath. I meant it for a pause, to give me time to gather my thoughts in response, but their scent filled my head and I found I couldn't think. I felt uneasy in my own mind.

"You couldn't stop the attack. You couldn't have saved them. But you still blame yourself, don't you?"

I turned away, still not opening my eyes. If I did, I was worried that the tears that were dammed up there would flow, and that I would lose all control.

"You think it's your fault they died, because they wouldn't have been there in the woods, lost and vulnerable, if it weren't for you. If you hadn't lost control of yourself."

"Please stop," I think I whispered.

Eelie put their arm over my shoulder, and it was all I could do to stay upright. I wanted nothing more than to bury my face in their chest and sob.

"Arin, it's okay. It's not your fault."

In that moment, their words took root in my mind and I believed. For the first time in the almost five years since their deaths, I could breathe and know that their deaths were not of my making. Tears came then, and I did press myself against Eelie's chest. They wrapped their arms around me, and if they spoke I had no mind to listen to the words, only the soft murmurs and rumbling echo of voice through their body. I felt warm and protected and loved. I felt safe in a way that I couldn't recognize because I may not have ever felt it before.

I don't know how long they held me like that. How long I wept. When my grief was spent, they grasped my shoulders and straightened my body, pushing me back and turning me to look me in the eyes.

"Shall we walk?" they asked.

I nodded, standing and collecting my book. I saw them glance at the book in my hand with a slight frown. I thought of leaving it behind, but they said nothing so I kept it. They put their arm protectively around my shoulders and we began a meandering walk through the garden. I paid no attention to our direction, content to let Eelie guide us.

When they spoke again, their voice was somber, "I'm sorry that no one here thought to give you such reassurance."

My heart leapt to agreement, and my mind followed. Why hadn't Turin, in all the sessions they had sat with me, never given me such a simple, clear reassurance? I felt a pain growing in my hand and realized I was gripping the book so hard that my knuckles were going white. I felt a sudden urge to throw it away from me in rage. Why had Kari and Migs and Chan never held me and given me the permission I needed to grieve my family's deaths without blaming myself?

There was a small, quiet part of my mind—it struggled to be heard under the weight of indignation welling up inside me at my friends' and counselors' failings—that tried to recall that they *had* said so, if not in so many words.

But that was precisely the point, I thought, shouting down that voice. Why had I struggled for years in pain and self-blame without any realization from the vaunted healers and counselors of Reft that I needed the plain absolution that Eelie had provided? My mind was reeling and I began to feel the same anger rising that I had felt the evening before at table with Kari.

"Don't be too hard on them, Arin," Eelie said. "It takes someone who has experienced that kind of hurt to recognize the signs and to know the toll it can take." Their arm was still wrapped around me, and they squeezed my far shoulder gently. "If they couldn't see the depths of your pain, it doesn't mean they don't care for you in their own way."

It was true, I realized. For all that they were my friends, their journeys to Reft had not involved the same loss or violence as mine. Chan had run away from their family, true, but that had been their own choice, born of abuse and a different kind of trauma. And Migs and Kari had both left theirs in relative peace. Kari even wrote to their parents now and then. How could they possibly understand what I had been through?

I leaned my head against Eelie's shoulder and decided that I should forgive my friends for not knowing what I needed.

There was an odd feeling in my mind. We were inside the mountain now, on the fourth level walking down Wind hall where the guest quarters were. It was like a hum; a vibration; a pressure that throbbed behind my eyes.

"Where are we going?" I thought to ask. It was becoming difficult to think, and it was even hard to get the words out.

"I thought we should have some privacy," Eelie said easily.

I tried to process this answer. My thoughts were thick and languid, but it made a kind of sense, I thought. I had been talking angrily about Turin's failings as a counselor, hadn't I? I tried to remember if I had said anything out loud that they or the Council might take amiss. Better to say such things in privacy, with no stray ears to hear. Something struggled to rise to the forefront of my mind, but it slipped away.

I leaned closer and placed my hand on Eelie's chest, feeling the play of firm muscle beneath their tunic as we walked. "I'm glad you found me," I mumbled. It was so easy to simply relax into their embrace.

We were in a room and Eelie was sitting me on a chair in front of a bed. They were pulling away to sit before me on the bed. I couldn't understand why they were so far away. The room swayed as I leaned to reach them.

"Fuck, you're strong," Eelie muttered, consternation on their face. They pulled a long needle from their belt and sank it into their own forearm, gasping. They pulled it out and a bright bead of blood welled up. I fixated on this. The red was beautiful against their pale skin.

I tried to think, tried to understand what I had done to upset them. Tears came once more to my eyes. "I'm sorry. I'm sorry I'm strong."

"Don't worry, Arin," they said, reassuringly. "It's okay, I'm your friend. You trust me, right? We were talking about how frustrated you were with your friends and counselors, remember? About how they didn't really understand you here in Reft?"

They leaned forward and our knees were almost touching. Their fingers were stroking my thigh and I wanted to hold those long clever fingers, to entangle them and kiss them and—

I wanted to ask them a question.

I wanted to ask them... something about freedom. I had a feeling about being trapped in Reft, and about clouds.

It kept slipping from my mind. The pressure increased and the question tried to form again. Something about Reft, and something about Savat.

There was a thought, a fragment of memory that warred with that question. It was a memory about memory. It was a fear, a nightmare. Shadowed and murky and I was gasping for breath.

Eelie was there, their gentle, possessive hands stroking my shoulders, easing me down onto their bed.

"Maybe this will be easier," they said quietly.

They were lying beside me and I could feel their body next

to mine. Our hands explored each other and a different kind of pressure filled me. It was a need, a drive that came not from my mind, not from my heart, but from my loins.

We fumbled with clothes, trying to get closer than the thickness of fabric allowed. I had their tunic off and they had my trousers down around my ankles. I could feel the air cold against my thighs. I kicked off my sandals and the clothing that tangled my legs. I tried to lean towards them, to meet their lips and lose myself in a kiss, but they pulled away. As urgently as I touched them, I could feel them hesitating, holding back—not unsure, but somehow unwilling.

They were stroking my face and stroking my belly and the question came again, struggling to rise to the forefront of thought.

I wanted to ask. It was important.

I wanted to—

I wanted.

I reached up and touched their beautiful face. The pressure increased and there was pain in my mind and I thought my head would burst.

I wanted.

My thoughts were mired in thick fog, in suffocating shadows. A question came into my mind. It was not *the question*—of clouds and oaths and freedom—but it was suddenly vitally important to me. I thought—in as much as I could think at all—that if I could ask that question I would have all the answers I needed. I concentrated, trying to ask. My tongue didn't want to move, my lips didn't want to form the words, but I forced them to, struggling and stammering.

"Y... you... l... You... love h... Love him, don't you?"

"What?" Eelie said, recoiling in shock, pulling away from me.

There was a fine single thread of clarity in the fog like a ray of sun cutting through heavy storm clouds. I still couldn't think. I couldn't remember the important memory, but I had a thread to follow.

"Savat," I said. That was the name—having said it, I could remember it. "You love Savat. He doesn't know, does he?" The thread became stronger, thicker. I was aware of awareness—I could remember memory.

The memory I had tried to recall was one of memory suppressed, of conscious thoughts drowning in the ice-cold depths of drugged sleep. It was Neme's medicine and the spinning, dizzying haze of the tea she had given me for pain. It was the herbs forced on us by Cal and his men to keep Beaty and me pliant and sedated and easy to control.

"No! I... Arin, listen to me! I'm your friend and you trust me."

My thoughts tried to slip away again as the pressure in my mind rose, blooming into a cruel pain that sparked and radiated through my mind.

Part of me tried to shy away from that pain.

But I knew what to do with pain.

I embraced it, let its forking, coruscating tendrils trace through my being like lightning as I surrendered to it. And in that torrent of roiling anguish, I thought of that single ray of sunlight breaking through the clouds of my mind, burning off the fog. My eyes snapped wide open.

Eelie grasped both sides of my face, leaning close, their eyes fixed on mine and desperate. Their face held concentration and anger and fear.

I put both hands on their chest and with the pain and power filling me, I pushed.

The force flung Eelie from the bed, crashing into the chair

and rolling to the floor.

I rolled off the bed and tried to stand. My limbs were still slow and my mind confused. My bare feet were cold on the stone floor. I was in a room—Eelie's room? I looked at them as they stood, leaning on the upended chair for support.

"What... what did you do to me?" I demanded. My hand went to my head of its own accord to try to keep the room from spinning. Could they have drugged me? When?

Eelie smiled their crooked, grim little smile and shook their head.

"Fuck, you're strong. Slow... witless... but strong as an ox."

The pressure increased behind my eyes.

No, I realized. They hadn't drugged me. I shook my head trying for clarity. Trying to dislodge their hold.

They were inside my mind.

Eelie's smile widened, turned more grim. "I didn't think this would work," they said to themself.

I bit down hard on my lip, the pain giving me a center—an awareness of reality. My hands were both holding my head now, holding me steady; pressing to keep my head from flying apart.

I thought of Kari, of what they had tried to tell me. I thought of the anger and the distance that had been rising between us since Eelie had come back. A thought sprang unbidden to my mind fully formed, and I spoke it aloud, sure of its truth even as the words came to me.

"This is what you did to Kari, isn't it? When they wanted to tell what you were planning. When they were worried about you. You weren't turned out by the Council because you were going to do your own Reshaping. They expelled you because you tried to *stop* Kari from telling."

Eelie looked stricken, their eyes going wide and their smile lost in an expression of horror. They stumbled back.

"Get," I said through clenched teeth. "Out." I rode the rising pain, pulling power from it and my voice grew stronger with each word. "Of." I thought of the hurt I had caused Kari by ignoring their warnings. "My." The anger that had been bubbling in my mind these last days, planted there like the seeds of a noxious weed by Eelie. "Head!" I loosed the power between us, a blazing firestorm that raged through my mind and theirs, burning the tendrils of connection that Eelie had entangled in our thoughts and memories.

My vision went white in the conflagration, and the last thing I saw was Eelie's head thrown back and jaw locked open in a wordless howl of pain.

Shattered fragments of awareness of the time immediately after fill my memories. I have never been able to put them into any whole coherence. When my friends told me later what they witnessed, it was only a tale told of someone else's experience. For my part, this is what I do remember:

I remember wandering the stone halls of Reft, barefoot and bare legged. I had no idea where I was or why, and the only sensation I could name was the cool air on my legs and the colder stone under my feet.

I remember Fanti's arm around me, guiding me down Branch hall. I laid my head on their chest as we walked and I felt comfort and safety. They murmured to me in a litany of reassurance and calm questions.

I remember lying down on a broad couch in a pleasant sitting room, the balcony open to a northern view over the Vale. There was a soft blanket covering me, and unfamiliar decorations filled the room with color. Elegant vases of cut flowers in a riot of golds and pinks and fabrics in a multitude of shades and textures draped over every surface.

I remember the voices of people that I loved around me, discussing softly whether to seek help. I remember looking into Kari's eyes as they held my hand and apologizing for every wrong thing I had said to them. I remember begging them not to tell anyone else, or to go for help. I remember reassuring them all that I would be okay with some rest.

I remember a plate of food and Kari's gentle hand feeding me small morsels of cold chicken dipped in mustard. I remember a sip of wine, and thinking that more than anything I needed sleep.

When I woke I was feeling much better, more myself. I could see the sky darkening to sunset through the open panel to the balcony. Fanti was sitting in a chair nearby and saw me stir.

"Arin, you're awake. How do you feel?"

I moved to sit up and the world teetered. I ignored it and straightened, cradling my head in my hands. I tried to find an answer to the question. How did I feel? I felt whole, except for the pain in my head. I could think, and I could remember everything that happened up to expelling Eelie from my mind.

My face grew hot as I remembered the feelings they had stirred in me. I wanted to hate them. I wanted to denounce them for violating my mind. But even so, there was a small, cold, crystal clear sense deep within me that as much as they had manipulated my feelings and emotions, they couldn't have manufactured attraction that wasn't there.

I had ejected their presence from my mind; broken their hold and burned them out. In the stark light of that cleansing fire, I could see my thoughts and memories for what they were.

I could distinguish the feelings Eelie had forced on me from those that I felt of my self. Those that I still felt.

Those feelings burned in me shamefully even now. Kari had been right, Eelie had something rotten at their core. But there was something simple and real and sharp that I could not deny: I had desperately, genuinely wanted their touch on my body and wanted to touch them. That feeling was not one that they had forced on me. I had felt it from the very moment I laid eyes on them years ago, though I hadn't been able to name it then. Despite everything, I could still feel the memory of that lust.

And they had pulled away. Whether sex was a line they were unwilling to cross while they pulled my strings, or whether they held themselves back for some other reason—or some other person—they had held that line. I could thank them for that much at least.

"I'm okay," I said, and saying it, I felt it more truth than I would have guessed.

There was another thing I could thank Eelie for. As much as their words had been advancing whatever game it was they were playing with me, I couldn't deny the truth in them. I *was* blaming myself for the deaths of my family. I *was* unconsciously trying to make of myself a person who could not only survive such an assault, but respond to violence and hate with skill and... ruthlessness, was it? I would never again be a victim, but more: I would defeat any such assault, saving those I loved from whatever harm. I was no longer that scared little child.

Kari returned some time later, and brought the news that Savat and his retinue—including Eelie—were leaving in the morning. That Eelie was alive and hale was no real surprise to me. That they would risk making a Bridge in only a few hours was. I still felt unsteady on my feet, and the thought of any use of power at this point made my stomach clench unpleasantly.

"Kari, I..." I faltered, trying and failing to find the words.

Kari shook their head and sat next to me, not too close. They lifted their hand tentatively, as if they wanted to touch me, but hesitated, looking me in the eyes.

"Arin, I'm sorry. I should have told you what they are. What they did."

I took their hand and held it between mine. "I should have let you."

Twenty One

I knocked on the door to Turin's rooms, and at their call I pushed it open and entered. Turin gestured me inside with a warm smile. "Arin, good to see you. How are you faring since last we spoke?"

"I am well," I said, smiling.

It was now more than five years since I had come to Reft, and little had changed in Turin or their chambers. Their calm, peaceful eyes were the same, and their reassuringly cluttered office was still the place of reflection and healing I remembered, even if the chair I moved to sit on had been re-stuffed and reupholstered.

"I've been assigned a new training cohort, and they're properly impressed with me," I laughed. "Little they know how long it took me to learn to read." Turin smiled with me.

We were now meeting only once a month, with the bulk of my days filled by my training and duties in the Watch.

If little had changed in Turin, I had certainly grown. I had reached my adult height, and now our eyes met at the same level. My body had strengthened and my shoulders and limbs were well muscled by sessions practicing sword and long runs through the halls and stairs of the mountain and across the Vale. I was as comfortable in my own skin as I felt I could be, at least before my upcoming Reshaping.

Over the next half hour, they laughed in all the right places as I told them of my difficulties in teaching a gaggle of youngsters how to move with precision, the basics of strategy, and the rudiments of healing.

"I never thought that I would *teach*," I said wonderingly as I finished catching them up on my activities of the last month.

"Did you not? We knew you had it in you." Their smile turned wistful, "I have known your potential since the day you walked into the reception room on the slopes of the mountain."

"I thought I was happy and at peace then. I thought I wanted nothing more than to travel the wilds with Sem forever. I had no thought for what I might become, to what purpose my life could bend." I sat with this for a while.

Turin sat with me, saying nothing.

"It has taken a long time to find enough peace with myself to be of use to others," I said quietly.

"And have you? Found enough?"

I worked this over. I still had nightmares now and again of waking up in the dark, rotting fort, surrounded by Cal and his men. I still saw my family's death in my mind, and not only when I called upon the memory.

Turin seemed to pick up on my thoughts. "Nightmares?"

I shook my head, denying their weight and power. "Only sometimes. They're not so bad anymore."

"What you endured, Arin, is more than anyone should ever

have to. That you came out of that whole and able to function, is a testament to your strength and resilience. That it causes you ongoing pain, or that you struggle sometimes to move past it means nothing more than that you are human."

I shrank back into my chair slightly. I still had trouble accepting kind words. Turin didn't press it.

"You hold something in your mind now. Would you like to talk it through?"

I hesitated, but Turin was easy with long silence, and waited until I spoke. "I've been thinking more about my family lately. Not their deaths, but the time we had before. The time when I was young and the worst thing I had to worry me was a day of hoeing the garden patch." I glanced at Turin and saw them nod. I continued, "I've been thinking of Ranji. Of what he would have been, and if he would be proud of me now."

"Do you have cause to worry that he wouldn't?"

"Nooo..." I stretched it out, thinking. "Only, I'm trying to do right by him, by his memory."

Turin let me sit in silence for a moment before prompting, "Have you visited these memories?"

"I have," I admitted. "At first, I went seeking... comfort, maybe. Now, I worry that my path is too settled, that I have found peace and they have not."

"You think you do not deserve peace?"

I shrugged. "Didn't he?"

"The philosopher Mallier wrote that any peace found while living was flawed, for we can never escape the worry over what will come, and the loss of what has passed; but that a flawed peace is peace still. Perhaps Ranji has found a more complete peace than you." They shifted in their seat, leaning towards me. "What turns your mind to your brother now, after so many years? You did not carry these worries at our last session."

I grimaced. The reason was clear to me, but I also felt foolish about it. "One of the new training class. Their name... is Ranji."

Turin sat back again, nodding slowly. "It can be difficult, faced with a living memory without choosing to be."

"They... they're the same age as he was..." I shook my head. "I shouldn't let it affect me like this. It's not an uncommon name among Freelanders. It's only chance that I haven't met another until now."

"Why shouldn't you let it affect you? Does it diminish his memory to recognize the pain of his loss? Does it diminish your love or your loss to admit it to yourself? Surely by now you have understood that the pain we feel is as much a part of ourselves as our hearts and minds. Would you disdain your right to either of those?"

"No," I said softly. As usual, Turin was able to frame my intractable knot of feelings in a way that made the answer obvious.

"If it helps you, I can say that *I* could not be more proud of what you have done here. In some ways, you came to us broken down and hollowed out by the events you experienced. I know Sem had their part in your salvation. I like to think that I played a role as well. But there are many paths you might have taken even here."

Turin looked down for a moment meditatively. "Some before you have fallen into despair and contempt at our ways. You have flourished here at Reft. You made your oaths first as a child, and have renewed them each year since, and more: You have embodied them. It has been a privilege to work with you, to watch you grow into your power and take your place among us."

By mutual silent accord, this felt like the right note to end on, and I smiled my thanks and stood. Turin led me out of their rooms and we parted with a promise to meet again in one month.

I made my way to the eating hall to meet my friends for lunch. Our circle had expanded in the intervening years, but the four of us were still close. Some closer than we had been.

As I entered, I spotted them at the end of the far table. Kari, Migs, and Chan. With Heiu, who sat hip-to-hip with Migs, and the addition of Brenin who seemed to occupy the same space as Chan, our circle had expanded indeed.

And then there was Fanti, who looked up at me from beside Kari and smiled their dazzling smile, their face lighting like the dawn breaking over the mountains. I returned their smile and sat down next to them, our hips touching. I leaned my head against Fanti's shoulder.

Kari leaned forward to look at me, "You're not eating?"

I smiled and shook my head, "I'll grab something on my way out. I can't stay long, but I wanted to drop in and see everyone."

Kari sighed, "All business, Arin. You need to slow down, unwind… the mountain won't crumble if you take a break and relax now and again."

I relaxed for a few minutes, taking in the energy around me and Fanti's comforting warmth. I closed my eyes and let the voices wash over me, simply enjoying the sounds of banter, the smells of good food, and the little movements of Fanti's body beside mine.

Fanti gave me a kiss as I moved to stand, and so I lingered a moment to finish it properly. Then I stood and moved around their back, trailing my fingers over their shoulder to stand behind Kari, who bent their head back to look up at me, smiling. I bent down and met their lips upside-down.

"Tonight," I whispered. "Tonight you can unwind me."

Even as quietly as I had said it, this was still met by our friends with whoops and cheers that made me blush.

"Kari and I will hold you to that," Fanti said from beside me, their hand resting on the small of my back.

I smiled at them and disengaged, heading to the serving shelf to pick up a mushroom-filled pastry to take away for lunch. I had to finish planning for the afternoon's exercises with my training group, but I couldn't help smiling as I walked.

I emerged from the spiral stairs into the shelter of the watch tower, moving to the opening that faced north. Behind me my trainees came up, blinking in the afternoon sun. Froley stepped out first, followed by Berin, and Ranji brought up the rear.

As they assembled, I turned my back to the view of the Vale and looked them over, resting my hand on the short sword at my belt. All three were of an age, though their stories and journeys to Reft were very different.

Froley and Berin both had the pale coloring common to Torfall. The former had arrived the year before, escorted to Reft by members of the Watch in a chain of handoffs from Quarry East where they had run away from home.

Berin's experience was different in nearly every way. He was a boy for starters, not *nyssa*; the oldest son of five *nyssén* parents who were among the second wave to come to Reft twenty-some years ago—they lived in the Vale and worked one of the collective farms there with their four children. He had lived his whole life in Reft, and had been dreaming of joining the Watch since he learned it was something he could aspire to.

Ranji was the smallest in body, yet I had learned over the last few weeks that they were the boldest of the three. Like their name, they were Freelander to their bones, and for all that they had grown up on a farm outside of Oakroot instead of Meers, it was a constant struggle for me to remember that I did not know the whole of their experience. They looked like my brother in so many ways that it became easy to overlook the differences if I let myself.

I shook my head and focused on the task at hand. "Welcome to your first watch. The first thing to know is that standing watch is *boring*."

They all laughed with me.

"Nothing will happen, and nothing will happen, and nothing will happen for so long and so often that if something does finally happen, you may not even notice. The main enemy you will face on any watch is boredom. You fight this enemy by moving, by looking around, and by engaging with your surroundings." I smiled encouragingly. "So, look around. Tell me what you see."

The three each wandered to one of the great views, taking in the vista.

"Everything," Froley said. "It's like I can see everything."

Berin was gazing down into the Vale beside me. "I can see my fam's house from here, but I can see over the mountains too. It's amazing. We can see forever."

I looked to Ranji, walking slowly around the perimeter and taking in the views thoughtfully.

"And you Ranji? What do you see?"

Ranji paused at the eastern view, leaning out over the ledge to peer down, before speaking. "I don't know. We can see a lot that we could not from down there. But... There's also a lot that we cannot see from here."

I nodded, smiling. "Good. It's an important point: No matter what you can see from a given vantage, every view has its blind spots. Froley, what *can't* you see to the west?"

They walked to the western overlook and peered out into the distance. A few moments later, they said thoughtfully, "We can't see the Red River or the valley it runs through." They looked southwest towards a distant peak glinting in the distance. "I can see Redwatch, I think, but not the valley below it."

"So, suppose we need to know what's happening out there?"

Berin spoke up, "We could post sentries in Redwatch."

"Certainly," I said, "that would be well. But suppose we didn't hold Redwatch? Suppose it was taken and enemies were massing a force somewhere in the Red River valley? Where should we observe from? Think back to what Sandiéne said in his treatise that we read on terrain and movements..."

The three of them thought this through. Froley closed their eyes for a moment, then turned back west to scan the horizon.

"There," they said, pointing to a peak just south of due-west.

"Why that vantage, Froley?"

"Because, it's one of the highest mountains in the range, besides Reft. And because it's well north of Redwatch, but has a good view of the river and the valleys." They smiled proudly, but then frowned a moment later, "If I remember rightly..."

"Well done," I smiled. "Not only for a good answer, but for admitting the limits of your knowledge. Anyone else have any thoughts?"

Ranji spoke up, "I think... I think Froley is right. That *is* the best spot to watch them from..."

"But?" I could see they had the answer.

"But they'd know that too, right? So they would have an

outpost on that mountain already."

I smiled, "They may well. If they did, where else might we observe from? Remember that there are things Reft can do that they cannot."

Ranji screwed up their face, thinking, "There's foothills on the western side of the Red River in Somiere. We don't need to be as high as they, because we can communicate with Reft directly by Pairing—we don't need line-of-sight to send signals."

Froley jumped in, "For that matter, we could put some agents in their camps."

"Good. All of those are very good options. Now, which would you choose? Berin?" He had gone silent and I could see him withdraw slightly at the reminder that while he was *of* Reft, he had limitations that we did not.

"All of them," he said simply.

"Why?"

"Spies sent into the enemy camps could be caught, or might be too close to see the whole picture, so having others in the western foothills will give a broader vantage... fewer blind spots."

I nodded encouragingly.

He continued, "and if we didn't even *try* to watch from that mountain, they might wonder why. That might make them more careful of spies in their midst, or lead them to worry about the west."

I smiled again. "Very good, Berin. Well done."

I turned now to face north. "Now, a new problem. Suppose we get word of raiders in the Vale? What do we do?"

They came to stand beside me, looking out over the farms below. The Vale was so broad that it was easy to think of it as a valley, though in reality it was a lush expanse at the floor of a massive ravine. The distant sheer cliffs made formidable walls for miles around.

Ranji spoke first, "How would they get in? The only way in or out of the Vale is through the mountain."

"That's not actually true," Berin said slowly, "There *are* passes up to the heights from below. They're just very difficult, and hard to find from above. But we've had goats and sheep try those trails. I've been up one or two myself. A small group could find their way down..."

"Another vital point to remember," I said, smiling. "No matter what you think you know of a place, there's *always* someone who knows it better. Personal knowledge is vital. Even if you have good maps of the terrain, nothing can replace your own personal experiences of it.

"So, back to the question, raiders in the Vale: What do you do about it?"

"We could sound the alarm, call everyone into Reft..." offered Froley.

"Send the watch out to confront them?" Ranji said.

"How many are there?" I asked. "How are they armed? What are they after? Have they gone to ground or are they moving through the Vale?" With each question, I could see their eyes widen, starting to understand the scope of the problem. "If you act without information, your actions are likely to be the wrong ones."

They thought about this for a moment, but Froley pressed, "But sounding the alarm?"

"And what if their goal is to invade Reft? By sounding the alarm, you will have shown them the ways in *and* provided chaos and confusion to cover their entry." I saw them digest this. "The problem I've given you is large and complex. The questions I asked a moment ago need to be answered, yes?"

"We can send scouts into the Vale, try to spot them," said

Ranji tentatively.

"Ok," I said. "Who will you send? Organized how?"

Berin spoke, "The farmers know the Vale best. We should send members of the watch, not to do the scouting, but to organize scouting parties from among those who live there."

"Good! Remember that we of the Watch are not an army or a militia. We are too few to do all of what is needed. Our role in a situation like this is to lead, and to rely on the skills and knowledge of our fellows." I looked from Ranji to Berin to Froley, checking their faces for understanding. Froley's eyes seemed to be caught by something to the east. They gazed off distractedly. I was about to speak when they called out.

"Arin, look," they pointed.

I turned, no faster than the others. Looking down the eastern slope, there was a disturbance in the air just above the trail.

The air shimmered and coruscated, thickening from one breath to the next into an archway, a view from the slopes of Reft to another land—dark stone along a violent seashore. It was a scene that was deeply familiar to me, and I could feel my shoulders tense and the short hairs on my scalp stand on end. My voice was calm despite the churning in my gut.

"Froley, good job spotting it. Ring the watch bell, please."

My eyes were locked on that doorway. I knew what I was about to see, and I couldn't turn away. I heard the sharp sonorous clanging of a wooden mallet against the walls of the long bronze tube which hung just over the stairs. The sound filled the tower, but the bell was situated so that most of its call echoed down the shaft into the mountain.

The stoneworkers had done their work well in shaping the halls and shafts to carry sound. Before the third strike of the bell, the door below us was opened and there were two armed *nyssén* standing below, waiting. By the fourth ring, three guardsmen were coming through the Bridge dressed in black with Tamar Savat's orange and purple colors.

"Well done, Froley. You can stop now." The bell rang once more and the tone carried on, diminishing gradually, but still reverberating in my bones.

"Who are they?" Ranji asked from beside me. Berin was at my other side, and Froley promptly left the bell to stand beside him.

Savat himself emerged, followed by two more guardsmen. He paused just over the threshold, looking back over his shoulder, and then continued. And finally, the face I knew that I would see.

Eelie stepped through, hand-in-hand with another that I didn't recognize, though they both wore identical livery. Even from above, I could see tension and concentration on both their faces, but nothing like the extremes of agony Eelie had inflicted on themself the last time I had seen them make a Bridge. They must be drawing power from this new companion, I thought. Savat had recruited another *nyssa*.

As the two stepped over that uncanny threshold, it vanished, taking arch and light and the distant seashore with it into nothingness. They relaxed visibly as the Bridge disappeared.

I took three deep breaths, trying to calm myself. Then I remembered that my trainees were beside me. Ranji was still waiting for an answer.

"Visitors," I said. "They are visitors from Fall." My mind was still on what I had seen below, and I felt like I couldn't think clearly. I watched Savat, Eelie, and the newcomer disappear into the welcome building with the pair of Watch members. Savat's guardsmen dispersed to the stables as if well-practiced, but one of them lifted a brass-bound chest from panniers on the back of one of the horses and followed with it into the building behind Eelie, seeming hesitant.

I took another breath and shook myself free of my worries. They had come. I would find out why in time, or I wouldn't. There was little I could accomplish now by fretting. I turned to the three youths and their expectant faces. That final note of the bell finally faded.

I could sense that they had more questions about what they had seen, and about these visitors. I didn't feel up to talking about it, but I had questions too. What brought him this time? Some politics, certainly. Kari was sure to learn something in their clerkship.

"So. You have caught me out, it seems. Exciting things *can* happen on watch after all." I grinned, and they laughed with me. "I promise you it won't often be so."

I turned back to the northern view. "Ok. So, we have raiders in the Vale. We've organized scouting parties to search for the intruders. What else?"

The three trainees looked to each other for a moment, clearly disappointed that I was not telling them more about the visitors. Finally, Froley spoke, "We... need to close the entry points into the mountain. We don't want them slipping past the scouting parties."

Berin and Ranji spoke almost on top of each other.

"We should draw back the families into defensive clusters..."

"...we should try to identify the path the raiders used..."

Twenty Two

I woke with my face pressed against Fanti's shoulder. The room was dark and might have had the chill of early morning, but for our three bodies tight together. I could feel Kari's weight on my back, and their arm encircling my waist to rest on Fanti's thigh. By their breathing, I could tell both were still asleep.

There was a wetness under my cheek, and I realized with embarrassment that I had drooled a little as I slept. I shifted slightly, kissing their shoulder and neck. I wanted more than anything to stretch out. My muscles were tightening in the cool air, and I didn't want to waste the relaxation I had found in the long activities of the night.

Whether by my movements or in some dream, Kari rolled over and I was free. I slowly crept out of bed, careful to not disturb them. I stood for a few minutes looking at the two of them and I smiled.

They were wonderful even as a couple, and the feelings I felt when I saw them share a kiss or touch each other with love and heat were thrilling and comforting. There was no room for jealousy for I was filled with love for both. When I was with either alone, I was in awe of them.

Kari's brilliance and compassion and joy in life. Their soft body and softer lips. The care and dedication they applied to every task and every relationship, and their ability to bring those strengths to bear in support of those they loved.

Fanti's calm confidence and skilled hands, their warm nature and firm strength. I knew in the very center of my being that I was safe in their hands—more, that I was cherished in their hands.

And when we three were together... There was no one and nothing else in the world in those moments. Time spun out into forever in a reeling spiral of joy and pleasure and peace.

The door into the living space of our shared apartment was ajar, and I could see the earliest hints of sunrise lightening the balcony. I didn't want to leave the comfort of the room, but I had to get ready for my morning shift. I walked down the dark hall to the shared bathing chamber. My bare skin pebbled in the cool air, but once inside I felt the damp warmth of the narrow room.

Back in my room, I saw Fanti and Kari were still asleep and I smiled involuntarily at their intertwined bodies. I turned to the wardrobe at the far end of the room to dress. Beside it I caught sight of myself in the mirror, and paused.

I traced the lines of my body with my eyes. From my feet planted surely in the woolen carpet up the taut muscles of my calves and thighs to my hips, I was proud and confident in the shape I had taken.

I was taller than when I had left Anbress with Sem, and that height had come with a sturdiness that spoke to my Freelander heritage. My hips were still wider than my shoulders, but my shoulders were strong and I held myself with a straight back, despite the curving breasts that felt so out of place to my mind. They were not so large, Kari would say; but large enough. Even though after long training I had given over the slouching stance that I had taken to in an unconscious attempt to hide their growth, I still cringed at the protuberances; they felt like something foreign had grown from my body, extending beyond the envelope of *self* that my mind constantly reported was *me* with every movement.

For the ten-thousandth time, I looked in the mirror at my chest and imagined what it would feel like to have there the flat muscular planes that my mind told me belonged instead of these soft curving mounds that seemed to quiver with every breath.

Soon.

I pulled my gaze away and looked my own face over. The frown I wore faded as I let myself move past the discordancy of my body and take myself in. Short fuzz of dark brown hair, pale skin with a tinge of olive, the long scar that had faded to a thin ridge of slightly darker skin, and eyes that were picking up hints of bright blue in the morning light.

I watched my lips quirk into a little smile as I remembered Fanti tracing my scar with their fingers while they kissed me.

"Why can't you stay in bed?" came a voice from behind me, still full of sleep.

I shifted my gaze over my shoulder through the mirror to see Kari stirring in bed, struggling to sit up.

"I have a Council chambers shift this morning, remember? Can't be late."

That seemed to bring Kari fully awake and upright. They sat for a long moment looking at me.

I pulled my clothes from the wardrobe and began to dress. The wide gray trousers in a multitude of pleats flowed as I moved. Over these I pulled a skin-tight brocade tunic in deep blue that Fanti had crafted for me. The color they had chosen to bring out the blue in my eyes, and the weave was enhanced with their skill and a little bit of power to hold my chest tight and flatten the breasts that I hated to feel when I moved. The pressure against my chest was just enough to be noticeable, but not enough to constrain. I felt like I carried their loving hug around throughout the day.

"I can tell you what is discussed, you know. You don't need to be there."

Finished dressing, I lifted my sword belt and short sword, turning to face them. "You *do* know that I don't have any thoughts for *them*, don't you? You said it yourself. Their heart is... ugly."

Kari looked down, their hands clenched in their lap. "I don't trust them. Either of them. You know that. He... there has always been something off about him. Why he comes here, and what he wants of us. I know the Council thinks so too. They just can't afford to offend or refuse him."

I smiled at them. "All the more reason for me to be there, watching." I weighed the sword in my hands, debating whether to wear it. Finally, I slipped the sword from the belt and placed it back in the wardrobe, leaning it beside the wooden sword Sem had made for me so many years ago.

I looked down at Fanti, shaking my head ruefully as I buckled the belt on. The mountain could be crumbling, falling down upon us and the very earth breaking open to swallow us, and Fanti would still not rise before the sun was fully up. They had rolled over on their back and the muscular planes of their naked chest—adorned as usual with the small bronze pendant necklace they could not be separated from—filled me with yearning. I wanted desperately to climb back into bed and rest my head on their chest.

"I'll be fine. And I'll be back, never fear." I nodded to Fanti as I slipped on my sandals and moved to the door smiling. "Ravish them for me, will you?"

"Thank you for seeing me," Tamar Savat said, making a little gesture of a bow towards the elder *nyssén* sitting about the chamber.

Despite the seriousness implicit in a full meeting of the Council of Reft, such meetings were rarely formal. Today, the seven members were arrayed on various comfortable chairs and couches around a room layered in rich carpets and upholstered furniture. The far wall opened out by a system of sliding panels to reveal a broad garden balcony overlooking the Vale. The western horizon was darkened by the iron-gray clouds of a fast-moving storm. The panels would need to be closed soon.

"The least we can do for such generosity is grant an audience, your lordship," Atua said. Even from my post by the door I could sense the kind, respectful words were undercut by a tone of cautious distrust. If Savat noticed, he had the grace to ignore it.

"Please, do not mention it," he said with a dismissive gesture. "It is nothing compared to what I ask your assistance in."

"And what would that be?" asked Deme, their imposing form folded into a great wingback chair against the wall.

"I would like to know as well," said Turin from the couch they shared with Filla. Their eyes were on the brass-bound chest that lay on the low table in the center of the room. "It has been long since you graced our mountain with your presence, and now you come bearing gifts that would make a Duke blush."

I glanced around the room again, briefly taking in Eelie who stood to the other side of the door. If they noticed me they didn't show it. Their eyes were locked on their lord.

"It is a simple matter, my friends. And yet, of the utmost importance to me personally. It is a question of justice."

"Justice," Atua said, as if tasting the word. "It is no small thing to ask, and no small thing to grant. Many who would seek justice find that they have no stomach for it. Some who receive justice find they have cause to regret it. And one who would mete it out may yet feel its sting."

Savat bowed formally to them. "I am ever appreciative of your wisdom. And yet, I have a deep need for justice in this instance. Items of great importance to me—and little enough value to anyone else—were stolen from my estates in eastern Fall. I would have them back, even to the cost of beggaring myself."

Savat took a half step forward. "A collection of heirlooms of my mother's line. They are... precious to me. I ask the Council to conduct a Finding that I may locate the thief and track down these items."

Filla tilted their head and spoke, "A Finding. And yet, have you not followers of your own capable of such a feat?" their mouth quirked into something between a smile and a grimace as they glanced at Eelie. "Why have you not made use of *their* talents to find your thief?"

Again, Savat seemed to ignore the slight, though I thought I noticed Eelie tense and straighten. "Indeed, we did try," Savat said quietly. "At first we tried to find the items—I cared not for the thief. But it seems that by the time I had received word of the theft, they had been scattered or sold. That or my...followers...were not strong enough to locate them.

"Then, we tried to find the thief himself—one of my guardsmen, who I brought with me here, saw the man fleeing." Savat shook his head sadly. "But it seems the contact was too brief, or we could not bring enough power to reveal him. Eelie tells me that it will take a great Circle to find him."

Savat looked from one face to the next. "I do not ask for Reft to mete out justice on my behalf. My own people can capture this thief and track down the items he took, if they could find him. I ask only for the Finding."

The seven Council members looked to each other then. If they deliberated their decision there was nothing voiced between them. Watching from my position, it seemed to me that there was little they could do but come to the decision that Savat wanted. It was clear that they were reluctant to openly refuse him.

I was expecting Atua to speak first, so I was surprised to hear Deme's deep voice announce the decision, "Bring your man. We will conduct your Finding." Savat turned to nod once to Eelie who ducked out of the doorway without a glance spared for me or the room. Deme focused on me for a moment, "Arin, you will join us please. Your strength will be welcome."

As I stepped forward, Savat glanced at me and smiled—the first acknowledgment he had given me. I nodded, unsure how to respond in this setting, and unsure how I wanted to respond. I still remembered Eelie's words and deeds on their last visit to Reft and the memory made me queasy and drew the muscles between my shoulders into a tight knot. There was a brief flash of distant lightning from the horizon.

The others were standing and beginning to move towards the balcony. It appeared we would do our work here. Atua peered to the west as we assembled and seemed to speak my thoughts, though I don't think they intended for anyone to hear. "We will have a clock counting down on our labors. The storm comes."

Eelie returned with the guardsman who I had seen carry the chest into the mountain. He followed them, eyes wide and tense, clearly uncomfortable around so many of us. He was young, enough that his pale face was unlined with age or sun or worry. A mop of fine black hair stood askew from his head as if he spent a great deal of time running his fingers through it. One hand hovered near his hip where a sword hilt might hang, though he was unarmed.

I watched his eyes dance from his lord to the assembled Council members warily. His gaze darted to me, catching my empty sword-belt and my practiced stance as something famil- iar. When he took in the fine scars on my arms and the bold scar running down my face, he flinched and shied away as if struck. He kept his eyes to the floor after that.

We formed a circle. Though it was strictly unnecessary—we could easily have done the feat from where we were in the room—there is sometimes a comfort in ceremony and formal- ity. Eelie brought the guardsman to stand in the center, and then took a position across from me. Savat remained just in- side the room, leaning against the opening to the balcony.

Deme spoke to the guard, "Take your thoughts to the night this thief fled your master's estate. Tell us what you saw."

The guard looked to Savat, who nodded encouragingly, and then down to the floor again. He began to speak in a small, halting voice. "It was night, your... ah... um..., it was night— some three weeks gone. We had pulled in the patrols—it was a storm, a bad one from over the sea—and well, nothing ever happens on watches—" He gulped, wide-eyed and glanced up to his lord again, suddenly wary of what he had said.

Savat smiled gently and nodded. "Go on Jaem, we've discussed this. There is no blame here for you or the house guards, and you will not face any judgment on it. Simply tell them your memories."

Jaem nodded and swallowed. His eyes returned to the stone at his feet before he continued. "It was quiet but for the storm, and we was in the barracks—by the stables? We had a fire going to hold the chill back, and we were taking it in turns every few hours to walk the house—inside, you see? The housemaster hated for us to go 'tromping through' as he said, and only let us in one at a time."

I heard Atua speak softly under the guard's narration. "Embrace the pain."

I was well practiced at this by now, and it was second nature to visit those dreadful moments in my mind that I knew would never leave me.

Father's face covered in blood. Cal standing over him drawing the knife. Ranji leaping to his feet and the look of shock in his eyes as a feathered arrow appeared in his chest.

"I was coming to the end of my rounds, just past the library, and I saw a light in there. I knew wasn't nobody should be in there. The light was just a flicker, like a candle..."

The life leaving those eyes just as Father's lifeblood left his body—the one fading to darkness and the other fountaining in violence.

"I crept to the door and peeped in, and there was someone moving around along the bookshelves, and then I'd noticed one of the great windows that open out to the gardens was unshuttered and open. The rain was blowing in on the carpets, like. That's when I saw that it wasn't no maid or servant being nosy."

Father flailed helplessly at his throat while Ranji crumpled to the ground.

The pain of their deaths filled me and I felt it stream away into the Circle. I heard soft gasps from the others as my power joined theirs and felt their collective pain wash back upon me—greater, but not overwhelming. I had grown much in my power over the years, and it was a shock to realize that I was the strongest in this Circle...by some measure, aside from Eelie.

Our memories flooded together then, and I was Turin. Deme was me. There was neither me nor them, we were all one. The memories were a little easier to distinguish from my own than the first time I had joined a Circle, but it took a level of concentration that I didn't care to exert.

"...it was a man, all crouched and dressed in dark, dirty clothes. I opened my mouth to shout, to raise the alarm and I rushed in..."

I was Atua and Gesh and Purun. I could feel aches in my bones and arthritic joints and the little daily fears that my body was failing me. I remembered the sensations of birthing a child and the manifold grief of the deaths of loved ones I had never actually known.

"...he turned and had a tiny lantern in one hand and a sack in the other..."

And I was Eelie. The shock of it was almost enough to make me sever my link, but I held fast. It felt like I had run headlong down a grassy hill in the bright sunlight and stumbled into a dark, tangled wood that wasn't there until I tripped over the roots. Their mind was close, claustrophobic; overgrown with tangling vines and briar and odium. As far into that wood as I could peer, there was only more tangle. With each breath I was nearly overcome with an impression of seething hostility.

"...he dropped the lantern and drew a knife. But I had my

sword and I weren't worried, but I shouted... well, I cussed him 'cause of... he dropped the lantern on that fine carpet..."

I steeled myself against the pressure of Eelie's mind and tried to focus past the dense animosity they were projecting. It seemed... yes... within that horrid tangle of creeper and unwelcome, almost within sight, there was... a wall. I wondered what lay behind it.

"...and then the lightning flashed outside, and I got a good look at him..."

In that moment I felt Atua seize the power that streamed through the Circle and direct it in a flood into the guard's memory, and I could see the scene in the library. Even while the storm raged and rain sheeted outside the window, every detail inside the room was frozen perfectly in time and we were all there, standing in our circle, with the guard and the thief in the center, never mind that the thief stood against the bookshelves and the guard by the door.

The rich woodwork around us was filled to bursting with books whose bindings were tooled in leather and gilt—I could read each and every title. Here and there between the books was a small chest or a dazzling geode or a small sculpture in bronze or marble. I could picture each perfectly and count the myriad crystals that twinkled within the geode in the lightning flash.

The thick, lush carpet was woven of the finest wool and dyed in rich shades that looked especially dramatic in the stark lighting. I thought I could identify every whorl and scroll of its weaving. The lantern lay on its side at the thief's feet and a flame was just catching on the pool of spilled oil, no larger than my palm. That flame was reflected hundreds of times over in each pane of intricately cut glass in each frame of each window along the windward side of the room.

The window that the thief had forced was open front and back—its storm shutter that would have protected the delicate glass from the elements was blowing back and forth, rattling in the fierce wind—and its panes caught both the purple flash of lightning from the storm and the orange spark of fire from within.

The thief was perfectly illuminated, dressed in filthy threadbare clothes, stained or dyed dark, it was impossible to tell. His scuffed boots left muddy marks along the rich carpet. He had dark greasy hair and a rough scrabbly growth of beard from days gone without shaving.

But his face was clear. It is a face I can never forget—how could I? I see it every time I remember my family. I see that face in every nightmare of my past and every time I draw on my power. It is as familiar to me as my own.

With a sudden certainty I knew I had to lock away my recognition, and I knew how to do it. I had learned it from Eelie.

I siphoned off the slightest trickle of power from the flood that carried me. I wound that around my memory and willed it to grow into a bramble of thought. A dense tangle that could hide what I had realized. That part of my mind was no longer available to the Circle, and I hoped no-one had noticed.

Thunder crashed around me and I couldn't tell if it was in the storm of the memory or the one descending upon us on the balcony. Atua wove the power from our Circle into the thief, through his body and around his limbs, tying his being to ours, tying an unbreakable thread of Finding to him, and awareness bloomed in our minds.

"...an' he ran out and I yelled, 'Stop! You can't get away! We'll find you!...'"

Atua released the flood of power, and I could feel minds

disengaging from the Circle. I could feel relief in everyone around me. I could also feel the tension in my shoulders and back redouble. I had walled the memory off from everyone else, encapsulated it under a veil of scar tissue like a cyst. For a moment longer, I could pretend I had hidden it from myself as well. I wasn't sure if I was breathing.

I knew he was alive and I knew exactly where he was.

Around me, I could sense that the gathering was breaking up and moving back into the chamber. Though it was still late morning, the storm clouds brought a darkness and I could hear the patter of raindrops not far away. It was blowing a sharp chill ahead of it.

We entered the room and Gesh and Turin were closing shutter panels behind us. I thought of the library room with its carpet stained with rain and lamp oil and muddy boots.

I saw Savat and Eelie with their heads together. He said something, and Eelie nodded and smiled. Then he turned back to the Council.

"Thank you for your aid. You have done what I asked, and I have accomplished what I came here to do. By your leave, we will remain in Reft until the storm passes. With any luck, what we have done here today will bring some justice."

With a few more words exchanged, the three of them left, Savat and Eelie to their guest rooms, and Jaem back out to the stables, I was sure, thrilled to distance himself from so many witches, even if it meant cold and wet.

"Arin, are you okay?" Turin asked from behind me.

"I'm fine," I said numbly, "If you don't mind, I will return to my rooms, I have a bit of a headache." My mind churned with tension and possibility, so that I had no need to pretend. I nodded to the rest of the Council and left just as the fury of the storm began to rattle the shutters.

Alone in the hallway, I allowed that cyst in my mind to burst, and let my thoughts touch its contents. My breath was heaving, and the tension in my shoulders and back was only increasing.

A face as familiar to me as my own. A face forever entwined with the faces of my family. A face from my nightmares.

Savat's thief was Cal.

And I knew exactly where he was.

Twenty Three

I walked the halls of the mountain in a daze while the storm raged. I wandered aimlessly. Whichever way I walked, I was not going where my body wanted to take me. *I knew where he was.* I knew *exactly*, down to the very motes of dust in the air he breathed.

I felt as if my body was not my own; I was watching someone else stride through the stone passages. Nameless dark emotions were churning just out of reach and I could neither grasp them nor feel them fully. Images and feelings warred with any sense of being and awareness.

The blade slid casually across my father's throat and blood fountained in a gory spray, dark and violent in the dwindling sun. Cal straightened from his knife-work as I walked past, his rough beard and greasy, unwashed hair dripping with rainwater as the lightning shattered the night just outside the library windows.

My awareness seemed to spiral out hazily into the distance.

I watched from behind fogged glass as another self frowned in worry following another me who strode down the hallways with grim purpose, anger and fear and pain and fury seething somewhere between us. Too many selves. Too many unconnected senses and too many disjoint intentions. I felt a panic rising somewhere within one of those selves.

"Bacon and eggs every morning, Pips! What do you think of that?" One of me startled, looking around for Father, but the only ones there in that hallway were me. My breath was heaving, panting. Somewhere, one of me could not fill my lungs.

I reached the central stair and ascended. I thought maybe I lost some of my selves then—I went up but they went down. From this level, there were one hundred and thirty two steps to the top. One hundred and twelve steps to the bottom. But the shadows stretched endlessly down into the depths of the earth.

There was blood everywhere, and I couldn't figure out where it came from. I splashed in it with each footfall. My feet squelched in my sandals. Cal strode beside me and tried to speak, but no sound came out of his mouth. He gestured with his hands instead, alternately pleading and raving. His throat was sliced open and blood was spilling from the wound like water from a spring, flowing over the stone halls and tumbling down the broad spiral stair like ten thousand waterfalls.

It was another me who knew this wasn't true. I was watching myself dream the gore and blood and I spoke the words that the bloodied Cal was trying to say.

"Alright, lovelies, time enough," I said to myself in a whisper.

I passed through the doorway into my rooms. Empty rooms. My hands were shaking with the tension in my back and shoulders. Empty. It wasn't lunch yet, and Fanti or Kari might come back before or after. If I could just hold myself still long enough, they might come. They could help me. Help stop...

Lightning flashed and thunder echoed down the mountainside. The panel to the balcony was open, and some rain slashed through onto the carpeted floor. Cal crouched just inside, a sack in one hand and a knife in the other. His eyes were wide in fear and shock. His greasy hair and beard dripped with water, and mud was caked on his scuffed boots. The small lantern at his feet dripped a pool of oil.

"The lantern spilled its blood," I said, chuckling at the joke.

I was in the bedroom standing before the wardrobe. The wardrobe was open and my sword was there in front of me. The sword was a gift from Marki. If I could find Marki, perhaps they could stop...

A hand was reaching for it. One of me didn't want it. One of me needed it.

"What are you, Arin? Really?" I turned and Ranji was looking at me. The right side of his face was bruised, with a dark purple ring puffing around his eye and more bruises along his jaw. His lip was split and bloodied. His eyes looked sad and concerned. A fletched shaft stood out from his chest, and he idly stroked the feathers with one hand as he bored into me with those soft, sad eyes.

I was gasping for air. My back was buckling in tension so severe that I could barely stand. I was running back through the room, part of me following more slowly, weighed down by fear and worry. I reached the sliding panel onto the balcony and brushed past Father who was crouched there with a sack in one hand and a knife in the other. Smiling, he drew the knife across his own throat, careful to catch the spill of blood in the sack.

The other me threw back the panel with one hand while another me tucked the sword into my belt. The slow me shrank back, but we all reached the balcony together and leapt.

Rain and storm and violence and fury and wind.

We hurtled through the air downwards to the garden platform far below. We embraced the horror at what we were about to do. Ranji and Father flew with us, trailing feathers and blood. We took that pain too and wound it within ourselves, through our limbs and into our bones.

We struck the platform with enough force to shatter bone and rupture skin, but the pain and the power buoyed us over the shock and hardened us to the impact, and we stood lightly, feet only slightly sore.

As we stepped away, we left behind a pair of ruined sandals, the force of our landing having burst the straps and shredded the leather.

"First one, then two," someone said in satisfaction. One of us flinched away and wept.

Rain was sheeting down. Lightning burst above and thunder exploded in a show of violence, but it was diminished by the fury that was burning in one of us there among the greenery.

"Please," someone was pleading, begging the others. My knees were sodden, sinking softly in the muddy grass as I knelt.

"I don't have to," One of us said, thoughtful, worried.

"I know where he is," someone said, cold and grim.

Breath was hard, a struggle. Icy bands encircled my chest. Pain and numbness with each gasp.

I could point to him. I knew where he was, *exactly*, down to the very motes of dust that floated in the air in the dark dingy room in the wretched little house lit by the lightnings of the storm hammering the squalid cluster of huts on the outskirts of a fishing village on the rocky sea far to the south.

I *knew*.

Ranji stood to my right, his bruised face and cut lip shining in the rain, his tears lost forever. The arrow stood proudly from his chest.

Father stood to my left, his face a mass of blood and his nose broken. His throat gaped and blood washed down his chest to mingle with the rain and mud at his feet.

Mother knelt in front of me, her head bowed in sorrow and an arrow sticking from her neck, her arm draped protectively over Beaty's shoulder, whose life was stolen as surely as mine.

"Not stolen," one of us said with assurance, "destroyed. Ravaged. Ruined utterly."

And I knew suddenly why they had brought me here. I had known all along. Here, where I knelt in the mud—I had practiced my movements here on this platform every morning for years. I knew every inch of this platform, every blade of grass and every dip in the soil and every stone.

I tried to think of an argument; some way to convince me that we did not need... I tried to think of... My breath was coming in gasps and I couldn't think well enough to make sense of it.

I tried to think.

There was no thought.

There was nothing real to hold on to, only this: I *knew*. *Here* and *there*, I knew. Know two places intimately enough, and you can always find similarities.

Father and Mother and Ranji and Beaty all lowered their heads and sighed as we drew in the pain of their death and ruination. I wove them in and out of the places *between*. A running stitch that tied *here* to *there*.

And I drew them tight, cinching that thread between the

places and found that it was easy. Rage and fury was everything as the Bridge opened in a coruscating frenzy. I stood and took two steps into the dark room.

The sounds of the storm changed, diminished. Rain drummed against the roof of the shack but it was muted somehow. I could hear only breathing... gasping, desperate breaths.

He was sitting in the darkness on a mean looking cot, head cradled in his hands, not even a candle to give light. His beard was longer than the memory from the library; his hair just as unkempt and greasy. The room smelled of old food and unwashed man and half-full chamber pot. Beside the cot was a rough sack lying half-open and spilling antique treasures onto the dirty floor.

He lifted his head and looked up at me. His eyes were sunken in misery and worry. Recognition did not come to him at once. I gave him the time to find it, calmly standing straight, staring into those wretched eyes. The sound of gasping breath filled the room.

Moments passed, and then finally he saw. He understood. He straightened and his eyes widened.

"He said someone would find me. Never thought it would be you." His gaze darted between me, my scars, and the mind-bending doorway behind me. He laughed then, a wheezing, dreadful laugh. It was full of hopelessness and irony and satisfaction. "Oh fuck! If you only knew... It's such a joke..." He laughed and laughed, cackling maniacally as if at the finest jest.

The breathing was ragged, each gasp anguished and pained.

Fingers gripped the sword hilt. Forearm drawing it forth just so. The blade left the scabbard.

Gasping, labored breath.

The tip of the blade hovered in front of his face. His eyes

never left mine.

"Go on then," his voice grated, "time enough."

Water flowed down over my chin, and I realized it was tears. My shoulders and back were clenched and cramping.

"Do it!" He gasped.

I shook my head. I couldn't speak—I wasn't in enough control of myself for that. I was stretched tight, like sinew pulled to the breaking point. Acting now would be acting on his terms. The part of me that wanted his death raged at the idea of his acceptance, that he could welcome this end. I drew back. Not much—the smallest, almost imperceptible movement of my shoulder. He was not allowed to *choose* death.

His eyes widened and his face relaxed, perhaps seeing some measure of compassion in my retreat. A chance to explain, to beg. He opened his mouth slowly, and I could see a thought forming in those eyes.

"I know it don't matter," he said softly, sadly, "but I'm—"

Shoulder flexed, hips pivoted, wrist turned. A flash so fast that the blade tip stayed clean.

A gasp of breath and his throat opened. He didn't even move his hands in that desperate last reflex to hold in his own lifeblood. It fountained forth, streaming down his filthy shirt in dark rivulets. His eyes stayed on mine as his breaths came shorter and shorter, wheezing and gurgling through his ragged throat now instead of nose or mouth. Gasping, desperate breaths.

We remained as if in a tableau. I was still, blade extended to the side, eyes locked on his, watching his life fade, watching his eyes darken and become wooden, slowly. Listening to each gasping dreadful breath.

Cal died, and somewhere in my mind the small awareness of his location winked out. The moment came and went, and then I was alone—alone, but the gasping breaths continued.

In a sudden panic, I glanced around the room, looking for the source of the sound. There was no one. I was alone in the room. The only sound was the rattling of raindrops, and that horrible, desperate gasping.

I turned and strode back through the open Bridge, letting it go as I stepped over the threshold. I sank down to my knees and let my body sag. The tension in my back and shoulders was still increasing. I felt I might double over backwards in cramps and my stomach began to clench.

The gasping continued. It was a sound rooted in horror and agony.

The rain was slowing as the fast-moving storm passed over, and my tears were slowing as well. Despite the water all around me, I felt dried out like a withered husk.

I tried desperately to hold off the knowledge of what had happened. It was someone else that had done it, it had to be. It was another me. The me who had stood back calmly watching and thinking shook my head sadly. I looked on in confusion and dread as the me who had acted so boldly smiled a grim smile. I watched my crumpled form holding myself, desperately trying to catch a breath and unable to straighten enough to fill my lungs.

Gasping.

Twenty Four

By the time I had recovered my breath, I was seated stiffly on the couch in the living space of our rooms. There was a fire smoldering on the grate, but it did little to ward off the chill left by the storm—the sliding panel to the balcony was still open.

I don't recall walking back to the apartment. I don't remember laying the fire or starting it. I don't even remember sheathing my sword, though it was propped neatly in the corner beside the fireplace. The entire experience might have been a dream, a vivid nightmare of madness and vengeance.

Except my sword leaned against the wall, instead of tucked safely in the wardrobe.

Except that my sandals were gone, and there were red marks on my feet from where the straps had burst.

Except that my feet were bruised and flecked in dried mud.

I forced myself to breathe, slowly and calmly, focusing on my heartbeat, timing the rhythms and slowing down as much as I could bear. I let my eyes wander over the space, naming out loud the things I could see: A book Kari had left open beside the fire. The piece of needlework Fanti had been working on each night for the last week. The water pitcher, half full. The leg of a wicker-work chair on the balcony that I could see from where I sat. A blanket folded over the arm of the couch.

I found my center and was finally able to think. I tried to worry the problem over; tried to find a loophole that would mean it was not true. But after several minutes of futile, feverish thought, I coldly forced myself to take stock of the situation.

I had broken my oath. Perhaps not to the letter—I had not strictly used my power to kill Cal—but I knew that hair would not split so fine with the Council.

I had abused the knowledge gained by my place on the watch.

I had used my power to Bridge the divide between us.

I had killed—murdered—with the sword given to me by the Marshal upon attaining a swordmaster's rank.

The Council must know by now that Cal was dead; they would have noted the dispersal of the Finding. Eelie would know, and so then would Savat. Could they know how? I scoured my memory, trying to find any hint of observer to my actions. I could remember none, but could I trust that when I couldn't remember my path back here?

What would happen to me if they learned? Censure, and removal from the watch, certainly. Expulsion from Reft? Eelie had been here and had been... even if not actually expelled, still I had met no one who expressed sorrow at their departure. And as foul as their transgression had been—violence of the mind was still violence—it was well short of murder.

Turin's words came back to me, "Some before you have fallen into despair and contempt at our ways." The thought of losing Turin's respect, of losing everyone I had come to love here brought fresh tears to my eyes and a coldness to my heart. I could not allow that to happen.

My actions over the next hour were intentional and certain, even if I don't recall planning or deciding them.

I took up my sword and, checking that the blade was clean, returned it to the wardrobe along with my sword belt. I changed my damp and muddy clothing for fresh, using the still-wet trousers to scrub any mud off my feet and a spare clean shirt to dry my hair and body, and to wipe clean any marks of mud I had left on the floor

It had become our habit to keep most of our clothing, not returning it to the common stores. Much of what we wore was made by Fanti for each of us and was personal and bespoke. Since laundry was still a task that I found relaxing, once a week I took the clothes down to the main laundry on the fourth level and washed them. My muddy clothes went into the bottom of the basket that we kept beside the wardrobe. No one else but me would look there.

The sandals were a problem. I couldn't remember how long it had been since the rain stopped, and now I worried someone might find the ruined sandals and wonder. I put on a pair of slippers—bare feet might draw comments—and wound my way down the three levels to the platform I had Bridged from. I felt every glance and every eye upon me as I walked through the halls, trying to project a sense of calm. I was sure they could see my guilt written on my face and in my posture.

When I reached the platform, I slipped out of the slippers and walked barefoot along the wet stone that edged the garden soil, conscious of the open space around me with each damp step. There was still no one about, though the storm had passed. Carefully picking my way out on rain-slick stepping stones, I found the spot where I had landed.

The sandals were there, half-buried in the mud and in tatters. I pulled them out by the broken straps, and checking that no one was watching, I spun them in a tight loop and flung them over the railing far out into the distant rocky valley below. With one last glance around, I turned and made my way back inside, stopping by the common stores to collect a fresh pair.

By the time Fanti returned after lunch, they found me curled up on the couch with a copy of Sandiéne's *Position and Intent*, scribbling notes for my next training class with a steel pen and an inkwell balanced on my knee. They bent down for a kiss and I returned it, desperately hoping they could not see through my mask of calm to the roiling worry and guilt beneath.

I passed the next days under the pressing weight of what I had done. It colored every waking moment and woke me in the night. A part of me that seemed to resist all reason felt bitterness that even in death, Cal had managed to take from me something precious: my nightmares of the deaths of my family had been supplanted by visions of his blood spilling from his throat and over my hands.

I was withdrawn and irritable, quick to anger and quicker to tears. Kari and Fanti noted the changes in me. Fanti seemed to take it in stride and accepted at face-value the excuses I gave of not sleeping well. Kari thought they knew better. They brought me daily updates of what they had gleaned from handling the Council's reports.

The Council was meeting each day now, and the reason was

buzzing through Reft's gossip mill: Savat and his retinue were still here. When they had lost the Finding connection to the thief and Savat reported that Eelie had not yet taken any action, it could only be assumed that the thief had met his end by some accident or mischief.

The second morning after my crime, Kari had confided that Eelie and their companion Tanith had traveled by Bridge to the last known whereabouts of the thief, and returned to report him dead by violence. I flinched at the news—it was a blow, and only in that moment did I realize that I had been harboring a desperate hope that my fractured memories were nothing more than a vivid dream.

My reaction to the news seemed to plant a seed of chill and distance between us. That Kari thought I cared about Eelie's actions or was tense because of their continued presence in Reft was agonizing. There were moments where I desperately wanted to tell them the truth, but fear of losing them over it held my tongue.

Yes, I wanted Savat to leave, because that would mark an end of the episode. With Savat and Eelie gone, no one would give a second thought to the death of Savat's thief and I could begin to try to forget my own actions. Until then, I couldn't help but worry at every moment they remained, wondering when someone would question why he had been murdered mere moments after the Finding. I avoided Turin, worried that seeing me would remind them of my distant behavior immediately following the Circle.

I struggled to achieve a sense of normalcy. I attended to teaching my trainees, standing my watches, studying, and practicing my skills. I sought any distractions I could find. I came to cherish these moments of focus.

I was called to aid a carpenter who had misjudged the grain

in a timber, throwing her adze astray and slicing a deep gash in her thigh. We found her pale and weak, in shock from the loss of blood and shaking. Talking Ranji, Froley, and Berin through my decision to add some of my own power to the patient's pain to heal the nicked artery, while relying on needle and thread to close the bulk of the muscle, I was able to set the weight of my guilt aside for a few precious minutes while my attention was on saving a life.

When I led the trainees through movements on the sandy training platform, coaching them to achieve correct posture and form distracted me for a time. If I could not lose myself in the rhythm and flow, at least I could help them towards that peace.

In the midst of my worry and guilt, the days marched forward towards the date I had set for my Reshaping. Some weeks before, I had consulted with Atua, deciding to perform the work myself. They had judged me fit and skilled enough to achieve what I desired without supervision.

Before Savat and Eelie's arrival, before the Finding, it had been holding as much a space in my mind as the excitement at the coming of the highest feast day. Kari and Fanti, and Migs, Chan, Brenin, and Heiu had all cleared the day of duties so that they could join me in a Circle. It was contribution, moral support, celebration, and expression of love all rolled into a single unifying act.

When the day came I was filled with anticipation and anxiety, and it might have been enough to banish the weight, except that it carried with it a new worry: when they joined themselves to me in the Circle, my memories would be open to them. I had spent the night before awake in the darkness, planning and thinking through the implications of what I would do.

That morning, I asked Fanti and Kari to give me some solitude, giving them the excuse that I wished to practice the visualizations of the changes I would make to my body. They both accepted this with equanimity, leaving me alone in the bedroom.

I relaxed on the bed and let my mind drift.

I tried first to use the fresh anguish I had been struggling with these last few days. To draw that pain into myself and leverage its power. I let myself feel it, the pain in my chest, the struggle to breathe, the dread of what I had done.

But as much as it filled me, I found I could not make it bend to the task. Perhaps pain is a living thing, and has its own purpose and will. Or perhaps, as Sem had told me once, you cannot fill a hole by digging at it.

I gave up on that approach, wiping tears from my eyes. I spent some time in slow, even breaths, trying to recenter myself.

Eventually, I could lie to myself no more. I was hesitant to draw on the pain of Father's death, of my family's deaths. Hesitant because I was afraid that after what I had done, after what use I had put it to, that the power in those memories was too tightly entwined with my guilt and fear; a well poisoned by my actions.

Tentatively, I let myself think of Ranji, of his panic as he leapt to his feet, grasping the hatchet. His desperation to stop the violence that he saw unfolding before his eyes, and the shock as the arrow struck him in the heart. His soft, bright eyes fading to dull gray as the life left them.

I felt that pain and knew that I could still draw on it. And so I did.

I started with the moment of recognition. Everything spiraled out from there, a sprawling bolt of jagged fractured memory, each edge and corner sharp enough to lacerate. I knew that a great wall of briar would be nearly as damning as the truth if anyone were to encounter it, so instead I was delicate, subtle.

"Mind magic can be an especially subtle blade," Turin had told me. I needed it as sharp and fine as it would hone. I drew a fine thread of power, winding it through my mind.

It is difficult to describe what it was that I did; I was operating by instinct more than any skill or knowledge. That shock in the moment that I recognized Cal, I... adjusted, turning it just so and chipping away at the edges. In the same way that a shard of clear glass can reflect like a mirror in the right light, that memory would now dazzle and draw the mind to other thoughts unless approached *just so*.

From there, I traced through the memories that branched from that point, my panicked, disoriented progress through the hallways, my arming myself, my descent to the platform, the Bridge to the south...

Cal's murder.

It helped that those memories were already shadowed and dream-tinged. My conscious mind had not been fully in control, and so the memories were fragmented, disjointed much like those shards of memory from my first breaking.

It took only a few nudges here and there to re-cast them as a dream—a nightmare born of a Circle-wrought headache, the visions induced by the guard's narrative, and the thunderstorm.

When I was done, even a moderately deliberate examination of my memories of that night would see that I had left the Council chamber with a headache, returned to my bed, and slept through most of the storm, plagued by disturbing dreams of my family's death at Cal's hands.

I only wished that *I* could forget as easily, but whatever it was I did to change the connections from thought to thought didn't diminish my own memory or confuse the course of events for me any further than they already were. It would have to do. I could rely on my own focus and concentration to keep this moment from the Circle.

I had done what I could in my mind, and now, it was time for my body.

My friends surrounded me. This was as it should be. I took comfort in their presence, their proximity. Kari and Fanti knelt on the wide bed to either side, their hands grasping mine in support and love. Migs and Heiu, Chan and Brenin filled the small bedroom and made the air close and warm.

It should have been stuffy and claustrophobic. Our small bedroom—even at double the size of the one I had found so luxurious when I first arrived in Reft—was too small for seven people. But that it was *these* people, these that I had come to love as a new family, made that warmth feel like a sense of home and that closeness into an intimacy.

"Are you ready?" Kari asked.

I looked into their eyes and the steadiness and love and pure acceptance they showed me almost brought tears to mine. I looked to the other side at Fanti who gave me their broad, open smile that always made me want to laugh in joy. I squeezed their hands for comfort. For support. For reassurance.

"I am."

I closed my eyes then, and let myself feel the air on the fine hairs on my bare arms. I let my mind wander. I knew where I ultimately needed to go in my memory, but I wanted to give myself some few moments of relaxation before I embraced the pain. I breathed slowly.

I could sense from the changes in breathing around me that the others were waiting for me, so I let my memory drift back to the moment where the arrow found Ranji's heart. The pain of that moment was acute and devastating and elegiac. I felt the weight of it fill me and the power in it buoy me up. I rode the waves of that pain for a breath or two, and then I reached out with my mind.

It is a peculiar practice to draw others into a Circle. It's an act of purest empathy, of understanding at that deepest core of being that the pain they are feeling may well be yours. One must genuinely and unreservedly seek that pain, welcome it and embrace it. It is not a thing that people are disposed to do, and takes immense practice and dedication.

The Arin of five years ago—who had hesitated with the knife a half-inch from their arm unable to make that leap of imagination and will that would allow them to purposefully receive pain—could not have done it. Our bodies do their utmost to evade pain. It's a thing of the viscera, involuntary and below the consciousness. We have no memory of physical pain when it has passed, and so each instance is new and unique and overwhelms the senses. It's a part of why Reft teaches the revisiting of traumas within the memory: the memory of the event itself—deliberately and consciously accessed—helps to buffer us from fresh wounds.

But taking on another's pain and bringing it into a Circle is more akin to that burst of wild, unknowable somatic agony that defies memory. It's the violent heat and visceral fury and shocking *otherness* of the anticipated injury, but with the intimacy and inescapable proximity of remembered trauma. It cannot be held at a distance because it is coming from within oneself, never mind that its true source is another member of the Circle.

And with it comes wave upon wave of those other selves as we merge.

The flood of pain filled me and I rose through it. I felt the power from those I loved permeate me and nearly wash me away.

...

I grew up in The Lange with Mother who took in washing and did embroidery work to support us—my father had left well before I was born. I remembered playing vicious games of chase with other urchins who spent their days on our narrow street, until the one day when they saw my dressing in the odd colors and fabrics that I chose out of the scraps Mother found for us for what it was—that I dressed how I felt and I didn't feel the way they saw me. They turned on me then as a single, terrifying organism and I knew in that moment—if I survived the beating they meted—that I did not belong in this place, and that I would take Mother away and never return.

I remembered the painful, endless journey upriver. The fear and alienation I felt in Two Runs, holding to Mother's arm as I guided her through the churning mass of people. The slow, desperate fade of Mother's memory. The horror I felt on the first night, sheltering under a hedge on the side of the winding path north of the river, when Mother didn't remember where we were or where we were going.

My heart wrenched and I nearly came undone at the memory of the first time I lost my mother, when she woke screaming that she didn't know me, that I wasn't her child. A bitter sob lodged in my throat at the second time I lost her, when she didn't wake at all and I could do nothing but build a cairn over her small quiet body in that rocky place that I would never return to. I saw my own fingers gently removing the bronze necklace—Mother's only treasure—and tying the leather cord around my own neck.

...

I remembered the night when I first realized that Mother's fair skin did not bleed and bruise on its own, but bloomed in pain whenever she stood between me and Father's rage. The words he hurled at me in fury and hatred: *mixie* and *slip* and *witch*. I remembered her loving hands and his brutal fists.

That last night, I lay in the garret shaking, hearing Father storm and rage that no *son* of his would reject the birthright of his manhood—he would bury the boy first. I had no plan, only the thought that if I could take myself out of this place, perhaps Father's anger at Mother would subside. I could spare her more pain.

I felt the cold dawn air as I wandered through the woods miles away from the cottage, miles farther than I had ever traveled, cold and damp and beyond fear. I remembered the sound of falling water crashing over rocks, and thinking: This is where I could end—a cold wet burial in sparkling water, washed down to the sea in the traditions of my people.

I recalled the voice that brought me away from that frozen sleep. Babi Fen and their horrid face, scarred and weathered. Their rancid breath and rotting teeth. And their loving, accepting embrace that made me feel for the first time that I was not the problem with the world.

...

I remembered everything. Every moment and every word and every deed and all of it at once. My mind reeled in pain under the very weight of memory. Of Mother and Father finally accepting that there was more different about me than my quirky way of thinking and my annoying tendency to object to every other word spoken—correcting the statements of others in a tone that said "that's obviously not right."

I did not understand why grown adults could say one thing, and then four years later believe—truly believe, and argue!—that they had said something else... and even if they accepted their mistake, excuse it with "Oh, that was years ago," as if something as irrelevant as time passing could diminish what *was*. I was always *that child* to everyone. The one who didn't fit and no one wanted to be near. I wasn't actually *disliked*, so much as I made people uncomfortable.

I remembered explaining to my parents—for the thirteenth time, the last attempt being four months and three days before, over a lunch of meat pies that had used the last of the butter for the week—that I was not a girl and could they please remember that this time? And their response to please not say such things where others could overhear.

I remembered the trip to the city with my parents, somber and sad, but still loving me. I remembered them leaving without me, leaving me with the stranger who explained, not unkindly, that there was a place that welcomed those like me, and that they would take me there.

...

I remembered the heartache at leaving my mother and Father, my two sisters and brother, the thrill of the caravan journey into the unknown tempered by the realization that I may never see those I loved again. I remembered Father's tears, openly weeping at seeing his oldest child off to the only safety he could ensure.

I remembered the joy and freedom and tedium of the endless trek east across the Somiri wilderness. The pain and shock of being kicked by a mule in my uncle's caravan; the humiliation of recovering from those injuries amongst the seasoned caravaners who were not likely to ever let me forget my foolishness at stroking Fellény's ears—some of the boys were younger than me, yet still far more experienced.

I remembered my anxieties at arriving in Reft, of meeting others like me. I remembered the pain and fear and horror at feeling Eelie inside my mind, making me feel—lightning and blades flaying my mind, I *remembered* this—at odds to myself, making me agree with them.

I felt once more the joy of meeting Arin, the slight flutter in my breast that I felt at their smile. The pain in my gut as I began to lose them to Eelie's machinations. The flood of pleasure and wash of happiness and love when I melded myself with them.

...

I accepted their power, their pain and I sank it deep into my flesh.

Under the sleeveless linen robe that covered me, I felt my skin prickle. I willed myself to float on that ocean of power. I had talked through what I was about to do with Atua, and practiced endlessly in my imagination over the last several weeks.

I wove the power through me, found the tissues in my breasts that had grown to nourish children that I never wanted and would never have. I was aware of the skin and shape and tension in that place in my body, of each and every element of life that strove for constant renewal. I Shaped, feeling my own body flow like wet sand, like clay, like memory. I drew the stuff of myself into that liminal space between the parts of the Circle. I let it become energy and rejoin the universe as love and joy and belief.

I could feel the brushed linen of my robe settle onto flat planes of my chest, the skin alive and aware and sensitive, but taut and firm now with muscle and nothing else.

Half of the work done. My awareness drifted down now to the more difficult part, more delicate. What I wanted here was subtle, and here was where my advanced studies with Atua were of moment. I spun a fine weave of power through my womb, finding that essence of the tidal quickening and reshaping the finest motes of life that directed my body to prepare itself anew each month to grow a child. These I silenced, gently absorbing the life-giving energies and directives into the flow of power, releasing it into the world as peace and contentment. I would need moon tea no longer.

With a deep breath of satisfaction and peace, I released the Circle and tears came unbidden to my eyes as I looked on my family. They were all smiles and joy, and I felt a peace and contentment so acute that it verged on painful.

Twenty Five

The following morning I strode through the halls of Reft with confidence. I felt more at peace in my own body than I had ever felt in my life. I wore a snug—but not tight—tunic. Thin and light, it draped cleanly over my chest with no constriction or awkwardness.

I was feeling happy and satisfied with myself, and even better: news had come from Kari at breakfast that Savat and his people were leaving Reft this afternoon. I would be free of Eelie, free of worry, and free of the subtle tension that had arisen between me and Kari. The sun shone brightly through the channels cut down into the mountain.

When I reached the door to my watch post, I pulled up suddenly short. Marki was there, and by the look on their face, they were there to meet me.

"Marki," I said. "Good morning."

"Good morning, Arin. Walk with me, if you will."

We fell in together, me matching my strides to their longer

legs with little effort. We moved back through the hall to the main stair, ascending. There was a tension in the air between us, but I could not tell if it was real or imagined.

"How do you feel about your duties in the Watch?" They asked, breaking the silence.

"I feel good," I said slowly, "I am enjoying teaching, though I'll admit that I did not expect to. Froley, Berin, and Ranji are clever and quick learners. They'll do well."

Marki nodded absently.

"Where are we going?" I asked.

Marki said nothing for a few moments as we walked. Just before I realized which chamber we were approaching, they said only, "Your presence has been requested by the Council."

We came then to the door—the formal Council chambers, rarely used. My stomach churned on itself and I felt my face warm. Marki knocked twice then pushed the door open, leading me through with a hand gently on my back. I stepped forward in a daze, noting the full Council arrayed in their chairs.

The room was arranged in a semi-circle, with a chair for each member of the Council, each chosen for their own comfort. In the middle of the arc of chairs, Atua sat with a calm intensity. I scanned the room briefly, noting the others. Gesh, Fenilin, and Purun seemed ill at ease, shifting uncomfortably. Filla looked at no one, their gaze held by the view of the distant mountain ranges to the north. Deme and Turin each seemed to find something of deep interest in the carpets. Atua alone met my eyes, and their look was piercing and hard.

"I see that you performed your Reshaping," they said. "It went as planned, I trust?"

Their words were at odds with their tone, and the muscles in my shoulders were tensing just as my stomach clenched. I could only nod. I was unsure if I could speak if I tried. I can't say how, but I knew exactly what was coming next. What would be asked and why. Atua spoke, and I closed my eyes, hearing the words and feeling my breathing strangely calm and easy.

"Where did you go after the Finding we performed for the Viscount? You left the chambers immediately after the Circle was dissolved. Where did you go?"

"I went back to my rooms," I said calmly, softly. I might have expected myself to stammer, to struggle with breath, to tremble in fear. I did none of those things. My mind was clear and I could feel my reality narrowing inevitably down to this moment. This is where I had been moving since that flash of lightning on the library windows.

"And where did you go after that?"

"My memory is... clouded," I answered honestly, "fragmented. It is difficult to remember." All true.

Deme spoke then. "Arin, this situation is serious. Honesty is *required* here. Do not lie to us or try to dissemble."

I nodded.

"What did you do after leaving the Circle?"

I found then a simple quiet peace inside myself. I was unaccustomed to the feeling. I would not lie. But I also would not damn myself from my own lips. I said nothing.

Someone sighed at my silence. I thought it was Turin.

Atua's voice cut sharply, "Bring them in, then."

My eyes snapped open and sought their face. Bring *who* in? Were my attempts to cover my own memories for nought? Had one of my chosen family here seen what I had done and felt compelled to report my actions? Part of me was desperate to turn, to watch Marki move to the side door that opened into a retiring chamber, to see who it was they brought forward.

Another part of me was still calm and resigned. I knew what would happen next and next and next. I could see my paths narrowing down to a single thread, and it was one that I should have expected from my first step in slippered feet from the ruined hall of Ma'am's house in Anbress. Was I not destined to lose each and every future I felt that I could belong to? To see my life collapse around me time and time and time again?

And yet another part of me knew exactly who would step through the door that Marki opened. I didn't need to look because I already knew and there was no surprise in it: Their pale skin and pale hair—almost white—caught the morning sunlight and made them shine against their black livery slashed with purple and orange.

Marki brought Eelie to stand beside me, facing the Council.

"You brought this accusation. Speak now before the accused. What did you see?" Atua said. It had the cadence of a formal ritual, but there was a thread underneath the words; a discontent as if the very air in the room was distasteful.

Eelie seemed not to notice, and gave their testimony in a clear, calm voice. "After the Circle, we returned to our guest rooms, just down the hall from the chamber in which we had all met for the Finding. I was feeling unsettled for some reason afterwards and left my rooms, thinking to go to the eating hall for something to calm my stomach. I saw Arin in the halls, and tried to call out to them, but they didn't hear or didn't acknowledge me. They seemed to be in distress, so I followed for a time, but I lost them on the stairs. I returned to my rooms, and opened the panel to the balcony, because I enjoy the sounds of a storm. I felt something from below that drew my eye, and I could see on one of the lower platforms: Arin had opened a Bridge to somewhere. They stepped through. While they were gone, I sensed the Finding dissipate. When they returned they held a bare sword in one hand, and they collapsed to the grass, crying it seemed."

There was silence in the chamber for several moments.

Turin spoke, "Why have you waited until now to speak? Surely you might have connected these events you say you witnessed with the loss of the Finding?"

Eelie shrugged, ignoring the spoken slight. "I spoke to my lord of what I had seen. He asked me to hold, in the hopes that I—and by extension, he—would not be required to involve ourselves directly in an internal matter concerning citizens of Reft. We are the outsiders here."

Turin's lips twisted at this all-too-reasonable response, and they opened their mouth to reply, but Atua raised a single hand and they settled back again.

"How will you answer this account, Arin? Did you leave your rooms after the Finding? Did you form a Bridge and carry through a sword? Did you murder the object of this Finding, as your accuser implies?" Atua's voice was cold and sharp, demanding some response.

I opened my mouth, not quite knowing what I would say, and the words that came were both surprising and easy. "I will not answer their account. I have nothing to say, in explanation or in defense, for they have accused me of nothing. They have simply said they saw me out in the rain."

As I spoke, I noted several sharp breaths among the members of the Council. They certainly expected a defense or a denial. Perhaps they hoped for one or the other.

But I would not lie.

As I walked back from the Council chambers to my rooms, I felt numb and empty and light-headed. I had neither guard nor escort for there was no justification for either. The Council would debate my fate, but they were stymied by my refusal to either deny Eelie's account or plead my own. They sent me to my rooms like a wayward child while they did so.

There was a feeling welling inside me that I did not want to accept, refused to acknowledge. But it was a feeling that with each step I took, I also couldn't ignore.

I was walking the halls of Reft for the last time.

I reached the rooms I shared with Kari and Fanti and pushed the door open. The sitting room was empty, silent and dim with the closed balcony panel providing meager light. There was no one to greet me, to comfort me. I walked to the couch and sat, finding my eyes full of tears that now began to stream down my cheeks.

I could put a name to what I felt. It was an ending.

The very structure of this life that I had built here was crumbling and falling down around me. Reft itself might be stable and hale, but my life within it was fractured, struck right through with faults and flaws and spreading cracks, and I knew that it would not stand long.

I railed at fate, at my weakness, at the unfairness of the world. I wasn't ready to lose those I loved, but I knew something would fail here today, whatever the Council decided.

I pulled a sweater that Kari had left lying on the arm of the couch to me and buried my face in it, curling up with their scent and their warmth and sobbed into the wool.

I don't know how long I wept. Hours. Moments. However long, I was startled by the sound of knocking at the door. I sat up, and wiped my eyes, wondering if I had imagined it.

The knocks came again. Kari or Fanti or any of my friends wouldn't knock, not in the middle of the day... they would simply open the door and enter.

I rose from the couch and tried to tidy myself, giving my face one last wipe with the back of my hand, and made my way to the door. I did not expect the face I saw when I opened it.

Tamar Savat bowed a slight little bow, and when I stepped back in some shock, he entered.

"Arin, please forgive my intrusion. I am aware of what you are going through, and I want to apologize. It was never my intent to put you in such a position. I tried to keep myself and Eelie out of this for as long as I could."

He wandered slowly through the rooms, and found himself at the balcony panel, which he slid open absently.

"If I had known... All I can say is that I am sorry I brought the issue of this thief to the Council. I won't ask what happened. It's none of my business and if I could do things differently... Well. Let us say that it was poorly done on my part, and I apologize."

I simply shook my head. I couldn't explain; I wasn't sure I wanted to.

He continued, "I don't know what your Council will do. In my own experience with them, I've found them to be mercurial at best. But if my coming here has the result of harming you or the life you have built for yourself here, I will be deeply saddened. I cannot influence their decision, and I fear that trying would only make things worse for us both in the long run."

He turned to me then, and looked me in the eyes. "I will say this: Should they turn you out, or make your life here uncomfortable, you will always have a place in my service. All you need do is ask."

Something in my mind twitched at this. There was a memory, a deep long-forgotten question that had almost formed in my mind, but it was ephemeral. I couldn't grasp it, couldn't even find the edges of the question—it had no shape. It was like the vague smell of smoke long after a bonfire has been extinguished.

"Thank you," I said. I could bring nothing else to mind. The idea of serving him, beside Eelie each day, doing... whatever it was they did... It turned my stomach. "But no. I do not believe that would be wise."

"You can't be content with endless training and training, reading and talking about strategy and skills which you may never use... In my service, I can promise you that your skills will be applied, you will be valued and highly placed in my interests."

I cannot say why, but I had never been as sure of anything before. "No. Thank you."

He frowned slightly and seemed disappointed. "Well, if you are sure... Should you change your mind, only send me word; my offer stands." He bowed again, then, and let himself out.

I sat for a time afterwards in the silent, empty room. I could feel a sort of certainty solidifying around me.

Again, there was a knock at the door. I was standing at the open balcony, staring out into the open expanse of the mountains, at the place the hazy blue-gray ridges met the unfathomably clear blue of the sky. I felt like I could lose myself in that endless blue. I imagined setting out and just walking, taking step after step into forever. Seeking... what? Freedom? Absolution? Peace? If there was a pattern, I was becoming increasingly sure of its shape.

"Come in," I said over my shoulder, just loud enough to be heard. The door opened and someone entered. I didn't turn around. I was certain of who it was by the sound of their gait and by the very rightness of things. "Hello Turin."

"Arin," they said.

"You've come to tell me what the Council has decided?"

"I've come to ask you to talk to me. Please, Arin, tell me what happened. Why won't you explain yourself? We all on the council know Eelie of old. I know you know some of their history here. There is no trust in us for their accusation. You only have to deny it. We would choose to believe you over them."

"And where would that leave the integrity of the Council?" I asked calmly. When I continued, my voice was quiet, and my eyes were still tracing that horizon. "When I came to Reft, I was broken and lost. I didn't understand my place in the world, I didn't understand what I was for, what I could do. You helped me to find myself, and for that I thank you."

"You have no need to thank me, Arin. But *talk* to me."

"I did kill him. I murdered. I broke the Oaths of Reft and I took a life."

I felt more than heard Turin's sharp intake of breath. After a few moments, they asked quietly, "Why, Arin?"

"I can't say. I don't mean that I won't say. I mean I can't. I wasn't entirely myself. It was too much, seeing him. Call it my *third* breaking if you like. A joke, he said. What are the odds, really, when you think about it? Is it some cosmic pattern that bends our lives into endless circles? Or is there some hand at work?" I turned to face them then, and met their sad, troubled eyes. "It was *Cal*."

I watched their eyes. The fine muscles of the face and eyelids are infinitely expressive. I could see their mind at work assembling the pieces, and the moment when those pieces resolved into understanding. I held their gaze until they turned away.

"Arin, I'm sorry. I failed you. Perhaps I should have seen

with better clarity how you responded to that Finding. Perhaps I should simply have known that you were not ready, or…"

"You did *not* fail me. Who could have known that the thief was Cal? That I was brittle enough that seeing him alive and knowing exactly where he was would be enough to push me over that edge? Who could have known even that I would be in that Circle?" I shrugged. "What happened, happened. I've tried—for the last few days—tried to take it back. Tried to disbelieve, to cover it up, and to erase what I did."

I turned around again, my eyes pulled back to that view of deep, endless sky. "This is better. This calm and the peace of truth. Of clarity and understanding and honesty. I know now…"

Turin waited for me to finish, and when I didn't, tried to prompt me. "What do you know?"

I smiled a sad little smile. It was much like our sessions. "That I don't belong here. I needed to be here, I needed to learn what I've learned. I needed to find the peace I found. The love and the acceptance."

I turned back to them. "I made a new family here, and I love them dearly. I always will. But I can't live here among you. It hurts me too much to feel this much joy."

"Arin," Turin began.

"I assume the Council is waiting for you to return with me?"

Turin hesitated, then nodded. They seemed unsure of how they had lost control of the conversation so quickly.

"Please give me a moment to collect my things," I said, moving calmly to the bedroom where I had my wardrobe. Turin followed slowly, staying in the sitting room as I reached the door. I opened it and stepped through, saying over my shoulder, "Whatever the Council decides, will you please tell Kari and Fanti and the others that I love them and that I'm sorry? They won't understand." I closed the door softly behind me.

I moved to the wardrobe. In the back, at the bottom was a small pouch with a shoulder strap. I pulled this out and checked inside for the small folding knife that Sem had given me. Deep in the back on the top shelf, I found Neme's tiny mortar and pestle. I gently packed these into the pouch.

I took out a pair of clean trousers and a fresh tunic—the deep blue one that Fanti had made for me. I stroked the rich brocade of the tunic, thinking of Fanti. I rolled them and put them in the pouch. I found the fine silver chain that Kari had given me, the one piece of jewelry that I wore when I especially wanted to feel their love. I tucked it carefully into my pocket.

I reached into the wardrobe where the sword Marki had given me stood. I hadn't touched it since the night I used it to kill Cal. I let my fingers rest for a moment on the smooth scabbard, giving a silent thanks to Marki and Ciala for the training they had given me. I reached past it and pulled out the wooden sword that Sem had carved for me out of a spare piece of firewood on the way to Reft. I tucked this into my belt and draped the pouch over my shoulder.

"Arin?" Turin's voice came from the sitting room.

My heart was breaking slowly, excruciatingly. The pain was too much. Tears flowed down my cheeks and I made no effort to dam them or wipe them away. Let the tears come. Perhaps they could wash me clean of what I was about to do to Kari and Fanti. I didn't think they could.

The pain was too much, and the pain was just enough.

I wove it back and forth between the spaces *here* and *there*. Here in my bed where I had slept the last year or so in love and comfort. Here in the bed where I had finally become... where I had finally *become*. Where I had shed the lie that my body tried to tell my mind.

There, where I had slept the first night after leaving An-bress, full of fear and disquiet and loneliness. There, where I had cut off my braid, finally shedding the lie that I had been living for years in Ma'am's house, the lie that I had tried to tell the world.

I wove the power back and forth like a running stitch, and pulled it taut, drawing that distant lonely forest clearing just outside of Branmoor and my bedroom deep in the heart of Reft together until they were exactly the same place, and the air before me came alive in a frenzy of angry coruscations.

"Arin!" I heard Turin shout from beyond the door. Heard their footsteps approaching.

The tears filled my vision, but I could see well enough to step through the Bridge into the far away woods. I let the Bridge dissipate before Turin reached the door.

Epilogue

My rumination over the past must seem self-indulgent to you. Sitting here this night, staring into this fire has turned me maudlin. This fire, here on these flat stones; the iron gray clouds over us as the sky darkens to night.

It makes me think of another fire, long ago.

Many years had passed before I saw that place again.

I found the ruins of the fort first. It took months of wandering through those ancient hills. At first, I couldn't admit to myself what I searched for. But as I closed in on the narrow valley, as I dredged the dimmest, smallest clues from my somatic memory, I knew in my bones what I sought.

It was far smaller than I remembered. It was a sad tumble of tortured stone and the ghosts of rotted timbers. I could only just make out traces of the bones of its past.

It should have risen like a watchtower. From its foundation, it reminded me of Redwatch—which you have yet to see. Perhaps Redwatch as it will look to someone a thousand years from now.

I walked the remains of the once-proud fortress and found the traces of the small, fetid camp where we had been held. There was little enough to mark it, but the feel of the place was dark and close and haunted.

As I left that place, I drew on my shrouded memory of smothering dark dreams and the hurt and fear that still permeated the air. There's a modest, somber kind of healing in wiping the land clean of such monuments to despair.

I poured that power like a flood into the very stones. The foundations, the blocks tumbled down and standing in walls, and the earth beneath it, all shivered and collapsed into a dust so fine that the meager wind took it up and spread it out over the land. There was nothing left and no evidence there had ever stood a fortress here. No one else would seek dubious comfort under those stones.

Let it be forgotten along with its name.

I thought of some hint of that dust being blown down and down to Anbress, where I hoped Beaty had found some form of solace and peace. It was the best I could do for her. I hope she knows she need never wake in that dark place again.

It was another week, perhaps, before I found the place where I lost my family.

I don't know what I expected. Some part of me was prepared for the horror of finding their remains, irrational as that is. Those hills aren't barren. Even apart from years of exposure to the elements, there are—

—There are wolves. And any number of smaller creatures that would find life in such a bounty of death.

There was no sign of the violence and destruction that visited us that evening. No marker stands to honor them or to accuse the men who killed them. Not even a stain of blood on those stones.

The only evidence that I was not the first person to ever set eyes on that riverbank was the mark of soot that still attested to countless camp fires that human hands have set there. It had been the evidence that gave my family some comfort that others stopped over at that lonely place in the mountains above our home. It had led us to camp there, where Cal and his men came to take our lives.

I didn't stay there long. I was past mourning for them. All that I had done by then had more than paid—in pain and blood and guilt—for their deaths. There was little enough I could have done to honor the place that marked such a pivotal moment in my life.

Between tears and the power they raised in me, I wiped that place clean of any mark of human hands. The deep stains of soot and ash; the indelible sign of untold ages of life-affirming warmth—I drew it from the very elemental essence of the stone, unwinding its memory and history to a time before people walked that land.

Perhaps no one will find that place again. Or if they do, they won't find comfort in an unknowable history and will press on. Someday, perhaps that lonely place can weather enough time that the ghosts of the past no longer haunt it.

Read on for a preview of
the gripping conclusion to the
Paths of Memory
duology

THE DAY WAS waning as I neared the edge of the wood. The tangle of creeper and low foliage that intertwined the lesser trees along the perimeter was as imposing a barrier as the rumors of ghosts. Despite its appearance though, there was a narrow footpath that wound through into the darkness within. It took walking my Warding line to see it.

The nature of a dense forest is deception. Standing at any point beneath the arched canopy, the wood beguiles with imagined paths leading away, just straight and clear enough to hint at an exit, winding just enough that that exit is forever out of sight. Truly though, few of these are paths; the natural rhythm of shadow and light tricks the eye into seeing order in the chaos.

I strode between the trees with the same confidence that the farmers north of me walked their fields. The transition from grass and earth to the thick, damp mat of dead leaves under my bare feet was comforting. This wood was my home.

Deep in the heart of the wood, protected by its own more forceful and more *aware* Warding, was a shambling ruin of stone and moss atop a low hill. The foundations of some watchtower or fort that had burned centuries ago—and had stood for centuries before that—was now a low mound of tumbled stone, overgrown and decrepit. I was confident no one alive remembered it. Only the oldest and most obscure maps I knew of marked it, and those only with a simple sign that meant "ruins." It made a perfect home for the dark and mysterious hedge-witch who roamed the haunted hills.

As the stone mound became visible between the trees, I smiled as always at the dense shrub perched precariously over the shadowed entrance. I had taken it as an omen and a welcome when I had found it, tending and encouraging the fierce roots in their struggle to grapple with the crumbling stonework and survive.

My hedge.

A flutter of wings drew my attention and I paused. A flash of brown and white, and a finch alighted on a branch close to my face. It peered directly at me with one eye and squawked three times. Then it shivered, ruffled its feathers and preened for a moment before a quick hop to a further branch and a panicked burst of flight back into the canopy.

I stood still, watching. My breathing slowed to the pace of the earth and I made myself as still as the stone atop the rise. My cloak of drab homespun wool, caught and snagged with brown leaves and twigs and brush as it was, was ample camouflage for anyone who might have braved the ghosts of this place.

I closed my eyes and reached out with my mind. I drew on the pain that resided ever in my heart, that limitless well of self-inflicted pain born of the devastation I had wrought on those I loved.

This wood was full of life; full of memory. A quick skim of the surface memories of that life showed me the face of the intruder into my domain. Seeing the world through the mind of an animal, even for the briefest moment, is disorienting and vertiginous. For all that the biological structures may resemble ours, there is nothing alike in mind or perception. Seeing through dozens of minds at once... well, I was practiced at it, and still it was a struggle to avoid losing my own perception of self.

I sighed as I let go my brief touch on those alien minds. I continued up the hill to my home and stepped down the weathered stone steps under the low lintel. I pushed open the wooden door, rotted and ruinous on the outside, and clean and polished inside. Despite the outward appearance, I had expended considerable efforts to refine my remote home into a comfortable, if austere, space.

I had reworked the interior of the ruins, drawing living stone from the earth beneath me to reinforce the crumbling foundations, dividing the space into four distinct rooms. The door I had made myself with fresh timber, scrubbing the inner surface with sand and oiling it to a smooth luster while encouraging lichen and moss and fungus to occupy the outer surface.

The stone ceiling of my home broke into multiple layers, each placed strategically so that one slab of stone, which from the outside looked to have fallen in rot and ruin, formed a clerestory, letting a soft, dappled light filter through, even in the gloaming.

As I closed the door behind me, I shrugged out of my cloak and hung it on a peg beside the door, leaning my walking stick in the corner, and noting the large pack that already rested there. The satchel of herbs and mushrooms I had gleaned on my encirclement of Evans Hill and surrounding lands, I lifted over my head began to unpack. I carefully laid each find into appropriate jars or baskets filling a low shelf along the far wall. When the satchel was empty but for a couple of small wrinkled apples, I hung it on the peg beside my cloak. I didn't immediately look at my visitor, but spoke to them with resignation and not a little annoyance in my voice.

"Why are you here, Sem?"

On every path, there comes a crossroads

In Reft, Arin learned that their magical abilities are rooted in their own pain and trauma. Since leaving, they have struggled against the chains of their past to make something of their future.

When a face out of memory returns to challenge the delicate peace Arin has found in their life, they must journey deep into a land rife with prejudice and torn by war. Along the way, they'll need to find the strength to make new allies and to transform themself into a healer, a warrior, and a champion.

But the threads of the past run deeper than Arin can imagine, and their ties to a new rising power will lead them to a terrible choice: To embrace their nature as a witch and outcast, or to help reshape reality itself—and in doing so, erase their own destiny.

K.N. Brindle

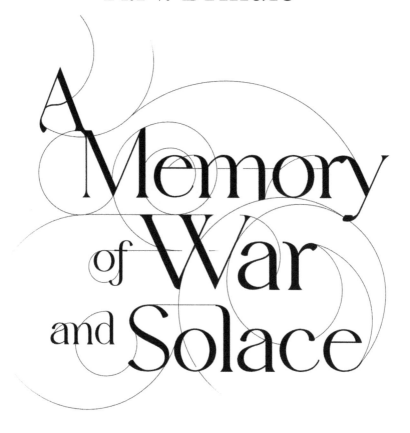

A Memory of War and Solace

Follow K.N. Brindle for news and updates at
www.knbrindle.com

Acknowledgements

Arin's story began in the summer of 2021, in the midst of the global COVID pandemic and just a few weeks before I was starting a graduate program. The timing, to be bluntly honest, wasn't very smart of me. My program was very writing-heavy and in an entirely different discipline from the one I had spent the last twenty years practicing.

But when Arin's first words came into my mind in that very first opening line, I had no idea what was starting. I only knew I had to write them down. A week later, I had written almost fifteen thousand words. I had no idea if those words were any *good*, but they *felt* good. I sent the very rough draft to a friend with ties to the publishing world, and she told me in no uncertain terms that I needed to finish it.

There are countless people I need to thank for the existence of this book. First and foremost, my partner who put up with my long nights of writing. A variety of friends and colleagues, and the members of the writing discord server that acts as my writing community, who cheered me on, read excerpts as I wrote them, and listened to my evolving attempts at reducing the complex idea of this story to a pitchable blurb. My therapist who managed to help me navigate the stresses of my graduate program, a head-spinning career change, and also was able to pick out the autobiographical elements of Arin's story and help me analyze and process them as the writing went on.

I also need to thank my beta readers who read the finished draft and gave me important feedback: G Stalica, Jordale, Ellery Baxter, Samantha D, Sara Codair, and Terra. Also deserving of great thanks is my editor, Shannon, who helped me polish the work without losing any of its emotional weight.

For much of this story, my role has seemed like little more than documentarian: writing down what Arin showed me they were doing and thinking. Through the writing, I watched Arin grow up, and I watched them develop their sense of identity. I watched them come into their own agency and power. I watched them make difficult decisions and terrible mistakes.

Even though I did a fair amount of planning for this story once I had started writing it in earnest, and even though I figured out where it was ultimately going from quite early on, I still was surprised when that somewhat passive relationship with Arin's story began to extend to other characters. Eelie, for instance, appeared nowhere in any of my notes or outlines until the day that they showed up for a scene, tapped me on the shoulder and insisted that I write them into the story.

Miraculously, while navigating my masters degree program over the course of 2021 and 2022, I managed to continue to write. Along the way, this book came together, largely in the form that you have read it. Indeed, it turns out that working on this story served me as a sort of stress-relief valve. The higher the academic pressures I faced, the more prolific I became in depicting Arin's life. Somewhere along the way, this story became a novel, and then the novel became a duology.

This is book one, and Arin's story is not over.

About the Author

K. N. Brindle has worn many different hats in their life, which is impressive considering how difficult it is to find one that fits their extra-large head. They've worked as a graphic designer, and in the industrial design and architecture fields. They've built telecom equipment. They've been an app developer and a software architect, and have taught software engineering. They're most recently a licensed therapist.

They are fine with any pronouns when used with respect, though they *really* hate being called "sir."

They live in the southeastern U.S. with their partner, children, and just the right number of cats.

A Memory of Blood and Magic is their first novel.

Author Portrait by @mimesatwork@wandering.shop